Advance Pra

"A strong, character driven book, and all (weird, wild, quirky and wonderful that I can t wait to see where they all go next."
-S. M. Beiko, author of *The Stars of Mount Quixx*

"A.W. Glen, like a deft composer, writes wonderfully. There is a speed and exuberant thrust in the novel's playful plot, in the back-and-forth rapidity of its dialogue, and in the characters themselves. ... Never trust weirdo music bloggers, but certainly go read Bukowski's Broken Family Band."
-Steve Schmolaris, author of *Bad Gardening Advice: Winnipeg Music Reviews from Artist Redacted to Zrada*

"'So what genre are you anyway?' A.W. Glen's debut is a sharp-witted skewering of the Winnipeg underground music scene against the backdrop of a spooky murder mystery. It's a hilarious and enjoyable mix of Hard Times meets X-Files, with horrific murders and supernatural curveballs befalling a struggling band just trying to get a good paying gig."
-Kent Davies, CKUW 95.9 FM

"Gripping. A page-turner. Six thumbs up (at least)."
-Sam Thompson, host of Witchpolice Radio

BUKOWSKI'S BROKEN FAMILY BAND

A.W. Glen

Copyright © 2024 A.W. Glen

All rights reserved.

ISBN: 978-1-0690028-3-9

Released by Transistor 66 Record Co. in Winnipeg, MB.

Cover by Alexis Flower.

All characters appearing in this work are fictitious. Any resemblance to real persons, living or dead, is purely coincidental.

Dedicated to all Winnipeg's indie kids, punks, and weirdos.

Dramatis Personae

The BBBFB
Jaymie Brzezinski – lead vocals, keyboards, rhythm guitar
Jo Connors – lead guitar
Rex Brzezinski – bass
Aaron Brzezinski – drums, backup vocals
Garrett Kliewer – drums (July–October 2019)

The Ballet Llama
Michaud Dubois – lead vocals
Jo Connors – lead guitar
Olivier "Three-Chord-Oli" Martine – rhythm guitar
Jake Lowes – bass
Alexandre Valliere – drums (2009–2011)
Hannah Chen – drums (2019)

The Bukowskiphiles
Maggie – CEO
Shahla – CTO
Stan – research analyst
Ayla – junior member

The Arts Collective
Miranda – admin
Steve – aspiring painter
Juniper – aspiring pianist
Evelyn – aspiring writer
Ronan – aspiring journalist

The McLeods
Leonora – the Brzezinskis' mother
Anika – the Brzezinskis' first cousin on their mother's side
Dorothea (Dory) – the Brzezinskis' aunt, Leonora's sister
Farida – the Brzezinskis' aunt

Local Bands and Artists
Allene Elvira – folk singer-songwriter and mandolinist
The BMI Babies – Motown cover band founded by Three-Chord Oli
Daffodile – indie pop singer with a small but loyal international following
Dead Zebra Beach (DZB) – punk-jazz fusion; poised to blow up
Gunt – long-time lo-fi duo led by Casio Bob
Lost, the Show, the Band – experimental conceptual performance art project
Lucas Yarbrough – music writer and critic
Michaud Dubois – former *Ballet Llama* frontman, now performing solo
Shifty Principals – punk band formed by Oli Martine and Alexandre Valliere
Tornado Tornahdo – surf rock cover band

Part One

The Pumpkin Thieves

1
Jo

Jo's new band was in the process of stealing every one of the round, ripe pumpkins vine-nestled in their former drummer's backyard garden. The group had been making some changes to their lineup.

It had been six weeks since the Bukowski Brothers, in search of a lead guitarist, had plucked her from a local musicians-for-hire website. She'd attended thirteen rehearsals with their now-scorned percussionist, but tonight—an hour before her first show with the band—she found herself waiting in the shadows of his back alley in the passenger seat of a getaway vehicle. She cracked her window to expel a breath of smoke into the soupy dark, then slid her pipe back into her bag. Beside her, the driver was having a panic attack, as she'd been informed he would.

Aaron Brzezinski, the band's once-and-future drummer, had been restored (reluctantly) to his rightful drum throne earlier that day, replacing the banished pumpkin gardener. Aaron did not cope well with stressful situations.

"Why did he have to fuck everything up?" he mumbled into the steering wheel, massaging his freckled forehead against it. "Everything was going fine. He's a better drummer than me. It should be him playing tonight."

"You're doing a good job?" Jo tried. She'd been introduced to Aaron less than half an hour ago and unofficially delegated as band therapist around the same time.

She wondered how her other bandmates were doing with the pumpkins; the drummer must have grown a bumper crop, judging by the size of the empty crates Jaymie and Rex had disappeared through the gate with.

"This is a terrible idea. We shouldn't be here," Aaron muttered.

"Well, it wasn't my idea." Jo tried to keep the accusation out of her tone, reminding herself that Aaron couldn't be held responsible for the whims of his mad twin. He didn't reply.

Outside, the alley was silent under a swampy October sky. Snatches of conversation floated from the street, where people wandered to and from Friday night events, unaware of the theft occurring just beyond the fence. Behind a garage roof, a ruddy harvest moon lurked, feigning ignorance about the pumpkins and likely to deny any involvement later.

Jo settled into her seat and investigated the glove compartment for CD options. Aaron stared out the window and began a compulsive rhythmic tapping on the wheel, likely without any awareness he was doing it.

Jo had been in unconventional bands before. She felt that most good bands were unconventional by nature, or else they probably played boring garage rock in front of boring audiences. She was determined to take Aaron's eccentricities as a positive.

A dog barked twice. She glanced up from a handful of CDs clearly collected from local DIY shows—The BMI Babies, Shifty Principals, Gunt—but concluded that the sound came from too far away to have been caused by her bandmates' misdemeanours.

"Oh my god, we've gotta go." Aaron was working himself into even greater agitation, and Jo felt a pang of alarm. She sat up straighter and checked that the alley was empty before reminding herself not to get caught up in the energy of his fear; being stoned always made her susceptible to catching other people's vibes.

"It's cool, that pup's way down the street. Hey, do you guys listen to the Ballet Llama?" She held up one of the CDs. "Did you know I played on this album?"

"What? Sure. Oh shit!" Not to be redirected, Aaron twisted around to monitor the zone behind the car, and jumped as the dog barked again.

"Jaymie and Rex must be almost done by now." Jo tried to sound reassuring.

"No, we have to—we can't—" A sheen of sweat threatened at the edges of Aaron's pale face. "I'm afraid of dogs," he admitted.

"Oh. OK, well, it's outside the car …"

Jaymie's instructions had been simple: "Aaron, this is Jo. Jo, Aaron! He has a panic disorder! So, you guys stay here and do something ... calming. Remember, this is fun!" And then, pointlessly, "We're all a band now! Yay ..." He'd given the kind of sparkling wink characteristic only of talking cartoon animals and Jaymie Brzezinski, then hefted the empty boxes into his arms and darted after Rex into the darkness of the unfortunate gardener's yard.

"Want me to drive?" Jo asked, trying to think of a way to help.

He sized her up. "How high are you?"

"Barely."

Aaron grappled visibly with the choice between trusting a stoned driver versus handling a car while dealing with the grim knowledge that dogs exist, but finally he said, "Yes. Please."

Jo tossed the CDs back into the compartment and reached for the door handle.

"Omigod don't open that! There's a dog out there!"

She was at a loss. She closed her eyes and allowed herself a synesthetic vision of the guitar line that began the first track on the new EP, the hook that had charmed her into this band and made her excited for her first rehearsal. She moved her fingers over imaginary frets, and a comforting contour of melody rose and fell before her closed eyelids.

She forced herself back to the situation at hand. "Should we ... switch?" she asked. Aaron drummed his palms on the wheel, calculating and accurately assessing Jo's hips to be wider than his own, her body more unwieldy.

"You just hop over the middle," he instructed. "I'll go overtop." He slid the driver's seat back and climbed onto the dashboard, nimbly folding his slight form between the dash and windshield. His legs stretched over the gear shift in the gap between the two front seats.

"You don't want to just jump into the back seat for a minute?"

"It's too late for that now."

Grumbling, Jo pulled her feet up onto the seat, then swung her left sneaker over Aaron's knees. She hoisted her hips over his shins. A thigh cramp caused a retreat; a satisfying pop in her hip got her back on track. Her shoe caught in the loose seatbelt.

"If you just—"

"Here, I'll slide over."

"Ow, just wait, I'm almost there!"

"Sorry, I'll—"

"Ok move your foot. Not like—never mind!"

And she was free, about to descend gracefully into the driver's seat, when a tap on the door startled Aaron into a headlong sprawl against her chest. Two bearded and beer-toting Friday-nighters hailed them from outside.

"Never seen it done that way before," one of them commented, as Jo further lowered the window.

"Sorry to interrupt," said the other. "But there's a house party one street, three blocks over. Two seventy-one Lipton." He gestured down the alley. "Costumes encouraged. Sick band playing later. We're trying to get lots of people out. So. When you guys are all finished …" He raised his eyebrows at them. "Also, not the best alley for this. Lots of foot traffic."

Jo, stoned enough for a bit of hazy paranoia, tensed, thinking he knew about the burglary occurring a few feet across the fence, but then remembered she was sitting in the dark with her feet splayed across the dash and a headlights-frozen deer of a man in her lap. She relaxed.

"Two seventy-one. You'll hear it!" He set off, cheers-ing his twelve-pack in their direction as Jo gave a bland grin and Aaron nodded dumbly in her arms.

Her new bandmate might take some getting used to. But then, they all took some getting used to. She deposited him in his seat and pulled her right leg over the stick shift, settling in.

"Feel any better?" she asked.

"Distractions always help."

A moment later they heard the click of the trunk opening and felt the soft shudder of the car accepting several heavy pumpkin crates. Into the back seat tumbled an exuberant Jaymie, followed by placidly smiling seventeen-year-old Rex, the youngest member of the Bukowski Brothers' Broken Family Band.

Jaymie leaned into the front, arms circling Jo and Aaron's seats, freckles dancing in the dim alley light, his face a fuller, crooked-smiling version of Aaron's.

"We got our merch," he beamed. "You kids ready to play a house show?"

Jo Connors was Rex's new favourite thing about band practices—mostly because she was terrifying. She was the sort of formidable musician woman

Rex might have wanted to grow up to be in five or ten years, if Rex still expected to grow up to be a woman, which Rex—*they/them*, or *he* if you felt like it—no longer did.

Jo had the enigmatic charm of someone who either has a complicated past or has simply spent all of your encounters with them politely concealing how inebriated they are. She was six foot one—taller than any of the three Brzezinski siblings—and with her slippery black hair and seemingly unshakable poise, she was also the most intimidating of the four band members.

But what really delighted Rex was Jo's angular, jangly lead guitar playing. Rex loved to have something interesting to lay a bassline under, and it didn't hurt that Jo's history included a brief era playing in one of Rex's favourite defunct local punk bands. As far as Rex was concerned, Jo was a monster on her instrument and a wonder to behold on stage and too high most of the time to have a real conversation with, which only added to her allure even more.

The *Bukowskis* made it out of the garden with no altercations, drove back to the jam space to swap the car for their van and gear, and still had time to draw thirty-six *BBBFB* logos in black sharpie on thirty-six stolen pumpkins before heading to the party at number 271.

Now, as Rex maneuvered their too-heavy bass amp through a kitchen packed full of stylish twenty-somethings, they were especially grateful for Jo's presence ahead of them. She carved a wide path with her amp, guitar, and the suitcase containing her pedal board. Rex estimated that the pumpkin picking might have gone in half the time with her helping, but knew that Jaymie was trying to be considerate about the amount of illegal activity they involved their new guitarist in.

Rex's best friend, Maggie, appeared at their side with Rex's bass on her back—she'd no doubt encountered their van on her way in.

"What a bunch of hipsters," Maggie muttered into Rex's ear. "Kill me if I'm dressed like that at twenty-five." She jerked her chin derisively at a woman wearing an ocean-blue onesie and ten thousand wooden bangles. Maggie was barely sixteen, but Maggie had Lived.

"Your mom let you come!" said Rex, instantly more at ease among the polished (or intentionally unkempt) strangers.

"She had nothing to do with it. And since when have I ever missed a *Bukowski* show?" She did another scan of the room, upon which the mid-October Halloween spirit was overlaid like a subtle Instagram filter; about half the party-goers had taken up the costume suggestion, and a few vampires, personified puns, and skimpy cats mingled with those sporting more conventional autumn finery.

They brought the gear to the living room, a carpeted space without furniture. The walls were a mosaic of cult horror film posters and hand-drawn art that depicted warped humanoids with too many eyes and noses and gave the distinct impression of being not just seasonal décor. It screamed *artist house,* and Rex felt a swell of excitement at the venue's dingy glamour.

"So, I heard Aaron's back in the band? Didn't he, like, bail on you guys and swear never to play another show or something? And Jaymie untwinned with him and then they weren't best-friends-slash-brothers anymore? What's the deal?"

Maggie knew everything. Maggie being out of the loop on band intel was unthinkable; Rex knew she was just looking for another take on the drama.

"Tell you later. I have a bunch of pumpkins to set up. Want to help?"

Maggie said, "Hmm," and conveniently caught the eye of one of the few other teenagers with enough cred to know about the show. She waved him over.

"So who's the band?" asked her new conquest. He had a red toque pulled low, and Rex vaguely recognized him from school.

"*You don't know?*" Maggie cried, as though being unfamiliar with an on-again-off-again local indie band were the worst faux pas imaginable.

Rex smiled, gave a teenaged-yet-tasteful roll of their eyes, and set off to find the merch table as Maggie zeroed in on her victim. Behind them, Maggie's voice was swallowed by the din as she said, "Ok, I'll tell you."

Maggie, as the founding member of the *BBBFB*'s official fan club (four members and counting), was intimately aware of their history. The band had been formed two years and ten months ago by the three siblings, whose origin she also knew the gist of: they'd been born Jaymes, Ayryn, and Rybecca Brzezinski—in that order—to serve as sidemen in their mother's various musical projects. A celebrated jazz musician, Leonora McLeod had need of a backing band who would not require payment. Such were the times for professional musicians.

The training of Leonora's accompanists, as Maggie liked to tell it, had taken longer than anticipated, and in the meantime she'd taken on a semi-permanent gig with a Cirque du Soleil show in Las Vegas, which kept her away from her family for gradually increasing chunks of each year. Her offspring, unable to eschew their intended destiny, had compulsively maintained regular rehearsals, which were mainly directionless (and occasionally combative) improvised jams, until the day her eldest had commandeered the band to his own ends.

Rex, quiet and amenable, had taken to the bandstand since the day their bass was placed in their infant fingers, but of the identical Jaymes and Ayryn, only Jaymie had inherited his mother's passion for the performing life. Aaron was less than enthusiastic.

Just out of earshot from where Maggie regaled her friend with his life story, Aaron grudgingly set up his battered kit on a grubby carpet, in a house slathered in trashy posters and garish homemade art and filled with people who were mostly drunk and unnecessarily loud. Halloween had been half-heartedly splattered across everything like a spreading stain.

He adjusted the cymbal height. He dutifully made sure the snare was off so it wouldn't bother Jaymie during his stupid introductory soliloquy. He placed a stash of drumsticks easily accessible for when his nervous hands inevitably dropped or flung the ones he started with.

Then he went to see if Rex was still setting up merch in the front hall, only to find that all thirty-six pumpkins had disappeared and the man charging cover at the door was slumped over the cash box, his tiny, circular glasses askew, quite dead.

A slender band of blood striped across the man's neck. Aaron's pulse quickened. He felt the too-familiar pressure in his chest, like his ribcage was a room in a sci-fi movie, rigged so its Jenga-block walls would fold in piece by piece until his heart and lungs could either agree to work together to solve some kind of depraved puzzle or else be crushed to death. He wished, not for the first time, that he had more control over his body's adrenal impulses.

He exhaled harshly, ran his damp hands through his hair, and tried to steady his breathing. Situations like this were *exactly* why he'd quit the band in the first place.

2

The Bukowski Brothers' Broken Family Band

Maggie's account was a charming one, but who are the *Bukowski Brothers*, really?

First, more on Leonora. The Brzezinski siblings' mother was a notoriously sarcastic freelance saxophone player from the vibrant neighbourhood of Transcona. Everything Leonora did—from her choice of fashion accessories to her improvised melodies—had a tinge of irony to it. Though she almost never missed a gig, booking agents often made sure they had a backup plan because they couldn't tell if her acceptance to play was sincere or not.

She'd received two degrees in music and played masterfully, though her stage banter was terrible. Listeners memorized song titles as she introduced them, only to find later that the names led only to Gregorian chants or ancient polkas; on her albums the songs were titled only with serial numbers. Audiences left her shows exhilarated by the joy of music but with an uncomfortable feeling they'd been insulted at some point and hadn't noticed. Growing up with such an influence, it was hardly surprising if the Brzezinskis' music occasionally blurred the lines between artistry and farce.

Their father was a Polish private investigator. In his twenties he'd worked as a police officer, and he'd arrested Leonora for public indecency while she was on a European tour. She'd gone for a celebratory post-show swim in the river Vistula, then hung all her clothes on the Warsaw Mermaid and lain beneath waiting for them to dry throughout the summer night.

The unwitting man made the mistake of confessing to her an amateur passion for the clarinet, somehow allowed her to allow him to buy her a drink upon her release, and sobered up to find himself imprisoned in the poorly-lit wastes of central Canada with a couple of precocious toddlers. Such things could happen in the company of Leonora.

Brzezinski got his wits about him and planned an elaborate escape back to Poland. Warsaw could also get cold, but it was a kind of cold he could comprehend and come to terms with. He caught a plane.

In subsequent years he became disillusioned with police work and started his own P.I. business, expecting mostly to track down wayward teenagers and stalk cheating spouses. He was soon being celebrated throughout the country for catching all kinds of under-the-radar serial killers and minor psychopaths, details of which he clipped out of newspapers and faithfully mailed overseas to his little boys. He maintained a polite correspondence with his former partner but never quite understood that chapter of his life.

Years later, Leonora took another tour in his general direction. The cultured cities of Europe were calling to her, and North America was not buying what she had to sell. The trip resulted in the conception of Rex; it was never confirmed whether Leonora was still in love with the detective or just having trouble finding a bass player. The poor man was as baffled as anyone. He resolved to do a better job of keeping in touch—he made sure to email the children monthly, and never failed to send them each a jazz-themed Christmas card.

"So what genre are you, anyway?" A woman dressed entirely in horizontal black and white stripes had taken a promising interest in Jaymie as he carried his keyboard inside.

"Whatever genre you want me to be, baby."

The woman had been speaking to Jaymie for about five minutes—the amount of time it takes, upon meeting an attractive stranger, to generate a rich backstory in your imagination and cast them as the hero of it. A certain 'benefit of the doubt' results, whereby any lapse of civility can be excused as self-aware and innocently flirtatious. Jaymie was aware of this phenomenon. He also guessed the woman was a few years older than him and clever, which he always felt exonerated him from anything he did to encourage the fantasy.

"How about acoustic sludge metal? With some throat singing thrown in?" she asked, sipping something rose-coloured and narrowing her long-lashed eyes at him. "No wait, I'm in a tranquil mood. An hour of binaural beats?"

"I get nervous playing my binaural set, but maybe if you can get a drink or two in me …"

Jaymie stepped closer to her, then cringed as Aaron materialized at his side, pulling on his shirtsleeve and looking about as frantic as usual.

"Jaymie Jaymie Jaymie, the door guy. The door guy is dead."

Jaymie had always known there was something off about Aaron that went beyond the simple pain of being the slightly less handsome and charismatic twin. He knew at some point something had shaken Aaron up enough to interfere with the DNA chemistry that could have cultivated similar personalities in the two. But he never brought it up, out of respect, and he tolerated Aaron's idiosyncrasies with all the tenderness and patience of unconditional love.

"Fuck off, Aar. I'm busy."

"Did you hear me? He's dead!"

"I heard—hang on, what? Sorry." He glanced in apology at the woman. "Who's dead?"

"The guy working the door—somebody killed him! And the pumpkins are gone! We need to get out of here, Jay. There's some bad shit going on." Aaron bounced on the balls of his feet and rubbed his knuckles, which was never a good sign.

"OK, calm down." Jaymie knew about eight different tactics for de-escalating Aaron, and he chose one at random. "People die, Aar. We can't quit music just because that's a reality. It'd take a fucking worldwide zombie pandemic to stop this band! Right? I mean, obviously in that case we'd take a break, for the safety of the general public and—I digress. Look, the door guy, you said? I'm sure someone's on it. In the meantime, you know what's a good distraction?"

"Seriously?"

"Sharing the power of rock and roll! What ills could possibly befall us in front of a whole crowd of people?"

"Why did I think you were the right person to come to about this?"

"No use worrying—"

"Just habit, I guess."

"You know what?" Jaymie clapped him on the back. "Round up the others. It's time!"

"Yeah, no. I'm gonna call the cops and ask our kid sister to talk me through this."

"*Sibling.*"

"Sibling! Kid sibling." Aaron's incredulity over this exchange appeared to have diverted him from his panic attack, which Jaymie noted with a sense of victory.

"Do you feel better?" he asked.

"Yeah, I can almost breathe again. Thanks for fucking nothing, Jay."

The thing with anxiety, Jaymie mused, is that it can seriously sap your creativity. Chronic nerves could burn through countless watts of the precious energy that would otherwise be put toward things like songwriting, or developing hopes and dreams. But it wasn't as though Aaron was a lost cause. Some people just needed a little extra care and reassurance.

"Sorry about that," he said, turning back to the woman.

He needn't have apologized; she'd used the extra minute to process the fact that the adorable man she'd been flirting with had an adorable look-alike and they were probably together all the time and maintained a constant adorable ironic rapport and gave people déjà vu whenever they passed a few minutes apart. There was no number of dead door-people that could stop her from giving him her number by the end of the night.

"It's OK. No, actually I'm offended—whispers of death on a night like this! How will you make it up to me?" She tugged at the hem of her stripy dress and cocked her head to one side.

"I'm going to change all the names in our songs to your name," Jaymie suggested. "Even the murder ballads."

"Am I the murderer or the murderee?"

"You're the murderess. Of ... myy ... heeaaaarrrtt ..."

It was hard to tell, with musicians, whether they were perfectly enchanting or the absolute worst, but at least she wouldn't be bored. Before he could fully burst into song, she laughed in his face, took his hand, and led him to the kitchen to share a delicious ironic raspberry vodka cooler with him.

Garrett, ex-drummer for the *BBBFB*, stood in his backyard with a scotch in hand, staring at the pumpkin-less vines that gripped the expanse of his garden. He was indulging in a vision of his plants as a sleeping beast, ready to awaken and rise from the earth, tentacles writhing into the alley as the monster mourned the loss of her babies.

Full of fury and retribution, she'd roil down the block toward the conveniently close house party, where she'd exact her strangulatory vengeance, bearing her victims home to be digested in the depths of the dirt. And Garrett would stand with his whiskey, and watch.

Unfortunately, the garden lay still, and Garrett knew that if he wanted justice he'd have to go out and demand it.

He also knew the *Bukowskis* hadn't expected him to discover the missing pumpkins until the next day. He was supposed to be playing three sets with another band, and then he was supposed to go home and collapse into bed without ever glancing at his backyard.

But the bar had been shut down by health inspectors because of a bizarre fungus proliferating in an unmaintained grease-trap, and the show was cancelled.

Two days ago, Garrett had received his final email from the *BBBFB*, whom he'd been playing with as Aaron's replacement for the past four months. It read only, "We no longer require your services." And while Garrett knew the reason he'd been terminated, he still felt bitter that he'd never had an opportunity to share his side of the story.

Not that he still wanted to be in the band. He was a professional-level musician, and if there were more session work in the city, he'd be making a living at it. As it was, he'd practically been paying to play—their meagre payout from shows went in the band account, and practices cost him at least two nights out of his week. This was not the sustainable gig he needed. But he did need those pumpkins. Market-gardening in his large back and front yards supplemented his income enough to take the holidays off and go home to Steinbach for Christmas.

He drained his glass, pulled on a jacket against the growing chill, set off toward the party and, like a sane and reasonable person, called the police.

"Jo! Have you seen Rex? Actually, hey, look, oh my god, OK, I know this sounds crazy, but the guy charging cover at the door is for sure dead."

"Dead? Dang. Let's go take a look," said Jo, who'd just gotten freshly baked for the show and was feeling amenable and up for anything. "You sure he's not sleeping?"

"His eyes were wide open!"

"Or, like, took acid and wigged out? People do dumb stuff at these things. Could be ketamine, could be TwiLite …"

"He was all white, and there was blood—and his mouth was wide open—he was—I don't—he wasn't breathing—his fingers were like—"

"OK, don't panic. That sounds rough."

She followed Aaron through the throng to the front table, where a person in leopard print was accepting the ten-dollar "suggested donation" from new arrivals. A young couple stood nearby with their heads close together, speaking in furtive whispers. Jo remembered Jaymie greeting these two earlier; they were the organizers of the show.

"Oh my god, he's gone," said Aaron. "Nobody will ever believe me. Everyone will think I'm even crazier than they already do—"

"Hi! We're so sorry. There was a death. We've taken care of it." One of the organizers moved close to Aaron and Jo and put a hand on each of their shoulders, as though to console them. "Sorry everything's starting late. Life is full of unexpected ebbs and flows," she said.

"We adore your music, BTW," said the young man.

"We're super excited for the show."

"Please help yourself to some artful beverages from the back porch. And feel free to share your tunes whenever you like."

"Thanks, man. We will," said Jo, suddenly loath to disappoint the earnest couple. As she spoke, she felt the itch to have her guitar in hand, and she imagined the soft click of her delay pedal as she tapped in the tempo of the first song. She glanced at Aaron, who didn't appear placated. "But about the … ah … death. Is everything …?"

"Like, did someone call the police?" urged Aaron.

"Oh!" exclaimed the woman. "Police. Yes."

"Most def. First thing."

"Nobody loves cops—"

"—but sometimes it's the right thing to do."

"We just thought since the night was going so well."

"*So* well. And no need to call off the music, when …"

"It's just this has been happening lately …"

"People sort of know the risks by now."

"We figured we can't just stop having shows, right? Unless you're not … If you don't want to …" The woman looked up at Jo with pleading and very creatively outlined eyes.

"Yeah, we'll play," said Jo.

"Excellent, excellent. Don't worry about anything. It's all under control."

"Totes."

Jo looked to Aaron. He shifted back and forth, patted an agitated beat on his thighs, and finally shrugged and nodded.

They made their way back to the living room to find Jaymie adjusting his synths and Rex brandishing cat-ear headbands and syrupy-looking face paint in their direction, and they took up their guitar and drumsticks to play a show.

3
Legend of the Bukowskis

"On March ninth of the year nineteen ninety-four, at 1:40 in the morning, the greatest novelist in America passed out of this life and into legend."

Approximately half the people milling around the room quieted and turned toward the corner where the band was set up. Laughter and conversation drifted from the kitchen and front hall; a man's voice could be heard proclaiming "Not even!" repeatedly and loudly enough to sound amplified. Jaymie, clad in a mailman costume, turned toward the drums.

"Dear brother," he said into the microphone. "I'm concerned that these good people will miss an important part of the story. Perhaps if the two of us chime our spoons against our teacups both at the same time—"

A resounding smash ricocheted through the room. Several people jumped. A man screamed delicately and a woman plagued by tinnitus clapped a hand to the side of her head and fished around for earplugs. Aaron sat watching Jaymie from behind the drum set, his hands in his lap and one knee vibrating. The ride and crash cymbals quivered and hummed, soothing each other and bracing for his next sneak attack.

"Thank you. Allow me to introduce myself. My name is Jaymie Bukowski, and I was born in the same instant that my ancestor, the great writer Charles Bukowski, slipped away into the afterlife."

Jaymie had their attention.

"Bukowski was not ready to die! There were drinks to be drunk, sunrises to stay awake for, women to be rejected by. His soul sought a vessel in order to cling to the earthly realm. Ladies, gentlemen, and other classy people, I am that vessel."

Jo struck an angelic harmonic on the high E string.

"A descendent born at the very moment of his death! Bukowski's spirit understood what was meant to be."

As Jaymie described the infant days of his ghostly possession, Rex adjusted their bass to a clip-on tuner and spun the volume knob. They looked around at Jo, now fuzzy-eared and whiskered and swaying serenely with her guitar, and at Aaron, who slouched over his kit wearing a sardonic expression on his own cat face.

The audience began to assemble, the first few rows seating themselves on the carpet while more reluctant listeners lounged against the walls. Rex flashed a smile at Maggie, who grinned up at them from close enough that Rex could have reached out and tousled her hair.

"There were always signs. At the age of four I got into the schnapps and wrote a treatise on the absurdity of existence. In crayon."

Rex began a gentle pulsing in the key of A.

"Knowing instinctively of my destiny, my mother raised me on German folk songs and the works of Henry Miller …"

Aaron flipped the snare switch and began the softest possible rolling march.

"I never knew my father! Outcast and scorned by other children, I comforted myself with the knowledge that I was meant for greater things. A memory of my former life called to me—haunted me."

Rex began a more urgent rhythm, locking in with Aaron.

"By twelve, I had discovered alcohol. My nights were spent in solitude, writing. My first poem was rejected by all the major periodicals. It was about loneliness."

Suppressing a smile, Rex glanced at Aaron, who had shared a bunk bed with Jaymie until well beyond the age of twelve and could confirm that Jaymie hadn't been lonely a day in his life.

Jaymie Brzezinski was, by Maggie's calculations, the fourth most brilliant human alive today, and an idol much more worth meeting than the three that surpassed him.

"My brothers and I stand before you, the bluebirds in our hearts bursting to escape, smiling through our sadness with a set of almost-made-up songs! We're the *Bukowski Brothers' Broken Family Band* …" The band cut out and the room thrummed with a charged silence. "… And you can find us on most streaming services and social media platforms."

He winked. Aaron coaxed the snare into a great swell and finally crashed into the beat of the first song. Jo hit the main riff.

Maggie leaned against the red-toqued boy from school, letting the familiar music wash over her. She chanted under her breath as the band launched into the verse of "Most Poets."

"I take it you've seen this band before?" asked her new boyfriend, not understanding that the volume absolved him of the responsibility to make conversation.

She sang, *"I'll write you a poem if I wake up on time / most poets can't write a single fucking simple line …"*

"Ha, I like them too."

"I got famous 'cause the other writers never understood / it's because they're all so bad, not because I was so good!" Maggie shout-whispered the words in his ear as Jaymie crooned them into the microphone.

Red Toque appeared to be picking up her signals, or had at least acquired the expression boys get while piecing together a potentially romantic situation: Probably she liked him—or she just really liked this band—how could one tell?—maybe they should kiss?

Jo kicked on an overdrive pedal for the bridge section and Maggie let go of his arm to yell, *"Fuck Tolstoy!"*

"This is the worst band I've ever heard," said a petit man standing against the back wall of the living room. His companion, an equally petite woman, giggled.

"I like them," she said. "Is this what they call, like, alt-country?"

"His voice is like that guy on the X-Factor."

"They sound like Vulpix, but with words, you know?"

"Yeah, I know." He didn't.

"Do you wanna go make out?'

"Yep."

They left.

The band was decent, maybe even decent enough to live up to the hype generated by the show's promoters. But god, what a stupid band name.

Lucas Yarbrough, sovereign scholar of the local indie scene, sat cross-legged at the side of the room, covertly jotting notes into the phone balanced on his knee. He deleted something, grimaced at the screen, then remembered he was currently Making a Living Whilst Having Fun! and bobbed his head in time. His music blog had been getting a lot of traction lately, but the new ad revenue made it harder to sit back and enjoy the show.

I can't help but feel a deep contentedness settle over me, he lied, *as the band breaks into their fourth song, "No Responsibility."* The guitarist turned on a delay pedal and sent soft bubbles of sound floating over the heads of the crowd. She really could play.

Bukowski (if that is, in fact, his real name) leads them into a gentle ballad that, upon closer listen, seems to be about its narrator's penchant for "getting drunk and jacking off in bed." Could he publish that, now that he actually had readers? He tried again.

Be assured, your boy here will not let the mythology influence the review, even though the only thing I've heard about JB is that he dropped out last minute on a Dead Zebra Beach tour to focus on his own music (he must be sore now, considering DZB's success at NXNE), and that his twin brother once inexplicably screamed, kicked over a floor tom, and fled midway through an audition for the BMI Babies. Delete delete delete. Lucas's was not a gossip blog.

Though the term "indie rock" is too broad a category to be descriptive, the BBBFB's guitar- and synth-centred sound falls firmly on the darker side of this genre; JB presents the lyrics with a frantic theatricality that hearkens to bands like Of Montreal, Mother Mother or godddddd I don't want to write this right now

He tapped backspace in sync with the ticking hi-hat, breathing a sigh that was swallowed by the synthesizer. The guitar sighed back in sympathy, exhaling a spiral of sixteenth notes. A girl in a blue onesie waved from across the room, and he rose, casting a regretful look at the band. She'd sent him early mixes from her upcoming album, and he'd promised her an interview. He pocketed his phone, missing the days when he and his friends went to shows to get deranged on spiked energy drinks and didn't worry about remembering the details later.

"I can't decide if this is, like, cosmic nihilism, or if he's just trying to get attention."

Jaymie was midway through the chorus of "Professional Drunk."

"Well, the real Bukowski would never have considered himself a nihilist. There are certainly themes of pessimism and absurdism in his writing." Two college students in *Daft Punk*ian helmets hunched in the far corner of the room, hands shoved in the pockets of their skinny jeans, trying to decide whether or not to enjoy themselves.

"Where'd you hear about this show, again?" one of them asked the other.

"I keep up with things. Heard there's a singer in town claiming to be the next Charles Bukowski, so I figured we should check it out," her companion replied, his voice muffled behind the solid black of his mask.

"Well, this guy's read the Bukowski Wikipedia page, I'll give him that."

"If it's nihilism, it's more *existential* than cosmic. There's a lot of hope in Bukowski's shit."

"There's a lot of literal *shit* in Bukowski's shit—"

"Hm, I should read more Bukowski."

"—And death and depravity and misogyny—"

"This is catchy, though, right?"

"Which *is* what matters, when you really get down to it."

"They're so legit!" The show's co-organizer clasped her partner's hand and bobbed on her toes to see over the heads of the audience members packing her living room.

Her boyfriend nodded, but couldn't focus on the music enough to share her delight. His mind kept wandering to the small guest bedroom off the upstairs hallway.

Righteous band, no doubt, he thought, *but how are we going to deal with that legit dead body?* Putting on an indie show never turned out to be as simple as you expected.

"This is exactly like that scene in *Infinite Ends*." The petite woman pushed her companion against the wall of the staircase. The band had drawn most of the aimlessly fluttering party attendees into the living room, and the upstairs was quiet.

"I know exactly what you mean," said the man, running his small hands through her hair and wondering if she'd just invented a movie title off the top of her head. He untucked her blouse from her jeans and felt the skin of her back, briefly pausing to calculate that this was an acceptable move three minutes into this particular make-out session.

She angled her head in a non-verbal cue to kiss her collarbone, which he proudly caught. He involuntarily took the sort of deep, shuddering breath that could come across as either repulsive or irresistible depending on the kind of mood one was in, and then waited to see which way she was going to take it.

"Let's find a bedroom," she said.

At the top of the stairs was a hall with a door on the left opening into darkness. They groped at the walls for a light switch, but soon gave up. There was a vaguely visible mattress on the floor, surrounded by oddly shaped piles of junk or debris. A single square of pillow was lit by a streetlight shining through the curtainless window.

The woman pushed him into the room and pounced. He tumbled, laughing, onto the bed, but instead of soft sheets, he squelched into something cold and wet with slime. All around him, clammy, slippery ooze moved in, soaking his clothes and hair. His fingers grasped a handful of the stringy mucus and held it to the light.

He screamed.

Garrett leaned against the doorframe, listening to the songs he'd grown so used to drumming on in rehearsals. It was strange to hear his parts in their original form, stripped of his unique ornaments and fills. He noted with satisfaction that, of the two of them, Aaron was the inferior drummer.

The *Bukowskis* had hired Garrett on a recommendation from their cousin, whose musical opinions they trusted unquestioningly, so he'd never actually seen them play live before his first practice. It was the first time he had a view of the band from an audience perspective.

The twins were good-looking, if musicians were your thing. They were floppy-haired and lightly freckled; identical and identically dishevelled—yet somehow Jaymie always looked like he'd just given a vigorous performance on a stage or in a bed while Aaron gave the impression of having just barely outrun the cops.

Besides being a little scrawnier and a little more likely to wear the expression of someone having a dream where everyone is clothed except him, Aaron had one subtle distinguishing feature from Jaymie, which was a small scar on his left cheek, mostly concealed by a wave of hair hanging over his face. Jaymie wore his hair the same way either out of solidarity or because he liked having the option of impersonating Aaron.

The band executed the hard stop at the end of "Don't Do It" and started into "A Place in the Heart," which featured a great chorus hook and lyrics almost too emo to get away with. Jo played an arpeggio pattern that traversed the entire neck of the guitar and back.

Jo had intimidated Garrett at first with her size, her straightforward manner, and the facility she had on her instrument. He'd even had a bit of a crush on her, until he'd realized what a complete deadbeat she was. Jo seemed entirely unambitious when it came to money or musical employment—besides the online profile that had gotten her this gig—and yet conveyed the self-assurance of a person who has done much more with her life than just play the guitar and watch TV in her parents' basement. Garrett couldn't tell whether she'd perhaps been overly drug-happy in her teen years, or if she really just didn't give a shit.

Jaymie sang a line about the irremediable emptiness of the soul and gave a little flourish on the keyboard. He jogged a lap of the stage, stood by the drumkit for four bars doing a shoulder stretch, and then yelped into the mic, *"There's no help for that, n-n-n-n-no, no help for that ..."* which, repeated sixteen times at different volumes and with one dramatic modulation, made up the outro of the song.

Jaymie had boundless energy. Garrett had never seen him tired or downtrodden or at a loss for words, though he'd frequently seen him elated, furious, enraptured, or grief-stricken (for instance, when one of his favourite bands released a bad album). Jaymie moved like whatever pitiful square of floor he'd been given to perform on was a spotlit stadium, and like it never occurred to him not to be confident.

Little Rex played simple, solid, and perfectly in-time bass parts, which mostly meant you didn't notice them much. They even adjusted tempo unflinchingly along with Aaron's dicey drumming. Rex wore their usual uniform of band T-shirt and jeans. Their blue-streaked hair was gelled into a spikey frame around their face, and one of their painted whiskers—applied by a careless or shaky hand—wiggled snakily down their cheek. Garrett liked Rex. Nice kid.

"What the hell are you doing here?" A curly-haired woman had appeared from nowhere.

Garrett cringed. He should've foreseen that Anika would be here.

"Came to see a show," he said, without looking at her.

"Right. You came to see the band, for fun, after you *cheated on their cousin*. Or maybe you forgot the family connection. Would you have made different choices, had you recalled you were dating the cousin of the people whose band you're in? Sorry—*were* in." Anika's tone was academic, but Garrett caught the vitriol.

"It was an open relationship, Nik. Like *you* wanted," he said, and winced as Aaron played a fill where, in his opinion, a fill should not be.

"Sure—conveniently open, from that moment onward."

Garrett was not interested in revisiting the same conversation they'd had for the last four days in a row. "I had thirty-six pumpkins," he said evenly. "I came to pick them up."

"Seriously? You expect me to believe you came to a house show looking for a bunch of pumpkins? Look around! See any vegetables? You're jealous or something. You know what? Good luck. I hope you find your goddamn pumpkins. I'm not letting this ruin my night." She was gone as quickly as she'd appeared. Anika had an uncanny aptitude for silent entries and exits.

Garrett stood undaunted, and Jo hit a wrong note that only he noticed, and Jaymie sang, *"Hey, you don't like it? Then get your ass out of here ..."*

At a quarter to one, the *Bukowskis* finished playing "Dirty Old Men," their final song, and began to either pack up, seek a drink, or mingle. Garrett considered this to be perfect timing, because at 12:50 the police showed up to arrest them.

4
Uneasy Thieves

"Honestly, officer, we were going to call 911 as soon as the show was over," said the young woman.

"We didn't want the guests becoming alarmed," said the man.

"The band was already playing. It was so loud."

"Or rather, their drummer found him beforehand—"

"They were just starting. But whoever killed him must have been long gone by then."

"I'm glad you were called. Enforcers. We weren't sure what to do."

"The body's safe, we put it upstairs."

"Truly sad this keeps happening at shows."

The police officers stared down the young promoters, whose imploring silhouettes in the doorway of their punk house gave the impression more of middle-aged parents defending a vandal child than a hip marketing team trying to save their first big show.

"Body?" asked one of the cops. "We got a call about some stolen pumpkins."

"Oh. Well yes, whoever did it took the band's pumpkins too." The girl must have noted the officer's skeptical look, because she added, "It was their merch. Was it their drummer who called you? He saw the body. I think he was pretty spooked."

The second officer responded, "Yeah, he said he was a drummer. I remember because I was thinking, 'Why would I care that you're a drummer?'"

"The show's over," the first officer told the couple. "Get the names of everyone here. Don't let the band leave yet. I want to see them, about their … pumpkins. And this death."

The young woman grumbled something at the order to shut down the party, but disappeared into the living room. The policewoman took their names from the young man and asked what he knew about the incident, which wasn't much. He showed them the table where the body had been found, explained how they'd immediately carried it upstairs out of the way, and endured a brief and too-late lecture about tampering with a crime scene. The other officer pulled out a walkie-talkie and said some things into it about starting a murder investigation and so on.

"OK," said the first officer. "Take us to the body."

The man led them to the staircase, just as another couple skidded down it and tumbled out the door, their faces blank with terror.

"So, it appears they found it." He gave a sheepish shrug. "But in our defence, it's not great etiquette to hook up in random people's rooms at a house concert, just saying …" The cops adjusted their expressions to a higher grade of Unimpressed and followed him upstairs.

The promoter found Jaymie wrapping the cord of his sustain pedal, effortlessly engaged in conversations with three different audience members at once.

"That's our newest song, glad you liked it … Yes, that really is my last name … No, I don't consider myself a nihilist—cool helmet, by the way …"

"Jaymie? Sorry, but the police want to talk to you. About the stolen pumpkins." Seeing his expression at the word 'police,' she added, "I know, right?"

"Uh oh, cops! I believe it's time to bail," said Jaymie, misunderstanding most of the situation. He hastily fitted his synth into its case, then remembered an important detail. "Did we make anything at the door?"

"Over three hundred!" she trilled. "Thank you so much for playing. We'll e-transfer you. The security answer will be 'Bukowski.' Sorry someone died at your show!"

"Such are the risks of living and of leaving the house," said Jaymie, with an appropriate amount of noble wistfulness. "I'm sorry as well. Thank you for hosting." He winked at her, and she blushed and moved away to clear out the guests.

Aaron was disassembling his drumkit and watching him in disbelief. Jaymie braced himself.

"Are you fucking crazy?" Aaron hissed. "There's a *dead body* in the house, and you want to make a run for it? We just stole a shit-ton of pumpkins!"

"Stole? Our pumpkins are covered in Bukowski logos. They look nothing like the ones that poor man lost!"

"Jaymie!"

"Plus, our pumpkins have conveniently walked off. It sure bites to be at karma's receiving end—I have new empathy for Garrett's loss—"

"Jaymie, I swear to god—"

"OK, you're right, it might look suspicious," Jaymie conceded. "Well, I've talked my way out of tighter situations than this. I once had to convince a gorilla-like bouncer I was good friends with Burton Cummings, even though the age difference between us is significant—"

"Yes, and you met the whole fucking *Guess Who*—you told me fifty fucking times, Jay, so will you just fucking go and—"

"Hey! Guys!" Anika broke in. She'd been standing beside the PA for who knows how long. "Good show, as always. Did you rob Garrett? He says you robbed him. He called the cops."

"Shit, he's *here*? That's just fucking perfect. Jaymie, you said he had a show!" Aaron was getting worked up again, and Jaymie sensed that it would be best for him and everyone in his vicinity if he were off the premises as soon as possible.

"Hey, Rex! Can you and Aar finish loading? I have to talk to some cops real quick."

Rex and their friends had formed an animated bubble of after-show euphoria, which they dutifully steered back toward the stage. Rex directed Maggie and Red Toque in teamwork-maneuvering the bass amp through the living room door. Anika picked up Aaron's cymbal bag and followed them out, muttering to Jaymie, "Good luck."

With the performance complete, Jo had promptly packed up her Jaguar and gone to find the free drinks their host had mentioned. The "artful beverages" turned out to be a few mixed cases of craft beer on the floor of the back porch. Pleased, she bent to select one, then rose and gave a small start—a tall, broad-shouldered man had come in behind her. He immediately offered his hand.

"Great set! Sorry to startle you. You're very skilled."

"Thanks. Thank you." She braced herself for the familiar tension of post-show encounters; she felt slow and scattered after playing, the hour of output having so depleted her social energy that only time or alcohol could replenish it. She twisted the cap off her beer.

"Did you used to play with the *Ballet Llama*? Eight or ten years ago?" the man asked, and Jo laughed in surprise.

"Yeah, when I was, like, eighteen. Wow, someone actually remembers that band?"

He grinned. "You guys were the best! My friends and I used to mosh at your shows. I barely remember it, honestly, but I know we had fun. Guess we were pretty drunk at the time."

"Us too," said Jo, trying not to sound too nostalgic.

"Yeah, I know. One show I remember, your bass player's strap came off, and he was too messed up to get it back on—he ended up cross-legged on his amp like he was meditating!"

"Yup, sounds like Jake. He fell off near the end, right?"

"Yes! His leg fell asleep, I think. Played the last however many songs lying on his back on the floor!"

"Those were the days," Jo deadpanned. She moved aside to let a costumed attendee leave through the back door.

"Nice suit—*Daft Punk*, right?" Lucas waved him out, then lowered his voice. "Whatever happened to that band? Dramatic breakup or something, right?"

If it was bait, Jo didn't rise. "We're in touch. Thought they might come tonight, actually," she mused. "But yeah, drifted apart. Our singer, Michaud, got a government arts job—"

"Seriously? So much for 'damn the man.' That guy was wild—glad to hear he lived past twenty!"

"Yeah, he cleaned up. Most of them still play, but in more chill bands. Jake's becoming a doctor or something. Got it out of his system, I guess."

"But not you?"

"I think my thrashing days are done, at least."

"This band suits you. You'd be wasted in punk."

Jo examined the man. He had a nice face and a neat goatee. He wore smart-looking black-rimmed glasses and an unpretentious button-down shirt. He was taller than her, which she found appealing, though she reminded herself that height is no indicator of character, and it's what's on the inside etc. etc.

He must have noticed her checking him out, because he too looked down in consideration of himself, and then cleared his throat and gave an awkward laugh. Jo was used to awkwardness, since she herself, like many musicians, was frequently awkward. Musicians have a particular skill: whether conscious of it or not (and Jo was not), they are able to make any non-musician they engage with feel as though the awkwardness is somehow their own fault—that it is they and not the musician who is gracelessly floundering.

"Nothing wrong with power chords, of course!" said the man, recovering from being subjected to the full brunt of this phenomenon. "… I'm Lucas."

"Jo. Do you play too?"

"No! No, I wish. Always wanted to be in a band, but I never had any rhythm. Actually, I write about live shows! I'd like to tell my readers about you guys, if that's OK. All six of them." He laughed. "They aren't critical reviews, it's all positive—not that I'd have anything negative to say! It's about promoting the scene. We need more people out at shows these days."

"Cool," said Jo. "Get your six readers out here."

"Maybe a few more than six."

"The more the merrier."

"Shows are more dangerous now, obviously. I guess this is the—what, the fourth or fifth death? I mean, of course you know that. But a lot of people want to keep coming. We want the music to keep happening."

"We'll keep the music happening, Lucas."

"Good. It was nice talking to you, Jo."

Jaymie was psyching himself up for a conversation with the police when Jo returned from the porch. She'd caught only the tail end of his and Anika's conversation, and she pointed at the ceiling and raised her eyebrows.

"Yeah, cops're up there."

"I'll come with you," she said, probably guessing her more imposing presence would be a comfort in a confrontation, and likely forgetting about the little ears and little whiskers tempering that presence.

"Thank you," said Jaymie.

"It's about the pumpkins?" asked Rex, who lingered in the doorway, teetering between following their friends outside and staying to provide Jaymie with support/supervision.

He realized with some relief that Aaron hadn't told Rex about the murder after all, and he decided to let them enjoy their performance high. "Yep, the pumpkins," he confirmed. "Don't even worry about it."

Rex nodded and looked around the room. "Sure cleared out fast in here."

The organizer had successfully dispersed the audience by telling them that *Noble Pirogue*, an illustrious and beloved local band, were playing a surprise show at a bar on Portage Avenue. By the time someone discredited the rumour, the party attendees would have spent fifteen minutes retrieving their footwear from the shoe-eating vortex of the front entrance and would likely go find somewhere else to drink.

Jaymie and Jo climbed the stairs, then hesitated in the hallway a few paces behind the police officers, unsure whether to announce themselves or wait to be called upon. Ahead of them, the promoter led the cops to the bedroom, stepped inside, and turned on a dim lamp on a bookcase, revealing the contents of the room.

The body had disappeared. Or rather, it had transformed. Surrounding the mattress in a neat semi-circle, the twenty-four pumpkins that remained intact stood keeping vigil. The other twelve had been eviscerated, their exoskeletons broken and reduced to blunt shards. The remains had been formed into the shape of a man, his body built from curved pumpkin slices, his lacerated vegetable flesh glinting in the low light. Barely contained within the fragments were the disgorged innards of the pumpkins, like fresh entrails leaking from countless wounds. The carcass rested on a bedsheet shiny with seed-laden juices, its faceless pumpkin head propped on the wet pillow, leaking stringy orange brains.

Jo stood transfixed in horror, while Jaymie backed away. As he retreated, he bumped into Garrett and yelped in surprise. Garrett, who had followed them upstairs to officially accuse them of the theft, took one look at the grisly scene and fled wordlessly back down the staircase.

"We have definitely not seen these pumpkins before," said Jaymie. "Never in our lives."

5

Compromise

The police were unable to locate the *real* body; a thorough search of the house revealed nothing out of the ordinary, besides the eerie pumpkin man. The remaining pumpkins were taken to be checked for fingerprints, with the promise they would be returned to their owners. The *Bukowskis'* drummer remained incorrectly credited with calling the police, and the band's claim to the produce was supported by the fact that every pumpkin was marked with the *BBBFB* logo.

When asked to confirm these facts, their singer had nodded slowly and said, "These are, in fact, our pumpkins. I was a little startled, is all. Poor pumpkins. Someone has broken them." The police sympathized with the unsettled musician—there was something about him they just trusted—and pronounced him free to go. The show's organizers then needlessly intervened to explain that the band was loading in when the body was found, and were therefore innocent, and should definitely not be sent to prison where there was probably no decent indie scene.

The cops agreed—besides, this problem was bigger than one newly emerging band. Over the past year, four murders had occurred at music events around the city. First, a college student received a very clean stab wound to the heart at a dreampop show on Osborne Street. Then a guest at a popular art gallery/venue was found propped outside, the ink of her hand-stamp still fresh, while a shoegaze band played blissfully on within. In early summer, two bodies appeared at the Jazz Fest's outdoor stage during 'Indie Night'; one was a mini-donut vendor, the other a trombone player. There were exactly zero witnesses.

The police, with no leads, didn't know what to do. Could you shut down a city's music scene? It would simply move underground and become more dangerous. Station cops at shows? Expensive and incendiary—and house concerts like this one wouldn't even make it onto their radar. Sponsor self-defence training for musicians and show-goers? The demographic statistically least likely to enroll for voluntary exercise? It wasn't in the budget anyway; they were saving up for a second helicopter.

There was no solution except to hope scenesters would be deterred by the danger and inspired to find a new, more productive hobby.

Jaymie and Jo returned downstairs to find Aaron, Anika, and Rex outside the locked van with the heap of gear, waiting for the key. Rex's friends were saying their goodbyes and admitting they had curfews and concerned parents after all.

"So, the cops said we can keep the pumpkins," said Jaymie. "When they're done taking Instagram photos with them."

"Jesus, do we even want them back?" said Jo, shaken by the scene in the bedroom.

"It's great merch," reasoned Anika.

"So, the police took away the, uh …?" Aaron glanced at Rex and avoided saying "body," or maybe "corpse" or "carcass" or "pumpkin cadaver"—Jo shook her head, longing to get home to a bedtime toke and her soft pillow.

"It wasn't exactly … I'll tell you later," said Jaymie. He unlocked the trunk and picked up an amp. "But yes, they're taking care of it. We're all good."

"Oh really? Are we all good?" The screen door banged shut behind Garrett.

Jo had, frankly, forgotten all about him. Her one strategy in a conflict was to stare down in confusion at her aggressor until they calculated the odds of beating her in a fight and apologized for whatever they'd demanded of her, but Garrett had recovered surprisingly quickly from the bedroom scene and didn't appear fazed even at being outnumbered five to one.

"Hey, Garrett. Thanks for coming out," said Jaymie.

"Anything to support the band," said Garrett. He picked up the heavy bass amp and set it in the back of the van with an ominous thunk. Rex, perched inside the vehicle, backed into the shadows and emitted a nervous "Huhuhuh OK."

Jaymie was undetermined. "Did you pay cover? You know we'd have put you on the guest list."

"Must've missed the set—did you start early?" Garrett shifted a few of their drums around, unreadable in the darkness. Jo didn't think he'd get violent, but she hadn't known him long, and his life's work was, after all, hitting things.

"Liar, you watched the whole show," said Anika.

"Stay out of it, Nik," said Garrett.

"Oh, bad move," said Jaymie.

"Stay out of it?" Anika snapped. "You want me to *stay out of it?* Maybe you should have thought of that at Harvest Moon Fest when you stayed after your set for a *'chill night at the campfires'* and then took shrooms and got naked with that hippy chick!"

"There it is," said Aaron. Rex let out a startled snort from the van. Jo relaxed, shook her head, and hefted two guitar cases into the trunk.

"For the last time, we were in an open relationship!"

"Maybe *you* were! I'm pretty sure rule number one of polyamory is you let your girlfriend know you're polyamorous!"

"Drummers, am I right?" Jaymie muttered to Aaron, as the two stacked the components of the drum set into the van in tandem.

"*Let you know?* It's what *you* wanted!"

"Yeah, and *you* hated it and *you* wanted to be monogamous, and *I* told the hot tattooed guy from my arts admin class, 'Sorry, but I'm with someone and it's very serious and committed—'"

While the two fought, Rex scuttled around the van fitting the gear into the space, which was a particular skill of Rex's. The others passed up the floor tom and synth cases, offering advice or congratulations as things jigsawed into place. Finally, Anika reappeared beside them.

"Garrett says he won't press charges if you give back the pumpkins." She sighed. "And he wants the door money, to make up for the broken ones."

"You worked all that out just now?" said Jaymie.

"He says …" She winced. "He thinks the police will be a lot more suspicious if they know you stole a few hundred dollars worth of produce right before someone got killed."

"Someone got *what?*" said Rex.

"Some poor guy dies, and all he cares about is blackmailing us about his stupid pumpkins?" said Jaymie.

"Yeah, and about the pumpkins ..." Anika smiled contritely. "I still think it's hilarious and I appreciate that you did it."

"Do we have a deal?" called Garrett from behind her. "Or should I tell those officers about how smashing up pumpkins is exactly the kind of thing this violent rock band is into—and I should know, I played with them for months. That's why I quit! Too aggressive. Who knows what they're capable of?"

Anika said "Fuck you," at the same time that Jaymie said "We *are* into the Smashing Pumpkins."

"And sure, you *probably* won't get a murder pinned on you. I mean, obviously you didn't do it ... Right?"

"You saw what was up there!" Jaymie cried. "I don't even think a human did that!"

"How would someone get that body downstairs without anyone seeing?" Jo shivered. "And to make that ... sculpture? Within the time of our set? That was, like, three sets worth of detail." She was recovering from her initial shock. Aaron and Rex, who hadn't seen the pumpkins since their transfiguration, exchanged confused looks.

Garrett was less interested in playing detective. "Fine, you were too busy singing to kill anyone," he said. "But either way, you'll sure as hell have to pay for those pumpkins. Everyone who knows us knows they're mine."

Jaymie threw up his hands. "Yeah, fine. They wouldn't have sold anyway."

"Good. How much did you make at the door?" asked Garrett.

"Fifty bucks," Jaymie replied without hesitation.

Garrett had seen the full living room and looked understandably skeptical, so Jaymie continued, "Promoters have to pay for their posters and Facebook ads and stuff. Why is this a thing with you? If you want money, go play country music."

"Whatever. I want them back by Monday. And the fifty."

Apparently satisfied, Garrett left them standing in the street. Jaymie kicked at some dead leaves. "Well, I think that went well! Considering."

"Thanks for taking my side," said Anika.

"Of course! *We* don't care *who* said it was an open relationship *when*. Right guys?"

The band quickly murmured assent.

"What an asshole," said Jo.

"Sucks about Tattoo Guy from your summer class," said Rex.

"Oh, we went out yesterday! Found him on Insta—he's kind of a big deal, as it turns out," said Anika. "… Sorry about Garrett."

Jaymie shrugged. "He got us through a few months, but I wanted Aaron back in the band anyway! I get all funny if we don't hang out enough. I descend into emotional turmoil, pretty soon I'm an alcoholic—you know how it is." He gestured offhandedly, as if they could all relate to the separation anxiety of being temporarily Aaron-less.

"Oh, almost forgot—while you were upstairs. For you," said Aaron, stuffing a scrap of paper into Jaymie's hand. It was a phone number.

"That's really sweet, Aar, but I do live with you. I can still talk to you whenever I want."

"Ha ha. The girl dressed up as a sexy fugitive."

"Oh, is that what she was!"

"Mira … Mika … She told me her name but I forget. I'm sure you remember though." He smiled insincerely at Jaymie, who did not remember.

Jaymie looked down at the wavy dashes and loopy zeros. He put the paper in his pocket. "Thanks, Aar. I appreciate you giving me this, rather than impersonating me, going on a date with that beautiful woman, marrying her, and living a lie for the rest of your life."

"As you would have done to—"

"As I would have done to you."

The exhausted *Bukowskis* got the last gear Tetris-packed into the van, and Rex drove them to the large house where the siblings lived and jammed. Rex hadn't asked about the murder, trusting Jaymie to provide a dramatic and overly-detailed explanation at home.

They left their equipment in the kitchen, to be unpacked in the morning. Jo drank a glass of water and dug for her car keys while Jaymie lit his last cigarette of the night. Rex slouched and sang a Cat Came Back bassline under their breath. Aaron broke the peace.

"This was the last one, Jay. It's dangerous and it's fucking tiring. And, as I've told you more than once, I'm busy. I'm going back to school."

Rex tensed. As much as they wanted both brothers to be happy, it was simple and obvious that they should all be a band together. They waited for Jaymie to resolve the issue.

Jaymie tapped his cigarette into a dead petunia still hanging by the door from summertime. "Yeah, right," he said. "You'll be bored out of your mind. They'll kick you out of Psych 101 for compulsively drumming on your little lunch kit all day. You'll flunk Intro Logic because you won't be able to find a rationale for meaninglessly sitting there hour after hour. You'll drop math once you put two and two together that you'd rather—"

"I'm not taking math! Have you ever once asked me what I'd study? No, because you only think about yourself. It hasn't even crossed your mind that I'm not just a duplicate of you who exists to be your helper for whatever stupid plans you've come up with. Maybe I want to take … Biology! Or … I'm not sure …"

"Biology? That's *nature*. You're afraid of nature! You know what nature includes? Dogs! Stick to your comfort zone, Aaron—you're barely even comfortable there."

"You think *this* is my comfort zone?" Aaron's whiskers had commingled with nervous sweat into a chimney-sweep smear, and the sooty line of makeup connecting his nose and upper lip blurred like a nosebleed. He was breathing heavily, and Rex hoped he was working out some anger rather than initiating another panic attack.

"You know what?" said Jaymie. "I never asked because I know you so well that I don't need to! You'll drop out, and—"

"No, fuck this! Quit blaming me for—forget it. I'm leaving."

Jaymie finally lost his composure. "Leaving! Where the hell are you going to go?" He gesticulated wildly with his cigarette, alarm clear on his face.

"To bed, Jaymie! It's fucking three in the morning!"

"Oh … OK goodnight. Love you."

"Love you too goodnight." Aaron deflated, half-heartedly slamming the door behind him.

Jaymie stubbed his cigarette in the petunia and smiled contentedly at Jo and Rex. "Good show, friends! He'll come around. We're going on tour!"

Garrett's pumpkins were declared fingerprintless, picked up by one Brzezinski or another, and returned to him, as promised, along with fifty dollars. The sharpie-pen logos on them were distinctly off-brand. Still, the remaining twenty-two sold at the next farmers' market and went to new homes in time for Halloween.

The pumpkins missed Jaymie Brzezinski terribly. From pantries and front porches, they reflected on their brief time with him, remembering the feel of his arms around their middles and his voice in the back seat of the car and his synthesizers weaving haunting melodies from the crowded living room. From 12:00 until 12:05 every night, each pumpkin could be heard quietly singing the *Bukowskis'* opening song, and each, when carved into fearsome Jack-o-lanterns, mourned the concealment of their beautiful band logo and rotted immediately in protest.

The *BBBFB* Instagram page received nine new followers after the show, and twelve more after the farmer's market. One buyer liked the logo, and he looked them up, appreciated their musicianship, and messaged them about playing a tribute show he was organizing in December. So, all in all, it could be considered a successful night.

6
Interlude 1

Bukowski Lives!
By Lucas Yarbrough. October 15th, 2019.

The Bukowski Brothers' Broken Family Band (their actual band name) has cornered the market on indie bands fronted by dead writers. Spirited frontman Jaymie Bukowski (his actual name, according to social media) claims to have been born the moment Charles Bukowski (probably not JB's actual ancestor) died, a story which this reviewer can so far neither confirm nor deny. Whether or not there's credence to his tale matters very little in light of the performance the BBBFB delivered Friday night at a house show put on by Lo Wave, an up and coming local promo team.

The show begins with JB monologuing about his at-birth Bukowski-possession. For a guy whose youth has been a continuation of the life of a curmudgeonly, gambling-addicted septuagenarian, JB is surprisingly energetic. The first song, an upbeat scorcher, is about how terrible every writer except him is— a Bukowski sentiment if ever there was one.

Though the term "indie rock" is too broad a category to be descriptive, The BBBFB's guitar- and synth-centred sound falls firmly on the darker side of this genre—JB presents his lyrics with a frantic theatricality that combines an indie aesthetic with punk rock performance art. Four songs in, he appears to be wasted (but is, I suspect, not actually wasted) and is yelling a nonsensical drunken diatribe against whichever god controls the outcomes of horse races in California, with no accompaniment but a tipsy walking bass line, the band's tight pop sensibilities set aside for a freak-jazz meander. It is, in a word, madness.

Guitarist Jo Connors (maybe an actual genius) may be known to some for her stint circa 2009 in The Ballet Llama, the kind of band that made me wish I was in a band. We're 25 minutes in and she's shredding scales and notes and assumptions and etc. while JB performs an onstage costume change (mailman Bukowski to journalist Bukowski). Connors has left behind her days of rage-y power chords at blistering speeds, but she hasn't lost her intensity. Hey Jo, can we go on a date? Just kidding, it's 2019, and that's inappropriate.

JB's wardrobe change fortunately doesn't include his underwear, which, it is soon revealed, are horseshoe-patterned. The enraptured faces in the front row suggest that this is the type of classic manic pixie dreamboy young fans love to lust over. He has somehow captured the hearts of both literary-referencing intellectuals and trendy teenagers alike. (And, of course, the rad young and young-at-heart within that Venn diagram). Mind you, there may be no one outside those demographics that the band would appeal to—they're just too weird.

JB trades his synth for an electric guitar and manages to play it while jumping up and down on the balls of his feet and spewing a ceaseless stream of lyrics naming and describing his 9 cats, almost too fast to make out, for an entire song. If he breathes, I don't catch it. His backing band, costumed as 3 out of 9 cats, never misses a beat.

We're nearing the end, and JB leads the rhythm section (his actual family) into a gentle ballad about the narrator's penchant for 'getting drunk and jacking off in bed' (an actual line from the bridge), and I think to myself, why are we all here? We're going to get ourselves murdered.

You'll have no doubt heard about the tragedy by now. You'll have heard another outburst of warnings to stay in and let the scene founder and die. But we will not stay in. I may not be in a band, but this is the next best thing, and I know you: rockers, trend-setters, and music lovers of all kinds, I remind you (not that you actually need it), this is a city that supports their friends' band in the thick of a January blizzard, and threats of (actual) danger won't stop us either. Shows like this are the reason why.

Bukowski finishes the set slumped on the floor, the band executing a live fade-out as his voice diminishes to a whisper. The audience cheers. This young Buk has proven that our music scene is far from dead.

RIP Kenton Weins

Part Two

The Band Books a Tour

7

Fans

From the back of the stage at the back of the dim cavern that was Rookies Sports Bar, the beat was speeding up and slowing down like a treadmill set to a heavy-duty interval cardio routine. It vaguely registered in the mind of Jaymie Brzezinski, who stood behind the keyboard, that his drummer might be having a panic attack, but he was imagining they were in some big city playing a major showcase, and the showcase must go on.

In front of the stage was a checkered dance floor, which was vacant. In the sound booth further back was a slightly drunk but very focused man who seemed to have made mixing for empty rooms his life's work; the low end was rich but not overwhelming, the highs pristine. Behind him, several pool tables and VLTs had attracted slightly more attention than the band playing. Left of the stage was a long bar at which a few regulars sat heavily on their stools, patiently tolerating the set of young musicians who frequently intruded on their habitat.

Between the dance floor and sound guy, a smooshed and drooping couch crouched, like an animal that had hunched its way in from the cold and tried to appear inconspicuous. Fortunately, it had found its niche and been accepted for who it was by the three people watching the show from the comfort of its decrepit cushions. These onlookers were familiar with the couch, having seen this particular band at this particular bar countless times—together they made up three quarters of the Bukowskiphiles.

The *Bukowski Brothers'* fan club was nearly as prolific as the band themselves. At its core were Rex's two best friends from school, and their stan, a middle aged man whom none of them had known personally before forming the band and who, as far as they knew, was actually named Stan. They had yet to test whether he'd defend them to the death.

In the peripheral circle were BabyBFBgirl, a regular contributor to their forum, and Bukfan69, who may have signed on believing it to be a fan page for the real Charles Bukowski. Ahem, the *former* Charles Bukowski.

Stan sat wedged between Rex's friends, a Mike's Hard Lemonade in one hand and a camcorder in the other. Maggie and her co-founder, Shahla, didn't seem to mind—they'd known the risks of starting a club, and his fanaticism could only add to their legitimacy.

Likewise, Jaymie had known the risks of forming a family band. With unpaid backing musicians, you had to accommodate a few quirks, and Jaymie knew how to be flexible, even when the beat had itself become so flexible as to be all but lost forever. He turned away from the keyboard and yelled, "Drum solo!"

Aaron, drenched in nervous sweat, looked up in disbelief and stopped playing all together. Rex and Jo lowered their hands from their fretboards, relieved for the struggle to be over. Jaymie winced and tried again, more quietly, "Drum solo?"

Aaron blinked, communicated telepathically that he had quit the band once and for all, and launched into an erratic, hysterical drum solo.

"Free jazz …" Jaymie whispered into the microphone.

Aaron lost a stick over his left shoulder and snatched another one from his stockpile, his playing unfettered by such constraints as timing. It was a deranged, lawless music, frantic and cathartic. From the chaos of the kit a turbulent soul was unleashed, howling a furious celebration of its misfortunes. The toms took on a jungle timbre, and then—an explosion from the crash cymbal—he accidentally dropped both sticks at once, grabbed another pair, and rose as a phoenix from the flames playing perfectly metronomic skipping sixteenth notes on the hi-hat.

Jaymie was euphoric. He had caused this tragically temporal work of art! He faced the audience. Rex's friends were laughing at a meme on one of their phones, their heads nearly meeting over the protruding stomach of Stan, who was too busy troubleshooting his camcorder to express his usual enthrallment at Jaymie's impromptu act of brilliance. The bartender wiped a glass and watched the stage with an expression conveying skepticism at Jaymie's life choices.

Maybe they weren't at the right venue for this. He cued the rest of the band back in for the last chorus of "With or Without Pay," the beat solidly in place.

"I'm booking us a tour for next month!" Jaymie exulted.

"Thought I was gonna die up there. Played here a million times, don't know what came over me …" Aaron alternately gulped water and sipped from a glass of whiskey.

"One show is already confirmed! I got the email today." Jaymie fished a cigarette from his pocket and slid it behind his ear.

"It's like, I suddenly wondered if we'd finish up and someone would be dead in the back room or something, you know?" said Aaron.

Rex sat between their brothers, a textbook open before them. Pages of pencil-scrawled solutions overlapped on the sections of the bar not occupied by Jaymie and Aaron's drinks. Rex held an orange juice containing a half-shot of tequila that Jaymie had splashed in from his own glass—unbeknownst to the bartender, who had known Rex too long for them to implement a fake ID, and allowed them in as a band member, provided they didn't drink.

Rex's friends, who had completely convincing IDs made by Shahla, had already been demanded at home by parents conscientious of their circadian rhythms. Rex occasionally wondered what it would have been like to have a curfew; perhaps Rex would have been more rebellious, had they been provided a rule or two to rebel against.

"Pretty sure it takes, like, three months to book a tour," said Aaron.

"So cynical, Aar," said Jaymie. "Haven't I proven myself capable of a little thing like an express-booked tour?"

"And have you forgotten our sister has school? They have to do their—" He glanced at the textbook, "—numbers."

"'Brother' or 'sibling' is fine," monotoned Rex, whose Pronoun Grace Period, generously implemented for the benefit of loved ones struggling to adjust, was drawing to a close. "I know it's new, but like … try."

"Sibling! Sorry, Rex. I just had a cardiac arrest on stage, if that's any excuse."

"I'm confident our new baby brother is back on track enough to miss a few days of high school," said Jaymie. "Who says they can't learn algebra on the road? Right, Rex?"

Rex shrugged in reluctant hope. "I'll tour. But ... I shouldn't miss jazz band concerts."

"Dammit Rex, when'd you get so well-adjusted! You could drop out like we did and do music for real! Mom would approve."

"Jesus, Jay, they're *finally* back to doing a regular school week. You know he's kidding, Rex. You keep adding up those x's ..." Aaron slid a sheet of equations over for a closer look. "Where would we tour, anyway? Toronto? With the highway getting all icy in November ..."

Rex was wary of getting their excitement up when it came to the *BBBFB*, yet they felt, deep down, that the band was great. They had little interest in expanding their horizons to other musical projects, even though their mother often reminded them that competent bass players were in constant demand; the world would soon be their oyster, etc.

Despite Rex's undying loyalty, there always seemed to be more setbacks than successes. That spring, Aaron had quit drumming to finish his abandoned high school diploma, and Jaymie had been so angry he'd moved to a hippy friend's couch for ten days. The couch was too short and only had springs on one side, so he'd foregone sleep, lived off Adderall and vegan pâté, and penned from scratch a full-length concept album about a brave writer subjected to a deep betrayal, until his siblings had driven the nine blocks to Kildare Avenue and rescued him.

They could play their own neighbourhood bar as often as they liked, but when they landed a real gig, it always seemed to be in spite of things rather than due to planning and deliberation. It had occurred to Rex that this was why bands who could afford it got a manager.

"Not Toronto. What if I told you we were going to ... Poland! Free tickets from Tato!"

The effect on his siblings was instantaneous. Aaron gulped from the wrong drink and sprayed a geyser of whiskey across the counter. The bartender glared.

"*Are you crazy?*"

"We're not going to Poland," said Rex.

"Poland is full of psychopaths!" said Aaron.

"It's all creepers and drug lords," said Rex.

"Did you even read the last email? He barely stopped a terrorist!"

"I'm kidding," said Jaymie. "We'd literally get kidnapped before stepping off the plane."

"Free tickets. Jesus. If Dad wants to see us, he can come here. All *we* have to deal with is the odd murder." Aaron found a napkin and dabbed at Rex's notes, which had been caught in his spray.

"Maybe if he came here, he could catch that killer," Jaymie said thoughtfully.

"Yeah, pitch that to him," said Rex.

The Brzezinskis didn't admit to outsiders that they were afraid of Poland, but it had long been a means of freaking each other out. When Rex was a child, the twins had regaled them with made-up Poland horror stories, based loosely on their father's news-clippings, postcards, and the anecdotes he delivered with a bit of fuzz and a time-delay over the phone.

"No," said Jaymie. "This autumn, we go west!"

"B.C.?" Rex asked hopefully.

"Close, Rex. Close …" He timed his pause for the sweet spot when both his brothers clearly wanted to shake him but hadn't yet stormed off. "Regina!"

Aaron rolled his eyes and pushed away his glass. "I'm going to pack my drums," he said. "And maybe rescue Jo from Stan."

Jo had been cornered before she could make it to the bar and was now being long-windedly—though not unkindly—informed which famous male guitarists she sounded most like. The Brzezinskis had decided to allow Stan some time with her, in the interest of keeping their biggest fan happy. He'd been thrilled at their choice to add lead guitar.

"What a snob. Am I right?" Jaymie jerked his head in Aaron's direction and rose to go smoke. Rex sipped their weak tequila sunrise and returned to their homework.

The next morning, Jo was awoken at 6:51 by a relentless knocking at the window over her bed. She lived in a basement apartment in West Broadway, and the intrusion on her sleep reminded her to ask her landlord about getting a double-paned window—for quiet and warmth—as soon as she'd paid rent on time for a month or two and was back in the good books.

She sat up, turned on the lamp, and immediately collapsed back onto her pillow, one arm slung over her eyes, head feeling like a balloon blown too full. She'd had one too many drinks after the show. It happened more often at shows with poor attendance and low stakes—times when there was little reason to celebrate besides the fact that Rex had been offered up as DD.

She'd also indulged in a couple of Jaymie's cigarettes, if only because, as most musicians know, it's important in life to show that you're able to do a number of things that make you feel physically ill.

She groaned and rose. Jaymie stared back at her through the cloudy glass of the window. The streetlights were still on and the reluctant sun had yet to reach the narrow stretch between Jo's window and the brick wall it looked out on.

She jimmied the pane open. Jaymie immediately took this as an invitation to slide through and drop down onto the end of the bed. He tugged a heavy-looking messenger bag after him, barely keeping its contents from spilling out the top, and sat against the wall, his hiking boots—the most practical thing Jo had seen him wear—dangling over the side of the mattress.

An odd, hungover thought crossed her mind: her band of thieving weirdos was stalking her, and now that they'd dropped her off and knew her address, she'd lost her last opportunity to get out. She quickly reminded herself that bands were a thing she was trying to get back *into*.

"Dude, what are you doing here?" she asked. "We just got home, like, five hours ago."

"I'm delivering your mail!" he gestured at his scruffy bag.

"You're *actually* a postal worker," she said dully. She slumped down next to him on the bed. "Of course you're a postal worker. Like Bukowski."

"I've decided not be offended that you've never been interested in how I pay for our equipment, but yes, I work for Canada Post. And I just got switched to your neighbourhood! Fortuitous, no?" He bounced a little on the bed. "Hey, did you move recently?"

Jo had moved shortly before joining the band, following a stay in her parents' basement. At one point she'd quit her job, decided to 'make a go of it' in music, promptly failed to find any paying gigs, and needed the free rent at her folks' until she found part-time work.

Since moving, she'd unpacked exactly one and a half bags. In fact, Jaymie was her first visitor. She wondered what he must think of the small space, scattered with cardboard boxes.

She rubbed her eyes. "Aren't you on some kind of delivery schedule?"

He ignored the question. "Jo! It's good to get up early! You can get so much more done—more than people who sleep the same amount but stay up late. Studies show!" He rifled through his mail bag. "You have ... an angry letter from your internet provider—uh oh!—aaand ... the Long and McQuade Christmas catalogue. Early on it this year, aren't they?"

"There's nothing I need to get done today!" she protested. "I was going to sleep in. Since we played that show last night? And loaded all our gear in at one a.m.?"

"A success is no reason to give up, Jo. In fact, the opposite is true!"

"How many energy drinks have you had?" As she asked it, she wondered if there was something stronger giving Jaymie his zest.

Jo wasn't exactly unmotivated. It was just that once you've learned an instrument, you realize you'll never be good enough at anything in your life. Any new interest is an unending commitment. How did anyone decide to, say, *learn French*? When would you be done learning French? You'd have to spend the rest of your life on it, or forfeit and admit defeat. Sure, she could spend the morning cleaning her apartment, but would it ever be *clean*? It all seemed distantly overwhelming. Besides, she didn't mind having time to be bored now and then.

Jaymie Brzezinski had not been bored since 2012.

"No energy drinks until after 12 p.m., that's my rule. I ate a ton of Lucky Charms this morning though." He winked. "It's not healthy, but it is lucky—I manifested us a tour!" Jo burrowed back into her warm blankets. "What's his secret, you ask? His secret is *The Secret!* Laws of attraction. Creative visualization. And a complete breakfast—of cereal marshmallows! Youcangetthemwithouttheactualcerealnow ..." Jo turned off her lamp. "Imagine how much you could practice the guitar if you started at seven a.m.—"

At this, she'd had enough. She knew how to practice the guitar. She rolled out of bed, grabbed Jaymie's mail bag, and thrust it out the window. Before he could protest, she grasped his arms, hefted him up to standing, and got her palms under his heel for a boost. As she stuffed him back out the window, he delivered the message he'd come to report.

"We have a mini-tour in two weeks! Two shows in Regina. One's a bar, with a two-fifty guarantee. Gas money! Then another house party, which is always great for a built-in crowd—but you know that, obviously. Kinda kooky folks, but nice, I think. We're gonna make bank! 'Get that bread,' as Rex says. Plus—fans! Okseeyouatpractice!"

Jo slammed the window shut and tumbled back onto her mattress. She squeezed her knees into her chest until her slight nausea subsided. Trying to maintain her annoyance, she thought of all the reasons why a seven-hour drive for two shows was barely worth the trouble, and yet, after a moment, a small, satisfied smile curled its way across her face.

8
Band Practice

Jaymie slept for the entirety of the following day. He was late for band practice and they all assumed he'd been delayed at work or had gone out and lost track of time, until Rex had the inspired idea to check the loveseat in their enclosed front porch. They found him curled up under all three of the Brzezinskis' ancient cats and two ratty blankets deemed too decrepit for anyone's bed, but acceptable for evening porch hangouts. Jo had walked in right past him.

The Brzezinski siblings were the third generation of their family to watch over the old house on Pandora Street. Their Grandma and Grandpa McLeod had bought the home in the sixties and lived there until their retirement, then left it to their itinerant eldest daughter and moved to Florida. The three cats had opted to stay and watch over the house rather than snowbird away to a warmer locale; they were estimated to have moved in around the same time as the grandparents and likely didn't have another relocation in them.

The home was two and a half stories, had an outward appearance of slight dilapidation, was cluttered but clean within, and boasted a cozy and well-furnished basement jam space.

Herman, a massive long-haired tabby, creaked down the stairs as Jaymie haphazardly arranged himself by his keyboard and guitar. Two of three cats had gone deaf in the early 2000s and as a result now enjoyed participating in band practices. The third sang along from the safety of the main floor in a voice that didn't quite approximate syllables or a steady pitch.

As Jaymie set up, Aaron made sure no one had curled up for a nap in the bass drum and began a quiet swing beat. Rex walked a bassline and Jo tried out some dissonant jazz chords.

Jo had realized at her first real practice with Aaron that the house concert hadn't been a fair representation of his playing. At the time, she'd been disconcerted by his inconsistency, and was troubled to think an unsteady tempo could compromise a band with so much potential.

She'd since upgraded her opinion—Aaron was entirely competent, and at times inventive in ways Garrett's steady hands hadn't been, provided no one had recently been murdered nearby, *and* he had to believe no one was *going* to get murdered nearby by the end of the night, which seemed to be difficult criteria to fulfil lately.

Fortunately, they were leaving the province, if only for a weekend. Regina might have its share of challenges, but at least no active musician serial killers they were aware of.

"Today, a new song!" said Jaymie, gulping coffee and incorrectly plugging and re-plugging cables into a vocal effects pedal. "Then we work on our cover set." Aaron groaned. "—And quit that highbrow music snobbery, Aar. Sometimes you have to give THE PEOPLE …" His voice was magnified as he succeeded in connecting his mic to his pedal to the PA. He clicked the delay on. "… what they want." *What they want they want they wantwantwa*

Jaymie had been trying to convince his siblings to learn a country set to supplement their musical income. He'd been inspired toward this more commercial route after attending an arts career workshop that preached the benefits of selling out (without using that term).

"You know who loves family bands?" he'd lectured his family band. "Country fans! Well, folk fans. But we already play one genre that doesn't make any cash. So."

Surprisingly to some—considering her punk background—the only one not inconvenienced was Jo, who was already a shredder and promptly learned to chicken-pick with a gusto that kept her stone-cold sober for at least two or three hours out of every day. The other two protested the effort and/or indignity, and so far only three covers had been mastered.

"What's the new song?" asked Rex, their usual calm expression taking on a similar but slightly upturned variation that Jo was coming to recognize as enthusiasm.

"Yes, thank you for asking, T-Rex. I just wrote it! In the front porch a few minutes ago."

"You were passed out cold," said Rex.

"You know there's no use contradicting him," said Aaron, clicking an impatient rhythm on the rim of his snare drum.

"What's it about?" Rex asked.

"Yes, Trent Rex-nor. Again, good question, thank you." Jaymie adjusted his levels on the mixer, cleared his throat into the mic, struck a chord, and sang, "Mira, Miiiiiiiirrrrrraaaaaaa …"

The Bukowskiphiles were also having a productive day, having decided on a gesture to send their favourite band off on their first tour. In attendance at the gathering in Maggie's living room were Maggie, Shahla, and Shahla's twelve-year-old sister, Ayla, who was visibly too young to go to shows and therefore only held the status of 'Junior Member.'

Stan's presence would have been too difficult to explain to Maggie's mother, but he would soon Skype in to give a presentation on references to the novel "Ham on Rye" in the band's single, "Ramen High," and no doubt express his glowing opinion on the new guitarist.

The three girls had strewn the carpet with craft supplies while the *BBBFB's* self-recorded EP played on repeat. Maggie had painted the four *Bukowskis* as woodland animals, onstage with their instruments in their paws. Ayla had written her own and Jaymie's initials in perfect gothic calligraphy script, surrounded by an expanding network of marker-drawn hearts that gave the impression of a very affectionate acid trip.

Shahla had coded an AI fed with all of Jaymie's lyrics and a selection of Bukowski's poetry, which now outputted its own original *BBBFB* lyrics in varying degrees of lunacy.

Next on the agenda was to research the tour stops. This was an important part of staying on the same page as the band, since they couldn't be with them in person. The first venue, an unremarkable-looking pub, was easy to find.

The second proved more of a challenge, since it was privately organized. Shahla had no choice but to hack into the *Bukowskis'* Facebook messages, find the relevant correspondence, infiltrate the show planner's personal account, determine her address via a grocery order confirmation, and execute a thorough examination of the house using Google Street View. A fan's gotta do what a fan's gotta do.

The host lived in a huge house on the city's outskirts. It was light blue with white trim. Shahla made a note of this in her spreadsheet.

Stan was having trouble with his internet connection, and she absentmindedly scanned through the hacked email account while they waited. Maggie finished her artwork and sent a text rated approximately 18A to the boy she'd befriended at the house show.

"Hey, look at this." Shahla spun her laptop around to face Maggie, whose eyes darted over the screen, narrowing as she scrolled.

"Who are these people?" she asked.

"I don't know. Like, *all* her emails are like this." Shahla clicked back and pulled up another message. "Do you think we should tell Rex?"

"I think we should go to this show," said Maggie.

"Pretty sure I won't be allowed to drive to a different city for a show," said Shahla. "Especially at some stranger's house."

"Can I come?" asked Ayla, pausing mid-reapplication of the lipstick she was using to make kiss marks on her card.

"Did you hear what I just said?" Shahla contemplatively lobbed a glue stick at her sister, already imagining an email, sent to her mother from her programming instructor, about a youth tech conference in Saskatchewan which would enrich her young web-developer mind …

"We can take my dad's car," said Maggie.

"I'm not sure." *Your child, having shown strong potential for a career in Computer Science, is invited to attend the Canadian Youth Conference for…* No, *The Western Canadian Conference of…* She'd have to design a website for it and everything.

Just then, Stan unplugged his router and plugged it back in again, and the deities of internet connection looked up from their cat memes and smiled upon him. The video-chat ringtone piped out of Shahla's computer.

"Hey Stan," said Maggie.

"Greetings," said Stan. "Today, I want to talk to you all about symbolism …"

The band played their three covers and ten originals, then ran the new song four more times, reworking the structure, adding an extra chorus, lengthening the guitar solo, subtracting the extra chorus, changing the pads in the second verse. They left the vocal harmonies, the development of which usually involved some amount of controversy and abuse, for last.

"You want me to sing a third above the entire time and then randomly drop, like, two octaves mid-line?" Aaron jittered the hi-hat, tossed a stick in the air, and failed to catch it.

"Yes, correct, so glad you understand. Let's take it from the bridge?"

"Jay, that doesn't make any sense. I'm already singing the higher part. If I just stay there, then we're not both suddenly making a huge switch."

"I just, this is how I hear it." Jaymie shrugged.

"You just like that line better! It's the *one* part where the harmony moves more than the melody. You can't stand not being on the more interesting part for even one line!"

"No, that *is* the melody. They swap registers," Jaymie insisted. "That's how I wrote it."

"You didn't write it! I *just* came up with that harmony while we were singing! Like two minutes ago!"

"Right, but it's how I *imagined* it—that's why I told you to sing it a third above!"

Rex broke in. "Guys! You have the same voice. Literally nobody will know the difference."

"The difference is in the delivery, Rex," said Jaymie adamantly. "No one who has heard us would mistake us."

"Everyone who's heard the EP thinks you layered your own harmonies."

"What!" said Aaron.

"There are obviously two of us!" said Jaymie. "And I don't like when people sing their own harmonies—you can hear the ego!"

"Jo?" asked Rex, and Jo was taken off guard at being pulled into the dispute. Maybe this meant she was officially part of the band.

"Yeah, I figured you multitracked yourself," she admitted.

"Goddamn it," said Aaron.

"Well," said Jaymie, looking at Aaron in defeat. "Arm wrestle for the higher part?"

"Tenors," muttered Rex. "God."

Aaron rose in resignation from behind the kit. Rex rolled their eyes and swung their bass off their shoulder. "Food break?" Jo nodded and set down her guitar.

Jaymie was slightly bigger than Aaron, but Aaron spent many hours of his life beating on inanimate objects with sticks, so the two were perfectly matched in strength. The real suspense of the contest lay in whether Jaymie would get distracted by something before Aaron started to worry about the health ramifications of prolonged strain on a muscle group.

Rex led the way upstairs and into the kitchen, where Diana Ross lay in the middle of the floor like a forgotten bundle of dishtowels, exhausted from making her octave-above descant audible from one floor away. Jo touched her side when Rex wasn't looking, and was reassured she was alive by a purr beneath her fingertips.

Rex opened the fridge, on top of which sat an impressive collection of marshmallow-filled cereals.

"This is your mom's place, right? Do you guys pay rent?" asked Jo, to make conversation. Young people, even if only five or ten years younger than herself, made her self-conscious. Even nice ones like Rex could throw her off. It was something about their limitless potential, coupled with their (she assumed) propensity to judge her lack thereof.

"No, but we look after it for her, and the cats." Rex found salsa and cheese whiz in the fridge and rummaged in a cupboard for chips. "The guys cover bills and whatever. But I'm, like, in high school. She pays *me* my allowance, to stay there."

"Right, duh, you're a kid. No, sorry, I mean … So, she's travelling, right? A musician?"

"Yeah, she has a gig in Vegas, or she'll get on with touring shows in the States." Rex poured salsa into a bowl and checked the expiration date on the jar with the weary habit of someone who has learned the hard way to check expiration dates on jars.

"But, so, if she's down there, you weren't just raised by …" Jo glanced at the staircase. The twins could be faintly heard trying to psych each other out. Rex laughed.

"If you think *this* is obnoxious, you should see them when they're getting along. 'Come jam with us Rex. Come jam with us Rex. Did you eat today Rex, did you eat today Rex.' Everything twice."

"Looking forward to that."

"But no, we stayed with our aunts when she was away. Anika's moms. A and J moved back here full time when they dropped out of grade twelve. Mom didn't travel so much when they were kids, but I'm *mature*, apparently. I was allowed to move home from the Aunties' a couple years ago, as long as I keep up my grades. I was always over here practicing anyway."

"Cool. Your dad's not in the city?"

"He lives in Poland. We want to visit him someday. But I wouldn't go there unless it was with a big music project. Like, with security."

Jo was confused. "Rex, uh, you know Poland is a developed country, right? I think they have a pretty decent standard of living?" She flinched, wondering if, in her curiosity, she'd accidentally grilled a queer kid on their modern-family setup and then mansplained Poland.

Rex made an unreadable teenager expression at her, and she quickly volunteered, "I moved a couple months ago, out of my parents' place—again. Must be nice to be in your own space long enough to set up all the instruments and everything."

"Oh, are you from here? What school did you go to? Did you meet the *Ballet Llama* there? Is it true somebody died in Quebec?" Rex asked, and then grinned in embarrassment at this lapse in their impassive demeanor. "Sorry. Lots of time on tour."

Jo was instantly more at ease. "Ha, rumours! Yeah, they were a couple years ahead of me. We didn't have as much in common, though, besides the music. Not like you guys."

A round of swearing from downstairs signalled the end of the battle for the upper harmony. Rex scooped up both dip bowls and the chips in one stretchy musician hand and plucked the limp cat off the floor with the other, then led the way back downstairs. Aaron was stretching and shaking out his arm. Jaymie rolled his shoulders and turned off the PA.

"I don't care who won," Rex told them.

"OK, well, one more thing. I wrote a song too," said Aaron.

"Is it about dogs?" Jaymie and Rex asked at the same time.

"No! Jesus, you think I can only write songs about dogs?"

"It's just that you write a lot of songs about dogs," said Rex.

"I need to work through things sometimes."

"What's the song about?" Rex asked.

"Never mind," said Aaron.

"We'll have to hear it next time, Aar," said Jaymie. "It's time for—"

"Snacks!" Rex said at the same time that Jaymie finished with "—an even bigger pumpkin heist to fund our tour—" and immediately corrected to "Snacks, I meant snacks!"

9

The Library

A day before tour, Rex accepted—on behalf of the band—the animal cartoon, Valentine's-themed card, and demented song lyrics presented by the Bukowskiphiles as good luck tokens; Jaymie lounged in Mira's bed promising to think of her every single day he was away (two and a half, if all went according to plan) and then never contacted her again, as per an unspoken mutual agreement between them; and Aaron tracked Jo down at the Millennium Library, where she shelved books for slightly less than minimum wage. He had misgivings he needed to confess.

The library, which had six floors—each with its own labyrinthine floor plan that didn't correlate to any of the other five—always made Aaron uneasy. It took hours of wandering to find anything he was looking for, and next time he returned everything was rearranged and he had to relearn the entire landscape. This, coupled with the fact that you never knew who or what you were going to run into in the miles of stacks, made visits to the city's downtown public library a source of disorientation and distress.

After an hour of browsing, stopping to scan the Music Biography section or succumb to a clickbait title in Applied Psychology, he found Jo shelving prehistoric-looking tomes in the Quiet Zone study area. She perched atop a ladder, hair in a long ponytail. A couple of butterfly tattoos attempted to escape the collar of her blouse and creep up her neck to peruse the shelves.

As he crossed the floor toward her ladder, he nearly tripped over a short humanoid concealed entirely in grey except for the lower half of his, her, or their face, which was just visible under a hood.

This being was a feature of the Quiet Zone, where it crept around on silent sock feet and paused at the nook of anyone working there. It extended a small decibel reader, and if the scratching of their pen, the tinny beat from their earbuds, or the purr of their congested breathing registered at above twenty dB, the person would wake up a few minutes later propped in an alcove in the Whisper Zone, with all their belongings in more or less the same position and no idea what had happened.

Yet another reason why Aaron never felt at home in libraries.

"Jo?" He'd reached the ladder. Jo checked the Dewey Decimal number on the grimoire she was holding and slid the dusty book into place. He wondered if she hadn't heard him, but then she looked lazily down and, as though waking out of a trance, descended the rungs.

"Neat coincidence, running into you here," he said as she stepped onto the grey carpet. "Just came for my book of … ancient satanic rituals." He squinted at the indecipherable gothic font on the spines of the closest books. "I put one on hold."

"Wow, you guys show up everywhere, don't you?" she said.

"I show up in very few places," said Aaron. "But I'm used to people saying things like that—it's widely assumed I have telepathic knowledge of Jaymie's comings and goings." Come to think of it, he did know Jaymie had visited her once or twice on his mail route that week, though he couldn't remember which of them had mentioned it.

"Sorry, rude of me. I'm not used to having conversations in the library," she said. "This is my first one. How are you?"

"Good! I love the library," he lied. "It's so nice and … quiet. Hey, do those guys ever make you nervous? The little noise ninjas?" He pointed at the diminutive quiet-enforcer standing motionless a few metres away, his or her or their decibel reader hanging limply at his or her or their side, directly facing him.

Jo shrugged. "They don't bother the employees much."

"Great. So, tour! Wow, is that tomorrow already?" Aaron knew his attempt at enthusiasm more closely resembled hysteria.

"Hey, you've never toured before!" Jo grinned. The noise-patrol gnome gestured angrily at her. "It's going to be great. I toured west once, had some good times."

"Yeah, I mean no, I haven't toured. Jaymie has. He's filled in on keyboard with a couple other bands. But not Rex and I."

"It's the most fun in the world," she assured him. Jaymie had promised the same thing, but somehow the things Jaymie labeled 'The Most Fun in The World' often didn't leave Aaron feeling safe and enriched.

"I'm not sure Jaymie knows what he's doing. He's never booked one himself."

"It'll be fine. You play some good shows and some bad shows until you have enough connections that they become mostly good shows. And that's touring." Aaron must have looked unconvinced, because she continued, "You deal with problems as they come up. Jaymie seems pretty equipped to do that, for all his … unconventional ways."

Aaron nodded, suddenly curious about Jo. "How far have you toured?"

"West to B.C., east to Montreal, and a few shows in the States. With my old punk band. We went south illegally, though—didn't bother with the visas. I wouldn't do that now. Have to think about the future, you know?"

"I know," said Aaron. The future was, for him, a topic of constant simultaneous avoidance and obsession.

The grey-swaddled creature, who had approached noiselessly without either of them noticing, now jerked an arm into the air, waving the decibel reader in front of Jo's face. Aaron jumped and clutched a hand to his chest. Jo rolled her eyes and muttered a few words to the gangly imp, then cast an apologetic smile at Aaron and resumed her shelving until he'd walked to the elevator and back a few times to calm down.

Aaron redirected his internal dialogue from a tirade about the pointlessness of leaving the house toward a congratulations on expanding his boundaries—as per the instructions of his cognitive behavioural therapist—and crept back to Jo's book cart.

"Sorry about that," she said. "It *is* the Quiet Zone, I guess."

"Right, no problem." Aaron took a deep breath. "The other thing is, I don't know if you heard already … There was a death at the *Tornado Tornahdo* show last weekend. That surf-rock band? It was their lead guitarist. Just so you know."

It was clear from Jo's expression that she hadn't heard. She set the book she was holding heavily down on the cart. "Well, shit," she said. "That guy had great tone."

Aaron nodded.

"Good time to venture out of town, I guess. Play some safer shows." She squared her shoulders and stepped a foot resolutely onto the ladder, like an explorer claiming a nice new rock that had probably already been 'discovered' a hundred times. "Too bad, though. You OK?"

"Yeah, but ..." Aaron fidgeted. "You don't think it'd be good to take a break?" He managed to look her in the eye. "Jaymie's thrilled you're in the band, and I feel like if anyone could convince him to lie low for a bit ..." Jo scuffled uncomfortably on the ladder, and he sensed it was a losing battle. "Rex is basically just a kid, and if anything were to happen ..." He looked at her helplessly. "He won't listen to me, because last time we had a tour planned, in the spring, I sort of bailed. It's a long story."

He tried to read Jo's expression, which looked like half pity, half annoyance or scorn or desperation or something entirely different that had nothing to do with him. (His cognitive behavioural therapist was encouraging him not to take things personally).

"If we stop playing, then whoever—or whatever—is doing this will win." She shelved a book determinedly and completely at random. "Nothing's going to happen to us. We'll be careful. People don't mess with me much. I guess maybe I'm intimidating, or something."

He had noticed.

"Don't worry about anything," she continued. "Especially not the tour." A look of excitement crossed her face, and Aaron couldn't help but be reminded of all the manic pep talks he'd received over the years, whenever Jaymie was in need of an accomplice.

He nodded and forced a smile. It occurred to him that Jo needed the band possibly as much as Jaymie did. Aaron wondered if she had many friends. Did she jam with other people? What did she like to do on weekends when they weren't practicing?

"Regina!" She air-guitared covertly for a second, and he understood that she had no desire to take a break.

"Well, I'll let you get back to work!" He jerked his head at the agitated decibel enforcer. "Before this little guy murders *me!* Haaaaa."

"See ya tomorrow." Jo lifted a hand in farewell, then hefted a fresh, potentially life-threatening tower of books onto the ladder.

"Bright and early." He paused at the stairs. "Pack for an extra day," he called, prompting another glare from the Silence Officer, who was actually a very young delinquent allowed to serve community service hours, in lieu of juvenile detention, by encouraging quiet in the study zones. "Something stupid and terrible will come up—it always does with Jaymie."

"Sir," she replied, "You're being too loud. If you must speak, you may do so in the Whisper Zone, one floor down from the Quiet Zone. I hope you find what you're looking for."

The next day, the Brzezinskis loaded their gear at the crack of noon, picked up Jo, and began the seven-hour drive west, unaware that their return home would be delayed much longer than an extra day.

10

The Great Journey West

The band travelled across five hundred and seventy-three kilometers of empty November prairie. A light snowfall overnight had turned the ground a dull white-grey and erased the horizon separating land and sky. A few snowflakes drifted casually downward like the last stragglers to leave on the morning after a party, having woken up on the living room floor, the host politely implying they had no breakfast to offer.

Jaymie drank three coffees and drove the whole way there, planning their next tour in his head and sharing non sequitur anecdotes. As they crossed the Saskatchewan border, he was coming up with a series of skill-testing questions to determine Aaron's tour preparedness.

"We played a show, and now we're getting a drink, and we realize we haven't seen Jo for fifteen minutes. We do a quick scan around the bar, and she's not there. Do you: A—freak the fuck out and call the cops because she's probably been kidnapped by some very large kidnappers, B—have a panic attack and curl up in despair, C—text her and check outside because she's probably just having a smoke, or D—relax and give it time because Jo is quite able to take care of herself, and probably needed a short break from us, as many people eventually seem to."

Aaron thought. "Well, she doesn't smoke cigarettes. Unless maybe *you're* also outside smoking a cigarette, in which case maybe *I'm* outside smoking a cigarette too …"

"Not a trick question, Aar," said Jaymie, rotating the radio dial. There were two stations available and both were pop-country. He fished for CDs between the seats and settled on the newest *Daffodile* album, which he'd bought at her show the previous weekend.

"Option C, but with a bit of the vibe of option B," said Aaron, satisfied.

"Either C or D would have been acceptable, but I'll give it to you," said Jaymie.

Jo unrolled her window and blew a soft, grey cloud into the soft, grey sky. Rex spell-checked a paper about Charles Manson they were writing for English class.

"Ok, here's one! We're being hosted by a friend's friend's parents who like supporting musicians. They tell us we have free reign over all the couches but we mustn't go in the basement. We should: freak the fuck out because A—our hosts probably lure bands in with promises of granola breakfasts and then lock them in the basement forever, B—they're messed up neo-Nazis who keep their paraphernalia down there and don't want us finding it, C—they're kinky 50-Shades people hiding their torture dungeon till they suss out if we're into that stuff—they didn't realize we're mostly siblings (or maybe they did!)—*or* we should D—relax because they're boomers who hoarded a ton of useless shit and they're a little embarrassed about it."

"Well," said Aaron, "Most of those answers aren't necessarily mutually exclusive, but I'm catching on to the pattern here and I feel like I'm not supposed to freak the fuck out …"

"Hey," said Jo, finally bored enough to have checked her under-used email account. "Message from my old bass player. I think we're … booking a show?"

"Jo, no!" Jaymie spouted. "You're with *us* now!"

She laughed. "Pretty sure everybody plays in everybody else's band in our town. We're the weird ones for not all having three different projects on the go."

"That's cool," said Aaron. "I like the *Ballet Llama*. Just a one-off reunion?"

"I think so?"

"Jo, you're too popular! The *BL*, Yarbrough …" Jaymie craned around so she could see he was teasing, and Rex made sound of protest as the car squiggled and straightened.

"Lucas? I might send him a message, you know? … But yeah, kind of a surprise to be in two bands, after a few years of nothing."

"Who wants to proofread my Manson paper?" asked Rex, pulling off the headphones they'd been using to block out Jaymie's lengthy hypotheticals.

"Rex!" Jaymie exclaimed. "Forget Manson. You should start your own cult! Teach your wisdom to the people! We'll all join! Right?"

"Sure, I'll join," said Jo absently, writing and then deleting a message.

"Rexientology," said Aaron.

"Rexistentialism!" said Jaymie.

Six and a half hours after leaving home, they arrived downtown. The pub they were booked at was on a street full of shops and cafes, and it took four laps around the block to determine which unmarked back-alley door was the right one to load into. A jovial bartender directed them where to set up.

The bar was packed with people entirely uninterested in a touring band. It was Friday evening and everyone was in a boozy Grey Cup haze, transfixed by the numerous screens systematically placed to allow the game to be viewed from any angle in the room.

The *Bukowskis* played their set—minus the monologues and costume change—to the oblivious drinkers. A table of six near the stage alternated between conversing rambunctiously or staring, engrossed, at a TV slightly above and to the left of Jaymie's head, which almost disconcerted even a pro like him. By the time they tried out the country tunes, their non-audience was too disgruntled by the game score to give more than one or two despondent yee-haws.

Afterwards, they were each provided a free meal and drink, and the bartender, who hadn't listened to a note they'd played, paid them their guarantee and told them it was a great set and they should come back any time they wanted. Another success!

As Jaymie victoriously finished his burger, the friendly barkeep asked where they were headed. He explained that they'd been hired for a house show the following night.

"Whereabouts?"

"Edge of the city." Jaymie told him the street. "Some kind of co-op house? I'm not sure. But they like us and they want to throw a party!"

The man had been wiping down the counter, and he stopped mid-motion. "Do you have a connection there?" he asked.

"No, they reached out to us!" said Jaymie. "I sent our EP to the college stations here, and they must have heard it. They sent a message inviting us to play there if we ever toured west. So I figured, we tour west!"

"Interesting." The man's boisterous manner had dissipated. "Interesting."

Jaymie glanced behind him; Jo and Aaron were tearing down their gear out of earshot. Rex was finishing their pasta beside him, a book of poetry open on their lap, but Jaymie wasn't particularly worried about Rex.

"You know them?" he asked.

"Not really. People know *of* them, but they don't leave that house much." He resumed wiping the counter. "I'm just surprised they'd hire a band. They usually seem to take care of their own … entertainment."

"Intriguing," said Rex, without looking up from their book.

"Religious devotees?" Jaymie grinned. "Will they feed us delicious baking?"

"You could cut out some of the swears," Rex suggested. "Increase the chances."

"I'll replace the raunchy stuff with stories about my favourite desserts."

"Oh my god, you found that one pastry stand at that one farmer's market and now you think all religious groups are bakers." Rex slurped their last noodle and slid a bookmark into their anarchist verses.

"And speaking of censorship, you know I'll always accept you, Rex, but your presentation is a little offensive. Religion doesn't care that it's 2019! You may have to hide that whacky hair and decide on a reasonable gender for yourself before the show."

"Kill yourself," said Rex pleasantly.

"I'm joking—you're perfect! I'm getting you warmed up for all the backward zealots out in the big world!" crowed Jaymie, obviously forgetting that Rex attended a high school. He downed the rest of his drink and vibrated with his usual excitement. "We've sheltered you too long! Tour, Rex! You never know what to expect!"

"Look," the bartender broke in. "I'm sure you'll be fine. Just … don't stay too long, OK? They get up to some weird shit."

"Like what?" asked Rex.

"I don't really know, but they got some attention over the past few years—there was a famous filmmaker or a writer or something living there. I heard about a few people going to check it out. I think they stayed and ended up abandoning their jobs or something."

"Well, they must be selling something good if they have that successful a conversion rate," said Jaymie. "Maybe we'll join!"

"Like I said, I wouldn't stay too long." The man moved to the other end of the bar, where a guy in a green jersey was urging his brain through a soup of alcohol and post-game disappointment to remember how his wallet worked.

"Gotcha. Don't drink the Kool-Aid, as they say." Jaymie winked and went to pack up his synthesizer. Rex reluctantly followed, clearly curious to hear more from the bartender.

"We'll find out tomorrow, Rex," said Jaymie. "If they're selling something, guaranteed we'll hear about it."

"Don't we seem like a weird choice for a band, if that's true? We're practically unknown, we're not commercial, we're obviously not Christian rock. And they didn't hire us for the three country songs."

Jaymie hesitated. His contact had assured him the *Bukowskis* would be paid, so they must have had their reasons for reaching out, which could only be …

"It's the music! Rex, have you forgotten we make excellent music? Have a little faith—speaking of religion!"

"Check it out, we won," said Jo, passing them on her way to the van. The buzz of the game had by now fully diffused into drunken melancholy.

"What! I didn't even know we were playing!" said Jaymie. "Poor suckers. We'll have to celebrate! What is it? Football? We'll get some wine on the way …"

They loaded out and found the address of their hosts, who *were* in fact a friend's friend's parents and had left a key outside before going to sleep. There was a large spare bed, a mattress on the floor, and a couch, all prepared with fresh bedding, and granola and bread set out for breakfast. A note on the counter urged them to make themselves at home but please avoid the rooms down the left-most hallway on the second floor. Jaymie slipped the note into his pocket before Aaron could notice it, and they all slept soundly.

Jaymie believed that a tour must be treated a little like a holiday in order to avoid fatigue, and the next day they slept in, went thrifting, ate at a trendy café, and explored a city park while the cagey sun poked a few long, sneaky fingers down from the concealing grey.

In early evening, they located the big blue house on the edge of the city and pulled the van into a driveway already packed with several vehicles. The property had spacious yards in front and back, and from the driveway they could see a back deck, gazebo, and a small kids' play area, all well-furnished with lawn chairs and swinging couches.

They were greeted by an affable thirty-something woman with a cropped pixie cut and round glasses that hugely magnified her eyes. She introduced herself as Miranda, led them into a wide front hall, and showed them the spacious living room through an arch to their right. It was lined with couches and armchairs, with big cushions placed in front of the "stage" (rug), much like their last house concert.

"We've told everyone the music will start around eight, but there's no rush," she said. "Do you need anything to eat? Would you like a tour? Perhaps you'd prefer to bring your instruments inside first. That's Steve, over on the couch. And Juniper, talking to him. Please tell us if there's anything you need."

She clasped her hands and blinked her magnified eyes. Steve, a middle-aged man with a thick beard, gave a serious nod and wave. Juniper, who wore a long skirt and looked to be in her early twenties, smiled in their direction. The room was clean, the walls adorned with framed photos, the corners decorated by a few tall house plants. It was, by all appearances, quite normal.

"The others are around, but I've asked them not to bother you while you're setting up. Bags can go here—" Miranda showed them a storage room on the other side of the entrance. Friendly-sounding conversation could be heard from down the hall. "It's so good to finally meet you, Mr. Bukowski," she finished, a little breathlessly. "We've read all your poetry."

Jaymie's bandmates blinked at him. He had not published any poetry.

"Wonderful!" he said. He wrote song lyrics, and that was basically the same thing. They went outside for their equipment.

***

"On March ninth of the year nineteen ninety-four, at 1:40 in the morning, the greatest poet in America passed out of this life and into legend." Jaymie left his usual one-beat pause.

"The greatest poet in America," said the audience, as one voice.

"My name, uh …" He stuttered in surprise and lost his thread, which had only happened twice in his life before now.

The first time, he'd been ten years old and playing Marco Polo in a swimming pool while recounting the plotline of an Aquaman comic that would form the basis for the next game, and he'd been kicked in the head mid-sentence and nearly drowned. He was dragged to the surface by a frantic Aaron, who'd been It but eventually opened his eyes when the Aquaman anecdote drawing him toward his prey ended abruptly, forcing him to start yelling Marco! again—without response. A lifeguard yanked Jaymie onto dry land, and, after coughing up a few gallons of chlorine-water, he couldn't remember where he'd left off and had to restart the story.

(Aaron was never given much credit for his part in the rescue, being the one who'd accidentally kicked him in the first place. After accounting for the kick, the rescue, the period of shaking Jaymie and screaming while the frustrated lifeguard attempted to do mouth-to-mouth, and the tearful reunion when Jaymie came to, it was determined that Aaron was It again.)

The second time, he was sixteen and playing his first show, and a girl from his drama class was standing near the stage. They were a cover band, and she had her eyes closed and was singing along, and he started watching her sing.

Nobody had ever sung with him for their own pleasure as opposed to being pressured to harmonize, and he and the girl bonded for a magical eternity that lasted thirteen beats, until she got the words wrong, and then *he* got the words wrong; he knew them, but he'd been watching her mouth and he second-guessed himself and didn't recover until the next chorus. By then, she'd wandered away for a snack.

You could never trust an audience member—they were fickle and had no true loyalty. You too would become unpredictable and flighty as soon as you became an audience member, no matter how hard you vowed to support the artist and not motor off as soon as you heard they were selling chocolate-covered beavertails at a stand across the field. Jaymie quit their shared drama class—and soon high school altogether—and swore never to slip up again.

"My name is Jaymie Bukowski, and I was born in the same instant that the great writer Charles Bukowski slipped away into the afterlife."

"The great writer Charles Bukowski," intoned the audience.

"Bukowski was not ready to die," said Jaymie, leaving more space between proclamations, acclimatizing to the customs of the crowd, finding his rhythm.

A.W. Glen

"Not ready to die," said the audience.
These people—these people really got him.

11
It's a Cult, of Course

After their performance, the band drank the Kool-Aid. The *Bukowskis* drank so much of the Kool-Aid that two members blacked out before midnight, one spent several hours playing nostalgic pop-punk songs on an acoustic guitar she found in a corner (surrounded by a circle of people whose tolerance of her was saint-like), and the fourth woke up with a headache.

It would be preferable to believe that practical young Rex, understanding the potential harm of alcohol on the developing brain, had abstained from it, but let's not kid ourselves.

They awoke in a comfortable bed, fully clothed including the sneakers they'd performed in, beside a sleeping teenager with long hair, a handsome face, and a luxurious unibrow.

This had never happened to Rex before. They remembered, vaguely, meeting him on a makeshift living room dance floor and having some kind of debate about free will.

They slid out from under the covers without waking the boy and walked softly to the window. Moving the curtain aside, they saw they were on the second floor, overlooking the driveway. Two people stood near the *Bukowski* van with their heads together. The young woman, Juniper, gestured toward the vehicle. The man, Steve, must have made a joke—they both laughed and walked toward the house, and Rex lost sight of them under the window ledge.

Rex found a mirror behind the bedroom door and re-spiked their hair. Yesterday's gel crunched between their fingers.

"And another thing," came a voice from the bed.

Rex whirled around. "You're awake."

He smiled winsomely, squinting in the light pouring through the curtain. "The question of free will isn't just whether or not humans have it—it's a spectrum! It depends on the maintenance of your own internal state! Is a person the source of their own actions? You have an intention, and in the end, you have to make a decision, whether it's the 'inevitable' one or not." (He made exaggerated air quotes with his fingers.)

"OK," said Rex.

"And that's why you should meditate."

"Oh."

"What do *you* think?" He looked at Rex in expectation, but then appeared bashful and adjusted his shirt, which had gotten twisted up while he slept.

"I don't think I maintained my internal state well enough to decide right now," said Rex. They had been warned about people like this, but hadn't expected to encounter one before college. Still, he was very cute.

"Of course! Free will is much lower early in the morning and later in the evening—Hey, I wonder if Bukowski had anything to say about it?"

"I think he was more concerned with free beer," said Rex.

"Anyway, it's time for breakfast. You probably need coffee! It's downstairs. Or maybe you like tea?" He hopped out of the bed, also fully clothed, and opened the bedroom door.

"Sure, thank you," said Rex, suddenly feeling shy. "We didn't, um, *do* anything, right?" They were fairly certain all of their memories were intact and the encounter had merely been friendly, but they hadn't been drunk all that many times, and they'd seen enough dated sitcom episodes to feel wary about waking up with a stranger.

"No, nothing at all," said the boy happily. "Neither of us was sober enough to give the other consent!"

"Oh, great," said Rex. "Glad we agree on that."

He seemed proud, and Rex wondered if, like them, he hadn't been drunk many times. Rex had always had the impression—gleaned from the collective unconscious—that getting drunk was a great achievement, until you reached a certain age, and then it was embarrassing—in the same way that sharing a bed with another person was something to celebrate, until you'd shared with too many. Rex wasn't sure what that age was or what that number of people was or who it was that got the privilege of deciding.

"I hope you didn't mind sleeping here. You seemed like you didn't mind."

"I don't mind," said Rex, and they really didn't. "But I forget your name."

"Ronan."

"I'm Rex. They-slash-he but mostly they."

"Yes, I remember. I use mnemonics."

Rex followed him downstairs to where a breakfast of bacon, eggs and toast was being laid out at a table long enough to seat at least twenty people. There was enough food for at least twenty people, and at least twenty people were meandering in from different parts of the house.

No one had gone home after the show. Not for the first time, Rex wondered what kind of place they'd just stayed the night in.

They claimed a seat beside Jo, who was staring bleary-eyed into a mug of coffee. She croaked a quiet "Morning," from under her hair.

The woman who'd first welcomed them, Miranda, greeted Rex and sat down on Jo's other side as Jaymie drifted in from the living room, grinning at the sight of the feast.

"That was the best couch sleep I've ever had!" he declared. "You people sure know how to own a couch. I don't even remember passing out!" He looked around for the nearest empty chair, then sat down, with a great show of elation, at the head of the table. "I did throw up on it," he confessed. "But I've already thoroughly cleaned it with supplies from the bathroom!"

"Well, Bukowskis," said Miranda, after those closest had congratulated him, "we hope last night was enjoyable for you."

Rex and Jaymie responded "Yes, thank you," and "I have no idea!" respectively. Jo gave a thumbs up and looked dubiously at the food on her plate.

"We also hope you've seen how nice it can be spending time in our home." The tableful of people watched the *Bukowskis*. They appeared to be of widely differing ages and backgrounds, but all shone matching beaming smiles at the bandmates.

"We hope you won't be in a great a rush to leave it today," said Miranda. "Or ever!"

"We loved the audience participation!" said Jaymie. "Sorry, what did you say?"

"You see," Miranda continued, "our little enclave has had a dearth of effective leadership in recent times …"

"Is this a cult?" Rex blurted out. They blushed, horrified. Ronan laughed loudly, spat out a piece of egg, and then blushed as well. He glanced at Rex, who glanced back a split second too late, and then he looked again, and Rex looked again—but he'd looked away again—and they repeated this process one more time before finally making eye contact, blushing even more, and staring at their plates.

"Adorable," said Jaymie, noticing this exchange. "Rex, of course they're not a cult. That's rude. Miranda, you were saying?"

"A cult!" Miranda laughed affectionately at Rex, who stuffed a forkful of potatoes into their mouth and slouched in their seat. A few of the others tittered. "No, no. We're an *arts collective*."

"That explains everything." Jaymie nodded sagely. "Not that I thought you were a cult—well, I did, but in a good way."

"Sorry," said Rex, now even more embarrassed. Was it not a dream of theirs to be involved in a real artists' collective and fill the world with zines and inclusivity? "What kind of art do you make?"

The table fell gravely silent. Rex wasn't sure what they'd done wrong this time, but resolved to take a vow of silence until they were twenty-one.

"Well …" began Miranda. "You may have noticed—these walls remain devoid of art."

"Not everyone is born an artist," came the small voice of Juniper, at the far end of the table. "And not everyone is born with the urge to create …" She stopped, seemingly overcome by a crushing timidity.

"But the worst tragedy," said Ronan, finally looking Rex in the eye, "is when you aren't born an artist—or, say, a musician—but you *do* have the urge!"

"And then you're helpless," said Juniper, and a large tear oozed down her cheek.

Steve, seated beside her, patted her shoulder. "In this collective, all of us are in that category," he explained. "It's what unites us. All we desire is to create beauty."

"That's the saddest story I ever heard!" exclaimed Jaymie. "We'll play a fundraiser to buy you supplies and guitars! Might have to start with cheap ones, but still—it's never too late!"

"The gifted ones never understand," said Ronan bitterly.

"Manners, Ronan," Steve reprimanded. "They are our guests." Ronan glared and crunched his toast.

"You see, we have all those things," said Miranda, her voice strained by the vast amount of patience she was exercising for the benefit of the confused musicians. "But we cannot use them. Some people have the gift, and others do not, and some—" she gestured around the table, "—yearn for it more than anything in the world."

A collective sigh fizzled through the room.

"… I don't mean to sound insensitive," said Jaymie, breaking the heavy silence. "But have you tried … practicing?"

Steve gave a humourless laugh and ran his hands through his greying hair in vexation. "We've all sat down to paint a portrait. Or, say, write a memoir, like Evelyn—" A middle-aged woman gave an ironic smile. "Compose a piece of piano music …" He again patted the shoulder of Juniper, who sniffled. "Or write a scathing political article—"

"To be published in an online news source!" said Ronan fiercely.

"The result is … It's too terrible to even show our friends and family." He put his head in his hands.

"For a political article, I don't know *creativity* is the most important element to …" Rex began, but they remembered their earlier blunder and changed course. "I'm pretty into DIY—like, 'do-it-yourself'—which says *everyone* can be creative, not just famous artists. Even if it's not amazing craftsmanship, it will speak to someone. Like, maybe it will reach even more people than if it was something really impressive and esoteric?"

They were met with blank stares.

"Rex is right. I'm not discounting your efforts," said Jaymie carefully. "But you might need to try it a few more times before …" He must have been sensitive to the raised eyebrows and volatile energy in the room, because he shifted tactics. "Do you know how many bad songs I wrote when I was a kid? At least two or three."

"You've written dozens of bad songs!" Rex contributed.

"OK, fine, it's true. I wrote at least twenty before I wrote even one good one. In fact, a reviewer at the university paper recently concluded that none of them have *ever* been good!"

"But you see, that's why we need you!" said Miranda, her already enlarged eyes growing behind her glasses. "Once you'd awoken your creative spirit, you began to make great music!"

"Thank you, but don't you think the 'creative spirit' could exist in all of you? Just buried a little deeper?"

"She means Bukowski," said Steve.

"Oh," said Jaymie, and for the fourth time in his life, he was at a loss for words.

"That's why we need your guidance, Jaymie Bukowski!" cried Miranda. "Please stay, and help us summon our own creative spirits!"

"When you use that word *summon*, I'm not sure I—"

"We'll stay," declared Rex, surprising even themself. They glanced at Ronan and mumbled, "I've always wanted to be in an arts collective."

Jaymie stared at them. "It ... sounds like ... we're staying!" he said.

Exclamations of delight circulated the table.

"What the fuck is happening?" Jo set down her fork, which contained a single piece of hash brown she'd spent the duration of the conversation woozily daring herself to eat.

"Jo, we're going to stay with this artist cult—collective—and teach them the guitar!" Jaymie announced. "We'll stay as long as it takes! Rex wants to!"

"I work on Wednesday," said Jo.

"We'll stay till Tuesday!" said Jaymie.

"Fine," said Jo.

Rex shared a smile with Ronan.

"Hold on, you know what's odd about all this?" said Jaymie.

"No, Jaymie, what could be odd about all this?" Jo winced at him over her coffee.

"No one is protesting." Jaymie peered around the table. "Where's my brother?"

Aaron woke, nauseous, under a cloud-choked autumn sky, in a field long shorn of its crop. The prickly remains of stalks of wheat or canola, blackened by farmers burning the prairies after harvest, scratched at his arms and neck as he gingerly raised himself onto an elbow.

He threw up. A harsh gust of wind blew over the empty land. He coughed and looked around, seeing nothing but more fields and a few scraggly trees in the distance. He had no idea where he was.

Alarm welled in his chest. A wave of dizziness warned of an encroaching panic attack—or maybe it was the hangover.

He suddenly knew without a doubt that the evil cult had kidnapped his family and friend and, finding no use for him, poisoned him and dropped him in a post-apocalyptic wasteland a million miles from civilization, never to obstruct their dastardly plans. He'd wander these fields, growing the ratty beginnings of a beard, living on burnt straw and haystack mice, perhaps finding a rickety porch to shout paranoid ravings from until he wasted away …

He gasped for breath.

He then more accurately realized that he must have gotten very drunk last night, believed his hosts to be an evil cult attempting to kidnap his family and carry out dastardly plans, freaked the fuck out, and ran for it. He'd probably been doubly uneasy when his escape went unhindered. He'd likely staggered the one block out of the city and promptly passed out in this field.

A semi truck roared down the highway thirty feet behind him.

"Shit," he muttered. "What an inconvenient illness."

Groaning, he got to his feet, stumbled to the road, and made his way back toward the city.

12

Rex Has Met a Boy

The *Bukowskis* did not leave the following Tuesday, or the one after that.

After breakfast, the cult (for that, by any reasonable definition, is what they were) began searching for their new leader's sibling. Jo watched from the comfort of the couch, which smelled freshly of cleaning supplies. The one hash brown she'd eaten churned in her stomach, and she felt sluggish and useless. She'd had her share of hangovers, but she couldn't remember the last time a party had left her this sick.

"He's about yea tall—" Jaymie held his hand at a height several inches shorter than either himself or Aaron and bounced on the balls of his feet. "He has brown hair, brown eyes, freckles …" His followers listened intently while he described himself. "Kind of a skinny face … Had on a black T-shirt … He looks like something bad might happen at any moment …"

"They all met him yesterday," Rex reminded him.

"He may have over-imbibed," Miranda reassured them. "He's probably still sleeping."

"There are quite a few rooms in this house," the would-be memoirist, Evelyn, pointed out.

"There you have it, Rex. You know how he can overdo it sometimes!" said Jaymie. "He probably got woozy and found a dark corner to curl up in. No need to be worried!"

"I'm not," said Rex.

"Good! Me neither. But let's go check out all the rooms immediately, OK?" Uneasiness flickered back and forth over Jaymie's features.

"I'll join your search party," Ronan told Rex, eliciting a shy grin.

"I'll look in the van," Jo said. "Maybe he checked out early last night and needed someplace quiet to crash."

She needed the quiet too. She had mixed feelings about spending the next three days with these people, especially considering her own mortifying behaviour last night. She was pretty sure she'd played "Good Riddance" more than once for the kind, patient folk that had gathered around her. She couldn't fathom what had come over her, or how they'd managed to stay so polite. She'd fallen asleep in that circle—perhaps mid-song, for she'd woken on the carpeted living room floor still holding the guitar, covered in a blanket, a pillow tucked under her head.

She didn't know it, but her band had, in fact, been poisoned. A little. Their drinks were laced with a mild sedative—enough to knock Jaymie and Aaron out in no time, although it had almost no immediate effect on Jo, whose old punk band had rudely but fondly referred to her as "The Tank." Fortunately for Miranda and her comrades, Jo had eventually knocked herself out.

The motive for this doping, of course, had been to ensure that the four bandmates wouldn't leave after the show. Even Rex—a minor!—had received a (much smaller) dose, which goes to show the level of villainy at play.

Jo sighed and reached for her phone, but her pocket was empty. She wondered if she'd left it in the van. She collected the keys from Jaymie, but found it unlocked. There was no sign of her phone—or Aaron—and she was about to lock up when, on an impulse, she sat down and turned the key in the ignition. Silence. She tried again. It was Sunday, which meant most garages wouldn't be open. They'd be staying at least a day, whether she liked it or not.

She lay back to rest her aching head, and let out a swift exhalation that formed a frosty cloud. She might not have much in common with these strangers, but Rex and Jaymie wanted to stay, and with a broken van and nothing waiting at home but cardboard boxes, she couldn't think of a reason not to.

Fresh air would help clear her head. She rolled a joint on the dashboard, imagining a peaceful walk through the pasture behind the house, and then tucked it behind her ear and crossed the backyard toward the bordering hedge. Beyond was the beige smudge of empty fields; the house was one of the last on the block before the city ended and the country began.

She was about to pass through a gap in the hedge when a hand landed on her shoulder, causing her to jump. Several people had followed her from the house without her noticing. Her skin prickled under her coat as a man's voice spoke in her ear, "Leaving so soon?"

Aaron prided himself on his sense of direction, which was completely average. Yet after hours of wandering, thirsty and cellphone-less, he hadn't located the blue house. He didn't know the address and had been too busy going over potential worst-case scenarios in his head to notice street names as they drove. He made a mental note to add "memorize landmarks" to his list of compulsive safety measures.

He kept his spirits up by reminding himself that walking increased blood-flow and therefore relieved hangovers, and he only briefly lost hope when he passed the same pair of leering purple and blue lawn flamingos for the second time, at which point he had a quick panic attack behind an austerely-trimmed bush before getting back on his way.

Eventually he encountered a corner store and stepped inside for directions. He described the place to the teenager behind the counter, who just blew a gum bubble at him, but a nearby customer tapped his shoulder, and he turned around gratefully. She told him, "Sorry, but I know where!", paid for her bag of Maltesers, and beckoned him after her. The customer was new to the country, and had been learning English one Canadian small-talk subject and several apologies at a time, as per the manner of conversation partners locally available.

"It's very cold, in winter, yes?" She powerwalked ahead of him.

"Yeah, it's cold where I live, too. Maybe colder," said Aaron. He resentfully eyed the bruisy flamingos as they retraced his steps. Leafless trees groped over them from either side of the street. "You know the house I mean? It's big and blue and they host events there?"

"Oh yes," she assured him. "Very popular. Pro … prolific, I think? … Do you like hockey?" She offered him a Malteser, which he queasily declined.

"I don't follow it much. … Popular? You mean a lot of people go to their parties?"

"No, no parties, sorry," she said, and thought for a moment. "It's very … excuses."

"Exclusive?"

"Exclusive! Sorry. More like *famous*. Like … Marilyn Manson. You know the actor?"

"Funny you use that example, because my sis—sibling was researching him," said Aaron. "They wrote a paper."

"You mean *her?*"

"They use *they.*"

"But researching *her* …?"

"They were researching … *him."*

"Sorry?"

"Oh … You meant Munroe. I meant Charles. I meant sibling. Sorry. We're both confused. Me much more so than you. Ha. Sorry." He smiled weakly and breathed on his hands, wishing he'd stopped for his gloves and toque during his frantic and totally unnecessary escape.

"Anyway, do you know what they're famous for?" he asked. She looked uncertain. "I mean, are some of them actors too, or … are they good at sports?"

"Many things! Movies, painting. So many things!" She nodded again, wearing a look he'd come to recognize as pitying encouragement.

"Well, good for them," he said, nonplussed.

"Music … Bands … Like Nickelsback," she suggested.

"Oh … good."

A gust of wind hit their faces, like the first blow of a pillow fight you weren't aware you were participating in. It was colder than usual, even for November.

"So cold here, and even colder soon!" said his cheery guide.

They'd taken a side-street that appeared to lead back out of town, when he spotted the *Bukowski* van in a long gravel driveway. He profusely thanked the woman, who responded with a gracious, if incorrect, "I'm so sorry!" and a chipper wave goodbye. He jogged the last stretch to the house, eager to be on his way home.

Rex was having a romance adventure. They lay on their side on Ronan's bed in a rectangle of golden late-afternoon sun, a curtain of boy-hair strewn over their shoulders, wondering how such interesting fortune could have befallen them only two days into their first tour. The warmth of Ronan's chest, and his polite hands, only just beginning to toy with the bottom of their T-shirt, provided a low-key buzz similar to that of being onstage—and if it wasn't *quite* as exhilarating as performing, the difference was made up for in novelty.

Rex had spent most of the afternoon kissing. As it turned out, you could find someone's philosophical ideas dubious and still be quite willing to make out with them—possibly more willing, if it kept them quiet. Rex filed this knowledge away in their archive of adult wisdom, to be reflected on later, once they'd put their sneakers and outer layers back on.

Ronan was also seventeen, and from a small town a few hours away. He had surprisingly decent taste in music, an inclination to make a difference, and political views that he expressed clearly enough to sound intelligent, and vaguely enough not to offend Rex out of his bed. It was enough. Rex moved aside a swath of his hair and kissed his forehead, experimentally imagining they were Aragorn and Boromir at the end of the Fellowship, but nobody was dying.

Rex was supposed to have located Aaron and started facilitating creativity workshops, but surely the members of their new arts collective needed some time to reflect on Jaymie's advice and finish building their altar. Also, it was worth giving Aaron a few hours before going into missing-persons mode; Rex's brothers were known to disappear now and then, and had so far always turned up, mostly unscathed, eventually.

"What's your story?" asked Rex, needing a break and not wanting to risk an argument about whether or not capitalism was an inevitable result of the natural course of evolution.

"I ran away from home six months ago," said Ronan, turning onto his back. "I was having an existential crisis, and I knew high school wasn't helping … I mean, there you are, wasting all your time on inanity, and you don't fit in because everyone's obsessed with absurd, useless things, and they're all total idiots about what actually matters."

Rex nodded. Rex too went to high school.

"When I found this place, it just made sense to me. Back then, Sheena was leading us. She was brilliant—a genius! There were already people here before her, but she's the one that got us all together doing art, and she was—she could make it work every time! It was amazing."

"Right on," said Rex. "Communal flow-state. Love that. Like being in a band."

"You'd have fit right in! If you'd just—I wish you'd been there—we were really making things! It felt like—I wish I could describe it—"

"That's the best feeling," said Rex, squeezing his arm in encouragement. "When you're having a really creative phase, and you're caught up in this wild energy—that crazy intense focus, like you're high except you're not—"

Rex was describing a feeling Ronan wanted to experience more than anything, inadvertently uncovering something irresistible; he became a flurry, his words like marbles he was trying to keep cupped in his palm, but that kept tumbling out between his fingers.

"Yes! That's what it's—there's nothing like it. I'm so glad you're staying. I can't wait for you to see it—that feeling is worth everything, even with what happens to—"

He stopped, his mistake exposed less by what he'd said than by his expression, which was that of a man who has revealed too much and is waiting to see if your empathy drive will override your self-preservation instinct and force you to politely change the subject rather than watch him flounder.

"Go on," said Rex, whose self-preservation instinct was intact.

"Nothing. You look nice."

Rex blinked, and then broke. "Oh god, it *is* a cult, isn't it?" They peeled themself off his chest and sat up, hugging their knees. Their beautiful arts collective dream had lasted fewer than three hours from start to finish. "Obvs too good to be true."

"Hey, no, it's not that …"

"A real artist collective … a cute person who actually likes me."

"No, no, it's nothing bad! We have a little ritual. For creativity. That's all. Sheena taught us it, but we haven't had a real leader since her. That's why we need Jaymie." He rolled back onto his side and touched their hand. "And we need you."

"I'm sorry, but a *ritual?*" Rex flopped back down on the pillow, wondering if they'd just pulled an Aaron. Rituals, after all, were lovely. Candles. Tarot cards.

"I can't really describe it. I hope you'll stay long enough to see it! I mean, I think you … will." He gazed into their eyes with his own large, guilty ones. Their square of sunlight wisped away as a cloud moved over the window. A draft crept through the room.

Rex's emotions slid through perplexity and alarm and finally landed on resignation.

"Are we trapped here?" they asked.

"... Na," Ronan confirmed. "We wouldn't."

"And when you said you were *making things* ... You do just mean art?"

"Of course! All kinds. I wish I could show you it!"

"It's a secret?" Rex was bewildered and deflated at the same time. Ronan nodded forlornly. "How long has this group been around?" they asked, mostly to keep him talking while they tried, with their limited experience, to gauge the seriousness of the situation.

"A few years. I'm the newest, besides you guys. I'll go home someday, but for now this is too important. I do miss my sisters, though. I have two sisters—nine and ten years older. Like how you have big brothers. But, you know, sisters."

Rex flagged the attempt at redirection, but asked, generously, "And parents?"

"Yes, parents too."

"Do you think they're worried about you?"

"Maybe. But they never understand."

"Ugh, mine either."

"Right? Wow, I just feel like you get me."

Rex forced themselves not to agree too wholeheartedly, even if he smelled like the most welcoming laundromat. "Are you going to ask if my parents will worry about me? If I stay?"

"Of course I am. Will your parents worry about you?"

Rex considered telling him that their parents knew exactly where they were, and that their mom would become frantic and call the police if Rex didn't return home that very evening.

"No," said Rex. "They won't have noticed I'm on tour. Our mom's not due home until next month. And it will probably take my dad ages to realize my letters have stopped. Unless I can call them?"

"Outside contact is a little, um, tricky at the moment ..."

Rex sighed. "Yeah, I figured. And it isn't just regular old art you make, is it? Like, I can't glue some macaroni to a Pride rainbow and go home."

"Ha ..." Ronan gave Rex the impression of a puppy who has innocently lured you in on behalf of a serial killer; he meant well, and, after all, it was your choice to start petting him.

"Seriously: did they lock up Aaron so we can't leave?" Their chest gave a pang.

He shrugged miserably. "I really, really doubt it?"

"I have to tell Jaymie. The ritual stuff he might take in stride slash possibly love, but not that. He might go to the cops."

"Rex, let me help you find your bro. If he turns up, will you trust us?"

Rex's mind raced. They wanted to trust Ronan; he clearly wasn't yet the pokerfaced political journalist he aspired to be.

"I really like you," said Ronan.

Rex hadn't dated much, because, so far, they'd rarely been invited to. They preferred to think this was because they were intimidating—in their personal style and musical skill, if not in stature. It didn't help that they were quiet, and spent more weekends hanging out with Maggie or jamming with their brothers than going to parties.

But in truth, they suspected their identity wasn't working in their favour in the high school dating market. They didn't live in a particularly progressive neighbourhood, their name and pronouns had not been adjusted outside their circle of friends, and some people even seemed to assume the change, now a couple of months old, had been intended to inconvenience them personally. Rex couldn't imagine dating most of them anyway. People a little older, whom they encountered through their brothers, had assured Rex they'd have more luck in college.

"OK. Do you want to make out again first?" asked Rex. College was a whole year away.

The band might be a bit stuck, but Ronan was charming, and Rex was the type to make the best of a situation, even while coming up with a way out of it. Rex was a competent multitasker; most musicians are.

Jaymie was rubbing his knuckles and conversing rapidly with Miranda and Steve when his brother arrived, late in the afternoon. He relaxed visibly at the sight of Aaron.

"Oh, you're back!" he said. "Where were you? I want to hear all about it. But first—you won't guess what happened! We're going to stay here. Why are you covered in hay? Wait, Rex is still looking for you." He yelled, "Rex!" into the stairwell. "Let's never be parted again! So anyway, we have to stay for a bit and help these people recover their creative spirit …"

He brushed the straw out of Aaron's hair, produced a glass of water from somewhere, and led his crestfallen but unsurprised twin to the living room, where an altar was being erected. The members of the collective were piecing together an oversized image of Charles Bukowski's face, which had been printed out in no particular order on many pieces of eight-by-eleven paper.

Juniper was in charge of the puzzle, overseeing Evelyn and two other helpers as they tried to determine if a piece of paper covered in porous, stubbly skin belonged to the left cheek area or the forehead. Aaron stared.

"And Aar, please don't do that again," Jaymie was saying. "I understand we should individuate from each other at some point, but far from home on your first tour is not the time."

"What the hell is this?" said Aaron.

"Oh, this was their idea," said Jaymie offhandedly, untroubled by the Bukowski altar, which included the merch table from the night before and a few tealights. "They're heavy on the *spirit* side of the creative spirit. But I think we can have some fun! We'll do workshops on songwriting, and Rex can talk about essays and journaling, and you still sketch sometimes, right? Or you could lead a therapeutic drum circle? They'll feed us the whole time, and provide us drinks—not as many as last night, ha!—and we can have a bonfire this evening and it'll be like a mini holiday—an artist residency, even!—with new friends and stimulating conversation and—"

"And let me guess. They worship you," interjected Aaron. He had no desire to stay with this odd group in their weird giant house, at risk of nervous-drinking himself into unconsciousness again.

"I truly missed having you here to finish my sentences. But no, what I was going to say is that Rex wants to stay," said Jaymie.

Aaron narrowed his eyes at this obvious attempt to play the Rex card. "Sh—they shouldn't be missing any more school. Remember last year?"

"Is travel not *at least* as intellectually stimulating as a school they barely tolerate?" Jaymie reasoned. "Maybe we prioritize emotional nourishment, for once. Rex wants an arts collective, and they might not find another one till they organize it themself midway through university, poor kid. And *you* can use this period of rest and rejuvenation to practice not stammering every time you say 'sibling' or 'they.' Since that's actually extremely important."

Aaron let out a frustrated breath.

Incidentally, he possessed at least five of the nine personality traits that make a person susceptible to cult indoctrination: his self-esteem, like that of most musicians, required frequent validation, and he could have benefitted from the built-in sense of community and identity that a cult environment offered; he was more of a follower than a leader, though this may have been a result of having Jaymie in close proximity his entire life; and though his sense of self-worth and hope for the future weren't entirely depleted, it was safe to say he was often discouraged. Not to mention his predilection for the occasional period of conspiracy theory-style delusion.

In short, Aaron could have been an ideal inductee for a cult run by anybody except the one person in the world he knew without a doubt to be completely full of shit.

13

A Band Meeting

Obviously, the *Bukowski Bros.'* fan club had missed the show. But why?

As it turned out, there really was some kind of hoity-toity Young Programmers conference being hosted in Regina that weekend, and Shahla's parents, after conducting an internet search to confirm its existence, were beyond pleased that their daughter had been selected to participate.

Dismayed, Shahla was forced to do an evening of dull research to back up her story. She determined who within the organization chose the participants, infiltrated their files—which were available online in a Google drive she accessed by hacking into their email—added herself to the list of invitees, and sent herself an email welcoming herself to the convention.

On top of losing almost an hour of her vibrant life to this project, she had to suffer the sting of not actually having been invited in the first place—small indignities like this were the downside to keeping a low profile on the computer science scene.

Shahla's whole family drove out, which at least had the benefit of appeasing Ayla. Her parents permitted her to bring Maggie, and so plans were made to sneak away from the hotel for the Saturday night *Bukowski* show.

This plan was also foiled by Shahla's mother, who bragged about her daughter to speakers from a panel about the future of AI, resulting in Shahla having to give an evening presentation on a project from the year before. (She'd disassembled and rebuilt her teacher's computer overnight and returned it with the ability to predict exactly which websites he was going to go to and at what time, and open the pages automatically a few seconds before he thought of going there—basically backpacking on already growing surveillance capitalism trends, but a little creepier. He'd reported a 92 percent success rate. Since the project was pretty basic, she'd also reassembled the body of the computer in the shape of his favourite animal, an English bulldog.)

So, on the night of the show, the three Bukowskiphiles found themselves partaking in rice crisps and non-alcoholic punch in a brightly lit conference hall surrounded by nerds.

"Ugh, I'm sorry," Shahla told Maggie, for the tenth or fifteenth time. She'd finished her presentation, followed by a question period, followed by some obligatory schmoozing with professor-type characters. She'd stood miserably rooted between her parents, her mother gripping her shoulder to keep her from sliding away.

She slumped in front of her napkinful of snacks.

"It's not your fault," said Maggie. She unself-consciously produced a miniature flask from her shoulder bag and tipped a golden substance into her Styrofoam punch cup, then offered the vial to Shahla, who shook her head.

"I'm bored," said Ayla.

"Why don't you do your, colour on your thing, your book," Shahla muttered to her.

Ayla unzipped her backpack and brought out her Bukowskiphile Bukowski File—a pink binder full of *BBBFB* notes and pictures—and pencil crayons.

"I've brought you to the most boring event in the most boring city in the country," Shahla whimpered to Maggie. "I'm a monster."

"I thought so at first," said Maggie distractedly, casting a half-smile over her shoulder at a boy in a sweater-vest who'd been staring into his laptop at the next table. He blushed.

"We should be hanging out with our favourite band and flirting with talented artists whose works have gotten top reviews around the country!"

"Relax. They're probably insufferable. Besides, you dilute your fan-girl worth by spreading it among too many *artistes*. And that's not slut-shaming, it's just time management."

Shahla sighed. "I'm choosing where we have lunch tomorrow. My parents owe me that. So, we can at least check out the pub where they played and interview the staff."

"You're a stalker after my own heart," said Maggie. She turned toward the other table and beckoned the boy with a finger. He looked behind him, pointed at his own chest, and looked behind him again. Maggie nodded. Shahla rolled her eyes. The boy picked up his laptop and joined them. A moment later, so did his mother.

Despite a very slight language barrier, Maggie had soon engaged them both in conversation on topics she knew nothing about. The boy was studying coding; his mother was the CEO of a small but successful app company.

Shahla despondently watched Ayla doodle a border around a grinning photo of Jaymie she'd pasted on a page of pink construction paper.

"Oh, I know him!" said the sweater-vest boy's mother suddenly, pointing at Ayla's book.

"You know Jaymie?" Maggie asked doubtfully. Shahla knew Maggie preferred to think the bands she liked were obscure enough that dorky moms wouldn't be familiar with them.

"Yes, I gave him directions! He was looking for the famous artists' house. A very nice boy."

Shahla and Maggie exchanged a look.

"Was he with the band?" Maggie asked.

"No, all alone, and getting chilly out." The woman nodded. "Scared and lost."

"That doesn't sound like Jaymie," said Shahla.

"That's the house we were hoping to visit," said Maggie. "Can you tell us about it?"

Ayla fastidiously sharpened a pencil crayon and turned to a clean page for notetaking.

"Yes, a little! But they're … *exclusive*." She smiled. "They like to stay inside just by themselves. Nice people, probably, but very … repulsive."

Aaron threw open the door of the bedroom.

"Rex, get off of that poor boy," he said. "We're having a band meeting."

Reacting on instinct, Rex cast him their best teenaged glare—a malicious cocktail of disgust and indifference that would have sent most parents to therapy—before remembering they'd been worried only minutes earlier that he was locked up somewhere. Fortunately, Aaron was not a parent; he mimicked Rex's squint and ushered them out of the room, unfazed.

"Ever heard of knocking?" muttered Rex.

"Question: How do you know when a drummer is knocking?" said Aaron.

"The knocking keeps speeding—"

"We don't knock. Who is that fucker? I don't like the look of him."

"That's not how that joke goes," said Rex.

"Jesus, I'm gone for one morning and suddenly you're grown up, cuddling neckbeards?"

"He's my friend, and it's none of your business," said Rex, but Aaron was already gearing up for a speech. He planted his hands on their shoulders.

"OK, look, Rex, I know you want to be in an arts collective," he began.

"It's OK, I—"

"But I promise you there will be other opportunities."

"Yeah, no, we should think about—"

"With people who don't have a hero-fetish for Jaymie—"

"It's possible we need to leave," said Rex. "Ronan started talking about some ritual? They're making something. If not art, then … something."

Aaron remembered his guide talking about the collective's "fame," and his uneasiness deepened.

Jaymie and Jo were waiting in the van, Jo reclining under a blanket in the front seat with her eyes closed, Jaymie jotting feverishly in a notepad. The meeting had convened.

"Jaymie, these people might not be as talentless as they're letting on," said Aaron.

"We need to plan a visual art workshop," said Jaymie. "I promised them one tomorrow morning. Do you still do those fun little monster drawings?"

"Listen. I talked to someone when I was trying to find my way back." He recounted the woman's fractured description of the house. Jaymie looked up thoughtfully for a moment, before going back to his notes. He'd somehow always been able to speak lucidly while reading or writing something completely different from what he was talking about. It drove Aaron crazy.

"Aar, you know that cliché in movies, where the girl is like, *Oh, I can't sing at all, I'm sure I'm just terrible,* and she refuses to sing, and then someone catches her singing all by herself, like in the shower or mopping backstage when she thinks everyone has gone home, and it turns out she's just amazing, and she gains self-confidence …" He crossed something out and chewed the end of his pen.

"Sure, I—"

"And maybe she gets famous and maybe she falls in love with the guy who was spying on her when she was singing all alone because he always had faith in her?"

"I'm following."

"OK, well. These people are not that girl."

Aaron sighed. "OK, Bukowski, so you're the only real genius here. But there still has to be more of an explanation for all this."

"They're completely talentless, Aaron. I hate to say it. They have even less talent than if you took a random group of twenty-five strangers and averaged out the talent among them. Like, I don't think they've even tried. Ever."

"I know how shocking that must seem to you," said Aaron wryly. Jaymie continued to scribble, and he lost patience. "Jay, if you don't start listening to me, I'm going to tell Miranda and her friends that our birthday is really January fifteenth. See if they still adore you when they know you were born seven weeks before Buk died."

"You'd never," said Jaymie, without bothering to look up. "The whole success of this band rests on suppressing those seven weeks."

"I'll show them my driver's license," Aaron challenged.

"I'll tell them you were born premature and that's why you're littler than me."

"I'm not—you're not even half an inch taller!" Aaron furiously objected. "And that's not even possible! You can't have *one*—"

"Aar, these people believe I've spent my entire life possessed by the ghost of a dead writer. I think they can accept one premature twin."

"Shut the fuck up for one fucking second Jaymie, I'm telling you, we've got to get the fuck out of here before some weird shit starts going down!"

"Right on cue." Jaymie put down his pen and paper and sat back, unsurprised.

"I'm not having a paranoid freak-out!" Aaron insisted, feeling his face redden.

"No, Jaymie, something's up," Rex broke in. "I got the vibe from Ronan that they weren't telling us everything at breakfast. They want us to watch this ... ritual. And we maybe can't go until then." Their voice caught in their throat. "This is my fault. I wanted to stay."

Aaron forced himself to swallow his anger. He squeezed their shoulder.

"Of course it's not your fault," said Jaymie, finally paying attention. He knitted his brow in consternation.

"Yeah, so, I went to smoke a J behind the house, and six of them, like, converged on me," said Jo from her hangover throne. "That guy Steve was like, *You better not be thinkin' about leavin.'* Something about limiting outside contact for safety and artistic integrity or some bullshit." She massaged her temples. "I was annoyed, so I pushed it—bottom line is, no stepping off the premises. They were OK when I gave up and explained I just wanted to smoke. Actually, they offered me some they grew. Better than the stuff from the store. But they're watching us. And there's a hell of a lot of them." The serenity with which Jo related this incident suggested she was still benefiting from the effects of the cult members' gift. "Also, the van's dead."

The four sat in silence. A minute passed.

"So, OK ... they've perhaps had some career success," said Jaymie finally. "How much, we're not sure. Because we cannot, at the moment, Google it."

"Because all of our phones have been stolen," said Aaron. "Right?" They all nodded.

"So, what do they want *us* for?" asked Jo.

"Well, obviously they've got writer's block, or whatever, right now," said Rex. "Or they wouldn't be complaining about not having any skills."

"Unless they're pretending," said Jo. "For reasons unknown."

"Maybe they're going to keep us chained in the basement as art slaves," said Aaron gloomily. "And sell everything we come up with and try to get famous."

"Our music doesn't make *us* famous," Jaymie pointed out. "It doesn't even make us any money. And it's not like they could perform it without us."

"I think that ..." Rex hesitated. "I think they genuinely need a leader. They're that type of people. And their old one seems to have mysteriously disappeared."

"What about Miranda?" asked Aaron.

"She's not a leader, she's an administrator," said Jaymie. "Leadership requires originality."

"Fuck it," said Jo. "I'm going to go hassle her. Even if I don't get any answers, it's something to do."

"I'll go with you," said Aaron. "Strength in numbers. And in, you know, strength." He gestured vaguely toward her bicep.

"OK," said Jaymie. Then he regained his pep. "Look, they haven't hurt us. They didn't lock up Aaron."

"That was on me," Aaron conceded.

"They brought us here to provide education. Which we haven't done yet. So, let's begin by doing what we said we'd do, and maybe once we've hammered home the '10,000 hours' idea, we can peace out. That's my plan."

"But if any of us gets an opportunity, we run for it and call the cops," said Aaron.

"Maybe, just to be safe," Jaymie agreed. "The cats will need feeding. And they did ambush our vehicle—not a great sign." He winked brightly at Rex, who still looked disconsolate.

With that, the meeting concluded. The band exited the broken van and gave awkward waves to the ten or twelve people casually watching them, pretending to rake leaves or trim dying tree branches or share a cigarette in the front yard.

There are a few things worth knowing about the "arts collective" Jaymie was now guiding.

First, the group didn't have twenty-five members, as the *Bukowskis* had approximated, but at least forty and possibly more. Secondly, they were not hopeless at the fine arts—not by a long shot. Not only had they created decent art, they had won four notable awards, received recognition in various literary and arts journals, and earned significant sums in payment for paintings sold, novels published, and a small business creating purses out of recycled Dasani bottles which had been bought by a larger company. One of them had designed a jewel-encrusted badger skeleton that must have cost a fortune to create. It was in a major gallery.

Some of this was discovered by Aaron and Jo a couple of days later, while Jaymie gave a workshop on stage presence and Rex shyly facilitated a writing circle. The rest of the weekend had passed in a flurry of activity and had, despite their lack of freedom, not been unpleasant. The residents were friendly and enthusiastic students. Rex couldn't help enjoying Ronan's company in spite of everything, and Juniper was so helpful and kind that none of them could stay angry with her for being complicit in their captivity.

The only sour notes were when Jaymie and Rex tried to test the boundaries of their confinement on the pretense of going on a cigarette errand and a jog, respectively, and were quickly and forcibly escorted back to the house by seven or eight apologetic residents; Jaymie's chieftain status did not exempt him from the rules. The gravity of their situation was officially confirmed when Tuesday rolled around and they were gently informed that they couldn't go home on schedule after all. They were needed. The cats, they were assured, would be fed.

Jo hadn't had an opportunity to interrogate Miranda, but she and Aaron did, on that third day, come across an old bathroom on the top floor with a sign reading "out of order do not enter." It was the "do not enter" that caught their attention.

The bathroom turned out to be filled with files, photographs, articles, and paperwork. Manila folders were stacked in the bathtub; piles of magazines teetered on the toilet seat and under the sink; books and photos were heaped on the floor beneath the chipped and stained white paint of the bathroom walls. Perched on the sink, a gold trophy shaped like a musical note was barely reflected in the grimy mirror.

The two bandmates sifted through the stacks, reading adulatory literary reviews about a book of railroad-themed poetry, perusing a magazine for bookmarked pictures from an award-winning photography show depicting rural Saskatchewan, and so on. They immediately thought to question the artists involved, but couldn't find anything from a current member. Less interesting but more informative were the contracts, sales records and, almost too conveniently, a copy of a letter responding to an awards gala invite and requesting about forty plus-ones. The names listed included everyone they'd met so far in the collective.

This information also helped solve the mystery of how twenty-odd people lived comfortably without ever seeming to leave for jobs.

They sat in silence for a few minutes, taking it in. "Prolific," Aaron's guide had said. No part of her assessment had been lost in translation.

"So, if this is our cult, where are the other twenty?" asked Jo, scanning the gala list. "Did they just leave before we got here?"

"Maybe they live off-campus," suggested Aaron, not looking like he believed it.

"Right, because this crew is so chill about people coming and going." Jo picked up a folder too carelessly and its paper contents spilled all over the bathroom floor. "OK, one option: you have to make a successful artwork, and then you're allowed to move out. Would explain why none of these awards are for people we've met."

"Option two: they stalked all these local artists and took their awards and somehow convinced people, like the lady I talked to, that the artists live here," said Aaron.

"Assuming the artists were bribed or met tragic accidents. But we can't Google, so."

"Rex said Ronan mentioned their old leader, Sheena. She taught them this creativity ritual, and now they need a new leader. So, maybe some of them left with her, or …"

"Great. Well, at least the mystery of the great ritual will be cleared up this weekend. When I've been fired at work for no-showing and the *Ballet Llama* has replaced me and my spider plant is dead …" Jo saw several expressions competing for dominance on Aaron's face and realized she was in danger of upsetting him. She stopped herself and gathered up the documents spread around the floor.

"We're never getting out, are we?" said Aaron, after a brief, quiet panic attack that Jo politely pretended not to notice.

"Maybe not," said Jo. "We could well die here. But, um, at least we're all … together?"

"Just like the other twenty members." He was still out of breath, and Jo was suddenly determined to give Miranda a good shake-down when she got the chance, as pre-revenge for herself and her possibly-soon-to-be-dead bandmates.

"OK. They probably aren't dead, because that'd be nuts …" She looked around, lost.

"There's no point trying to escape now, while they're all awake. What should we do?"

"Go back downstairs and drink?" Jo suggested.

Aaron sighed and wiped the nervous sweat off his face with a piece of toilet paper. "The thing about people who panic a lot," he said, "at least the way my cognitive behavioural therapist puts it, is that it's a sign you have a lot of … hope … about things …"

"Hope?" said Jo dumbly.

"It sounds tacky when I say it," said Aaron. "And it probably doesn't apply to things like PTSD. But if you didn't have enough hope to panic, you might just not care about anything."

"I admire that you care about things," said Jo.

"I might just be hormonally imbalanced," he admitted. "But still."

"I could really use a toke right now."

"Are you listening?" said Aaron. "God, it's like hanging out with Jaymie."

Jo looked at him in surprise. She suddenly remembered the conversation they'd had in the library, and she felt a stab of guilt. She'd made touring sound like a delightful adventure that Jaymie, their unfailing and indefatigable captain, would effortlessly guide them through, and instead they were imprisoned by a bunch of creeps. It was so easy to put complete faith in Jaymie's confidence and capability, even she'd fallen for it.

She shook her head clear and got to her feet. "We won't mention this to any of our new pals," she said. "You help Jaymie with his classes like nothing is wrong, and I'll figure out their intentions. People often let their guard down around a dumb stoner, you know?"

Aaron nodded in relief and picked up the gala list. He folded it and slid it into the pocket of his jeans. Then they headed downstairs, calmly greeting a woman who lurked in the stairwell pretending to wait her turn for the bathroom she'd forgotten was out of order.

If the band had been able to access their phones or laptops over the course of the days that followed, they'd have known about some important developments back home.

The siblings' mother announced the dates of her homecoming tour. Like them, she was busy, and trusted they'd respond when convenient. A booker waited to hear what band they'd be covering at his upcoming tribute night. A former girlfriend of Jaymie's accused him of attending a show back home and failing to acknowledge her, which, while she was mistaken, would later reinforce his own perceived ability to be doing everything, everywhere, all at once.

Rex received a zero for their unsubmitted essay. Aaron missed one text from one friend. Jo was not only fired, as predicted, but also missed Lucas's carefully crafted response to her carefully crafted comment ("good article, you seem cool"), leaving him to conclude he'd misread the signals. Her other band booked their reunion show without waiting for her go-ahead, trusting they could show up at her place with beers the night of and convince her, if need be. Her snooping landlord emailed to inform her that her spider plant was indeed dead, and that she was still behind on the rent.

Jo didn't need to know any of this to be fed up.

"OK, freak, what's your endgame?" She'd finally cornered Miranda in an upstairs office.

"I'm not sure what you're talking about." Miranda gawked through her bottlecap lenses.

Jo had never really confronted someone before. She'd scripted only that first line, and was now improvising in unfamiliar territory, and Miranda, a born organizer, was prepared.

"You're a—a kidnapper! What's this ritual thing we heard about!"

"Oh Jo, I'm sorry about the circumstances, but are you really having such a bad time? All we've asked is that you enjoy our hospitality for a few days."

"Oh, you 'asked,' did you? I'm probably getting fired, like, right now."

"Jo, I'm so sorry! Maybe we can compensate you. What's your work? Are you in audio production? Recording? A session guitarist? Missing gigs with other groups? A tour?" Something about Miranda's exaggerated concern led Jo to believe she knew Jo was not.

"I work at the—never mind! We have lives back home, you know!"

"Of course. And they must be much more interesting than this—even though *here* you're meeting new people, helping them work through struggles, taking on challenges … It's nothing compared to the thrilling life of a working musician! Which I'm sure you are, with your talent."

"I mean, I haven't exactly been—"

"You know, I loved the *Ballet Llama* in my twenties. Listened to you on my Discman all the time."

"Oh my god, we're not that old! Mp3 player, at most."

"I jogged to it."

"Ew!"

"But that was almost ten years ago—I assume you've been in plenty of great bands since then. It was obviously the start to a vibrant career."

"Well, I didn't exactly—I mean, the indie scene doesn't really work like …"

"Of course—a music career isn't as linear as other fields, is it? And you're young. There's still lots of time—and I assure you, you have fans *here*, at least! Jo, stay for the ritual. Even if you don't love it, don't you think it'll be something a little different? Refreshing?"

Jo tried to hold onto her anger, even as she felt it being replaced by a familiar feeling of depletion. "Are you going to kill us?" she asked limply.

"Oh my, artists do have such zany imaginations! The ritual is like a workshop. It brings us together to share ideas. And we're in dire need of fresh ideas."

"What about your former club members? The awards?"

"We've had residents move on to different pursuits, and we never hold it against them."

Jo sighed. Their captivity was alarming, but there were few signs of it being fatal. Had she picked up Aaron's neurosis? "Ugh, fine. If we stay until then, will you let us go?"

"Of course—you're not *prisoners*. Now, I have a very large grocery order to place." And though she was a foot shorter than Jo and probably had half the muscle mass, she successfully dismissed the disgruntled guitarist with barely a wave of her hand.

14

The Ritual

In a dim basement in a blue house on the edge of a small prairie city, twenty-eight people gathered on two rows of seats arranged in a semi-circle. In the centre of the room, a grand piano loomed out of the half-light like a broken slab of Stonehenge. Its open lid reached skyward, pointing out sacred celestial patterns in the stucco ceiling. Beside the piano, a tripod held a recording device emanating blue light, ready to document tonight's sacrificial ceremony—possibly to be uploaded to the gods in mp3 or even .wav format.

The ritual started innocently enough. A young woman in a light-coloured gown sat at the piano, a Steinway kept impeccably in tune. She took a deep breath, adjusted the bench, and smoothed down her skirt. Her posture, normally closed off and demure, was dramatically changed. Her shoulders were relaxed, heart forward to welcome cosmic inspiration, face serene, arms suspended before the keys as though afloat in a tranquil pool. The tips of two slender index fingers touched two keys as elegantly as a butterfly alighting on the headstock of your guitar at an outdoor festival gig.

She played F and G together, a discordant major second, six times. She expanded to E and G, a minor third, and repeated the process, her tempo shifting twice before the six strokes were finished. Her right hand missed as she moved to D and B, the new notes sounding only five and a half times. Finally, she reached the octave, stumbling once more as she closed the intervals, one by one, folding the gap back to F and G. Then she started again.

Watched by the twenty-eight utterly silent people, Juniper fumbled through "Chopsticks" two more times. Her audience barely breathed. The blue light of the audio recorder gave a deviant twinkle as it caught every slip and stutter of the piano keys.

Rex cringed. Jo stifled a laugh. Aaron shrank into himself and Jaymie thumped his head against Aaron's shoulder in defeat.

Then Miranda spoke in a low monotone, a string of incomprehensible syllables that tripped their way out of her mouth, collided with the heinous piano playing, and attempted an about-face to get back in. Twenty-three voices echoed the nonsense chant back to her. Miranda vocalized again, and the call-and-response continued.

Unperturbed by this interruption, Juniper flubbed away at the keys. She showed no sign of embarrassment at the brutal performance, her bearing as regal and unapologetic as that of a concert pianist with years of Alexander Technique study under their belt.

Then something extraordinary began to happen.

First, the chords of "Chopsticks" morphed into a richly voiced jazz reharmonization in 7/4 time. This shifted to an unrecognizable piece of music, somber and gentle and reassuring. And beautiful. The chorus of chanters fell silent as her song filled the room, expanding and diminishing, twinkling melodic arcs becoming rolling chords and then decrescendoing back to a pedal-point murmur.

Jo listened, dumbstruck. Mesmerized by the wonder of Juniper's fluttering fingers, it was some time before she glanced at the girl's face. It had grown dangerously pale. Her lips had a wet, blueish sheen. Her eyes glazed over and clouded. Jo suddenly saw how thin she was, ragged shoulder blades carving drastic angles in the folds of her dress. The harsh blue lines of her veins stood out vividly on fragile doll's wrists, and Jo felt herself stiffen in horror. The hands danced like skeleton spiders across the gleaming ivory. A limp ragdoll musician, a marionette, sinew stretching through ancient porcelain about to crack from strain and neglect.

In Jo's mind the piano was no longer a monument, but a dying beast. Its ossein keys were parched bone; its gaping lid revealed a criss-cross of innards, tight intestine strings reaching from its pins to the pelvic curve of its soundboard, inviting the dying girl who stroked it to crawl into the wound and warm herself in the steaming depths of its belly.

I'm having a bad trip, Jo thought. Had they drugged her? She reminded herself to take deep breaths—highs gone wrong were nothing she hadn't dealt with before. Then Aaron clasped her arm. He was frozen in fear. On her other side, Rex stared transfixed at Juniper, jaw hanging slightly open. They too were seeing the young woman's life leaching away. And Jo knew she was experiencing something more sinister than a bad trip.

Through the dread gripping her emerged the knowledge that she had to act. And quickly.

There was a dusty Martin acoustic in the corner—the same one she'd embarrassed herself with on the night they'd arrived. It was in need of new strings, but it was playable and stayed in tune. Jo rose slowly from her seat, hoping she wouldn't be noticed. Luckily, everyone was either watching Juniper or had their eyes closed in reverence, absorbed by the haunting melody that came from the Steinway. Jo moved like the shadow of a grizzly bear around the outskirts of the room, picked up the guitar, and pulled the strap over her shoulder.

She touched the low E string and a fraction of a note sounded, a tiny pianissimo unheard by the crowd. She half heard and half felt the note resonating against her ribs, and identified it as being a third below the root of the key Juniper played in. They were in G. The People's Key.

Juniper's piece was in standard four-bar phrasing; Jo recognized the progression as one she'd heard a lot in pop song choruses. Why did the most beautiful, haunting music you came across always turn out to be a four-chord progression you'd heard a lot in pop song choruses?

Jo waited for the next phrase, then plucked an E minor high on the twelfth fret. She voice-led to the nearest C, fingerpicking a soft pattern across the strings. From there, a few steps to G, then D, moving down the neck of the guitar, gently relieving the piano of the melody, working it into the upper strings while her thumb struck the root notes.

Heads turned in her direction. Miranda stood with fists clenched, likely unsure whether crossing the room to stop Jo was worth the risk of breaking Juniper from her trance.

Juniper broke anyway. The piano fell abruptly silent and she looked around, blinking. She stood, confused and shaky with her gown swirling around her, looking like a drunken zombie bride. Then she fainted over the piano bench. Jo finished the song for her, the blue light of the mic glittering away in the darkness.

"So you can see our problem," said Miranda.

Rex and Aaron huddled over Juniper, checking her pulse and cushioning her head. The other residents had relaxed and were leaning back in their chairs or muttering to one another.

"Uh ... you perform a terrifying demon-possession ceremony that murders everyone who does it?" Jaymie gulped.

"Yes, exactly." In the fuzzy lighting her eyes were invisible behind her glasses, and the blue glow danced on the lenses. "Well, not demons. Spirits. Ghosts, if you like. But only the talented ones. The chant summons those with great works of art or music or literature left uncreated in their lifetimes."

"But these *spirits* ... They can't possess someone long enough to make a good ... product ... without killing them," guessed Jaymie, struggling to grasp what he'd just witnessed.

"Correct," said Miranda.

Jo put the guitar down, looking stunned. "What the hell do you want *us* to do about it?" she demanded.

"Not you. Jaymie," said Miranda.

"Me?" And then it clicked. "Oh, shit," he said. "Right." His band stared at him.

"We don't want to die. But this work matters more than anything else. More than life," said Miranda. "So, you need to teach us the right way to do it."

"Because I got possessed without ... without dying," said Jaymie, his voice hoarse with dismay. Aaron surreptitiously face-palmed.

"Because, somehow, you keep doing it, writing song after song, giving performance after performance. And the next morning you wake up, unharmed. And we do not," said Miranda.

"I ..." Jaymie was out of words for the fifth time.

"So, what do you say?" Miranda asked, just as she had at the breakfast table days ago.

He looked around at the desperate, hopeful faces, and at the withered young woman unconscious on the floor.

"I don't know how to help you," he said.

Miranda didn't love the idea of imprisoning people, but she'd been certain that once the *Bukowskis* understood what her co-op was all about, they'd be enthusiastic to work with her.

She also, like any good follower, had total faith in Jaymie's leadership, loved all his songs, and adopted his opinions the moment he voiced them. But that didn't mean she trusted him not to abscond. So, for the course of the past week, her people had kept the band busy and under constant supervision until they could witness the miracle of tonight's ritual.

Miranda didn't feel particularly bad about soft-kidnapping the band. Art was the greatest work a person could do, and saving unfulfilled talents from being lost forever was the noblest of sacrifices. Surely, they'd understand now that they'd seen it in action.

"I don't know how to help you," said Jaymie.

"That's a pity," said Miranda. She wasn't prepared for this response and, not knowing what to do, she nodded to Steve. He didn't have a plan either, but he took a heavy step toward Rex, Aaron, and Juniper, and Jaymie, whose imagination had been morbidly stoked by the events of the last twenty minutes, cried, "No, please! Wait!" and put his hands up in surrender. "I'll do it. It's no problem. When's the next ceremony? We'll work it all out."

Miranda smiled, her faith in him unshaken. Still, she noted his hesitation and decided to keep up the watch on him, just in case. "I knew we could count on you," she said.

"Yeah. Of course," said Jaymie. He looked nervously at Rex and Aaron, whose faces only registered shock, and Jo, who was pale but nodded back resolutely. "Next ritual, we'll get you your masterpiece. No casualties." He knelt beside his brothers. "Now, can we get this poor woman off the floor?" The group hastened to help.

"What did it feel like?" Steve asked Jo in a low voice.

"What did what feel like?" said Jo, still distracted by her frightened bandmates.

"When the spirit was inside you! It took Juniper first, but it finished its work in you." He gazed at her in reverence. "A transition … and it was so seamless. And to have survivors! We've never had something like this happen."

This got Jo's attention. "Is it *that* hard to believe I'm just good at this?" she snapped, jerking her chin toward the guitar.

"No—I just thought because you both were playing the same song—"

"Some dead perv's ghost must be in me—"

"Without any sheet music—"

"Fucking sexist."

"OK, oversensitive."

"What's wrong with your brother?" Miranda demanded. "Is he possessed too?"

"No," said Jaymie dismally. "He's just having a panic attack."

15
Motivation

Over the next few days, the *Bukowskis* took turns visiting Juniper, who was enjoying a period of convalescence in bed. Her complexion brought to mind a child in the throws of consumption, but she was in good spirits and pleasantly surprised to be alive, and it was in her room that they learned the history of the collective.

It was founded ten years earlier by a group of artists who'd bought the home together. They'd discovered that cooperative housing suited people who wished for low rent and favoured community and creative projects over accumulating wealth. It was a noble endeavour, begun in the pursuit of artistic collaboration.

"I've been here almost since the beginning," said Juniper proudly. "When I was thirteen, I saw a play they put on for free, and I knew I wanted in. My parents cared more about money than about me—I'd call home, at first, but they barely noticed I was gone. This has been my family since then. But it wasn't till Sheena brought us the chant a few years ago that we started making great things. Suddenly we didn't have to work anymore. There was income from John's film soundtrack, and royalties from Magda's book."

"And John and Magda are now …" Rex let it hang.

"Yes, they're dead."

"As you saw, it's an unfortunate side effect," said Ronan, who Rex liked to think had become their constant shadow more due to affection than the fulfillment of surveillance duties.

The whole band was present; even Jaymie had taken a break from editing the recording of Juniper's song. (The *Bukowskis* all agreed it was lovely, though the cult weren't sure it could be Truly Great, having been only *half* composed by a ghostly conjuration.)

Their former leader, Sheena Wilder, Juniper explained, had been a Victorian scholar. She'd come across an incantation that called up the spirits of lost geniuses in a tome she'd found deep in a London archive while researching for a PhD thesis on 19th-century occultism. She'd tried the spell, for fun, at a séance-themed party with a handful of drunken grad students, and been amazed to find it actually worked. She disguised the ensuing death as a heart failure, left academia, and set sail home to the New World to share her discovery.

"Wait, so are these dead artists *British?*" asked Rex. "That's, like, even more colonial than it already was."

"We have no idea where they're from," said Juniper. "Our friend Carrie—she's dead—made some paintings that look a lot like this Newfie painter guy from the '50s, but who knows?"

"Long story short," said Ronan, "Sheena heard about us and came to offer her gift."

"She won us over right away!" said Juniper. "It was nice here, but none of our projects had the same ... *impact* ... as what we could create using the chant."

"And without us, the spirits' work would be lost forever," Ronan added.

"Honestly, we just weren't that good on our own. We kind of needed it."

Ronan and Juniper both seemed convinced of the righteousness of Sheena's chant. Rex wondered if the flock's former shepherd had been truly gifted in the art of persuasion or if each of them had always been a bit of a nut.

Aaron took the gala invite he and Jo had found out of his pocket. "So of the forty-odd people invited to this award ceremony, I'm guessing none of them just lost interest and left?"

"All of us have remained," said Juniper. "We are a family."

"And the twenty or so that aren't around here anymore ..." prompted Jo.

"They are with us, in their own way."

"That means they're dead," Aaron whispered loudly to Jaymie.

"And it didn't bother you that your *family* members didn't survive the creative process?" asked Jaymie.

"They will be rewarded," said Juniper serenely. Seeing the band's blank stares, she clarified, "After we do the ritual, we'll be reborn as real creatives."

"Oh jeez," said Jaymie.

"Convenient," muttered Aaron.

"It's true," said Juniper, looking wounded.

"How do you know?" asked Jo, less gently than she probably intended.

"Sheena said it was in her book."

"I bet she did," said Aaron.

"So you *wanted* to do it?" asked Rex.

"Of course!" said Juniper. "I volunteered! But … I have to admit I'm relieved to have more time. The life I've got is actually not so bad."

"Did your dear Sheena, ah … Did she stand to gain anything? From you all doing the ritual?" asked Jaymie.

"You mean besides all the royalty money?" Aaron reminded him scathingly.

"But she died too!" said Rex. "So, she was either crazy or she had a real reason to believe in the rebirth thing!"

"Died? No, no," Juniper laughed. "When it came her turn to do the ritual, it didn't work the same. It gave her a whole bunch of arts management skills and now she's an agent for theatre actors in Vancouver! She still shares the art of others. It made her what she was meant to be."

"I'm sure it did," Jo monotoned, as the Brzezinskis stared at Juniper or put their heads in their hands. "I'm sure it did."

In varying states of jittery helpfulness, the *Bukowskis* finished out the weekend and stayed on into the next week. They tried to make the best of it.

Jaymie genuinely enjoyed leading workshops, preaching his ideas, and making up rules, such as: before every meal, you should write a page of stream-of-consciousness prose about any topic. This and other inspiration hacks were immediately implemented as law.

Miranda had deduced that Aaron was the kind of person who was going to be slightly miserable wherever he was, and had done her best to provide him comfortable places to sit quietly or play his drums. He'd amused himself for a while trying to confuse the group with rules of his own invention, until they'd learned to tell him apart from Jaymie by his general air of discomfort or, if they glimpsed it under his hair, the little scar on his left cheek.

Neither Aaron nor Jo were equipped to be mentors—Aaron because he was too distraught about their situation to focus on lesson plans, and Jo because she was too annoyed about it to appreciate the humanity in her pupils. She fought a losing battle with resignation, and Miranda soon bought her off with a limitless supply of her favourite entertainments, which turned out to be mostly indicas and access to HBO.

And so Jaymie and Rex took over the bulk of the responsibility for educating a group of people who stubbornly favoured being possessed over putting in the work.

Rex, between lessons, spent much of the next week discretely exploring second base. The collective was happy to see Ronan with a friend, since the only other member his age had immortalized himself a year prior via a heart-wrenching country ballad that sold to an artist whose name you'd recognize. The songwriter himself, of course, was a one-hit wonder.

Everyone respected Rex's privacy too much to inquire what they were up to—except the twins, who did their best to express their emotional availability and to provide the sex talk Rex should have received years earlier and from almost anybody else.

("For the love of God, don't do it, Rex."

"Don't do it, Rex."

"But if you're going to do it, use a condom."

"Do you have some?"

"We've got some—he's got some."

"Yeah, let me see."

"But for Christsake, not with *him*."

"Not him, please, Rex."

"That's some Stockholm-level shit."

"Mom will skin us."

"*He* didn't kidnap us—he's a kid." (- Rex.)

"What about that girl you like from jazz band?"

"She's straight."

"Bad luck, eh? OK, take a few."

"You're too young, Rex."

"Shut up, Aaron. Sex-positive parenting."

"Fine. Be responsible, Rex."

"Aw, our little guy!")

Rex had understandably mixed feelings about their, er, feelings, but reasoned that as long as they and Jaymie succeeded in refocusing the cult, the imprisonment issue would clear right up. And everybody knew what happened between a cute dude and another cute dude when a problematic relationship dynamic resolved itself: unobstructed romance.

Jaymie still refused to forfeit his attempts to get the residents to cultivate their natural creativity. After dinner that Wednesday, he gathered the group for their nightly motivational talk.

"You can do anything, if you set your mind to it! Look at John Steinbeck—rags to riches! Look at Dickens! Look at, fucking, Harry Potter!" Rex glared at him. "Not that I endorse—just, a lot of us are millennials, and I mean, can we separate artist and—never mind, whole other conversation. Anyway, point is—*grit!*"

His disciples listened attentively, but he had noticed the malaise clouding many faces during these lectures. The rapture and inspiration he expected from them was missing. Somehow, he was still not getting through. A hand rose in the audience.

"Jaymie, I have a question. Do you mean that if I write enough dog songs, eventually I'll be able to write *really great* dog songs?"

"Yes, that is what I mean. I know you have some difficulty with self-confidence—"

"And are you saying that hard work is all it takes to transcend the barriers of race and gender and class?"

"You're a middle-class cis guy, Aar. I'm not sure why you're concerned."

"Are all the people in this room middle-class cis guys, though?"

"Well, no … Which brings me to my next point—overcoming adversity! Did you know that the most successful people actually had statistically *more* rather than fewer setbacks to get past …?" He sighed. "Yes, a question from the snowflake in the third row?"

"Jaymie, what if I have to choose between being an artist and supporting my family? Is art still the most important thing?"

"Fortunately, Aaron, you have no such choice to make."

A woman stood and left the room, head hanging. Jaymie narrowed his eyes. He knew his brother had a dangerous penchant for lurking around with his ear to the ground, absorbing the insecurities of others. He grinned at the crowd.

"Obstacles will present themselves from all angles. It could be in the form of poverty, overwhelming responsibilities, self-doubt, *siblings*—"

"Jaymie, if I devote my whole life to music but then at sixty-five I realize I was actually a mediocre musician no matter how hard I tried, what does that mean about my life?"

"OK you little fucking troll …"

And so on.

Miranda exited the room the moment the speech ended and caught Steve and Evelyn on their way out.

"Meeting," she said, and led them into the side room off the main entrance. The band's gear was still stowed there, and the three were forced to arrange themselves around stacked drums, guitar cases, and keyboard stands. Evelyn hoisted herself onto the bass amp, brushing off an animal cartoon and lipstick-stained card, and pocketing a printed sheet of Jaymie's lyrics.

"We're getting nowhere," Miranda said, finding an empty corner and crossing her arms.

"Well, what do you suggest?" asked Steve. "You said seeing the ritual would be enough to stir up his compassion, but he's still keeping the answers to himself." He nearly tripped on an oversized duffel bag full of metal drum stands, tried to move it, realized it was too heavy, and settled for lightly kicking it instead. "It's like he doesn't even *want* us to survive."

"Maybe he's still figuring out how it works?" Evelyn suggested. "He was just a tiny boy when he was possessed. He probably doesn't remember how it happened."

"Well, he should try harder! We should be having more rituals! Experimenting with different things!" Steve insisted.

"You know we can't have them too often," said Miranda sharply. "We'll raise suspicion. We've only gotten this far because we're careful."

"And besides, this was supposed to *end* the rituals. I don't want to lose another one of us. We shouldn't have to," said Evelyn. "We know he can help us. That's why we chose him."

"We *assume* he can," said Steve. "If we're right, then what's taking so long?"

Miranda massaged her temples. "Alright," she said. "We'll plan another ritual. If having that on the horizon isn't enough to motivate him, we'll get one of the brothers to volunteer—Rex, since they've been so keen about our cause. And less volatile than the other one."

"What if they don't want to volunteer?" asked Evelyn, her heels thumping an anxious beat against the face of the bass amp.

"Do you have a better idea?" Miranda gestured a little too aggressively and knocked a pair of drumsticks off a shelf above her. They hit Steve, startling him backwards into Rex's hard-shell bass case. He stumbled and thudded against the door. The case rocked perilously for a moment, then toppled and landed half on his knee and half on Aaron's open bag of cymbals, arousing a cacophonous duet of timbres from man and instrument.

Miranda apologized and helped him to his feet, but Evelyn was frozen in place. The slapstick performance had woken something. A phrase, "cacophonous duet of timbres," emerged as though transmitted from a higher plane, and a shiver of anticipation ran through her.

"I'm sorry, I have to go," she said.

"Where?" Miranda gave her glasses a skeptical nudge up the bridge of her nose.

"I'm ... It's very important." And she swept out the door.

Pressed against the wall of the kitchen, which was adjacent the storage room on the opposite side from the door, were two identical men who'd until very recently been preparing to shout curses at each other and possibly engage in physical violence. Instead, they stood rooted to the spot, listening. One mouthed the words, "I fucking told you so."

"I'm sensing it's time for us to depart," Jaymie said quietly, once they'd peeled themselves away from the thin drywall.

"No shit!" hissed Aaron.

"I just ... I guess I thought maybe I could help them. That if I could get them to listen and put in the effort, we could stop doing that freaky chant and killing each other." He clasped his head, the picture of a tormented martyr.

"What do you mean, *we* could stop? Listen to yourself! *We* are not *them*. Let the police stop them, Jay. Admit it, we're here because you love the attention. All these helpless lost souls salivating over you from their séance circle ..."

"Write that down," spat Jaymie. "It's good alliteration—maybe you're a poet after all."

"They wouldn't care if I was, just like they don't care that *you* are! They only care that you're a fake mystic back from the dead or however the fuck it's supposed to work—God! Have they even read any Bukowski? You're nothing like him!"

Actually, the group had discussed this incongruity and decided that, had Charles B. not had a childhood plagued by physical abuse, neglect, poverty, alcoholism, and the stifling expectations and gender roles of 1930s America, he might well have turned out more like Jaymie. Could anyone prove he wouldn't have?

Aaron bit his lip, resisting a full tirade. He surveyed the tidy kitchen, which had appeared so bright and benign on the first day they'd arrived, countertops shining and ripe fruit hanging in baskets. Now even the umbrella plant in the corner reached threateningly toward him.

"OK, relax! Hey, it's OK—don't have another panic—Christ, fine, we'll get out of here. I'm hearing you. We'll go tonight, OK?" Jaymie slumped against the wall.

Aaron took a shaky breath. "Man, I'm going to need at least a couple days apart from you once we're home and all this is over."

"Fuck that, I'll stay away a whole week. In fact, why don't you just quit the band again like you love to do?"

"Oh, do I have permission to quit your band now?"

"God, you're mean sometimes." Jaymie did a quick arm stretch and rolled his shoulders, and his face eased back into its crooked smile. "Come on, act natural. Let's go tell Jo and Rex."

They went back to the living room to look for the others, debating which of them had been meaner during this particular discourse, and narrowly avoiding meeting Miranda and Steve as they headed down the same hall less than a minute later.

They say that if a creative endeavour has resonated with even one person then it is worthwhile, and Jaymie's lecture—the last one he would ever deliver to these followers—had finally spoken to someone.

After her meeting with Miranda and Steve, Evelyn went to her room, placed a towel under the door to mute the sound of tapping keys, and sat down at her antique typewriter. She riffled a stack of pages she'd written over the past few days, glancing over her work and making the occasional pencil correction. As she went, she felt an excitement stirring within her.

She loaded a blank sheet of paper—an item that until this week had terrified her more than death—into the machine, and began to type.

16
Escape Artists

After the lecture, Ronan invited Rex to discuss, over a bottle of wine, the ideas Jaymie had presented. Rex accepted. They climbed out a third-floor window to a perfect view of the sunset and sat on the sloping roof of the house, gazing over the stripped fields, watching distant smoke spiral up from where a farmer was burning stubble on the horizon. A strong wind wafted the smoke eastward, like a stoner thoughtfully aiming the exhalation of his bong rip away from his girlfriend's face.

Rex opened: "I think he's right that anyone can learn new skills. But on the other hand, we're good at music because we've been playing since we were two ... which is maybe also why we're so weird."

"I like that you understand what it's like to be different," said Ronan.

"Yep, I understand," Rex agreed.

A magpie soared overhead, chattering about how lonely it was that all its usual victims for murder and child-abduction had migrated south.

"It's like, there're things you're wiser about than anyone I've ever met, like music and life in the city, and then other things you're kind of innocent about. In a good way!" His cheeks reddened and Rex detected a wine-sparkle in his eye. "I mean, did you kiss anyone before me?"

"I don't think there's a good way or a bad way about it. But I get kind of shy, I guess."

"I just feel like you're not like other—" At Rex's expression, Ronan rewrote his sentence midway through. "—prolific musical teenagers ... that I know."

"Being different means your life doesn't progress in the same order as, like, the kids on TV. Like, you start high school and you have all kinds of exciting hookups for four years and then it's yay college or whatever, assuming it's not Riverdale and you didn't die in an earlier season." Rex had thought about this more than once.

"Yeah, thank god. That you didn't die, I mean."

"Being different hasn't been too bad. There are a few idiots at school, but I don't really care. Still, I guess I'd like to stop being … so innocent … sometime."

"Cool." He offered back the wine bottle, which Rex just beheld contemplatively.

"I mean, virginity is a patriarchal, heteronormative social construct and it's totally fucked, obvs," they said. "But like. At some point."

"Like … today?"

Rex sighed. "I think … no. Sorry, I didn't mean to … I *do* like you. But I think I'm going to wait. Until there's less … captivity."

"Captivity."

"Till I'm not kidnapped. It's an awkward setup. Like. For a beginner."

"That's just kind of incidental, though."

"You haven't exactly volunteered to help me get away."

"It's just really nice you're here."

"Trauma vibes."

"Even with *me?*" He blinked virtuously.

"Are you pressuring me? Because I have two older brothers, and they might not look tough, but they *will* find some petty, nuanced way of destroying your self-esteem for a while."

"No! Nope. Not pressuring," said Ronan quickly. "I was kind of nervous anyway. I'd rather it be the right … I just really like you."

A warmth ran through Rex, even though they weren't sure how far they wanted things to go with Ronan, and even though they were still worried about being trapped, and even though they weren't sure Ronan actually *did* understand, and even though they couldn't help wondering if all their relationships for the rest of their life were going to be some confusing version of this.

They found themself oddly excited to discover that so many different attitudes could exist within them at once.

"I miss my mom," they said, completely surprising themself.

"I'm sorry. I'm sure they'll let you send a message at some point." Ronan looked away, and Rex knew he felt guilty for the circumstances, even while benefitting from them.

"And *you* won't even phone your parents to say you're safe?"

"My dad will just come get me, like, 'Why can't you just play hockey?' As if *that*'s more important than *this*. Know what I mean?" Ronan sipped his wine.

"I don't know my dad super well. My parents split six or seven years before I was born."

"Sorry," said Ronan. This time Rex accepted the bottle. "I didn't know."

"I wonder which annoying hobby he'd push on me if he lived here. Cadets, maybe. He used to be a cop." They squinched their face in a show of complicated disgust.

"Gross. You'd probably have run away here too, and then we'd have met a lot sooner." He winked in a way that wasn't creepy—a skill that Rex had thought only Jaymie, out of all the men in the world, had mastered.

"I sort of wish I had. I've had so little chance to rebel."

"I wish you had too."

"We can still make up for a bit of lost time," said Rex. Romance felt a little unnatural and scripted, but fun at the same time, like they were a dashing and confident actor playing a part in a movie. They leaned into the role, grasping Ronan's jacket by the fur of the hood and pulling him in for a last, long kiss as the magpie above practiced kill strikes on its shadow-prey against the backdrop of billowing smoke.

In keeping with the tradition of desperate escapes, the four prisoners waited until the dead of night and made use of a conveniently placed wooden trellis in order to avoid the assiduously guarded front and back doors.

"We're artists escaping!" Jaymie whispered up to Aaron as he climbed. "Does that make us escape artists?"

"Shut up, I'm concentrating," said Aaron from a few feet above, shakily navigating a vine-coated tread. He'd just had a near miss, his shoe sliding on the damp leaves and lurching him down a few rungs before he caught himself just short of Jaymie's head.

"Escape, artists! They're after you!" Jaymie murmured, but then obeyed his brother and focused on the lattice at hand.

It was a moonless, silent night, and Jaymie had the impression of descending into a vast inkwell. Someone was about to scoop him up on a giant calligraphy pen and use him to compose a poetic masterpiece. He shuddered, hoping fervently that none of his loyal new followers were … following.

The thing about being an influential figure, he mused, fingers deep in decayed leaf matter and rotten wood, was that it could be hard to establish boundaries. The more fans the better, but what about the ones who were in it for the wrong reasons? He dodged Aaron's slidey sneaker. There was a fine line between developing a following who'd defend and celebrate you and having to make a swift midnight getaway in fear for your life. But if you weren't ready to navigate the pitfalls of celebrity, then you might as well not go into music in the first place.

Rex, their skinny form as good as invisible in black jeans and hoodie, dropped nimbly to the grass where Jo waited, picking at splinters that had penetrated her gloves. She'd offered to go first, since she would've caused the most calamity had she fallen.

They'd slung on their backs only their most valuable and lightweight carry-ons: Jo's guitar, a tote containing the smaller of their two synthesizers, and Rex's laptop, upon which they hoped to access the internet as soon as they found a connection.

They picked their way over the lawn to the driveway, where their van still squatted invisibly, dark vehicle against dark night. If all went well, they'd return for it and the rest of their gear in the morning, with backup.

A shadow moved in the drive. Rex hissed a warning and they all froze. The van was being watched—Jaymie mentally kicked himself for not thinking about it.

They passed a tense minute crouched in a huddle in the yard. A second form moved under a poplar tree close to the bushes that separated the sidewalk from the front yard. Jaymie felt a rush of adrenaline. It was just like in those video games where you had to avoid the guards' flashlights or a whistle blew and you got sent back to the start of the level!

"Back, other way," whispered Jo. They turned around and skirted the house, hidden against the bulk of the building. A red ember floated like a tiny wicked fairy in the middle of the backyard; the silhouette of a small woman—Evelyn, the writer, Jaymie guessed—tilted her head skyward and exhaled a fog of smoke into the night. They held still until she turned her dragon breath toward the fields behind the house.

Jaymie longingly mouthed the consonants of "a cigarette," into Aaron's ear and sensed rather than saw Aaron rolling his eyes. They crept the remaining distance to the sparse hedge and picked their way through one by one, praying the snapping twigs wouldn't alert the sentinels.

They stopped again on the other side and listened, ears hyper-trained to adjust intonation and volume levels now straining for the sound of footsteps. Jaymie heard nothing.

"OK, this is actually really effing scary," he breathed. There was no point denying it. Rex pressed against his side, shivering. He squeezed them around the shoulders and made a mental note that for future tours he would hire musicians he didn't know or care very much about.

Then they set off again into the dark fields, hoping to skirt the street-lit neighbourhood and re-enter the city at a safer point. A cloud shifted and a smattering of stars appeared and vanished again, like a group of strangers who'd come across your show by accident, looking for a place to drink, but decided to go elsewhere once they realized there was a cover charge.

Aaron looked up, the brief starlight illuminating his features. He was strangely calm—or perhaps not so strangely, if you knew the cocktail he'd partaken in earlier that night.

Jaymie, in his explorations of the house, had located the commune's stash of Pentobarbital—the short-acting barbiturate they'd been sedated with after their show, although Jaymie could only infer this detail.

The drug, in controlled doses, dulls the senses and slows the nervous system, and has been found effective at calming anxious thoughts and curing insomnia. Though no longer widely available in North America, it is still marketed to veterinarians for its usefulness, in greater quantities, in euthanizing animals.

One member of the collective had been a vet tech in their former life, and became addicted while self-medicating a case of compassion fatigue. They eventually composed a poetry collection personifying rodents as representations of mental illness, which became Instagram-famous and was later distributed by a major publisher, but before their passing they'd illegally amassed a supply of the drug, and the group had held onto it for situations like that first night.

It's worth mentioning that the substance is *not* safe to mix with liquor, and it speaks to luck and the alcohol tolerances of the elder three *Bukowskis* that none of them suffered any serious health repercussions.

Tonight, Jaymie had offered his brother a mug of spiked chamomile tea. Fortunately, the concoction had the desired soothing effect, rather than throwing Aaron into a paranoid funk the way it had when mixed with marijuana and copious amounts of Crown Royal.

And so they began the trek across the barren field, four hooded figures cloaked by the smothering black sky.

After Rex had said goodnight, Ronan lay awake contemplating his favourite philosophical topics, which could be summarized as "Trolley Problem" and "Does Rex Make Me Gay."

Ronan hadn't met people his age who were interested in the same things he was; the house's other residents were past their teens, with the exception of a few children who'd been born in. So, having Rex around was a breath of fresh air. Not only did Rex see things more deeply than Ronan's peers back home, they were also, at least in his opinion, quite pretty.

He estimated that Rex looked similar to the type of people he'd been into in the past, if you got past the crazy hair and plentiful ear and eyebrow piercings. But Ronan understood that a person's appearance does not dictate their gender, and that was OK, even if it meant he had to be queer now. Not that there's anything wrong with that! Totally fine. Even if he didn't *feel* queer. He'd Google about it when he wasn't so busy trying to impress them.

Either way, he sure liked cuddling with the pixie-faced little punk. So, he was confused and alarmed when he knocked on Rex's door with the last quarter-bottle of wine and a really good point he'd come up with about utilitarian moral obligation and found the room empty.

Respecting people's desire to identify with whichever gender or non-gender they liked was something he could come to terms with—it was 2019, after all—but honouring their inclination to depart the shady consortium you've trapped them in for their own good and the good of those around them and the good of Western Culture at large was another thing entirely.

He did the only thing he could think of, which was to alert Miranda, awaken the others, and make pursuit.

The exhausted little family traversed the farmland, barely speaking except to occasionally confirm there were still four of them. A breeze stirred as dawn approached, thinning the cloud cover. The sky began to glow in the east.

And in the half light of the early autumn morning, the unfortunate bandmates saw figures keeping pace with them in the surrounding fields, calm drudges with heads bent, like labourers resigned and ready to begin early morning reaping duties, to scythe at the fruits of their enterprise, slowly, slowly closing in.

17

Doomed Cry-Face Smile Emoji

The fields shone golden-beige as the first rays of sunlight glanced off dead stalks of straw, as lovely as the final five minutes of a Bob Ross instructional painting video.

Less picturesque was the scene unravelling on that stark plain.

In the middle of the same field Aaron had woken up in two weeks earlier was a skeletal wooden structure, an empty triangle silhouetted harshly against the waxen sky. It stood on a makeshift platform built out of stacked pallets sunk into the near-frozen soil. The helpless *Bukowskis*, guided on all sides by a horde of silent figures, had no choice but to walk toward the awful contraption, though they all wanted nothing more than to run in the opposite direction.

Aaron couldn't help thinking it was some kind of gallows. If not, then something just as bad. These people were probably going to murder the band in terrible ways. He was about to live out his darkest nightmares—they'd make him choose one sibling to sacrifice and one to spare (you save Rex but kill yourself later, obviously), just as a cruel game. The *Bukowskis'* first adventure as a band would end in horrors so legendary that other bands worldwide would cancel their tours in fits of last-minute hysteria for years to come.

So why was he so calm?

Aaron couldn't remember the last time he'd been able to think clearly in an even mildly stressful situation, much less attempt to strategize while walking into near-certain destruction.

The last time he'd reacted to something with any degree of composure, their mother had been living at home, and she and Jaymie were arguing, and little Rex was listening in, and he was trying simultaneously to get the two to lower their voices and to calm down Rex, who was upset because they thought they were moving to Las Vegas, and *someone* (oops) had told them that slot machines wandered the city like triffids and hypnotized you into instant addiction, so they'd have to go around blindfolded or else become a little sad wastrel child-gambler, haunting the Strip, feeding pennies into the maws and waiting for the cherries to line up, which they never would, because Aaron had also explained the concept of "the house always wins," forcing Rex to assume all gamblers had been brainwashed by a conspiracy of slot machines, and they started crying because they didn't understand that sometimes adults just like to go have some fun, and come to think of it he'd somehow managed to have this entire flashback without deadnaming the pigtailed little guy in his memory even once, so he must be pretty on his game right now …

Anyway, in all the confusion someone had accidentally put the electric kettle to boil on the stove burner, and it started on fire, and without thinking he'd unplugged it and fanned the smoke with a tea towel, thus saving the home and everyone inside it, like a total boss.

Now he racked his brain, thinking of ways to distract their captors, trying to remember how far away and in which direction the highway was, estimating the time it would take to get there and how soon they might meet a vehicle, and wondering if it was worth risking another, entirely different, dangerous and terrifying prospect: hitchhiking.

Jaymie scanned the horizon for an opening between his followers, but he knew there were too many of them. He pictured a showdown against the rising sun, he and Aaron putting to use the forgotten two years of karate they'd taken as kids (an unsuccessful attempt to exhaust them of their energy), Jo in berserker-mode cleaving a swath of destruction through the bodies, Rex sprinting like the wind back to the city for help. But even he, for all his optimism, knew that four musicians were no match for two dozen people united by a Greater Purpose.

Then he saw what stood on the rickety dais. The wooden triangle was an easel, onto which two people were laying a large rectangular board. On one side was a bucket of brushes, on the other a low stool. He felt a pain in his gut.

"Welcome," said Miranda, the word shattering the long silence like unwanted amplifier feedback. "We're pleased you could join us for today's ritual. This must mean you've solved the hiccup in our creative routine." It was still too dark to see her clearly, but he could hear the ugly smile in her voice.

"Sure, of course," Jaymie grinned, his heart pounding in his chest. This was no problem. He'd get them out of this. He'd spent *lots* of time with a pounding heart; it was a side effect of his occasional caffeine overconsumption. Another side effect was that you came up with a lot of innovative last-minute solutions.

"I have a theory," he said, "which I'll demonstrate. No chanting involved. If I don't get possessed and make a nice picture, you can—you can do whatever. Lock me in the basement till the end of time." A hundred ideas jostled through his mind, most of them futile. If he could make the painting into a performance the way Jo had done with the song, perhaps the others could slip away for backup …

"Impossible," said Steve. "We need the chant to initiate it. And you already have Bukowski's spirit. You can't have two spirits in you."

"He's right, you can't," said Miranda. "We've tried."

"But we must all have at least one spirit in us even *before* we're possessed, if our spirits can come back and possess *other* people later—"

"Then you can't have three." Miranda's tone suggested that the logistics of the procedure were not up for debate.

"Fine, who wants to—" Jaymie began.

"Rex would be happy to volunteer," purred Miranda. "Since they were *so* enthusiastic to join our collective. And especially now that you've made the ritual safe. Right?"

"Right …" whispered Jaymie, and he understood that he was being punished for failing.

"Ugh, voluntold," muttered Rex bravely. They walked the last few steps to the platform and stepped stiffly onto it, shoes making hollow clunks against the wood.

Jaymie's mind went blank. Equally as terrifying as a gallows, the blank white canvas stood, flatly absorbing the light of the sunrise in preparation to swallow all the light in the world.

Jo had as realistic a view of their odds as Jaymie did, but she knew that if he hadn't come up with a clever way out by now then there wasn't much hope for a nonviolent solution. They wouldn't fall for her guitar trick again—and anyway, there was nowhere to plug in—and she was stone-cold sober and she was anxious and she had only one skill left to offer, if you could call it a skill. She set down her guitar case, strode up to Steve, and punched him in the face.

Jo hadn't fought much, because few would consider challenging her. So, having had limited opportunity to gauge her strength in the context of physical conflict, she erred on the side of destruction and put everything she had into it. Something crunched against her fist. Steve was thrown backward by the blow, and she shook out her hand. Seconds later, a force crashed into her, knocking her onto her front.

For a moment there was no sound except the tinnitus in her left ear. Her punch hand throbbed and she hazily wondered if she'd ever be able to fingerpick again. Then she heard yelling—one or both of the twins calling her name—and she wedged her hands under her chest and heaved up, bucking at least two bodies that attempted to restrain her. A boot kicked her arm from under her, sending sharp pain lancing into her elbow. She gasped. Several pairs of knees held her down as she struggled, spitting out frozen dirt and kicking against the hard ground.

She turned her head to the side and shook tangled black hair out of her face. She could blurrily see two men holding Jaymie's arms as he cried out indecipherably. Another, who she remembered had dreams of being a caricaturist, towered menacingly over a shell-shocked Aaron.

Miranda crouched beside Jo's head to deliver a statement she heard at least once after almost every show she played.

"I tried to learn guitar once," she spat in Jo's ear. "I couldn't get the hang of it." She stood and nodded to one of the men, who got out a roll of duct tape. Jo hissed something unrepeatable and decidedly unfeminist at her.

"Stop!" Rex shouted from the platform, where they'd been watching the fight with a look of intense distress. They fished for a paintbrush from the bucket. "I'm ready." They sat, pulled the stool closer to the easel, and gripped a thick, tapered brush in their long fingers.

A cloud, hoping to conceal the horrible scene, wrapped itself around the rising sun and tried to choke it. It was fended off.

Jo was allowed to watch with her wrists wrapped in duct-tape, kneeling beside a despairing Jaymie, who was still guarded by the two men, his mouth also taped to prevent his protests from interrupting. Aaron stood beside him, looking terrified but still able to breathe, not yet in full panic mode. Steve loomed behind, his nose crookedly dripping blood.

Rex leaned toward the easel, dipped the brush in black paint, and drew a large, shaky circle encompassing most of the canvas. Miranda began to chant. Morning light caught the purple streaks in Rex's hair, which was unstyled and sticking out at all angles as though trying to escape the young bassist's head. Their expression was obscured by the blinding rays.

Jo's breath caught in her throat. A protective impulse she hadn't known she possessed began to scream within her, and her heart hammered, and she understood what Aaron had meant about caring too much to function.

Rex added to their portrait two polka-dot eyes and a sweeping, lopsided mouth. A wet black splotch ran goopily from one of the eyes, creeping its way to the bottom of the canvas and then splatting on the wood planks. The chanting became a frenzied monotone.

It won't work on Rex, Jo thought desperately. *It only affects these talentless creeps, Rex is different*—

Aaron sank to his knees. He had a familiar stricken look on his face, and at first Jo thought it was a belated panic attack.

"I'm … back," he mumbled. "It's been … such a long time." No one had seen him pull the little synthesizer from the bag Jaymie had dropped. Jaymie reached his bound wrists out in anguish to try and shake him out of it, but one of the men blocked his lunge.

"Such a long time," he breathed. "… Since I put the lime … I put the lime in the co … In the coco—" He choked on the last word and turned on the synth, which contained a small speaker and backup battery for impromptu performances such as this. He activated the arpeggiator. "At last … My final great work …"

Rex dropped the brush. Tripping over their dirty sneakers, they scrambled tearfully off the platform and into Jaymie's taped-up arms. No one stopped them. They had all directed their gazes, and their chanting, toward Aaron, and Jo realised that she and her bandmates were not exempt from the malevolent spell this coven invoked. She watched him in horror, her thoughts diminishing to a single word, *No*.

18

The Swan Song of Aaron Brzezinski

"No, I can't forget that evening
　It was late as I was leaving
　And I stepped out in the street to brave the night
　It was calm but in the dark, bright eyes alight
　Yes, they alight"

His keyboard playing wasn't skillful, but the simple progression, moving back and forth between a few triads with the arpeggiator filling out the rhythm, gave the accompaniment a haunting, undulating effect.

"When I think about tomorrow
All my hours seem only borrowed
Since you had me there but then you let me go
Now I can't bear the fear that's building in my soul
It's in my soul"

"Ah, the metaphor. It's about strength in times of darkness," someone murmured.
"Yes," said Evelyn. "It's about facing your fears."
"It's about trying to make art!" whispered the woman beside her.
"That's the same thing," said Evelyn.

"And I can't live
Not knowing if you're out there

I can't live
I don't know what's in store
I can't live
Knowing that you're out there
I can't live
Can't walk through that door"

He had a sweet voice—Jaymie's voice without the sharp edges, softer and less certain. He'd grown pale ... Or did he always look that way? It was actually hard to tell whether or not Aaron was beginning to languish and wither as Juniper had.

The group stopped chanting and listened to the results of their incantation.

"And I fear that once you've woken
You will rise and leave me broken
Though you howl with the promise of a thrill
You'll take me from this life still unfulfilled
It's unfulfilled"

"It's about taking risks without knowing what the future holds!" an awestruck man suggested.

"It's about wanting to become what you're meant to be, but not knowing if you can handle it," someone else quietly conjectured.

"And I wake to feel you near
A soft breath that I can hear
And a warmth that promises to soothe my pain
But then your teeth are in my skin, and I wake again
I wake again"

"It's about ... the fickleness of fame?"
"The hidden costs of self-actualization?"
"Addiction, maybe?"
"And I can't live
Not knowing if you're out there"
"It's about sacrifice."
"I can't live

Don't know what's in store"

"But does it sound a *little* like that other song …?"

Aaron jumped the octave, his voice wavering into a falsetto so stupid that Jaymie nearly groaned aloud.

"I can't live

Knowing that you're out there"

"Yeah, the music is a little different, but it sounds like … the lime-in-the-coconut guy—what's it called?"

"I can't live

Can't walk through that door"

Aaron moved through the chord progression twice more, easing the volume slider down. The final notes faded. He looked up, his masterwork complete—still very much alive.

"It's about the struggle of finding your own way," said Juniper.

Jaymie shlicked the tape off his face and rubbed the rashy skin underneath. "No," he said, so quietly that only Rex could hear. "It's about dogs."

Aaron's audience didn't know what to make of the song. They couldn't even tell whether it was good. A few were discussing the meaning behind the lyrics. Others had grown suspicious that the quality was lacking, based on the fact that he hadn't died. A couple of serious music enthusiasts questioned the originality of the piece.

"Is it … kind of the same tune as *I Can't Live?* By Harry—"

"It's called *Without You,*" said Miranda, who knew a thing or two about popular music. "And yes, it is."

Aaron cleared his throat. "My name is Aaron Bukowski-Nilsson, and on January fifteenth, nineteen ninety-four, the same day my uncle twice-removed, the great singer-songwriter Harry Nilsson, suffered a fatal heart attack, I came into this world—" he looked straight at Jaymie "—seven weeks premature."

Miranda spun toward Jaymie, her expression wavering between awe and accusation.

"How did you do it?" she demanded of the wrong brother. "Can you have *one* premature twin? Steve, you get data out here, right? Check when Harry Nilsson died! Check if you can have *one* prema—" She looked around. "Steve?"

But Steve couldn't respond. He lay prone on the platform, his body stiff beside the stool he'd claimed moments after Rex vacated it. He'd perched there, a trance overtaking him as the group chanted at Aaron, and made broad, black strokes on the canvas, bold gashes of movement attacking the white emptiness, striking against the vapidity of Rex's sad smiley.

Inspiration had struck. He'd always wanted to be a painter; he'd been unable to resist.

The body on the platform barely resembled him. Years older than the Steve they knew, brittle and ghostly white, hands curling into petrified claws on either side of his head. One clouded blue eye leered sightlessly from under his hair. Fortunately, no more of his face was visible. The group gathered around, examining the painting. It was striking.

"It looks ... Japanese, maybe?"

"Can we still release it? I mean, he's a white guy."

"*Was* a white guy."

"It looks authentic, though. It's perfect, the juxtaposition between the inane soullessness of our culture of emoji communication, and the simplicity and truth of Eastern spirituality. The ghost knew what it was doing."

"But is that racist, though?" asked Ronan, expressing probably the most minor of the moral dilemmas he must have been having up till that point.

"It's certainly *appropriative*," said Evelyn.

"He's, like, *very* white," said someone else.

While they discussed the piece and checked Steve for a pulse that wasn't there, Rex quickly un-taped Jo.

"There's a highway across the field," Aaron hissed.

"You know Nilsson only *covered* that song, right?" Jaymie whispered back.

The collective remained fully absorbed by the new creation. "I say we release it under a Japanese name and never show any pictures of him," someone suggested.

"Isn't that ethically wrong?"

"The man gave his *life* for this painting, for god's sake!"

"And we do have to pay the bills."

"Hey, is someone checking on that Harry Nilsson date? Ronan!"

"On it!" said Ronan, looking dazed.

"Wait, so, the song—the spirit ... Is the secret that we have to know which talented person died the same day we were born?" asked Evelyn.

"And do they have to be blood-related?" asked Juniper.

"I don't know," said Miranda. "Jaymie?"

But the four *Bukowskis* had fled, pelting across the field to the highway, where they stood screaming and jumping up and down and waving their arms, praying for rescue.

Maggie and Shahla had been disturbed when their favourite band left on a two-day tour and never returned. Their Instagram had one new post, announcing an artist residency and social media detox. Rex only responded to their messages with a brief, "Having a wonderful time, staying a few weeks!" They'd immediately met to discuss the phrase 'wonderful time,' which was not a Rex-ism in any way, as well as the conversation they'd had at the tech convention.

The woman had told them the legend of an enclave that had produced as much nationally acclaimed art as all the other working artists in the province combined, and whose members never left, even after achieving local or national fame. Residents were occasionally sighted in the community, and all the successful ones were meticulous in answering fan mail, even if they hadn't emerged in years, and so rumours of disappearances went uninvestigated.

Maggie and Shahla had no intention of letting Rex's absence lapse into the status of rumour and legend. But the thing was, you couldn't file a missing person report for a Brzezinski; they were simply too often AWOL. Rex was the most reliable of the three, but if they were with their brothers there was no saying when they might vanish and reappear with anecdotes about how their mom had scored them all dirt-cheap last-minute tickets to Vegas and they couldn't afford roaming charges, or they'd been at home and Jaymie was high as a kite and had them practicing non-stop for three days for a showcase they might or might not actually be playing.

Maggie even did some light detective work interviewing Anika, who confirmed that they were incommunicado—but also that this wasn't out of character for her cousins.

But then something sinister occurred. Ayla's romantic card had been lovingly bugged by Shahla, who slid a recording device between the glued pieces of construction paper on the off chance it made its way out of their luggage and picked up the show. It sat in the closet picking up exactly nothing until the moment Evelyn almost sat on it and it fuzzily caught, "supposed to end the rituals … lose another one of us …" and "What if Rex doesn't want to volunteer?"

Alarmed, they enlisted the *Bukowskis'* reliable stan, who was actually named Stan, to drive to Saskatchewan and check out the situation.

Drawing near the address in his GPS, Stan strayed from the TransCanada to hit up a small-town hotdog shack he liked, and then took the Ring Road in. And that's where he was, a hotdog-wielding deus ex, going ninety kilometres on the dot and listening to Regina's irresistible 104.9 The Wolf, when he came across the four desperate *Bukowskis*, carrying a smattering of musical gear and barely keeping ahead of a small army of quirky maniacs.

In the car, the bandmates breathlessly related the main points of the story, in muddled fragments, to their rescuer. Stan nodded knowledgeably, told them about how something like that had happened to his buddy's band in Northern Ontario in the '90s, and loaned them his phone to call 911 and report Steve's death. (*"Yes*, I'm conflicted, but *this* is the kind of thing *police* are meant for," expounded Jaymie. "Controlling the goddamn *artists.*")

When asked whether he knew anything about auto repair, Stan said he'd picked up a few tricks, but he also knew a guy, and so they returned to the blue house, trusting they had about half an hour before their pursuers made it back on foot—longer, if the police acted quickly enough to intercept them. The band executed the fastest gear load-out of their lives while Stan consulted his "guy"—Shahla—on video call. Before long, he'd repaired the disconnected wire. (The collective hadn't wanted to waste a good van.)

Then they left, and they took Stan out for coffee. He'd earned it.

"What an adventure!" said Jaymie, as all of them gradually began to feel at ease.

"I'm never touring again," said Rex, sipping their hot chocolate.

"We'll certainly wait a month or two before booking the next one," Jaymie agreed.

"Touring isn't usually like this," said Jo. She was still shaken from her skirmish, but was unharmed except for a few sore knuckles and a bruised elbow. "We got bad luck this time."

"I'm with Rex. Never again," said Aaron.

"By the way, I have to congratulate you on your skillful employment of a dog song in a dire situation, Aar," said Jaymie.

"And I have to commend you on spending two weeks with at least ten women who worship you and not sleeping with all of them," said Aaron.

"Mhmm," said Jaymie, and there was a brief silence.

"… Oh. You did, didn't you."

"Not all ten! Perhaps one or two …"

"Never mind. Forget it."

"Jaymie, you were their *leader*. That's, like, pretty problematic," said Rex.

"Hey, *they* propositioned *me*. I explained that I would be leaving before long, and the short-term nature of the arrangement—"

"Tell me it wasn't Juniper," groaned Jo. "That sweet girl."

"Juniper! Do you think I'm an *animal?*"

"He likes them older," said Aaron. "Then they supposedly aren't naïve and he can feel like less of a bad person if he breaks their hearts."

Jaymie was indignant. "I will remind you that those people would have arranged ceremonious deaths for us, one by one, and profited greatly off of them."

"Oh, so now you're the victim," said Rex.

"Three words, Jay," said Aaron. *"Power dynamics."*

"That's two—oh, speaking of problematic, I drugged you without consent. Can you tell?"

"I think it's hitting more and more."

"That'll be the adrenaline wearing off."

Jaymie held up fingers for Aaron to count while their contented fan surreptitiously recorded everything, knowing Maggie and Shahla would appreciate it for their files. Then Stan said goodbye—aware that you never want to get to know your idols *too* well—and hit the road.

(The members of the arts collective had wisely delayed going home. They walked to a Tim Horton's, ordered twenty-four decafs, and tried to formulate a plan for dealing with the backlash from the botched bandnapping. Most knew, deep down, that without their fearless leader their campaign couldn't continue much longer, whether or not they could avoid jail.)

In the van, Jaymie was back at the wheel.

"Time to shave that rat 'stache, Aar, we're headed back to the real world! Fortunately, we don't need to be on the road again for a while, because we have lots going on at home!" he informed his exhausted bandmates. "I checked my email on Stan's phone—the tribute show is confirmed, and we have to let them know what band we're being!"

"Well, we've got seven free hours to brainstorm," said Jo serenely. She'd just discovered a stack of music magazines and the remainder of her stash under the back seat.

"Not only that, BUT—sorry Jo, I'm afraid this doesn't concern you as much—Grandma and Grandpa will be in town for a family dinner *on the same night!*"

"Great," Rex deadpanned. "G and G will sure approve of that."

"We're going to have to run speedily back and forth from the dinner to load-in, to dinner, to sound check—we'll swap out, of course, making fun excuses for each other's disappearances, and Aaron and I will take turns being both of us at once—back to dinner again, á la Katherine Heigl in the opening of Twenty-Seven Dresses, which is among my favourite rom-coms."

"That's pretty extra," said Rex.

"It's gonna be a doozy, folks!" Jaymie said happily.

"It sounds bonkers," said Aaron. "But I think we can manage it …"

"I appreciate that uncharacteristic optimism!" said Jaymie.

"… as long as something completely awful doesn't happen to one of us," he finished.

"That's the spirit!" said Jaymie.

"Don't talk to me about spirits," said Rex.

The November sun elbowed its way through the remaining clouds and retched weak light over the prairies, which unfurled dirtily before them like your living room carpet the morning after you've gotten very drunk and decided to give a haircut to your fluffy brown cat or your unconscious twin.

"One more exciting piece of news," said Jaymie. "Our home will soon be graced, for a short time, by the presence of Leonora McLeod." His announcement was met with skepticism.

"*The* Leonora McLeod?" asked Aaron drowsily.

"You mean the acclaimed saxophonist and composer?" said Rex.

"It would appear she has taken an interest in our artistic endeavours …" said Jaymie.

"And deigns to grant us an interview?" said Rex. "Is she auditioning session guys?"

"Thought you were over touring," said Aaron.

"I miss her though, don't you?" said Jaymie.

"I do," Aaron admitted.

"I don't," said Rex, who did. "I'm entitled a few more years of resenting her parenting style before I have to … I don't know …"

"Start appreciating her for following her dreams and being an inspiration to us all?" suggested Jaymie.

"Yeah, all that stuff you're supposed to do *instead* of having kids," said Rex.

"Well, you have to be glad she picked both, or you wouldn't exist, right?" said Jaymie.

"I'm seventeen. Existence is torment."

"Something on your mind, T-Rex? Besides nearly getting sacrificed for some pretentious pseudo-Buddhist garbage meme-art a few hours ago—and I am truly, truly sorry about that." Jaymie nudged the volume dial on the dash and a rich female voice eased its way into the conversation. Their last rotation two weeks ago had landed them back on the *Daffodile* CD.

"I think I almost had a significant other," Rex said in dejection.

"Some significant other he was!" said Aaron.

"Yeah, I hope you told him you weren't interested in exploring your *we/us* pronouns," said Jaymie. Rex did not laugh.

"You got lots of time, Rex," said Aaron.

"I'm practically an adult!" Rex protested. "Jaymie *did it* when he was fourteen."

"Rex! You know better than to believe the stories about him! He was nineteen. We both were."

"Same girl, too!" said Jaymie.

"It was *not* the same girl!" said Aaron.

"She sure sounded the same when you described her to me—"

"Look, just because we have similar tastes—"

"OK, whatever you say."

"If you'd bothered to remember the name of yours, maybe we wouldn't still be having this argument years later—"

"It's not my fault you got your cherry popped by a *Kaitlyn* and there are fifty million *Kaitlyns* on Facebook and a hundred different spellings and we could never find her again …"

Rex stared out the window, lips pressed tightly together, and Jo remembered a time in life when there were suddenly a thousand things you were supposed to have already done, and now you had to try to do all of them at the same time, as quickly as possible.

"Rex, you'll be fine," she said. "You're so much cooler than the chumps in that arts collective—which it *wasn't even*, by the way."

"What if the only people who are ever into me are culty weirdos?" Rex said quietly.

"There are way better weirdos out there who will be into you," said Jo, smiling.

"Nobody takes me seriously," said Rex.

"Rex, you always have the best ideas," said Aaron, tuning in to their distress. "And you make the right choices, and you take care of yourself, and you're always responsible, but not in a boring way." Not all of this was completely true, but somehow Aaron had an instinctive understanding that you have to tell young people that whatever it is you're trying to get them to be, they already are, or else they'll be crushed by the weight of trying to become it all at once. "And you have the best ideas, and you're responsible, but not in a boring way."

He also had the steady, memory-annihilating wisdom of Pentobarbital on his side.

"Oh my god, Aaron, drink some water," said Rex, but they settled more contentedly into their seat.

"You're going to get laid," said Jo.

Rex let out a self-conscious snort of laughter and picked up a magazine. "OK, thanks. And thanks for saving me with the dog song, Aar."

"No problem, Rex, sibling, kiddo. You're my favourite little buddy."

"And hey, no rush to let mom off the hook, either," Jaymie contributed. "Revel in the angst! We sure did. Aaron still does!" He paused for a few minutes, taking in the beauty of the cloud shadows that traversed the single valley they would encounter in the entire flat drive. "Jo!" he finally said. "You have to meet our mom. You'll love her."

But Jo had fallen asleep in the back seat, a *Rolling Stone* easing its way from her lap to the floor, and Rex soon followed her lead. Jaymie swapped out *Daffodile* for *Gunt* and spent the remainder of the road trip keeping Aaron awake, just to be safe—he hadn't had time to read the drug advisory label—listening to local legend Casio Bob put his guitars and synthesizers to appalling misuse, eating a bag of ketchup chips they found open between the seats, and discussing which band to cover for the upcoming show.

***

The anonymous tip received by the Regina police led them only to an empty easel in a deserted field. However, it spurred them into action. Investigations into the (finally confirmed) disappearances of eighteen former cult members eventually led to a number of bodies being dug up in the fields behind the blue house. All of the bodies were aged beyond identification, and only one, whose DNA was on record, could be confirmed to match a disappeared person; most were never officially located and the cases ran cold. All of the missing people had received some kind of recognition for their creative work.

Despite reaching a forensic dead end, the citizens of the city recognized foul play, and they were not about to let such an organization continue. The house, whose original owners were among the disappeared, was repossessed, and the remaining residents willingly dispersed back to home cities, and to jobs or families or other cults, depending on their next calling.

Ronan went home. In the time since he'd left, both his sisters had become investigative journalists and devoted most of their time to tracking him down. The elder became a specialist in human trafficking and worked for the government breaking up criminal organizations; the younger went back to raising her kids and taking on the odd small-town PI case, keeping it a side mission to watch out for signs of dangerous cult activity in Saskatchewan.

Miranda, following her bliss, took courses in accounting and business admin. She was an entrepreneurial woman who didn't believe in burned bridges, and she decided to pursue a career managing bands, starting with her very favourite one. Her potential client, recognizing skill when he saw it, said she was welcome to send gigs his way, provided he didn't have to pay her until the band made real money, and that she remain at least one province over, "Way *the hell* away from me and my family," forever.

Jo and Juniper's recording made it onto a Spotify playlist called "Chill Piano Vibe," and was then licensed for the soundtrack to a sensitive indie film about an orphaned teen on a pilgrimage to Portland, which cleaned up at the Sundance Festival. Jo graciously relinquished any credit for the collab, so that the royalties could fund Juniper's foray into the real world, and because she was embarrassed at having composed Muzak with an undead entity.

Juniper could hardly remember a time when she'd been free from the hive mentality and the guidance of a spiritual leader, and she found herself poorly equipped for independence. Fortunately, having moved cities to start fresh, she found the support and community she needed; she made a complete recovery from her near-death experience and enthusiastically joined the ranks of the Bukowskiphiles. She continued, all the while, to believe Jaymie Brzezinski really was possessed by the true creative spirit, i.e., Charles Bukowski.

19
Interlude 2.1

To: Evelyn Coyne

Dear Author,
Thank you for sending your manuscript for our consideration. We read it with interest, but I regret we will not be making an offer of publication.
Thank you for thinking of us, and we wish you every success in finding a publisher.

Yours sincerely,
Elena Antonopoulos
Penguin House Canada

Dear Ms. Coyne,
Thank you for finding me through the Saskatchewan Publishers' Group and for giving me the opportunity to read a sample of *Bukowski and Me*. I regret to inform you that I am unable to offer you representation.
Due to the high volume of submissions I receive, I cannot offer criticism on each author's work. However, I must depart from my pre-drafted rejection letter in order to inform you, Ms. Coyne, that your memoir is the worst thing I've ever read in my life.

Your account covers a time span of two weeks spent under the guidance of cult leader Jaimie Bukowski. Most of the book is less a report of his ideology and more a description of his appearance and his character and a list of things you would be willing to do in order to please him, though it is unclear if any of these things ever actually happened, and I hope, for his sake, and for your sake, and for the sake of all the readers you will never have, they did not. At one point you describe your leader in terms of a father figure; three paragraphs later you inform readers of the "erotic lustre of his gaze directed upon me," which is not only poorly written but also very disturbing.

It is also unclear, throughout the entire six hundred pages you sent us (written in a few weeks?—I have to give it to you, that's impressive) whether he is even there of his own accord. You speak of "keeping him with us" in a way that leads me to wonder, should I be concerned?

So many questions. Who is the guitar player mentioned only once? Are she and Bukowski a couple? As for the siblings, I don't know where to begin. The twin who, I think, reflects the darker side of Jaimie's personality—sort of a deceptive non-believer—what is the role of this character? I assumed he was a metaphor until 200 pages in.

The trans kid is the only part of the story that engaged my sympathy at all, but then we don't hear anything till page 491 when you're criticizing the kid's painting skills at some kind of questionable festival in a field. Honestly, these are highly unlikely characters and I'm having trouble believing they aren't fictitious. The truth is that a letter politely declining your book is not sufficient; I feel obligated to tell you to cease and desist. I hope you take these words to heart and think seriously about how much time you want to spend pursuing this craft further.

Now, to default back to my stock rejection email: I wish you every success with *Bukowski and Me*.

Yours sincerely,
Geraldine Grey
Literary Agent, Saskatchewan Publishers' Group

Ms. Coyne,

Thank you for submitting your manuscript to UTP. We are unable to publish your book at this time. Great story, though! We have met with our associate at Netflix Canada, and are happy to inform you that they are interested in doing a short documentary among next year's productions, most of which are filmed here in Toronto. We project a release date in early 2021, assuming we receive your consent to proceed. Please expect correspondence regarding your contract and interviews with a documentary crew in the coming months.

Best,

Arnold Stoker

University of Toronto Press

20
Interlude 2.2

Re: re: December visit
Leonora McLeod
To bukowskifamilyband@gmail.com,
aaron.brzezinski@hotmail.com, tearexx@gmail.com

Little ones, more news!
As I mentioned in my last email, Cirque decided to take this show on the road—for the past month our route has been carving a big old smile into the bottom half of the U.S. of A. Stops included L.A., Phoenix, Austin, Houston, New Orleans, Tallahassee, Atlanta ... to name a few. It's been quite a time!
I have to tell you a little tale from ten days ago in Louisiana. We decided to take a scenic route through the bayou (Pics attached!!), and what do you know but the tour bus broke down, so you have a group of 40-odd musicians and acrobats and clowns and etc. stuck out in the marsh with nothing but a handful of snacks and a day or two worth of cocaine to keep them going (R, I think you're old enough to hear this by now. Can't shelter kids forever). Can you imagine!
So, we're meant to play in Jackson that evening and the time is ticking while our driver tries to figure out what's up, and everyone's getting into makeup in the meantime because, as I've complained many times, the stuff takes three hours to put on and

almost as long to wash off. So everyone's painted to the nines waiting for rescue and finally some kind local folks come out and offer us a nice dinner of crabs freshly caught that day.

Well, it started getting dark, and it's looking like we weren't going to make it for the show. So we got into festivities with the good people of the marsh, and I can tell you, they know how to party. Soon everyone's dancing around the fire, jamming, cartwheeling, triple backflipping over the flames, depending on their particular skill, and suddenly someone asks where Lena and Ivan have got to—the trapeze artists—but someone else points out they were out of their minds an hour ago and they've probably gone off to cuddle somewhere.

Not long after that, we've lost a contortionist and a flutist and two percussionists, but everyone's used to people turning in or passing out at various intervals, and it's not till a third of the band and both the ladies who climb the silks are all gone that we realize something's up. Well, it turns out there's been a murderer on the loose out there for a couple of years, all kinds of disappearances, and he'd come out and thought all of us were sent to him by the swamp god, decked out for ritual sacrifice! Everyone panics, but it's the sort of drunk panic that doesn't get you far, so we mostly all look like a crew of little children running around screaming, dressed up for Halloween. Can you imagine!

Well, a couple of us still had our heads on straight enough to go look for the others, and we ended up half a mile away in these old stone ruins, decorated with all kinds of paintings of antler-monsters and things like that, and we had to chase the fellow through the maze while he's yelling nonsensical things, and the bus driver, Brian, and I finally got him cornered at the end of the labyrinth and informed him the game was up. He'd only managed to murder a few of the performers and we saved the rest. Still, we missed the Jackson date. What can you do?

Happily, our villain was arrested and we got it all sorted out—one can only hope your own murderer back home gets sorted in the same way! (Not *your* murderer, goodness gracious! You know what I mean ;)

I'm terribly sorry for not keeping better contact with you all. You know how busy things can get. I'm so glad to hear you escaped that odd cult—in some ways it's a blessing you weren't able to send me a message while you were there, I'd have been worried sick. J, I bet you made a splendid messiah. A., I'm sure you excelled at keeping him in check. R, lovely work on your English paper, I read it multiple times, never suspected Manson could be such a joy to learn about. It's been my only entertainment, besides binge watching TV shows on the bus—our driver, Brian, has the best recommendations.
See you dears in a few weeks!
Much love,
Mom

Leonora McLeod
Musician, composer, producer
"Music, once admitted to the soul, becomes a sort of spirit, and never dies."— *Edward Bulwer-Lytton*

21

Clone Collectors

It was a Friday night in early December and the Brzezinski twins were going through a happy phase in their relationship. They crossed the Provencher Bridge, sipping beers they'd packed in their coat pockets, headed in the direction of Osborne Street and a "secret" show they happened to have insider knowledge of. It was -33 degrees Celsius without counting the wind chill, but this had never deterred them before.

"What would you do if the murderer got me?" asked Aaron.

"I'd kill myself!" Jaymie said happily.

"What! I mean, I would too, if the roles were reversed. Maybe not right away—like, maybe I'd take a couple decades to process it first, but then I would, for sure." Aaron considered it while Jaymie dealt with important business on his phone. It was a clear night and the snow blanketing the broad Red River was competing with the moon to see which could shine more brightly. One of them would surely blow an important fuse in the next minute or two and the whole world would freeze over.

"You?" said Jaymie, looking up from an Instagram story he was crafting, which Aaron didn't know if he was included in and, if he was, whether it would be a flattering portrayal. "You *can't* die, actually—you're not a real person! I hate to break it to you, but you're actually an extension of my ego. I invented you to keep me company. You're my daemon! If I die, you just poof out of existence, like that." He snapped his fingers and winked casually at a group of women smoking under an arch at the centre of the bridge. They smiled and blew puffs of smoke at him that formed into hazy Christmas trees with gold shining hearts on top.

"How do you get them to do that?" Aaron asked, always a little annoyed by his brother's ability to avoid being seen for the sleazebag Aaron was certain that he was.

"Well, I just decide to believe in myself and in my own worth, and then …" Jaymie mulled on it. "No, I bet it's because I have a twin! Girls love that shit. They think it's adorable."

"I have a twin," Aaron pointed out.

"I guess that's true. And you have an even better twin—just kidding! I dunno, Aar. I think it's because I was born first."

They passed the restaurant perched over the river, nestled at the centre of the set of huge metal beams that made the city's most photogenic bridge look like a rocket ship straining to break free from a giant spiderweb. The scent of fries wafted through the frigid air. After housing a series of eateries specializing in gourmet French Canadian cuisine, the mid-bridge diner had reverted back to its original identity as a Salisbury House, where one could find a cheap but edible burger until late into the night.

"Actually, *I* was born first. I came out and they named me Jaymie and they put me in the nursery but then they got the labels mixed up and I've been Aaron ever since."

"That never happened—I was born first and I had to put on "Come as You Are" and coax you out with a piece of cheddar cheese. I remember, because Nirvana released it just that week."

"That album came out in '91, dumdum. And you can't even remember what we did last weekend, never mind being born."

"Sounds like a successful weekend." He stopped walking. "Aaron! That was over twenty-five years ago—being born, I mean—How have we not run out of twin jokes yet?"

"We have. I'm positive we've had *this exact* conversation at least once before." Aaron gulped the dregs of his beer and tossed the can in a Take Pride! bin set against the railing of the bridge. "I can't get too messed up. My drum student comes on Saturdays. It's our third lesson."

"Working from home, like a champ. Maybe this is the job that sticks!" Jaymie finished the post he'd been creating, which comprised a picture of Aaron making his signature "Things seem to be going well but it's probably a trick" face, a backdrop of fifty metal beams stretching stiffly into the sky like comic book energy lines emanating out of him, and the words "Aar Bear is excited to see a secret show!" in hot pink letters at the bottom.

"Like it? I can't change it. My fingers are too cold."

"Sure, cool."

"Cool. OK Aar, I'm afraid we have to part ways for a bit." Jaymie sheathed his phone in his pocket and began manipulating a pack of cigarettes with his mittened hands. Their breath was fogging so thickly that it appeared as though they were already smoking.

"What? Why?"

"I wanted to finish this conversation with you, to prove how much our friendship means to me, and also to post that story, but now I have to go back to the Sals." Jaymie put his non-cigarette hand on the shoulder of his brother's thick parka. "This is a networking emergency."

"Networking? What about the show?" said Aaron. The secret show was being held in a secret venue and featured two purportedly amazing bands, the names of whom were also a secret. (The struggle of keeping confidential the one name they'd been made privy to had been both delighting and destroying Jaymie.)

They'd received a lead that it was either in the sub-basement of Big Brother Coffee Co. or a loft above the karaoke dive above the taco shop in Osborne Village. Apparently, not even the bands playing would find out the location until load-in. Jaymie and Aaron had plotted a route that passed by both destinations and included the maximum number of pizza stops.

"I'll meet you there for the main event! Catching the opener has become second priority. Aar, did you see who was back there?"

"You're bailing on awesome music to flirt with some girls at Sals?" Aaron was skeptical but knew it wasn't a far reach for Jaymie.

"Not flirt, *network*—"

"Sorry, you're bailing on awesome music to *network* your way into bed with some—"

"Some *maybe* awesome music. Remember that time we went to a show with a surprise headliner and it was twenty bucks cover and it turned out to be that ukulele band that just does nineties punk covers?"

"It's a great concept. How'd they manage to screw up ukulele punk?"

"Well, you never know what you're going to get."

"Didn't someone die at that show too?"

"They did." The brothers left a moment of silence out of respect for the deceased, or perhaps because Jaymie was making sure his post had uploaded to the *Bukowskis'* Instagram and Aaron was sending a few feeler texts to see if the venue location had made its way into the collective unconscious yet. An ice-skating couple passed beneath them on the winding river trail and Aaron sighed out a cloud of frost, knowing that there would be no saving their plans from being unravelled by Jaymie's ever-changing whims.

"It's for the band," said Jaymie.

"I've been thinking about moving out," said Aaron.

"Making the right connections is as important as—wait, what? Move out? Why?"

Aaron guiltily savoured Jaymie's incredulity. "Our house can be kind of a rollercoaster."

"What the eff, Aaron! A rollercoaster? There's only three of us! OK, Rex can be kind of a slob, but—"

"It's you."

"So … you're just … ditching me. Again." Jaymie snuffed his cigarette against the frozen railing and tossed it over the side, to land atop the toque of a child skating below.

"You're literally ditching me *right now!*" said Aaron.

"I'm not *literally* ditching you, Aaron. What, am I putting you in a ditch?"

"No … but the murderer might."

"Jesus Christ! Can you chill the fuck out for one evening?"

"You know what? I think I'll go catch the opener by myself," said Aaron, bouncing slightly on the balls of his boots and rubbing his mitted knuckles.

"Well, good! What a perfectly reasonable thing to do!" said Jaymie. He pulled his scarf over his chin and clapped his own chilly hands together.

"I'll probably know some people there!" said Aaron, his voice rising in volume and pitch.

"You probably will!" said Jaymie, refusing either out of obstinance or misguided respect to acknowledge Aaron's apprehension.

"Jo will be there!"

"She one thousand percent will be!"

"And even if she's busy playing and can't hang, it's perfectly fine and normal to be at a show by yourself!"

"It literally is!"

"OK, I'm going!"

"You know, maybe you could just go do something like this by yourself *once a year* and you wouldn't be so frantic to move out!"

"OK, I'll think about it!"

"Well, good!"

"OK! Bye." Aaron set off toward the end of the bridge and the brightly lit walking paths beyond. Jaymie hesitated.

"Hey, you know I'd invite you to go back there with me, but …"

Aaron called over his shoulder, "I get it, I don't have your … whatever you have."

"You're wearing Sorels, for god sakes!"

Aaron turned back around. "It's forty below and your ankles are showing, you total fucking hipster! How are they not frozen?"

"I have fully lost all feeling in them."

"Jesus. OK, have fun."

"Aar!"

"What!"

Jaymie truly was underdressed for the night. He looked as dapper as if he'd just stepped out of a holiday-themed Brit-rock music video, but his socks were showing between his Chelsea boots and his rolled pantlegs and he was clearly feeling the weather. He rubbed his arms.

"Don't you want to know who's back there?"

"Who's back there?" Aaron asked resignedly.

"Daffodile! She was buying a Nip at the front counter!"

Daffodile had been a staple of the music scene since they'd first started going to shows in their teens. She'd hired a marketing consultant to help with branding in the early days of her career, with total success. Her logo, a yellow flower with doe eyes and a giant set of reptilian teeth, could be found stencilled or stickered or sharpied on the walls of every venue in the city.

Rumour had it she made her living composing minute-long musical numbers to be performed by the characters on a popular animated children's YouTube show. The characters were different kinds of fruit with eyes and hands, and they encouraged friendship and cooperation and moved in a delightful rapid-fire animation style that was inspiring joy and healthy eating habits in children across the nation, as well as triggering an acceleration of the nascent ADHD in that same demographic.

She'd been playing the festival circuit for years and was constantly touring, and yet she'd resisted moving to a bigger centre, and still played the occasional sold-out local show. A Daffodile sighting was a rare and precious thing.

"The singer? She'll think you're a joke. Jay, she's at least ten years older than you."

"And still as lovely as a man-eating flower. Goodbye, Aaron."

Aaron slouched his way to the river's far bank, his happy buzz dissipated. He had little doubt that Daffodile would be charmed by Jaymie. Perhaps they'd be opening for her next show.

It hadn't needed clarifying that Aaron wasn't invited on Jaymie's networking endeavour; he neither enjoyed nor had the knack for engaging with strangers, and, past the initial exploitation of the fact that they were twins, could only hinder Jaymie's progress.

He'd never understood how Jaymie seemed to have everyone instantly in the palm of his hand. Jaymie had a special way of looking at people that made them feel as though they were in on a secret conspiracy, just they and him. He gave the impression that he was at any moment about to offer you drugs, and you'd take them, whatever they were, in hopes that you'd hallucinate a dimension a little closer to the one he existed in.

Aaron knew his own face must be capable of the same expressions of coyness and warmth as Jaymie's, but he didn't dare try them on; he was sure they'd appear creepy or manic on him. A certain attitude was required which was not present in his bundle of their shared DNA.

The bridge ended at a park, and he sat down on a bench, ignoring the metal slats radiating cold through his jacket. He wondered if Jaymie actually believed he'd go to the show alone, or if his brother rightly suspected that the change in plans was enough to send him home for a quiet night of drinking with the cats, and whether Jaymie cared at all which option he chose. He pictured himself searching for the hidden venue alone in subarctic temperatures with a killer on the loose. He remembered an article he'd recently read about an oversized coyote sighted in St. James. A megacoyote. He opened his Transit app to find a bus homeward.

Then he imagined watching a full set of flawless punk rock guitar shreddery, and he thought of Jo and remembered how nice it is when your friends brave the winter to come to your show—and how disappointing when they don't. He stood up resolutely and faced downtown. After all, someone was bound to text him an address once the event was underway. And who would go out murdering in weather like this? He set off.

Tall shadows moved from behind a snow sculpture of a bison and followed him.

It wasn't until he was passing under the train bridge to Broadway Avenue that he noticed something was wrong. The sound of snow crunching under boots heavier than his own sent a shiver up his spine, and he turned around. Two hooded figures in matching black Canada Goose jackets blocked the path, staring silently down at him.

Aaron never wasted time deciding whether it was appropriate to panic. He was instantly covered in sweat beneath his coat. Breathing became difficult.

"Oh my god I'm being mugged," he stammered. "I don't have any money. I'm a musician." The beings exchanged a glance and smiled like dogs that have just had something plastic and peanut butter-filled placed in front of them.

"We're not after your money, child," said the one on the right, a strong-looking woman whom Aaron might have recognized as being one of the smokers from the bridge if he hadn't been too shy to get a good look.

"You're mistaken," he gasped, certain his face must be matching the red in his plaid scarf. "I'm an adult. No children here. All in bed by now."

"We've been watching you," said the woman.

"Ugh, no," said Aaron.

"You see, we're clone collectors." The man spoke, calm beneath his hood. "When you default on your clone, we come to collect."

"Default on my *what*?"

"Don't worry, honey," said the woman. "*You* haven't done anything wrong."

Aaron felt his limbs shrinking into his torso and decided to try edging backwards on the sidewalk while he still had working legs.

"It's a perfect likeness," said the man, looking him up and down.

"It has some damage to the left side its face," the woman murmured back, reaching her leather glove just short of touching the stinging-cold skin below his toque as he cringed away.

"Yeah, I—I got bit by a dog once," stammered Aaron. "And those aren't my pronouns."

Then he stared at her. "Wait, I don't know what you—do you mean, you think I'm—ha. Ahaha. No, big misunderstanding. I'm a *twin*. Not a clone." He gave a small, hysterical laugh.

"Sure, sweetie. That's what they all say."

Aaron yelled "*Jaymie!*" and ran for his life.

Part Three

Tribute Show

22

Reunion Show

A tribute show—but first, a reunion show!

The secret performance Jaymie and Aaron had been walking to see was nearly cancelled when the drummer from the headlining band turned up dead at the last minute. The band, after some deliberation, decided the show would go on. It's what he would have wanted.

Immediate action was taken to find a substitute drummer.

First the bandmates debated whether it was inauthentic and off-genre to hire a session drummer for a punk show. They reluctantly made some phone calls, but the freelancers they knew had gigs that night anyway. The band's singer thought of Garrett Kliewer, because he was so versatile, but the lead guitarist said he might not be keen to play with her again, and she mumbled something about pumpkins but wouldn't specify what the drama was, and they all just assumed she'd slept with him.

The singer reached a drummer buddy of his and it seemed the problem was solved, until they realized the guy was already too drunk to hold his sticks, much less perform ten songs he'd never played. And the guitarist suggested Aaron Brzezinski, but the singer wasn't sure because wasn't that guy crazy or something, like did you hear about when he auditioned for the *BMIs?* And the guitarist said: it's a *punk show* for Christ's sake, and no, at worst he was a little inconsistent, and as an alternative maybe they could cancel this show and go back to not being a band anymore, as they had peacefully been doing for the last nine years. Everyone agreed she was overreacting.

The bass player tried to keep the peace, suggesting that they borrow the drum machine used by the band opening for them, in response to which the lead guitarist and singer commanded loudly and in unison that he "Go back to med school, Jake."

Aaron wasn't answering his phone anyway, but it turned out the rhythm guitarist had a friend who had a sister who'd taken up drums only recently but had been working hard and could play in time and weirdly fast, and she was coming to the show anyway, because it just so happened that she loved the *Ballet Llama*.

That's how Hannah Chen got a gig with the *BL* even though she'd only ever had two drum lessons, and even though it was only a few days since she'd become old enough to legally set foot in a bar, and even though she only knew one and a half drum beats, and the second was really just a variation on the first where you added an extra kick on the "and" of beat two.

Fortunately for her, the four living members of the long-defunct *Ballet Llama* decided it was more punk rock to recruit a rookie than to cancel the show. They instructed her to play as fast as she could for as long as she could, and they'd take care of the rest. There were very few genres where this trick could work, and it was a long shot even for them.

For a killing to occur before a show had even opened its doors was unusual. The victim had arrived *early* for sound check—which everyone in the industry agreed was already suspicious—and had been abducted while loading in his kit, only to reappear half an hour later propped at the bar with an empty Standard in his fist. His head had been replaced by a rack tom.

The tragedy of the situation was amplified by the fact that, unlike some of his bandmates, Alexandre had mostly had his fill of the music scene by 2010, had gotten his life together, only ever played the odd show with *Shifty Principals* since the *Llama* broke up, and rarely went out.

The crime scene had been cleared away by the time Hannah arrived, which was fortunate because, as much as she enjoyed a morbid reminder of human mortality every now and then, she was already on the verge of puking just sitting onstage, fidgeting with the safety pins in her hoodie and listening to the band bicker quietly. It seemed inconceivable that in about a minute she would be making actual music with them. She desperately hoped she could reign in her nausea at least until the last song, so any projectile vomiting would come across as a climactic act of rock and roll rather than just disgusting.

Hannah had entered, carrying her cymbals and snare, through a coffee shop she'd visited many times without ever suspecting the secret housed in its bowels: a concrete-floored, mysteriously-stained, and many-stickered basement DIY space. Some musicians might have lamented at the cement reverb-trap they were being swallowed into, but Hannah was in the early days of her career, and to her the basement's scabs and splotches sparkled with glitz.

Now, seated on the drum throne behind the still quibbling singer and guitarist, she looked into the crowd. Two of her most rambunctious friends were pushing their way toward the mosh pit, which both comforted and worried her.

There were a few faces she knew as long-time denizens of the all-ages punk scene or the music world in general; hanging apart from the swarm she recognized Lucas Yarbrough, the music blogger and occasional Free Press columnist who'd long been hailed as the man with his finger most firmly on the pulse of the city, until he'd criticized the local group Youth Tambour for switching from drums to electronic backing tracks and been accused of no longer getting it.

The bass player, unable to get the other three to stop quarreling and begin the show, turned to her, shrugged, and said, "You can play now. Fast, please." So she did.

Jo thought the "secret show" idea was pretentious, and the new drummer was understandably terrible, but it was nice to be brought back to the days when the *BL* were first playing out; every performance had been in a secret and stupid location and nobody came anyway. She'd been the only one of the five to have any chops on her instrument, since the others were picking it up as they went, but back then she was just happy to be in a band.

Hannah's beat, which came in unexpectedly and as loud and fast as promised, interrupted Michaud's griping—something about marijuana not being an appropriate drug for punk music and how could she tap into the energy if she wasn't on the same wavelength as them?

She gave the gain knob on her fuzz pedal a quarter turn. She'd gotten used to the tidy overdrive the *Bukowskis'* music called for, and now the extra grit felt good. She laid a hand against her pickups as the amp fed back, and waited for the first chorus, when the two guitars would enter together. She shot a smile at Lucas, leaning against a wall at the back of the room.

Life had been a series of ups and downs since they'd gotten back from tour. Jaymie had returned to work, since his job was unionized and it would take more than a short stint as a cult leader to get rid of him. Jo was fired, but it was the holiday season and the library needed extra help in the gift shop, so she was brought back to gloomily sell cards and bookmarks.

She'd been on one date with Lucas. She'd received his reply to her message two weeks late, and then spent an afternoon deleting versions of "Sorry, was stuck in a cult, lol," and wondering how anybody ever ended up with anybody. Eventually, she pushed send.

Lucas grinned back and jerked his chin to draw her attention to some very wasted teenagers fighting over a bag of potato chips. She watched as one of the boys toppled backwards into a heavily stick-and-poke-scored young woman, setting off a human domino chain that took down four or five pierced attendees before flowing into the mosh pit.

When she looked back Lucas was tapping notes into his phone, as he'd warned her he would need to do sporadically.

Her back pocket buzzed. Texting onstage was never classy, but Michaud was still shouting incoherent greetings to his friends and making liquor demands in French, and Hannah's frantic drumming was evening out and settling into a groove in time with Jake's bassline.

"Jo Connors inspired mass chaos at a punk show on Friday night. The mere pre-show presence of this skilled (not to mention striking) guitar heroine was enough to send numerous inhalant-crazed partiers into infatuated hysterics …"

Jo rolled her eyes. She'd probably sleep with him; if not tonight then sometime. She put her phone away and snapped, "Mich!" and he said, "OK, relax, Jesus!" and started the show.

The band played one of their biggest hits right out of the gate: "C'était une danse, maintenant c'est un bloodbath," which felt appropriate. When it finished, Michaud waved at Hannah to stop playing.

"Hey, on est de retour!" he yelled at the audience. "Bienvenus, merci d'être venus, blah blah blah … C'est un Safe Space, OK? So you better fucking behave yourselves." With that, he cued her to start up again, and she played the drums, as hard and as fast as she could, for the next twenty-three minutes, which was the length of a typical *Ballet Llama* set. Any longer and they risked the need for an ambulance.

The mosh pit was in full swing by the second song, except for a girl who looked too young to have made it past the door, who stood texting right in the centre. It had formed a placid cyclone's eye to accommodate her without disturbing a hair in her perfectly twisted messy bun.

Hannah saw her friends, several drinks in and uninterested in responding to the nuances of the music. The taller one's spaghetti arms thrashed to the beat of their own drummer, which was understandable considering the drummer onstage had only been playing for two months.

A few people were forced to dodge out of his way; beside the oblivious messy-bun girl, a slight youth managed an artful backbend that just barely saved a fresh-looking septum piercing from being separated from his face by the windmilling limbs. He manoeuvred upright again, revealing himself to be the most beautiful boy Hannah had ever seen. Her sticks nearly skipped a beat, but they didn't, because by this time Hannah was a pro.

By the time they were playing "I Won't Go to Work (le travail est pour les morts)" Jo was re-accustomed to the genre and improvising on the familiar riffs, which she knew was going to make Michaud furious.

They stopped before the second-last song so that Michaud could toss a few obscenities into the crowd and thank them once more for coming. They let Hannah pound away underneath, since she seemed to be in the zone and they didn't want to break her concentration.

"Fuck you! Did you think we were gone forever? Vous aviez tous tort, motherfuckers!"

It occurred to Jo that he might be overdoing it. She wondered if he felt he needed to prove, at twenty-eight and with a comfortable job in arts admin, that he hadn't lost his fire.

"We're still on social media, if you want, I guess," he said. "Mais peu importe, so fuck it, who cares." He mimed spitting onto the stage. "This is Hannah, bienvenue Hannah, plus de cowbell, s'il vous plaît, Hannah!" The audience cheered or booed or screamed indifferently, it was impossible to tell. It was time for the last song, "Note pour moi-même."

"*I have to make a note ...*" he sang, the frayed remnants of his voice cracking on each word. He hadn't practiced the style enough in recent years to maintain his vocal stamina, but the crowd was eating it up anyway. The intro was supposed to be accompanied only by a gently descending bassline, but they hadn't told Hannah to stop, so she kept wailing underneath the slow lyrics. Jo liked the effect.

"Not to live the life they wrote ... for me." He skipped the next few lines to gulp his beer and cuss affectionately at some punks who were moshing with inappropriate fervor considering the mezzo forte of the first verse—or possibly he'd forgotten the words.

"I have no regrets / 'cause I know I won't grow up and forget ..." he croaked. Someone passed him two shots, for himself and the new drummer, but their instructions were lost in the din and he took them both at once in the three-beat break before the chorus.

Jo and Olivier shattered the lull of the drum–bass oasis for the set's climactic moment.

"I'll fight until I float / Je vais me faire une note!"

Hannah sped up, moved by the intensity of the chorus, and even Jo had trouble picking her palm-muted lead line fast enough. Hadn't they said this girl had only been playing a couple of months?

"Note! Pour! Moi-même! / Never to forget again!" Michaud lost his voice entirely on the sixth repetition of the line, kicked over the mic stand, and stumbled into the frothing pit, where the breakers descended on him and he was devoured by the current. Jo had once been impressed by his antics, but she'd been playing with Jaymie Brzezinski for the last four months and now it would take more than the old Sid Vicious shtick to catch her attention.

She finished the song and, feeling simultaneously triumphant and cliché, dropped her guitar against the face of her amp and walked offstage, leaving the amp feeding back shrilly while Hannah battered away at the drums and the room thrashed and howled its ecstasy.

23
Daffodile

The "acute stress response" is a component of human physiology designed by evolution (or God/etc., if that's your thing) to prompt a fight-or-flight reaction to immediate danger. It is activated by the sympathetic nervous system, which is known for mediating the body's adrenaline levels and priming one for action when survival is threatened. This sympathetic system was the only one of the two nervous systems that Aaron tended to use very often.

The trigger-happy SNS has a reputation for reacting to the mundane challenges of contemporary life with inappropriate enthusiasm, and in light of the fact that the modern human is rarely confronted by a crocodile or a pack of coyotes, many an overanxious millennial has commented that it might be best for evolution to scrap the entire process in favour of one that responds better to tedious workloads, school-based deadlines, and office drama. It's easy to agree—until you're forced to outrun a couple of frightening and unscrupulous employees from a suspicious collection agency; Aaron found himself with the opportunity to put his adrenal response to use for exactly its intended purpose, and it was doing its finest work.

He made it from Broadway to Portage Avenue in what must have been a world record for sprinting in Sorels. His stomach churned as he pictured his hulking pursuers. He'd gotten ahead—as it turned out, even two professional clone collectors couldn't match the pace of a wiry, panic-stricken drummer with surprisingly good cardio endurance for someone who never intentionally exercised. He skidded on the icy sidewalk as a powerful gust of wind hit his back.

The frigid winds at Portage and Main were so infamously forceful that the intersection had been closed to pedestrians many years before, to keep people from blowing into cars. The rule was enforced by a three-foot-thick, chest-high concrete barrier bordering the sidewalk on all four corners of the intersection for a full block. Aaron hoisted himself over it without hesitation. Fortunately, the traffic on that side of the street was halted at a red light.

Residents of the city who spent any time downtown were aware of the weather phenomenon at this corner, whereby the angle of the streets created a perfect wind tunnel, exponentially amplifying the gusts as they came—which they did, at all times of the day, any time of year, for up to a minute at a time, usually followed by about a ten-second period of calm. Anyone standing in the path of the wind would find themselves incapable of moving against it and, if below the weight of about a hundred pounds, physically lifted from the ground and carried as far as the Centennial Concert Hall three blocks away. There they'd pick themselves up, slightly battered, and go collect their toques and scarves strewn across Main Street, joking embarrassedly and receiving sympathetic smiles from passersby.

The Brzezinskis used to exploit this scientific marvel for the enjoyment of Rex, grabbing their hands at the last moment before they were carried off shrieking by the gale, until a few years previous, when Rex had become heavy enough to remain on their feet and too cool to plead for downtown adventures with their older brothers.

Aaron braced himself against the concrete barrier as the glacial breeze stung his cheeks and made his eyes water. A sudden cessation of the howling in his ears indicated the start of the brief calm, and he threw himself in front of the line of traffic. The light turned green. He pushed into a hard sprint. A truck turning left braked and spun 180 degrees.

Eight seconds later he was across the wide street, scrambling over the barrier, crouching on the other side, too winded even to middle-finger the honking cars he'd cut off. Had he looked back, he might have seen two large figures standing in the middle of the street, petrified by a new blast of wind, drivers yelling and steering around them until the storm died down.

Jaymie had made it back to the centre of the bridge, where a group of women still stood shivering outside the restaurant. They'd welcomed him into their circle, and he'd wasted no time lighting a cigarette and launching into a story about the time he'd dated twins.

When attempting to charm women you're meeting for the first time, the subject of your exes should probably be avoided at all costs, but Jaymie Brzezinski hadn't learned this rule because Jaymie Brzezinski had never had a failed conversation.

He said, "Yes, we are twins, thanks for asking—he had somewhere to be, though," and someone said, "Cute!" and someone else made a pointless comment about how they had a friend who was a twin, and within six degrees of conversational separation he'd landed on "But if you're thinking of dating a twin, I can give you some advice," and then he was off to the races.

Jaymie had been right that among his audience was the exceptional Daffodile, even with her identity obscured by her padded coat and a red carpet's worth of scarf wrapped around her head. She had a cigarette in one hand and her phone in the other, casually capturing the night view from the bridge in a panorama shot which, in one graceful arc of her wrist, included the sky full of stars, the frozen Red River, the classic downtown-at-night view on all the postcards, and her own opposite hand, elegantly flicking her ashes over the rail. She wasn't particularly interested in Jaymie's twin story.

Lack of interest had never stopped Jaymie Brzezinski! (Unless someone told him she was in a monogamous relationship, or was more into other women, or was asexual, or appeared questionably young, or had fallen head over heels for him and was sure to be a disaster, or said outright she only dated hockey players, or any of the other obvious reasons why seducing someone might be an absolutely godawful idea.)

"They were my first-ever girlfriend!" he said. "They were sixteen and we were fourteen, and we were still only like five feet tall and had all our acne and braces and everything, and we were getting over this major shaming from grade seven when there was a hurricane warning, and all the kids had to go sit in the gym, and then we heard the tornado had actually *touched down*, like, literally less than a block away, and Aaron made a pretty good argument about how we were going to die, and we got scared and held hands …"

He paused for his listeners to interject with "Aw," and "Oh my god so scary."

"Well, the local trees lost some branches, but the storm was over twenty minutes later and we were getting "twincest" jokes for the next two years. Kids are the worst ... Thanks, would you?" His cigarette had gone out, and Daffodile happened to have pulled out a lighter while he was talking. She lit him up, glancing at her friend and subtly raising her eyebrows in warning about the sort of people who'd rather have a conversation *at* you than *with* you. Jaymie didn't know it, but Daffodile had recently endured a break-up with a garrulous touring folk musician.

"So anyway, they were way out of our league. But they must have seen something in us—the heart wants what it wants, right?" He winked at Daffodile, who decided he was just polite and entertaining enough to tolerate until their ride arrived. She could imagine him having once been the sort of boy who wears a fedora and says "Milady," but if he was, he'd outgrown it, and he didn't seem to have the pushy, self-aggrandizing qualities that most annoyingly confident men did. She knew his type, but there weren't many who could pull off his type so well.

Aaron made it to the Millennium Library. He knew from Jo's complaints at practice that she was scheduled to work every day until New Year's, and he prayed that she might still be closing up shop before heading to her show. The downtown library had long evening hours.

He arrived at 10:36, five minutes after the front doors were locked. He pressed against the sliding door, fogging the glass and searching desperately for signs of life. A movement caught his eye in the dim courtyard beyond.

"Jo? Hey, hello? I need help!" he called.

But the motion had come only from the revolving door just inside, four slowly rotating panes of glass that hadn't yet been powered down for the night. It completed another turn. He let out a breath that stopped just short of a sob and glanced behind him.

A church loomed austerely from the other side of the street, its sign casting a glare on the scuffed yellowy snow of its lawn. Today the letters were arranged in a friendly "God Loves EVERYONE," and Aaron wondered, if there was a God, whether he or she had come around enough by now to also love clones, and the people who got mistaken for them. And speaking of clones, *what the actual fuck was happening?*

Two silhouettes rounded a corner, and another wave of nausea ran through him.

He turned back to the door and found himself face to face with the evilest Christmas elf he'd ever seen. It looked up at him, hands pressed against his mitts on the other side of the glass.

"Holyclusterfuckingchristalmighty—" Aaron stumbled backwards.

The library's diminutive silence-enforcer, who'd hidden unnoticed in the stacks until all the adults had left for the day, waved little urchin fingers at him through the cloudy pane. A pasty smirk peeked from under her hood.

The odd little person, a mischievous preteen who'd received a less-than-average amount of attention in her young life, was back on Community Service for the holidays. This time, she'd gotten busted playing Purple City, a game familiar to most people in the city. To play, you simply had to stare into the blinding spotlights that lit the Legislative Building for long enough that anything you looked at for a few minutes afterward appeared purple, provided you timed it so as to not go permanently blind.

That wasn't what had gotten her in trouble; while under the influence of the spotlights she'd attempted to reclaim the word "cunt" by handwriting it in violent lavender spray paint on the building, her purple cursive covering the entire rear of the huge, self-important edifice as well as several of the pompous-looking marble statues of men who'd done impressive and probably terrible things at some point in history. The graffiti mysteriously extended many feet higher than the young girl's arms ever would.

She was caught by a police force who probably should have had better things to do, but who recognized her instantly and already had her address on file, and who brought her into the security office and made her watch the video footage of her crime. She learned from the experience that the back of the building had cameras pointing at all angles except from the southeast, and that the spray paint had actually been white all along.

"Hey, open the door?" Aaron called, recovering. "Please?"

The girl, who, to him, was still a gremlin from an alternate dimension, cocked her head.

"It's just, I'm in a tight spot, and I don't want to die so please please please will you—"

The preteen had no authority over the library's locks, but had carefully observed the locking ritual and was enthusiastic to try it out, especially if it could provide the thrill of letting this sketchy-looking man, who was clearly fleeing the police, run amok in the library. She tapped an ID card swiped from security against the alarm and typed a password. The doors glided open.

"Thanks," Aaron panted. "I initially misjudged you." She held a finger to her lips and giggled. He dashed past while she unhurriedly relocked the door. Then she returned to the computer she'd claimed, its screen casting a window of light among the stacks, and resumed researching a new synthetic drug called TwiLite, which was popular at parties and raves and which she intended to acquire and sell to people much older than herself.

Later that night, the girl, whose name was Izzy, would find out she was to be entrusted into the care of an older sister who, after lengthy battles against a defective system, had won custody of her. She'd be cared for and sent back to school, where she'd channel her creative energy into healthier pursuits, while maintaining the lucrative side business she was currently getting off the ground.

Aaron was not to experience such a lucky break.

24

The Chase

"So, they were older and very pretty and, like I said, we weren't exactly a catch at that point in our life. But they wanted to try out having boyfriends, and they didn't get along with each other the way we do, so they were more limited in options. They were really competitive, so they had to have all the same stuff or it'd be chaos, right?" Jaymie stood in the middle of the Provencher Bridge finishing his story, his frostbitten ankles forgotten for the time being.

His listeners nodded along; they were in Friday-night mode and game for a high tale of high school drama.

Further down the winding river, the "secret" show had just gotten underway. The opening band had charged onstage, activated its backing beats, experienced technical difficulties, restarted their Mac, reopened Ableton Live, and re-kicked off the night. Hannah was arriving at the venue; Jo was arguing with Michaud over which songs to swap into the set in lieu of the ones with more involved drum parts; Maggie was mussing her already messy bun and establishing a position for herself and Rex close to the stage.

"Anyway, they were trying to make their friendship work, so they thought having twin boyfriends would smooth out any jealousy issues. We were pretty frightened of them, but we rightly suspected that the opportunity to be in close proximity to a girl would not arise again for quite some time.

"I went with the older one since I'm older too—that's how they chose who got who, since they didn't know us all that well—and we dated for about a month. Full disclosure: I experienced my first kiss in that time. But I guess they got bored, or maybe they each didn't trust that the other sister wasn't having a better time, because they started having some fun. And I don't mean to represent teenage girls poorly, because I had great female friends in high school, or like, you know, I talked to some girls a couple of times. But everybody's human, and sometimes people make careless choices, right?"

The four listeners nodded in sympathy at his disclaimer, now primed for the guilt-free slander of conniving teen girls.

"Well, they clued in at some point that we couldn't actually tell them apart. I guess we were supposed to know by their perfume or the call of true love or whatever. Also, both were suspicious that the other one might have the better boyfriend, so to satisfy themselves, they swapped us for a while."

His audience tittered, not sure whether to side with the empowered yet duplicitous female set of twins, or the boys too guileless to have bothered identifying the distinguishing features between their girlfriends.

"I guess that got old fast too, since at that age we were basically the same anyway. They couldn't bear to keep the secret forever—soon, we'd be hanging out with them and they'd be all, 'Of course I'm Natasha! ... Or am I?' and we were getting confused.

"But then one time I was going to a movie with whichever one was Tash for that night, just the two of us, which was nerve-wracking for many reasons, and I got the idea to send Aaron with her instead. This was before he got his dog scar—not that it's noticeable. Anyway, *I* met up with her sister instead of *him*, and you know what? *They* couldn't tell *us* apart either!"

Daffodile finished her smoke and stubbed it out with the toe of her boot. She hadn't laughed yet, but she'd made no move to go back inside either.

"So, we called them on it, which turned out to be a bad idea because they told the whole school we'd hoodwinked them to try and make out with each other's girlfriend. We were widely scorned for the trick, except for a few people who celebrated us, but those are *not* the type of people you want to be friends with. Never mind that we were so shy back then that we barely ever did more than hold their hand.

"Obviously we pointed out the hypocrisy, to which they responded that they'd only *pretended* to switch places, and actually we'd both been with our own original girlfriend all along. It might be true." He tapped his cigarette on a rusted metal ashtray mounted on a post.

"So, we all had a good laugh, except Aaron, who doesn't have quite the same sense of humour as I do, and we called it quits."

The audience was satisfied with the anecdote; they'd determined that no girls had been swindled in the making of the story and Jaymie came out as a good-humoured but endearingly clueless and notably handsome lead.

"Do you ever see them?" someone asked.

"No, never. One is in prison. They interviewed her in there and it turns out she checks most of the boxes on the Psychopath Test." He let out a long exhale of smoke. "We have no idea which one she is or whether the other one survived."

Aaron knew there were stairs to the second floor on the other side of Young Adult Fiction. He jogged through the stacks, one hand brushing the spines to guide his way in the dark. At one point he took a wrong turn and ended up face to face with a colossal cardboard Little Bear that loomed from the shadows of the Children's section. He yelped and cursed treacherous Little Bear, whom he'd regarded with great devotion twenty years earlier.

He stepped over a scattered assemblage of teeny chairs and dropped into a crouch behind a display of hockey books, struggling to catch his breath. He shuddered and wondered why everyone didn't just do their reading on the internet. A reverberant rapping came from the glass doors now far behind him. He jumped to his feet and navigated the last twists through the dark stacks to the stairs, and then took them two at a time to the second floor.

Because it was so cold for so much of the year, the city had made an initiative to aid pedestrians by connecting significant buildings via a series of skywalks that passed back and forth above the streets of downtown. This route generally backfired on anyone with a specific place to be and a certain time they needed to be there, but for urban wanderers and somnolent flaneurs it provided a lovely way to spend a winter afternoon.

Aaron was somewhat familiar with the twists of the tunnels, the crossroads and troublesome spots where you needed to go up a floor and double back in order to cross Portage. He'd pinpointed most of the places where you could see your destination through the transparent glass of the skywalk, but when you got to the other side you were just back in the central food court of the nearly deserted semi-underground mall from which all passageways branched off.

He found the skywalk leading out of the library—its doors still unlocked to allow exit into an event in the next building—and traversed the glass tunnel, lurching when an ambulance shot by under his feet, siren blaring. The passage led into the next block, which housed the city's hockey arena. And suddenly, he was free of the pressing silence of the stacks and surrounded by a great crowd of white jerseys. The game was over. At first stunned, but then relieved, he wove his way among a crowd of fans bearing sanguinely glazed expressions.

Then he saw them: two black-clad people standing out in the sea of white home-team attire like beady eyes in a giant mosaic of a polar bear. Unable to get in the library doors, they'd no doubt crossed the street and entered the stadium to head him off. Aaron realized he too was distinctive in his navy parka. He turned to the closest hockey fan and stammered a semi-lucid request for help, for directions to a security desk and assistance finding his brother.

"I don't carry change," came the muttered response.

"That's not—hey, do I look like I'm—and even if I *was*, you can be polite about—" He gave up and looked around again, but he no longer felt safer among the crowd. The throng was single-mindedly focused on their own escape, caring only about getting to their cars and heading home for a few more celebratory beers; this river only flowed one direction and Aaron's attire marked him as an outsider to their tribe. He felt an urgent need to be free of these people.

He wondered briefly if his opinion of them might be warmer had he not been imprisoned in a cult a couple of weeks ago, but didn't have time to dwell on it.

He weaved through the crush of people, ducking under the arms of massive men in white garb and barely avoiding treading on children they towed behind them. He veered down the nearest hallway, which branched off to another empty skywalk. He looked out over Graham Avenue—or was it Garry Street? Before he could decide, a pair of hands seized the back of his coat and stopped him short.

His story concluded, Jaymie tried to sense whether he was still welcome in the company of his target.

Daffodile had an inscrutable expression on her round, scarf-wrapped face. Then she let out a ringing laugh that echoed over the frozen river.

"That's the stupidest thing I've ever heard," she said.

"Wait till I tell you about the time I led a cult," said Jaymie.

"I'd love to stay and chat with you, uh—?"

"Bukowski comma Jaymie."

"Oh, I've heard about you. I'd stay, Jaymie, but I'm headed to a show." She lifted a foot gracefully and yanked the bottom of her tights down to cover the slice of frozen calf disappearing into her high-heeled boot.

"Is it a secret show?" Jaymie asked hopefully.

A car slid to a stop in front of them, and she checked her app. "That's our lift."

"Would you mind if I ...?" He glanced at the car.

"Will I be able to get a word in edgewise?"

"I'm going to be irrefutably silent, starting right now. You won't even notice me. Here—I'll chip in for the ride. I have, let's see ... one dollar, one eighty-five ..."

"OK, Bukowski, get in the car. I was just telling Alice, here, that—"

"Oh, can we take Waterfront? My brother is walking and my twin-sense just alerted me he's getting chilly. Thanks sorry thanks!"

Beneath his heavy parka Aaron was drenched in sweat. He gasped as he was jerked backwards.

There exists a hypothesis that drummers never actually tire; they simply accumulate perspiration in their clothing until they are forced to remove their shirts—usually onstage, with one hand, while the other maintains hi-hat duties. It took him less than a second to unzip and slide out of his jacket, abandoning it in the hands that had grabbed him.

He bolted down the hall he thought led to the last building on the route—a partially abandoned department store—and to Osborne beyond, but he emerged from the tunnel into the empty food court at the centre of the labyrinth. Brightly lit signs marked the unfrequented fast-food stops, their few listless employees leaning over the counters, sleepily playing on their phones. He fought against a hideous sinking feeling in his stomach.

A twisting pathway threaded between the tables, each of which had cumbersome seats attached by thick metal bars. Aaron ignored the path and climbed onto one of the tables, which were just close together enough to leap between. He took the long room table by table, wincing at the echo of his boots in the near-silent cavern. The restaurant workers barely raised their visors as he passed. Had he looked back, he would have seen his more ungainly pursuers a short ways behind him, forced to navigate the turns of the trail.

At the far end of the room was an out-of-order escalator—that is to say, a fully functional staircase with an "out of order" banner that he quickly ducked underneath. He skidded down the steps, nearly tripping headlong in his haste to reach the main floor.

At the bottom was an exit, and he gratefully took it. The cold air hit him as he oriented himself and then turned toward Portage Avenue, where he knew he'd find traffic and people and maybe even Safe Walk volunteers who could help him.

Then he remembered the swarm of inebriated sports fans that would be flooding the street by now, their crazed eyes passing over him as an easily ignored hindrance underfoot or, at worst, an outlet for their pent-up aggression.

In the opposite direction lay the river, the loneliest but most direct path to Osborne Street. He turned south, sprinted the last block, and took the wooden steps down to the ice trail, which ran ten winding kilometres along the city's two connected rivers, achieving the Guinness record for the world's longest skating rink.

The river was even quieter than the empty mall. The only sounds were the thumping bass of his boots against the packed snow at the edge of the ice trail and his rhythmic gasping breath, like someone tapping on a dull ride cymbal.

The silence bore down. He already regretted choosing the river; he should have braved the revelry downtown. He knew the hockey fans were regular people and that fear was compromising his decision-making ability. Now he was utterly alone in an arctic terrain soundproofed on all sides by rolling baffles of snow. If he called out, no one would hear a thing.

His foot fell too close to the ice and he stumbled and slid, treadmilling on the slick skating path. He caught his balance, dropping to one knee and fist to avoid a fall. This near to the ground, he could see through the first crystalline layer of ice, its network of tiny cracks spreading through the surface, a still, suspended universe of pale threads branching out like spiderwebs until they met the fierce current he knew rushed swiftly in the blackness below.

For a moment, he thought he heard barking. Did coyotes bark or just do that maniacal yipping? He shook his head. He couldn't allow his panic to take over. His chest ached from the freezing air and, seeing no one behind him, he lingered on his knees, exhaling nebulas of fog. Who was he running from, again? Some kind of collection agency?

Envisioning the two agents gave him a chill deeper than the one from the temperature. But now he considered a new threat, from below. Something shifted under his boots. A creaking whispered through the ice, like the gentle whine of a dog. The river groaned softly, expressing that it didn't care either way what happened to him, but he couldn't say it hadn't warned him.

And with that, the ice broke and he plunged neatly through the crack into the glacial water below, to be swept away by the current, as if he'd never been there at all.

25

Trials and Tribulations of the Modern Drummer

Hannah's new band was in the process of convincing her to stop wailing on the scuffed-up skins of their former drummer's kit; it was ten minutes past the end of their set and they weren't sure what to make of the newest addition to their line-up. What she lacked in experience she certainly made up for in enthusiasm.

Hannah, moved by the music and her own nervous energy, had unintentionally worked herself into a rage, and it took her some time to exhaust herself and snap out of it. She'd played for ten extra minutes by the time her bandmates finally convinced her to join them for a victory shot in the back room. None of the rioters and crust-punks in the pit had minded her keeping the show going, but the owner of the space wanted to close up by 1 a.m.

"Nice job, Hannah!" Jake steadied a cymbal as she disengaged herself from the drums. She followed him to the back room.

"Really? Because I only know one beat …"

"Our heroine, One-Beat Hannah!" cried Three-Chord Oli as he packed up his guitar.

"He means it," Jake assured her. "You were what we needed—tonight, anyway. The statement was: authenticity over virtuosity. This band has new life!"

"It's a pretty fresh sound," Oli agreed.

"Rest in peace, Alexandre," Jake added gravely.

The two were somber for a moment while Hannah blushed with relief at not having ruined their show.

"Hey, Monsieur Doctor, when are you setting up first aid? There's, like, four fractures and a black eye out there. Plus, a couple kids are wigging out on I don't know what. Mystery pills." Michaud had escaped the dancefloor. He staggered into the back room wiping at his bloodied nose, collapsed on a couch that looked like it had also survived a mosh pit skirmish, and seized one of their backstage beers.

"How many times do I have to tell you people, I'm getting my doctorate. Not becoming a medical doctor," said Jake.

"Can the *philosophiae doctor* still work a band aid?" Michaud shot back. "Hey, Joanne, reine de la guitare—you've still got it."

"Why wouldn't I?" said Jo, who was half asleep on a dusty loveseat. "Guitar is literally all I've been doing for the last decade."

"Yeah we get it—you're broke. Haven't you learned how to take a fucking compliment by now?" He slung his feet over the arm of the couch and gulped his drink. A curly-haired woman appeared seemingly from thin air with a napkin from a pizza box and dabbed his bleeding nose with it. He smiled sweetly at her.

"I take no responsibility for however this turns out," Jo muttered, as Anika cleaned him up. She stood, nearly stepped on Hannah, and looked surprised, as though she'd forgotten about her. Hannah realized she probably had. "Hailey—Hannah. Sorry. Thanks for filling in."

Hannah, who hadn't been a musician long enough to have mastered the skill of foisting one's awkwardness off onto other people, was suddenly aware of herself and her pigeon-toed stance and the fact that she still held her battered sticks in a sweaty death grip.

"Yeah, no problem. So, I was OK?" she asked. In another two years Hannah would have her own band, would know at least four more beats, and would be well on her way to familiarity with this dance. At present, she felt like a child.

Jo nodded and smiled absently. "Rock and roll," she said. She clipped her guitar case shut and left for the main room, where one of the moshers had hooked their phone up to the PA, much to the dismay of the venue owner.

Jake waved after her dismissively. "She's wasted. You were fine. The set was unconventional, but … conceptual. A palimpsest of the past and future scene." He grinned and then, despite his earlier protesting, traded his bass for a white plastic satchel and went to take over volunteer medical duties.

Hannah decided she liked bass players. She grabbed one of the beers she'd rightfully earned and followed him out.

"Feel like celebrating?" he asked, turning back to her and opening his first aid kit. "These are mostly Advil, but I keep a few fun things on hand." He wiggled his eyebrows.

She had a moment of confusion, and then quickly lifted her beer and forced a laugh. "Oh! I think I! Hmm, already celebrating. Might need to drive my friend's car for him later and I'm not—it's hard to gauge—"

"No presh." Jake smiled. "Go have some good clean fun. But here—as thanks for saving us last minute. Regift or sell 'em if it's not your thing." He placed two capsules in her palm.

Ahead of them and oblivious to the exchange, Jo lifted a hand and parted the waves of moshers without breaking her stride, soon reaching the far bank to greet her date.

The dancers closed in, trapping Hannah in the melee, where she found herself face to face with her final test of the night: the beautiful boy with the septum piercing.

Falling through the ice? Seriously? It was forty below, and the ice was two feet thick and frequently supported the small Zamboni that groomed the trail. Breaking through was the least of Aaron's worries. He stood up, angry and frustrated. It was just like him to lose control of his imagination at the moment he most needed his mental faculties. He looked behind him. He'd rounded a bend in the river and couldn't see whether he was still being followed, and it occurred to him that his pursuers might have predicted his route and planned to head him off at the Osborne Bridge. Still, if he was fast enough, he could get there first. He shivered and wondered how long he'd been kneeling in one place.

It had blizzarded a day before and then hit a record low overnight. The plummeting deep freeze made the snow-laden trees and scrub lining the river look like they were made from blown glass; the whole silvery landscape appeared as though it could shatter into pieces if you touched it. Standing still, he felt the full force of the cold. He'd entered this deserted northwest passage without a parka—he must have shed it somewhere along the way, though he wasn't sure when. He hastily retied his scarf. He'd lost his mittens with the coat, and he pulled the sleeves of his sweater down as far as he could. A layer of sweat was turning to ice against his skin.

He started jogging, pacing himself, trying to calculate whether the greater risk lay in losing stamina before he reached the bridge or freezing into an eerily life-like ice sculpture to be admired by skaters for the remainder of the season.

The icy air induced a deep and constant lung ache, but moving made him warmer, and he estimated that his strength could hold; Aaron had once, while nervous about a job interview, drummed along to a speedcore album on repeat for two and a half hours straight, so you couldn't say he wasn't in shape. (His neighbours to the east sold their home shortly afterwards.) He could worry about frostbite later.

He'd turned the last bend before the bridge when he hit another slippery patch of trail. His boots skidded out from under him and he careened backwards toward the frozen riverbank. He braced himself for impact against the hard-packed snow, already feeling his head cracking against the edge of the path—he'd be found in the morning frozen in a sad bloody ice cube—

He broke through the shiny outer crust of the bank and landed in a cradle of fluff, softly cushioned and completely unharmed.

I'm fine, he thought. How many times had he worked himself into a frenzy of terror over nothing? What was a "clone collector," anyway? It sounded exactly like something out of a psychosis episode.

From the riverbank, he had a clear view of the purple night sky, brightly reflecting the snow, and the sea of gentle white swells blanketing the ice. He wondered whether the whole city was just a white padded room protecting him from himself.

He took a deep breath and realized how utterly exhausted he was. Shifting in his cottony seat, he rested his head, one of the few parts of him still warm under his toque. Little rivulets of snow poured over his sweater and into his lap like sand in an hourglass, comfortably tucking him in until his time was up.

Columns of stars twinkled ahead. He squinted down the river and realized dazedly that they were the lights decorating the Osborne Bridge. He'd make it there soon, find Jaymie, and behold the wonder that was Jo playing shreddy punk guitar, just as soon as he'd rested his eyes.

He was still there several minutes later, passed out, when the two collectors, gasping with fatigue themselves, finally caught up.

"I'm going to need a drink after this," panted the man, who carried Aaron's coat under his arm. "This guy could win an Olympic medal."

"I'm sorry your first night on the job has been like this," said the woman, taking a bottle from her backpack. "Most of them come quietly."

"This is both mentally and physically taxing. And depressing," said her partner, eyeing the sleeping young man in the snow.

"Let's be quick—it's freezing out and we're not supposed to let them get damaged." She tipped the mouth of the bottle against a cloth as Aaron began to stir.

"As opposed to savouring the victory?" the man muttered.

"You feel bad at first, but you get used to it. It's a job." She handed him the bottle. "Funny, it's not usually the little skittish ones who clone themselves."

"Why not? Strength in numbers, maybe?"

"No. Too paranoid that a clone might turn on them. It's usually arrogant idiots who do it. The ones who think they're invincible. The irony is that the copy is just as bad as they are, and it *does* turn on them."

Aaron's eyes blinked open and widened in alarm, but only for a second, because before he could sit up, firm gloved hands were pressing against his mouth and the back of his head, and he was drugged into oblivion.

After the show, Jo was in no state to drive home. She mingled ineptly in the packed room, received a congratulatory kiss on the cheek from Lucas, and took him up on an offer of a drink. She said hello to Rex and Maggie and wondered if Lucas had noticed that her only friends in the audience were not legally allowed to be there.

Jo had expected to feel elated at the reuniting of the band that had constituted her only musical success (in terms of critical reception and a widespread fanbase), but all she could think about were the *Bukowskis*. After their tour, Jaymie had announced that the band would take an entire week off to rest and recuperate and learn a full set of covers, on their own time, in preparation for the tribute show. When rehearsals had started up again earlier that week, Jo had found herself hoping that something between them might have shifted since their shared ordeal.

She wasn't sure exactly what she was expecting—and it wasn't as though the dynamic had ever been bad—but she knew there was a certain bond between bandmates, unspoken and invisible to the outside observer, which she hoped might have been strengthened in some way.

Instead, Jaymie seemed intent on writing off the incident as a stroke of poor luck and a lesson in exercising caution on the next tour; Aaron was using it as further grounds in his bid to quit the band; and Rex, who Jo hoped was displaying their usual unfathomable teenage nature and not signs of repressed PTSD, was as calm and impenetrable as ever. Jo had spotted the black stenciled strokes of an amateur tattoo spidering out from beneath the rolled sleeve of their shirt, and she both admired Rex and felt a flutter of concern.

They'd managed to agree on a band to cover. (Or had Jaymie chosen, and convinced each of them it was their own idea? Jo wasn't sure.) Practices were productive. Everything was fine, and Jo felt a stab of shame for even noticing that Jaymie and Aaron hadn't come to her show. Rex had slipped away mumbling when Lucas returned with her drink.

The night was winding down; the rest of the *Ballet Llama* had departed. Michaud must have escaped under cover of Anika's cloak of inconspicuousness—apparently, her skill extended to others close in her vicinity—without paying Jo her cut of the door. Hadn't the reunion been *his* idea? She wondered if it was just a promotional move leading up to his solo release. And now she'd have to hound him for her hundred bucks, or however much it was.

Casio Bob from the band *Gunt*, who often used to open for the *Llama*, had greeted her with a tequila shot (putting her just over her comfortable limit) and asked her to catch up with him before she left, but last she'd seen him, he and Jake were heatedly negotiating something—probably substance-related—over the bassist's box of medical supplies, and they'd both since left for home or the next party. She felt a pang of post-show loneliness—the kind you get when everyone has told you how talented you are and then left together while you struggle with your gear up the narrow, dark staircase at the back of the venue, alone, in the middle of the night.

"Did you drive?" Lucas entered the back room as she stared at her neatly stacked equipment and tried to decide what to do with it. She was relieved he hadn't taken off.

"Yes, but then I had a few drinks, and a bit of weed, so …" She was careful to keep the slur out of her speech.

He laughed. "Well, I live about five blocks away if you want to keep the evening going?"

"Oh, at your place …?"

"Or I can get a car for you and your luggage," he added quickly. "Got the app here …"

"No, sounds great. I'll come back for it in the morning," she said decisively, not sure she could safely carry it up the stairs in her current state anyway.

They left out the back, into a night still bright and frigid. Jo shivered and Lucas tucked an arm around her waist.

His neat goatee tickled against her ear. *He must be 6'2 or even 6'3*, she thought, conscious of her own height. *Not that that matters.*

"Nice guys, your *BL* mates," he said. "Finally met them—I was too awkward to actually talk to them, back in the day. They seemed kind of …"

"Like pretentious dicks? They were," said Jo. "I mean, *we* were."

"Well, y'all don't seem that way now."

Jo considered it. "You're right. Jake and Oli have really evened out. Even Mich is OK."

Lucas exhaled into his scarf, and the breath fogged his glasses and instantly froze into a coating of ice that refused to be scraped clear.

It might have been the effects of her inebriation, but Jo let out a giggle, which was not something she did often. It alarmed her. She suddenly had a vision of the unfortunate *Ballet Llama* drummer—a man a little older than her whom she hadn't gotten along with much better than she did with the other band members, but with whom she'd made music for two years of her life—leaning over, headless, with his last beer in his hand. She'd barely thought about him all night. She'd worked late at the library and only arrived in time to see the ambulance leaving.

She hadn't known Lucas for very long. What were the rules about leaving a venue late at night, shortly after an unsolved murder, with someone you'd only had one date with? Jo had never really been afraid of anyone, at least not one person by themselves who wasn't, as far as she knew, in an arts collective. She wasn't used to the feeling. It passed the next moment, when Lucas nearly walked into oncoming traffic and she had to pull him back by his hood. Cursing, he gave up trying to clean his glasses and put them in his pocket.

"Alright," he said. "I'm blind. Take me home, please."

"What's your street?" she asked. Then, conspiratorially, "You can trust me. Whatever they've been saying about how I joined an evil cult—don't listen."

"If what I've heard about guitar players is true, I'm probably in trouble without even considering the cult. But what choice do I have? If that coyote story was real, I won't even be able to see it coming. I'll just hear *awooo* ..." He howled grimly and told her the address.

Jo laughed and took his glove in hers and led him toward his apartment building, where they arrived, shaking, ten minutes later. They stiffly pulled off their outer layers, and then some inner layers, and it was only once she was down to her Onstage Long Johns (thinner than Everyday Long Johns) and beneath the covers, long legs entangling with his and with his beard scratching pleasantly against her neck, that she could stop thinking of lost bandmates—dead or just hurtfully absent—and feel like this pointless punk rock reunion had been worth something.

26

Rex Has Met a Girl

Jaymie, on the other hand, did not go home with anyone that night. His evening did, however, take a surprising and romantic turn. To back up a few hours:

Once they were in the car, Daffodile asked if he'd really led a cult, and he was about to launch into the story when his social sixth sense kicked in. Perhaps he sensed the ghost of her hyper-extraverted folk singer ex still lingering on her, or maybe he was just taking slow steps toward maturity, but he said, "It's a stupid story, it'll bore you to death. By the way, we listened to your new album nonstop on tour. It's brilliant."

"OK, what's it called?" she demanded affably.

"Basilisk," said Jaymie, whose trouble with names did not extend to artists or albums.

Daffodile was enthusiastic to talk about the record because, she told him, she'd used some unconventional chord progressions, and she'd been thinking a lot lately about the balance between creative exploration and accessibility. She wasn't sure if she'd pulled it off, and she liked getting the opinions of musicians who weren't part of her band or production team. Jaymie listened to her speak without interjecting, except to ask questions at appropriate intervals, or assure her that it was indeed artfully pushing the envelope while remaining commercially viable, or to tactfully disagree on production techniques just often enough that she knew he wasn't being a yes-man to get into her pants or her band.

The car dropped them at Big Brother Coffee, where Daffodile's companion found a friend and went in ahead. They descended into the concrete basement, commenting wearily on how loud and muddy the sound was going to be, and Daffodile stopped, worried she might have forgotten her earplugs. While she fished in her purse, Jaymie had another stroke of good luck: two people recognized him on their way outside for a smoke.

"It's Charles Bukowski—in the flesh!" said one.

"Oh wow, you know me?"

"We were at your house concert in October," explained the other, offering a handshake. "We spoke briefly, but we had our costumes on—it's fine if you don't remember."

"Of course I remember!" said Jaymie, who didn't.

"We couldn't decide if you were a cosmic nihilist or an existential one," said the first. A fashionably gothy veil washed out her expression, but she sounded perfectly serious about it.

"It was an impressive show."

"The 'Ramen High' spoonerism—"

"I did a Bukowski self-immersion after that. I read his poetry, and *Post Office* ..."

"Also, you can sing, dude. I don't think you're a nihilist at all, actually."

"It's easy to frame everything in that context when you're doing a marking job for the Nietzsche unit of an honours class. It takes over your brain," said the man.

"And I was taking the class—philosophy influences my performance installations. Hey, your work gets philosophical—do you consider yourself a humanist?"

"I love certain humans," Jaymie confirmed.

"Are you intentional about absurdism? In your music, I mean."

"We're being annoying, aren't we?" the man beamed.

"Seriously? Flattered," said Jaymie. "You both know music, obviously."

"Well, the scene has taken a turn lately. Pop has always been about reusing the same formula and selling out, but now it's everywhere. What even is an 'indie band?' Everyone's a slave to the Spotify algorithm. Under three minutes, hook in the first ten seconds," said the man.

"I like to ask: does a good band embrace it? Subvert it?" said his companion.

"I try not to think about it," said Jaymie, and, sensing Daff might be getting impatient, he grinned and added, "Hey, speaking of bands that don't sell out ..." and nodded toward the final set of doors into the basement venue.

"The opener's still tearing down—we've got time." But they politely moved off, asking Jaymie's next show dates and promising to weigh in on the fan forum. He turned to Daffodile.

"I promise I didn't hire two established musicians to praise me in front of you, and that I didn't send a list of exactly which compliments might cast me in a favourable light in the eyes of a talented and intellectually astute pop singer," he told her.

"It's OK, I use that trick all the time," she said, and gave a vulpine wink. Then she confessed that she hadn't found her earplugs and wasn't up for social-butterflying around a loud venue quite yet, and wondered whether Jaymie would like to take a walk over the Osborne Bridge while she mentally prepped herself for the evening ahead?

Jaymie most certainly would.

"Oh, hey. You were really good," said the glowing, soft-voiced being who'd materialized from the havoc of the mosh pit to stand in front of Hannah in all his slender, sweaty sublimity.

"No I wasn't," she replied.

"OK, but I heard you've never even played a show before, so."

"I'd like to play a lot more of them," said Hannah.

"Me too." He smiled down at his sneakers, his cherry-red hair sweeping down to hide the top half of his face. "I play the bass," he clarified.

"Oh, cool. I like bass players. I mean, I like the bass." Hannah winced.

"Nice! ... Would you want jam sometime?"

"Would I want what?"

He blushed at her. "Like, to hang out and play music."

"Oh, I thought you were asking if I wanted to eat jam," said Hannah.

"Yeah, I should annunciate," said the boy, and rubbed at his piercing, which she could now see was either very new or slightly infected. "I was trying to say '*to* jam'... Also, I really like your hair."

"Thanks. I'm trying out this dyed part."

"Yeah, I love that style. Like Knives Chau." His eyes widened. "Wait, is that bad to say?"

"Whatever. I like your nose ring."

"Thanks, I got it done today."

"OK, let's have some jam." Hannah laughed nervously.

"Oh, ha, good."

He didn't get another word in, because at that juncture Hannah was nearly felled by the delirious affections of her two friends, who'd been largely responsible for maintaining the mania in the pit. They'd disentangled themselves to come and commend her on a show well done—or maybe it wasn't well done; they couldn't tell and didn't care.

By the time Hannah had recovered and congratulated herself on having spoken with him at all, the young man had slipped away and she was left to lament that, in a ridiculous sitcom-style blunder, she hadn't gotten his name or number and now had no way of finding him.

Jaymie and Daff crossed the same bridge that, a few minutes later, Aaron would incorporate into his last twinkling vision of hope before taking an unfortunate nap.

They trekked through the arctic gardens of the Legislative Building, which had been arrayed in dazzling golden Christmas lights (or purple ones, depending on your perspective) in loops and coils around the trees, in ostentatious robes billowing over the statues, and in towering three-dimensional wire formations of reindeer and beluga whales along the paths.

They shared stories of past tours and gazed into the bright spotlights around the building for as long as they dared. They shouted in wonderment and delight at the great mural of the word "cunt," which in this context somehow seemed friendly and empowering, painted in towering purple cursive on the back of the building.

The adventure stretched long past the setup time of the headlining band, and when Jaymie finally stopped checking the clock on his phone it extended into timelessness.

That's why Jaymie Brzezinski never made it to the secret show, and why he got home late and frostbitten and happy, and curled up on the living room couch under a blanket with Dick Dale as an eye mask and the other two cats entwined on his belly. He'd barely made a sound coming in, being unexpectedly sober and considerate enough to avoid waking the siblings he assumed were peacefully sleeping in their rooms by then, though of course they were not.

"I'm like, 'Is that bad to say?'—It's like, if it wasn't stereotyping, you just *made* it stereotyping! I've never said something like that in my life! And now this *one* time—"

"Oh my god relax," said Maggie.

"It was like I was twelve and I didn't know how to have a conversation with another human being!" They noticed Maggie was smiling. *"What?"*

"I'm sorry, I don't mean to enjoy your distress, it's just so rare that you're not, like, totally chill," she said. "You could ask her if being compared to Knives Chau made her uncomfortable and apologize."

"I just—'Would you want jam?'—what the fuck! She's so cool! *She plays the drums!*"

"Ha!" Maggie snorted. "Rex, calm down."

"I fucked it up, and—ow! My nose hurts."

"Stop rubbing at it! You know you'll make it worse—this is, like, your tenth piercing!"

Rex forced their fingers away from their face and ran them through their hair instead. They'd shaved the left-most third of their head and dyed the rest a vivid scarlet to celebrate the new piercing.

Rex was ready for grade twelve to be over. They'd quit all but their required courses because they were busy practicing for jazz band, and then they'd quit jazz band because it conflicted with the *Bukowskis'* next show, and they were ready to quit high school entirely, the way their brothers had, except that they were still considering university. At the moment, however, Rex had different priorities.

"OK, chill out, let's find her." Maggie pulled out her phone.

"I got awkward when her friends came, and I ran away. And I was an idiot and didn't ask for her Insta. Not that she'd have wanted me to, because I'm a total weirdo—"

"Just ask Jo," Maggie suggested.

"I can't, I'm too embarrassed," said Rex.

"Seriously?"

"I'll think about it."

"Well, in the meantime ... Hannah ... such a common name ... this is taking me a lot longer than usual ..." Maggie pursed her lips. Rex knew she would consider it a great personal failure if she couldn't locate the girl's profile in under a minute. Rex also knew that if Maggie couldn't find someone on the internet, that person didn't exist on the internet.

"I have some homework, I guess. But I *will* find her," she vowed. "Everyone has friends, and those friends all have friends, and I am friends with most of those friends."

"And then what?" asked Rex dolefully.

"Then you can add her!"

"I'm not adding her after that conversation!"

"OK, then *I'll* add her, and she can be *my* new BFF, instead of yours." Maggie grinned impishly. "That's what you wanted, right? A new best friend?" She looked back at her phone. "Hey, maybe this is her …"

"No, you're irreplaceable, you complete … frigging … jerkwad…" Rex made a few swipes at Maggie's phone and confiscated it. "No, this Hannah is in nursing and loves Christian rock."

"Oops, I didn't look closely. Not that nurses can't drum. Anyway, I overheard her drunk friends in line for the bathroom. They're on a gap year but she's in first year uni."

"She's already in university? Ew, she's so cool, I hate it."

"Let's see, she's in a punk band, so she's gotta be in, like, art school, or Poli Sci., or gender studies …"

"She can study my gender if she wants—know what I'm saying?"

"Rex, you're an animal!" Maggie squealed.

"I just said it and I already feel bad about it."

"I don't even know you anymore!"

"What's come over me?"

"Horny little Jaymie Brzezinski Junior over here …"

The exasperated coffee shop owner, whom they'd been ignoring for the past few minutes, finally succeeded in ushering them out with the last stragglers and locking the door.

"Well, we did it, we had fun," said Rex, bracing themself against the cold wind.

"Yes dear, it was quite the charming soiree. People will be speaking of this for some time, don't you think? A real *who's who* in there, wouldn't you say, darling?"

"Isn't Jo so good though? I, like, couldn't even talk to her after."

"Do you think she was born the same moment Jimi Hendrix died?"

"In 1970?"

"Yeah, and she just looks young! She's blessed-slash-cursed to keep reliving her twenties!" Maggie glanced behind her, as though protecting this unpatented hypothesis from eavesdroppers, though Rex knew she was really just making sure it was safe to pull her hood over her freezing ears without anyone judging her for the funny lump her bun made beneath it.

"An enchanted anti-aging serum," conjectured Rex. "Bestowed on her by the ghosts of the Twenty-Seven Club!"

"Yeah, because she's like fifty, deep down. You can hear it when she plays."

"Like how you're *technically* sixteen, but not *really*."

"I know, inside I'm twenty-three. And skinny. I'm trapped in the wrong body!" Maggie moaned.

"Fuck off!" said Rex, and shoved her into a snowbank. A handful of miniature plastic bottles spilled from Maggie's coat, sending the two friends burrowing into the powdery snow to retrieve them.

"Jager shots! I almost forgot I stole those," said Maggie.

"Never mind, you are sixteen," said Rex. "And clearly perfect. Me, on the other hand, I'm not quite sure what I am …"

"I'm more sixteen than you were ever a girl," Maggie agreed. "Here, there's two each and a third to split."

"Yikes, I'll do my best," said Rex. "Cheers!"

The two teenagers made their way across the blithely shining Osborne Bridge and disappeared into the night.

27

Jaymie's Lament

Jaymie awoke, removed the cats, and went to tell Aaron about his dreams, as he did most mornings. He soon discovered that his brother was nowhere in the house, nor was he answering his phone.

"Rex! Hey, Rex!" he called up the stairs.

"I'm sleeping!" yelled Rex, who'd made it safely home, late and tipsy.

"Rex, are you awake yet?"

"Go away, I don't care what you dreamed!"

"Hey Rex, did you see Aaron at the show last night?"

Rex groaned and rolled over, abandoning their attempt to block him out with the pillow. "No, he never showed." They stretched and shook themself awake, energized by memories of the night before. "Hey, I don't know why you guys bailed, but whatever you did instead was nowhere near as good as the *Llama*. Also, their drummer got murdered. … It was kind of crazy."

"But he wasn't there?" When Jaymie appeared in the doorway, instead of texting Rex or shouting from the kitchen, Rex realized something was wrong.

"Wasn't he with you?" they asked, propping themself on an elbow.

"We were supposed to meet there, but then I had to—something came up."

"'Kay, so, it sounds like *you* bailed, and he came home to watch TV."

"OK, yeah, but then where is he?"

"I dunno, Jaymie, maybe he saw a little terrier on the way home and took a detour and woke up the next day under a weeping willow in a graveyard with no idea how he got there."

"Jesus Christ, Rex! That was in the *summer!* It was fucking *forty below* last night!"

"Ugh, sorry. I'll be right down." They rubbed their eyes, threw off their blankets, and pulled on a baggy, knit sweater of their mother's before following Jaymie down to the kitchen.

"Holy shit," said Jaymie. "A drummer died? Oh my god. What if the killer was having, like, a *drummer* night, and Aar was walking there alone …" Jaymie couldn't finish the thought.

"How would the killer know he's a drummer?"

"The house concert!" The pitch of Jaymie's voice rose. "The fucking *pumpkins?*"

"Right, sorry, I'm not thinking straight … Why do people drink?" Rex shook their head and poured a glass of water. "OK, let's stay calm and think of all the possibilities—"

But Rex was too late.

"Oh my god he's been murdered. I knew this band thing was a bad idea. This is all my fault. Rex! This is all your fault—why didn't you talk me out of doing music? You know you're the only person I ever listen to—with great power comes *responsibility*. People were getting murdered! What kind of an idiot puts together a band in the midst of all that? And now he's—no way. There must be another explanation. We have to go and—oh my god, what am I going to do? There are just—Rex, there are certain things I need a teammate for. Like, who will remind me, when I'm making hot chocolate, you have to make a paste first! Like, with the powder, in the bottom of the pot? Because if you just throw it in there, there will be gross lumps when you drink it, and I don't keep track of stuff like that! I just, I have a lot on my mind and—shit! I shouldn't have left him to go home by himself. How could I have known! I didn't think he'd *actually* go to that show—it was loud and crowded and full of drunk teenagers—you know, by not going, I basically gave him an out! Because it's so awkward, especially if you're on your own, if you have a panic attack and you have to explain it to people, but you're busy trying to breathe and everything—you just need someone else there, to tell people you're just, like, choking on a skittle, or something like that that's less embarrassing than, like, panicking over nothing … And I know—I mean, we've all freaked out in our life. I've had—sometimes you drink one Monster Energy too many and all the sudden you're like WHAT THE SHIT IS HAPPENING?"

"Jaymie, I think we should—"

"Rex! Oh my god, you're right. We have to do something! We should go and—before he turns up all, you know, all made out of pumpkin shells or whatever …" He shuddered, sat down, and stared at the surface of the table. Then he jumped up again. "We'll retrace our steps! We were walking over the bridge, and then there was Daffodile and I—shit, I'm deplorable! What was I thinking? I never even heard his new song! The one supposedly not about dogs. Rex, I'm the fucking worst! And now I'm going to pay for it because who's going to wake me up in the morning if I have a radio interview or an appointment or, like, my *job* …"

"I can see you're stressed—"

"I'll be stuck with the guilt for the rest of my life! Which won't be long because who's going to remind me not to drive if I've had more than one drink per hour—that rule sounds conservative, I know, and that's how I feel about it once I'm four drinks in and I realize it's karaoke night at Cowboy's, but truth is, I'm not the greatest driver at the best of times."

"You're really not," said Rex.

"Shit. Rex! I don't know what to do! I'd gotten really fond of that guy, you know? It's like, I've only been sleeping in a room by myself for under ten years, and I just … I don't really like it. I don't know how you do it! Sometimes when he's not around, I say stuff expecting somebody to answer and then there's no answer and I'm like, Whoa, weird. And then I remember I'm by myself and I have to just text one of you guys, and it's fine or whatever. NOW THE WHOLE REST OF MY LIFE IS GOING TO BE LIKE THAT. Rex, you don't know what it's like!"

"Yeah, it's pathological," said Rex.

Early in life, Rex had wished for a twin. When you had a twin—Rex had observed—you never had to be alone. Fortunately, rather than terrorize them as Rex had seen some of their friends' older siblings do, or ignore them as one might expect from brothers eight years older, the twins in Rex's life had pitied their solo sibling and never denied them involvement in music-related activities. The perceptive young Rex had soon noted that brothers could be extremely high-maintenance, and then identified themself as an introvert, and the desire for a third sibling had gone away.

"I should just die right now," said Jaymie.

"OK, enough," said Rex. "He probably crashed at Anika's for the night. Or, like, he does have friends besides us! He could've gone to Adib's to play videogames. Or maybe he even, like, met up with a girl! Come on Jaymie, at least go through some of the possibilities."

"Right, because Adib and his boyfriend really want to spend Friday night playing Nintendo with our neurotic brother. You're right though! I'm being useless. I just—you know how I can get overwhelmed. OK. What are the options … I'll call Anika."

"Who's the kinda flakey girl he had some dates with in the spring? Does he ever hang out with her?" asked Rex, relieved to have gotten Jaymie on track without assistance from Aaron.

"Maybe. Do you remember her name?"

"I'll try to find her. You call Jo. … Also, which way would he have gone to the show?"

"Waterfront Drive, and then we'd usually take the river trail, if we were together. Was there a game last night? He might have wanted to avoid the crowd."

"The river at night? How could that possibly be less intimidating than hockey fans?"

"You'd be surprised," Jaymie said darkly. "I just remembered: he said he might be thinking of moving out."

"Oh … OK, so he's clearly pissed at you. That's kind of a relief."

"Right. Hopefully he's just being mean."

"Well, let's go get a coffee and make sure he's not *also* out getting a coffee, and we can walk on the river to downtown and stop in at the Aunties' and see if he slept there."

Jaymie agreed, mollified, but as soon as had Rex gone upstairs to get dressed, there was a terse rapping at the front door, causing him another bout of anxiety. He imagined police on the steps, with tragic news, and he stood helplessly for an infinite two seconds, unable to answer. Then it swung open, and a very young woman walked in, said, "Sorry I'm late. Played a wild show last night," and walked straight past him and down the basement stairs to the jamspace.

Jaymie stared after her, perplexed. "Rex?" he called quietly up the staircase. "Does Aaron have a teenage girlfriend we don't know about?"

Rex reappeared. "What? I mean, if he did, we definitely wouldn't know about it. Why?" A raucous drumming started up on Aaron's kit.

"Because that girl is for sure not here for me," said Jaymie. They stood and listened in bafflement for a full minute. The drumming sped up.

"She's not that good, is she?" said Jaymie, at the same time that Rex said, "She's got 'fast' and 'loud' down pat." The playing stopped.

"I practiced!" called the girl.

"Ah." Realization dawned on Rex's face. "He's teaching drum lessons now."

"Oh yeah, no kidding! Aw. That's our boy," said Jaymie, eyes watering. "Well, come on, Rex, no time to lose!" He pulled his boots on and skidded out the door, and Rex followed him as the agitated beat started up again.

Rex had never been too concerned by their brothers' absences. Occasionally one or both of them would party too hard and they'd end up on someone's floor for the night, or they'd have a fight and Aaron might go to their Aunts' house, or Jaymie would spend a few days with sketchy friends and return with a hangdog, heroin-chic complexion which—no surprise—many people found very attractive on him. And then there were the infrequent instances when Aaron got confused and woke up in a graveyard or a field in Saskatchewan, etc.

But the combination of the weather and the murdered drummer and the fact that Aaron hadn't even texted had set Rex on edge, and they knew they needed to track him down, quickly.

As they walked, they made calls and, when they realized it was Saturday and everyone was asleep, sent messages. The sky was as blue as a dreamy July beach day, but the cold was ferocious. Sundogs shimmered above the city, sending down violent golden rays as though initiating the Rapture. Comfortingly, the siblings knew that if any of them had been beamed up into eternity for their pure heart and acts of virtue, it would have been Rex, not Aaron.

Their efforts turned up no clues but kept them occupied and optimistic until a short while later, when Jo cleaned herself up and began walking to meet them, and on the way found Aaron's empty, snowy coat forsaken on the riverbank.

28
Jaymie 2.0

Jo awoke to a soft tapping beside her on the bed, like a drummer absently patting at the skin of his snare drum. Weak winter sunlight squirmed in through a curtainless window and shimmied groggily on Lucas's silver computer and bare chest. She shifted to get a better look. Her movement startled him, and he shut the laptop with a clap. She wondered if he'd spent the morning trying to figure out how you're supposed to write an honest review of a band's terrible show when you've just slept with that band's guitar player.

"Oh! Hey. Good morning," he said.

Jo yawned. "Morning. Are you writing your article already?"

"Yes, and it's a glowing one. I just posted it. Ahem." He opened the computer and read, "Dear followers, you'll be happy to know I'm giving my date last night five out of five cat-with-heart-eyes emojis, and yes—" He looked at Jo emphatically. "—I did get laid. Sort of. I'll report all the details and, as always, please share your thoughts in the comments. First, the foreplay—"

Jo grabbed the edge of the computer and spun it around on his lap—of course, it showed only his home screen.

"Did you think I would …?" he said, laughing.

"Five out of five? Your date was totally messed up at her own show, got herself off and then passed out within twenty minutes of walking in your door, and, I'm just noticing, hijacked your entire bed. How did you even sleep?" She plucked at the mussed-up blankets. She'd expanded while asleep and cornered him into the far quarter of the mattress.

"You were messed up? Damn, I didn't realize! I'm glad *you* initiated all the things we barely did before you said, 'You're nice,' and conked out immediately."

"Well, I can hide it pretty well. Years of experience." Jo stretched under the stolen covers, pleasantly impressed to find she had no hangover. "Sounds like I was at my classiest."

"I did notice you slurred the word 'pretentious.'"

"Oops. Who was I calling pretentious?"

"Nobody! I don't even remember. But speaking of the *Llama* ..." Lucas quirked a mischievous eyebrow, put the laptop aside, and slid down to face her, propping himself on an elbow and pointedly tugging her commandeered blankets back over himself.

"Oh shit, don't tell them!"

He slapped his forehead in belated inspiration. "Why, oh why, did I not take advantage of your compromised state to ask you *what broke up the Ballet Llama?* Idiot!"

Jo laughed and pulled her fingers through her hair, which had tangled into a hurricane overnight. "I told you, artistic differences."

"Yeah, right! That's not *even* what you told me. And what about the story of the corrupt manager who tricked you guys into selling him the rights to the French halves of each song?"

"Amazing—I hadn't heard that one yet!"

"You're really not going to tell me."

"No evil record execs, no drunk manslaughter on tour, no scandalous affairs within the band. Sorry to disappoint you ... But as consolation, I'll challenge your heart-cat system to see if it goes to a six. With your consent."

"Sober and willing."

She leaned toward him, but just then her phone buzzed from the floor. It had slid from the pocket of her coat, which lay in a heap by the bed, and she might have ignored it except that she could see Rex's name on the screen. She couldn't imagine why Rex would be calling her at all, never mind on a Saturday morning, except to tell her Jaymie had scheduled an emergency band practice for RIGHT NOW, or something bad had happened. Neither option seemed unlikely.

A minute later she was hurriedly dressing and hugging a disappointed Lucas goodbye, her tentative gaiety extinguished in the time it took Rex to ask if she'd seen Aaron. She skimmed her messages, which contained three versions of "Have you seen Aaron?" from Jaymie, Rex, and Jaymie again, all from within the last ten minutes, and one "Hey Jo, location location??" from Aaron, twelve hours earlier. Her abdominals clenched. She hadn't even noticed it.

She powerwalked back to the coffee shop to start her car and load her gear, only to find that her battery was dead. Swearing quietly, she looked around and saw someone making their way to the vehicle ahead of hers. They were snowsuited and moving fast, but they squinted their eyes, barely visible between scarf and toque, and walked over when she hailed them.

The person carried a fresh coffee, a bulging messenger bag, and a boxy instrument case, and she wondered if they were in the opening band, and whether they'd left the venue the previous night in the same condition she had. She considered asking, but a panicky guilt stopped her—she'd forgotten to introduce herself and ask the duo's names, forgotten to say "good set" afterward, forgotten to pay attention to whether the set even *was* good. So rude.

Instead, she simply asked for a boost, received another blue-eyed squint in response, and waited shivering while the stranger pulled their car up and attached the cables. It was to no avail; during the night the engine in the old car had forgotten the distant promise of springtime, given up hope, and expired. Jo's would-be hero shrugged and murmured through their scarf, then picked up their case and bag. She thanked them and waved them off.

She was relocking the car when she realized they'd set their coffee on the trunk. She was too restless to wait and see if they drove back—and she certainly wasn't one to turn down free coffee after a late night—so she kept it. A gift from the universe to a musician under-rewarded for her art.

She set off on foot down the quiet street and soon reached the bridge. There she left the sidewalk and picked her way down to the river, cringing as fresh snow slithered into her boots.

"Twi?" growled a small voice, as she passed by the underside of the bridge.

"Pardon me?" said Jo, looking around. Besides her coffee donor, she'd encountered no one on her way. "Hello? Are you OK?"

"TwiLite," said the little bridge troll, annoyed at not being immediately understood. She glared out at Jo, who peered into the darkness at her with snow-blind eyes.

"Like … the drug?" asked Jo.

"No, the kids' book," drawled the girl. She stepped into the light, most of her face covered by a black toque and neck warmer.

"I'm looking at you now, and it doesn't seem unreasonable you'd be talking about the book," said Jo, looming over the child.

"If you don't want it just say so!" she snapped.

"Hmm. What does it ... I mean, is it any good?" asked Jo.

"I don't know, I'm thirteen! My customers keep coming back, though."

"I'm not sure if—god, what am I doing? My drummer is—I have to find my friend!"

"Only takes a second. I can do e-transfer." The girl crossed her arms, challenging Jo to be brave enough to e-transfer her fifteen dollars for drugs.

Jo narrowed her eyes. "Hey, don't you work at the library sometimes? Lizzy ... Izzy ...?"

"It's Iz—I mean it's Jessica. Jones! Fuck—I have to go," Izzy sputtered, and she disappeared back into the shadows of the bridge, hissing, "Pussy," over her shoulder.

"Where's your mom!" Jo yelled half-heartedly after her.

"I know you get stoned at work!" the shrill voice retorted, and then she was gone.

Jo continued on her way. Mention of work had reminded her she had a shift in less than an hour, but this was just as soon forgotten, for it was as she was walking briskly along the river path to meet Jaymie and Rex, sipping the abandoned coffee from its paper cup, that she came across Aaron's jacket.

She almost didn't notice it. It had snowed again in the early morning, leaving a fresh topcoat on the city, and the only remnant from the land's previous layer was a few strands of fake fur from the lining of a hood, poking wispily from the bank like winter wheat groping its way out of the ground, three months premature. Jo spent a minute frantically pawing around for the rest of him, visions of poor Alexandre fresh in her mind, before she got herself under control.

She shook the coat out, wished fervently that she'd brought her one-hitter, and called Jaymie. Then, while he and Rex went to the nearest police station, she continued on foot and then by bus to their home and waited on their porch couch, blanketed by the lost jacket, nursing the coffee that had gone bitterly cold within two minutes of leaving the cafe.

***

Aaron woke up in a world that looked like a cross between a hospital waiting room and the children's play area in a fast-food restaurant. He sat up. He'd been lying on a gym mat in a corner of the large, well-lit room, and he had an unpleasant queasiness—a combination of fear at his unknown predicament and indignation at having been so unceremoniously chloroformed. Memories of the previous night blurrily returned to him, and he felt the stirrings of terror.

Fortunately, exhaustion won out over panic, and he got to his feet and went to look around for an escape route and/or snack.

Three people sat around a brightly painted picnic table nearby. Further off, two children—twins—played on a rug with stuffed animals and plastic food items. Several people napped or read magazines in almost-comfortable-looking armchairs in an alcove to one side.

Suppressing an anxiety that was part social and part fear for his life, he forced himself over to the table. The people conversing there turned their attention to him as he approached.

"Another new one," commented a middle-aged man. His neat silver hair and beard augmented a distinguished-yet-slick aesthetic, giving the impression of a high-rolling businessman or a crooked movie producer.

"The collectors have been active this week," said a slightly younger man, rumpled and tired-looking, as he adjusted a pair of cracked glasses and squinted at Aaron.

"They sent new notices at the start of the month," the first man said. "That means another set of deadlines is up." He addressed Aaron. "Yours wouldn't pay his fees either, then?"

Aaron stared back. "My what wouldn't? Who didn't? What fees?"

"Your Original … Oh, he doesn't know," the shifty gentleman said, and the side of his mouth twitched in mockery.

"Another one of *those*," said the disheveled man, but his tone wasn't spiteful so much as tolerantly anticipatory of giving a lecture he'd already delivered several times to students whose orientations were inconveniently staggered. He glanced with pity at Aaron before lowering his gaze to his hands, which fidgeted on the table.

"Probably an organ donor, poor thing," said a woman in a powder-blue suit sitting further down the bench. "Like you, Five-O."

"Certainly not," the first man objected. "He looks twenty-one. Millennials never think that far in advance. Unless his Original was much older and grew him from scratch, like these gems." He jerked his head toward the children on the rug, looking more than a little proud. "... But that technology is too recent for a full-grown result."

"Well, I often wonder," began the woman to her comrades, all of them unconcerned by the growing agitation of the millennial in question, "I wonder how some of them—the Originals, or whoever they hire to do it—manage to carry off the whole procedure without the Duplicate knowing. I myself wasn't told what I was, but of course I figured it out. See, I woke up one day and found myself thinking, Wouldn't it be ideal if there was another of me? I could literally be in two places at once. One of me getting the kids from daycare, and another answering clients and going to the gym and out for a drink with the girls ..."

Her two friends listened to her with the patient indifference of people who have heard a story at least once already but have absolutely nothing better to do with their time.

"Well, as soon as I had that thought, I remembered there *was* a way to do it, if you had the money, and just last week I'd been looking into a company that offered it! Then I thought, But why didn't I go through with it? ... And I had!"

The others chuckled politely.

"And as I realized it, it became clear to me that I was locked in my own garden shed! Cassie, my Original, had gone overboard and had more copies made than she could maintain, and I was ... redundant." Her expression turned distant and dejected. "And here we are," she informed the increasingly bewildered Aaron.

"Mine wanted a companion," the ruffled man told Aaron unhappily. "We were never good at making friends, never clicked with other people. But *together* we could apply ourselves doubly to our creative and scientific endeavours! Imagine having someone close to you who thinks the same way you do, who'd be there for you indefinitely, unconditionally, who could always be relied upon, because they had a mind identical to yours!"

Aaron felt a twinge in his chest that was somehow distinct from the many other anxious, uncomfortable, and confused feelings he was experiencing.

"Why did he get rid of you, then?" the woman asked bluntly.

"The fees!" moaned the man. "We were bankrupted by a government grant that never came through. It was entirely unrelated to the project that resulted in my creation, of course."

"A failed grant—is that the excuse he gave you?" the first man scoffed. "What a reliable soulmate. An eternal bond spoiled by a failed grant. *Unconditional love—*"

"I'll be out of here as soon as he gets his accounts in order!" snapped the disheveled man.

"They imagine a perfect BFF. No arguments. But it's never what they expect," said the other cruelly. "Say, Derick, did he give up his house first? His *laboratory?* Or you?"

"Erick will get me home by the time your kidneys are being harvested!"

"And you, 50117?" The woman interjected. "Tell him your story."

"Organs," the silver-haired man reported to Aaron in a tone that suggested this was the only logical reason for the existence of clones—for that is surely what these three believed themselves to be.

They waited for Aaron to take his turn. He drummed on his thighs.

"Well, I'll play," said the one created for his organs. "You're a youngster, relatively speaking. Your Original is either a whiz kid who did it himself and couldn't afford the upkeep, or an heir who had you made for a lark and found out, as most of them do—" He glanced at Derick, "—that it wasn't as much fun as he thought, and he got bored of you. Am I close?"

"He could be the Duplicate of an autistic savant!" suggested Cassie's clone excitedly. "Are you verbal, sweetheart?"

"N—no, there's been a misunderstanding," Aaron stuttered. "My brother wouldn't—I'm a twin and my—he's—"

"Of course!" She winked. "We're *all* a twin! —If anyone asks."

"I'm, like, a regular person … No offense." He watched them cautiously, but they didn't appear offended in the slightest. "And I have a social insurance number, and I've been alive for almost twenty-six years … and I remember most of it, more or less …"

"You can keep their memories," she explained. "It depends on the process, but many of us have them—Five-O doesn't have his Original's, but I have Cassie's, and Derick has Erick's."

"But they're *my* memo—"

"A SIN number!" Derick broke in excitedly. "I mean, I've got one too—at home!" He had a clipped, ecstatic speaking manner. "But just out of curiosity, how did you get it?" He stood and put an arm around Aaron, who cringed involuntarily. "I heard you can buy one on the internet … People your age know all about that stuff, perhaps I could get your contact …?"

"My brother will get me out," Aaron whispered to no one in particular.

The silver-haired man let out a barking laugh. "Brother? That's sweet. Mine only gave me a serial number. 50117. He didn't actually have fifty thousand copies, mind you; he just had a system for barcodes. Businessman. I hate to break it to you, but your *'brother'*"—his air quotes were dramatic enough that even a perplexed and possibly quite dull young clone couldn't miss them—"probably had a lovely dream for the both of you and then didn't have the work ethic to cover the costs, and ended up changing his mind and moving to the West Coast to follow his bliss and become a Youtuber."

Aaron cleared his throat. "Lack of work ethic is not something Jaymie suffers from," he managed to say firmly. "And he's a musician. He has *always* followed his bliss."

"Well, Jaymie Two-Point-O, I hope for your sake that your presence is a necessary component of either Jaymie's bliss or the continued functioning of his renal system, because otherwise you're in for a pretty grim future," said 50117.

"For fuck's sake, I'm not a clone!" Aaron looked to the fluorescent lights that studded the ceiling in a thick, nacreous pattern high, high above.

"Not to upset you, dear, but let's think for a moment: is your brother the type who might desire a copy of himself for any purpose?—And not necessarily a nefarious purpose!" the woman said, looking sternly at 50117. "Even, perhaps, just on a whim?"

Aaron sat down at the table beside her and put his head in his hands. His brother was exactly the type.

29
Notices

"Doesn't this go against basic human rights in some way?"

Aaron had calmed down after a short panic attack that hadn't surprised or troubled his three new buddies at all ("Quite normal. I experience something like that at least once per day," Derick assured him) and begun quizzing the clones—"Duplicates," to use the terminology they preferred—about the details of their confinement.

"They get around that pretty easily," said the woman, who'd introduced herself midway through his panic attack as Cassie 2.3. "A lot of us aren't real humans, depending on the cloning technique used. My skin is actually a thin polyurethane blend." She offered up a smooth-looking hand for him to admire the naturalness of the material. "There will be more regulations down the road, but the practice is new enough that they're still developing the laws around it."

"Great," said Aaron, confirming the softness of her hand with a light poke, and resisting detaining her palm to use as a worry stone. "And how do we get out if nobody comes to get us?"

"They have to register us and pay Duplication fees," said 50117 boredly.

"And if he doesn't come and pay the … the fees and registration?"

"We'll be dis—" Derick began, but Cassie 2.3 cut him off.

"They're starting a new program where you can be sponsored by a human and start your own life," she said.

"OK, but do I get my one phone call? How do I tell Jaymie to come pay the whatever?"

"They'll contact him," Cassie 2.3 reassured him.

"They'll give him at least four or five notices, usually a month apart, before they ... you know ..." said Derick.

Aaron didn't know, nor did he want to. "Oh my god," he muttered to himself. "I can't do five months here ... But he'll come as soon as they contact him, so it won't be that long. Plus, Mom is coming home tomorrow. Today? Anyway, she can prove I'm real. Unless he doesn't get the notices because they've made a mistake ... Which I'm pretty sure they have ..."

"Mine is working on getting a payment plan," said Cassie 2.3. "She *does* care about us, she just got a little carried away. As soon as she catches up with payments, it'll be back home for me!" She chuckled dolefully and played with the strap of a handbag that hung from her wrist.

"I was grown in a vat," said 50117. He spent the next two hours telling them of his glorious escape from the clandestine company who'd created him (for an exorbitant fee) and how he'd discovered the human world beyond his cage, how he murdered his Original—who had "no use for extra organs now!"—and his subsequent capture by the collectors while in the process of having two new clones of his own created. He was currently waiting to hear from his lawyer whether the murder could be deemed an act of self-defence, considering the circumstances of his birth, and if he could look for a sponsor and start a life.

Aaron zoned in and out, drumming on the table and missing all the things captive people miss, like his brothers and his mom and videogames. He wished he were more action-oriented; if Jaymie were in his position he would have orchestrated a grand escape for all of them by now, or at least scrutinized the hierarchy amongst the prisoners and established himself at the top of it.

Of course, he knew Jaymie would never have ended up in his position, because no matter how lonely Aaron got, he would never have thought of "duplicating" himself, and so would never have created a Jaymie to get clone-napped in the first place ... He shook his head and reminded himself that he was not a project of his brother's, and that this was a misunderstanding.

"It likely won't be long. He just needs to sign some things and pay." Derick had noticed his unease and was trying to be comforting, in his awkward, morose way. Aaron looked back into the watery, nervous eyes of the man who'd been painstakingly created for the sake of companionship and felt an odd kinship with him.

He thought of the fight he and Jaymie had had in June, when he'd taken a break from practicing five nights a week to go to evening classes and attempt to finish high school over the summer. Jaymie had melodramatically left home for ten days and written his most angsty hypothetical album to date. Of course, Aaron and Rex had soon rescued him and they'd compromised on a lighter summer performance schedule.

The two were often good friends, but they also fought, and that one had been particularly bad. The next time they'd disagreed, shortly afterward, Aaron had expedited the conflict process by quitting the band, and Jaymie, having neither the time nor motivation for a week hungry and sleepless on a broken couch writing another ten songs, had simply replaced him with Garrett; he'd hired a lead guitarist a week earlier, and he figured you might as well get your new players trained at the same time if you were going to change the lineup anyway. It might have been a permanent solution had Garrett's choices not offended dear Anika.

It had taken some time, after Aaron rejoined the band and helped with the pumpkin theft, for the tension to fully dissipate. He now considered whether Jaymie still harboured resentment toward him for not being an enthusiastic bandmate. Then he wondered if Jaymie even thought about him enough to harbour resentment, and how long it would take Jaymie to notice he was gone, and if, rather than come find him, Jaymie might just hire a more agreeable drummer.

"He's probably scraping up the money now!" said Derick.

"I'm not sure that's going to happen," said Aaron. He looked around the friendly dungeon and knew he might not be able to rely on a rescue. He'd have to fend for himself for now. An unexpected thought entered his mind: What Would Jaymie Do?

"My plan," 50117 was expounding, "is that people still need organs, right? And they're willing to pay good money for them! My kidneys are my ticket out of here, baby!"

"It's hard to find sponsors," Derick quietly explained to Aaron. "The program is new, so nobody knows about it, and even if they did, who wants to take in a potentially murderous clone they've never met?"

"My Original must have relatives who've pickled their livers and will sponsor me in return for half of mine! Even a non-relative—I'm type O-negative, and that's got to count for something!"

"No such luck for me," said Cassie 2.3. She looked down at her midriff and gave Aaron a sad smile. "I doubt I have organs."

Jo finished her cold coffee and laid down with her head on some mail that was stacked at the end of the couch. The three ancient cats flowed silently out of the cat flap into the porch, and slowly eased themselves on top of her as though believing that, if they were silent enough and slow enough, she might not notice. She cuddled them miserably.

The cats had survived the Brzezinskis' long absence in November. The cult had not arranged for their feeding (villainy!), and they'd finished their weekend's rations in the first afternoon, nudged their way out their little door, and slunk off down the street to seek their fortunes. By the time Anika thought to check in, midweek, they were long gone.

Dick, the eldest and a lover of comfort and good times, had immediately found another pet flap down the block, which was used by the dachshund residing in that home.

He'd entered confidently, disguised himself as a damp bath mat eternally hanging to dry—which each of the two human inhabitants assumed their spouse had, for some stupid reason not worth developing communication skills over, carelessly left there—and thrived cozily on dog food and bathwater, napping twenty-two hours per day until the Brzezinskis' van reappeared in their driveway. Then he extricated himself from the towel rack, creaked back down the block, and crept back into the bed of Jaymie, who was his personal favourite because he didn't wake up when Dick slept on his face. The hungry and confused dachshund felt great relief.

Diana, the second sibling, had made her way downtown and put her vocal prowess to use busking in front of a beer vendor on Main Street, in hopes of being discovered and booked at the cabaret/comedy venue across the street. The time was right; she'd been doubling the Brzezinskis' harmonies an octave up for the entirety of their lives, and she wasn't getting any younger.

She was promptly taken to the pound and scheduled for euthanasia— an appointment which was bumped up when she made her singing skills known. Her passion for music was infectious; soon the entire doomed menagerie had formed an ungodly choir from their various cages, and they might all have been exterminated at once except that a pet rescue initiative was doing its pre-Christmas rounds, and it swept them up and brought them to a no-kill shelter.

Amidst the activity, she slipped out of her cage and spent a week hiking in the Assiniboine Forest on an Eat-Pray-Love-style quest far more meaningful than the stardom she'd previously sought. She received a thorough petting from Jaymie's recent former-lover, Mira, who lived nearby and often walked in the woods to soothe her healing heart.

Then she returned home to the care and ministrations of the middle Brzezinski, whose name she had not bothered to memorize but whom she recognized by smell and touch as being the one who was home the most and therefore most likely to dole out meals.

Herman, the youngest, moved to Nashville and invested in a recording studio that was on the verge of going under. He had an ear for talent—or rather, he was stone deaf, but he'd seen many trends come and go in his long life, and he could recognize an artist with a certain attitude and look about them. He bet on the right up-and-coming country star, made a hit record, re-released it in Spotify-friendly one-minute remixes, and watched as the streams rolled in.

He frequented the classic venues, sired broods of kittens with felines decades younger than himself, forgot his old life (such is the memory span of cats), and might have continued building his empire indefinitely had he not attended a touring Cirque du Soleil afterparty where he was recognized—even with a lady cat on each arm—by the circus's principal saxophonist, who gave him a scolding and a snuggle and then anonymously mailed him in a cat carrier to the three Brzezinskis, who were relieved to have the last member of the household accounted for before the date their family was due to visit.

He forgot the whole charade and returned to his old hobbies of staring at the closet door for no reason and following Rex—who as a child had neither squeezed him too hard nor drummed on him—around from room to room, meowing, also for no reason.

Jo blinked awake as her empty paper cup slid from her fingers, hit the floor, and rolled under the couch. She realized she'd been dozing on the pile of mail. The black print on the letters blurred in and out of focus under her tired gaze. She shifted under the cats and kissed the largest on the nose, mumbling, "Did you invest in a studio? Yes you did *oh yes you did* ..."

Then the print on the top envelope fuzzed into view, and she noticed something very, very odd.

***

Aaron stared at a plate of food he'd curated from the lunch buffet set up nearby. The sandwiches and salads were neither very good nor the bland, sterile hospital food he'd been expecting. They were entirely inoffensive.

He knew he'd overexerted his adrenal system in the last twenty-four hours; his last panic attack had left him shaky, with a dull, nauseous coil in his stomach and a distinctly grumpy temperament. Part of him felt annoyed that in this entire ordeal he hadn't come to any physical harm except for the discomfort his own body was causing him in response to it. Still, he was fairly certain there was an official-sounding term for that in the future lawsuit he was planning.

"How long do we stay here after the warnings are given?" he asked his lunchmates.

The clones took conveniently large bites of their sandwiches, except for Cassie 2.3, who did not need to eat.

"It sort of depends," she said.

"Until they decide your time's up," said 50117 as he chewed.

"*His* time should've been up ages ago," said Derick. "He's been here months and months. We suspect he bribed the authorities."

"Suspect no longer—I *did* bribe them!" announced 50117, having apparently found the right moment to cash in on a mystery that had been unfolding over months, and which elicited little exclamations from the others, but which Aaron had no investment in whatsoever. "Gave them far more than the cost of registration would've been. Unlike *some people* nowadays, I actually *worked* while I was out there in the world. Did pretty well for myself! And money is power. Did you think of that when you decided to become a musician, boy?"

"You mean, did I imagine myself mistaken for a clone and in need of thousands of dollars to bribe the government?" said Aaron, feeling testy. "No, Five-O, I guess I didn't have your foresight. Hey—why don't they let us pay our own registration and be done with it?"

"Because of monsters like him," said Derick, glaring at 50117.

"I'm not ashamed of who I am! As soon as I'm out of here, I'm going to make more clones of myself! And harvest their organs and live forever!" exulted 50117.

"We've been here several weeks now," said Cassie 2.3, indicating herself and Derick. "Our Originals didn't respond well to the first warning."

"Erick and I tried to escape over the border and hide out in Fargo until the collectors gave up. ... They found us," said Derick, in a voice like a descending trombone glissando.

"As I said, Cassie hid me in the garden shed. I don't get cold, so at least there's that." She gave a short laugh and pulled a nail buffer from her bag to occupy her smooth, smooth hands.

"So, both our Originals had to give us up, for the time being, until they can finish the registration," said Derick, glumly watching her shine her nails.

"*Or* until all their warnings have been given, and it can be assumed they've abandoned you," 50117 reminded them.

"So, if your Original didn't do anything against the rules, like ours did, he probably would have received the notices while you were still with him," Cassie 2.3 explained to Aaron, ignoring 50117's provocations.

"He'd have told me, though," said Aaron. "I mean, I think he would …"

"*Unless* he showed signs of being an irresponsible or unsuitable clone owner—harvesting your bone marrow, training you as a secret weapon against his enemies—"

"No, and no," said Aaron.

"—Trying to escape with you or hide you in the shed …"

"Oh my god," Aaron sat up hopefully. "We toured to Regina and got kidnapped by this messed up cult—would that count as irresponsible?"

"Regina? It sounds promising," said Derick.

"If it counts, he won't have gotten the warnings yet. You just need to sit tight!" said Cassie 2.3, patting his arm. "Would you like to help me braid my hair?"

Aaron gave up trying to eat the over-dressed salad on his plate and said, "There must be a manager here. A supervisor. How is there nobody I can ask about it!"

"Of course there's somebody," said Derick, surprised.

"You can go talk to the Director," nodded Cassie 2.3.

"The Director?" said Aaron.

"Of Clone Services." Derick pointed. "He's down that hall."

"Do I need … an appointment … or something?" Aaron felt stupid, though he reminded himself that this was all entirely mind-boggling and there was no reason he should feel foolish.

"Yes, and you have one!" said Cassie 2.3 brightly. "We're all allowed a meeting with him when we get here."

"For clarification," Derick clarified.

"And to help get settled in," said Cassie 2.3.

"I think we've covered everything, honestly. But if it'd help you feel better ..." Derick again gestured encouragingly toward a hallway leading out of the room on the far side.

"Yes. It would help me feel better." With some aggression Aaron set down his plastic fork, which clattered through a slat in the picnic table and smeared greasy penne onto the fake grass below. "Fucking Director of ... You're shitting me ..."

He left the clones to their perpetual milling around and walked down a long, fluorescently lit corridor to find the Director of Clone Services.

30

Director of the Clone Department

Aaron found the office of the director, which was behind one of only a few doors and was labelled by a plaque. In a fit of indignant bravery, he threw the door open and strode in.

"Welcome! Please have a seat," said a clean-cut man sitting behind a large desk, typing at his computer. He gave a friendly smile. "Whichever chair you like."

"Oh," said Aaron, losing his momentum. "Thank you."

"Sooo … you don't think you're a clone …" he said, with the patient tone of someone for whom "Doesn't think he's a clone" was the most common duty in his job description.

"I'm not one!" Aaron snapped, pulling out the nearest chair. "I tried to tell them!"

"Right …" The man swivelled to face him. He picked up a pen, scribbled what looked like "DTHAC," on a sparsely filled out form, straightened some papers, and then grinned through steepled fingers. "Your Original is …" He glanced down. "Jaymie Brzezinski."

"Ugh, who are you, how do you know our names …" Aaron ran a hand through his hair and bounced on the edge of his seat.

"I assure you, I'm not an enemy. I'm middle management. I look after Clone Affairs."

"Clone Affairs …"

"And I'm working overtime on a Saturday right now," he added, as though Aaron should appreciate this sacrifice. "So, let's look at the facts! Jaymie. Does he look just like you?"

"Yes—he's my brother! We look alike, but we're just brothers, we're not—look, I can remember my childhood and everything. Unless you think somebody cloned Jaymie at *birth*, which is still ridiculous—although I wouldn't really put it past my mom, come to think of it. She really likes him. But then I can't see how either of us is to blame …"

"The only thing cloned in the nineties was Dolly the sheep," said the man offhandedly. "Our reports say he made you fairly recently."

"Jesus Christ!"

"And unfortunately, he failed to use the legal avenues." With a look of patronizing apology, he pedantically recited: "Without regulations, everyone'd clone themselves left, right and centre, wouldn't they? Babies everywhere that only exist to be harvested for their aortas—"

"OK, I get it! People want organs. Again, *my childhood*, though."

"Many clones are formed with the Original's memories intact. OMIs."

"No, my memories are *with* my Orig—with Jaymie! Not *as* him!"

"It's not impossible. Things happen as part of the process, especially if they used a sophisticated method. Artificial Regrowth, ARG, for instance. Some are led to believe they're a grandchild of their creator, when in reality they're going to lose their lungs to him or her at some point. It's a major crisis right now. Has your *brother* ever made any comments that suggest …"

"Like, 'Take care of those kidneys, Aaron, I'm going to need one some day'? Yeah, all the time. It's a *joke*. That's just what he's like!"

"Are you certain your *brother* wasn't being serious? Just to rule out the possibility—"

"Never," Aaron said adamantly. "He fully believes he's invincible." He thought about the Director's implication and got a feeling of horror. "You think he'd *plan* that … agh …"

"And that's the reason we exist." The man smiled. "We've saved many of that type of clone from abrupt and inhumane deaths. Did you see those tiny children out there? Imagine what would become of those poor GFIs without us! And, when we've expanded our budget, we'll start the rehabilitation program and all of them can have sponsors and integrate into society and, hopefully, live as contributing citizens!"

"I *am* a contributing citizen—I mean, OK, I'm a musician, I don't pay taxes. But still."

"Lovely …" The man typed up a quick email. "You know, I tried to learn guitar once—"

"OK, so will the sponsor stuff happen soon? I'm supposed to play a show tomorrow, and I have family coming to visit …" Aaron had little hope for the answer.

"It's in progress," said the man, deeply interested in his computer screen.

"So, you're just going to take someone's word for it that I'm a fake human, and I deserve to be locked up …" Aaron could feel another panic attack coming on.

"No, no! We always look at the paperwork."

"The paper—"

"Look, uh,"—the man glanced at a file in front of him—"Jaymie."

"Aaron!"

"Sorry, shouldn't have assumed. So many Duplicates feel most comfortable taking the name of their Original. Aaron, I can see you're upset, and I don't think you're lying. I can spot the ones playing dumb. Occasionally, an Original doesn't tell their Duplicate what it really is. Aaron, you seem like the analytical, critical-of-the-government, independently-educated type—"

"You don't even know me!"

"—which I admire. Government intervention makes many people uncomfortable."

"I'm all for public services—"

"Perhaps it'll be a comfort to learn that we *aren't* the government. I serve as a liaison, but the work is contracted out to us. We're a unique agency with sensitive specializations."

"Like a not-for-profit?"

"Right. But for profit."

"How is that supposed to be comforting!" Aaron brought his palms down on the desk with a papery smack, and the manager launched his swivel chair back a few feet.

"Let me take a different tack here. We've been watching you for some time now—"

"Aah, I hate it."

"—and there are often signs …" He pedalled forward again, letting the suggestion hang.

"… Signs you're a clone?"

The man clicked his pen. "Duplicates have differing lifespans, depending on the creation process. Some expire sooner than others. Like, Synthetically—well, let's just call them SMCs."

"OK, so?"

"Are there any parts of you … any elements … that have been, shall we say, *malfunctioning* in recent times?"

"Malfunctioning? What? No?" Aaron felt like a patient in the wrong doctor's office undressing for an operation meant for someone else.

"Do you ever have periods of time you can't remember?"

"OK, everyone gets drunk and blacks out now and then, it just takes a little less to get me there—"

"Find that your mind isn't working the way it should in a particular situation?"

"Yes, but—"

"Parts of your body won't obey you properly—"

"I have an anxiety dis—"

"And it's been getting gradually worse as time goes on?"

"I … but …"

"Tell me, would your *brother* ever—"

"Can you please stop saying *brother* like it's in quotation marks?"

"Is *Jaymie* the sort of person who might, even just on a passing impulse …?" The man's upbeat voice had taken on the lull of a zoned-out therapist directing a petulant client toward a particularly obvious minor epiphany.

"Yeah," said Aaron dismally. "He is, but—"

"Perhaps you want to think on it." The man glanced at his wrist and Aaron sensed that his allotted appointment time was running out.

"Do I get my phone call, or something? So I can explain this to him?"

"No need! He has been and/or will be contacted."

"Yeah, but can I just—"

"He'll be contacted," the man said with calm finality. "The situation will be explained with utmost clarity. Give it a few business days. Don't worry—we follow up with OGs at least four times before assuming they've decided to forfeit clone privileges. It can be upsetting for people to speak with their Duplicates if they *don't* have the intention of registering them."

"Come on, seriously? Can I call my other sibling?"

"Outside contact is restricted. It almost invariably results in an '*I'm* the Original—no *I'm* the Original' sort of standoff. It's very stressful for friends and relatives."

"So then what if he doesn't come get me?" Aaron asked in desperation.

"As I said, we've applied for an increase in government funding and are in the process of implementing and marketing a wonderful sponsorship system to find homes for abandoned clones. Unfortunately, government approval moves slowly, and until they get the protocols in place, we have to move subjects into the next phase. Otherwise, we get short on space."

"The next phase."

"TNP."

"Wait, do you have the clones *put down*? Like a pet you can't take care of?" Aaron tried and failed to keep his voice steady.

"All the pets here are well provided for until they die of natural causes! Which brings me to …" He beckoned over Aaron's shoulder. A tall man had been standing there, unnoticed by Aaron, and this man's sudden movement startled him. The man set on the desk a small, brown-freckled cat, which flumped onto its side on a pile of papers.

"This is Jane Dough—dough like playdough, ha ha. Janey, we call her!" announced the Director.

"Janey …" Aaron stared at her in vexation.

"She's our most popular pet therapy cat. As I said, we got an increase in funding, so it might be cushier here than you expected! Would you like to play on an Xbox while you wait?"

"… Yes please."

"Now, do you sleep?"

"What?" Aaron sighed in frustration. "Yes, I fucking sleep."

"Of course you do—but it'd be another sign you're a clone, if you didn't, wouldn't it! We'll assign you a room with a bed. Snacks? I'll assume you eat, as well. OK, you're not taken with the cat, I see …" He gestured to the other man, who reached to pick up the floppy animal.

"Leave the cat," said Aaron. He looked more closely at the tall man and recognized him as one of the collectors who'd chased him down. The oily pasta churned in his stomach.

"Ah, you've already met Spencer, from the CC Department. He's applied to move to the logistical side of the company. We're about to go through some paperwork."

Spencer gave Aaron a guilty smile, and Aaron understood he was being dismissed.

"Collections work can be demanding," the Director continued. "It's not for everyone. Some suffer burnout, even with the supports we offer," he told Aaron, who was not particularly interested in understanding the turnover rate for people who hunt down clones for a living.

"I'm going to end up with PTSD in this job," Spencer laughed self-consciously.

Aaron picked up the cat, which purred limply in his hands, cast the two men a last resentful stare, and went to find the Xbox.

Jaymie and Rex went to the police station, where Jaymie made a report that, predictably, took much longer than necessary and was so convoluted and full of digressions and reminiscences that the officer interviewing him decided it should be audio-recorded to determine whether Jaymie himself might be responsible for his brother's disappearance and, once that possibility was eliminated, to review later for the entertainment of himself and his coworkers.

When Jaymie and Rex—who had not had the opportunity to speak for the entire time—returned home later in the afternoon, they found Jo slowly freezing on their porch couch, huddled under her own and Aaron's coats and covered in cats. She shed them gratefully.

Once they were all in the warm kitchen, she produced a paper bag of bagels, saying, "I went to the place down the street … I'm not good at this … I didn't know what to do."

"We forgot about eating," said Rex, taking the gift.

"How could I possibly consume food at a time like this?" said Jaymie, still desolate.

"You should eat a bagel," said Rex.

"It might help keep your strength up?" tried Jo.

"No seriously," Rex muttered to her. "He'll have, like, a complete fucking tantrum and he'll be useless." Rex forced a bagel into Jaymie's hand. "Eat it!"

He sat and stared at the bagel, legs vibrating. "Were there signs of a struggle?" he asked.

"I don't think so. The snowbank might have been a little scuffed up … Or did I do that …?" She wished she'd looked more closely; it had been hard to think straight.

"It's like he just vanished! That murderer—! It's all my fault!"

"No," said Jo, surprising herself with her own conviction. "The killer's not a wendigo. Jaymie, you and I saw what that guy—or thing—does! It makes a big fucking horror spectacle of its victims! It doesn't just quietly vanish them and hide the body in the river."

"Oh god, Aar-bear in the river!"

"No, I'm saying that *didn't* happen …"

"The river is frozen, Jaymie," Rex reminded him. "Nobody is in the river."

"OK, what do *you* think happened, Rex? Because I notice you're pretty nonchalant about all this." Jaymie ignored his bagel and alternatingly rubbed the knuckles of his hands in a blatant signal of disrupted homeostasis.

"*Nonchalant?* I'm—look, if I got completely distraught every time I woke up and one of you wasn't around, I'd never get anything done!" Rex's own bagel sat untouched.

"OK, but *we* always know where each other is," said Jaymie. "Aar can't even go an hour without telling me what he's doing right then."

"Yeah, I think you guys should get that looked at," Rex shot back.

"There must be another explanation," said Jo, fighting against the contagiousness of Jaymie's despair. "OK, no judgement, but I've noticed Aaron gets kind of thrown off sometimes. And makes unusual decisions. Is that the right way to say that?"

"You don't have to sugarcoat it," said Rex. "It gives me a lot of hope at the moment."

"He always comes home, though!" said Jaymie.

"Yeah, but you guys disappear without explanation all the time—this isn't that different," said Rex. They turned to Jo. "When I was seven we went to this festival our mom was playing, and it was really loud and crowded and dog-friendly, and he disappeared for so long Mom thought he got abducted, but he was just camped out in a granary all day with his sketchpad. That's the year we got cell phones."

"His coat, though!" Jaymie reminded them. "It was freezing out."

"Couldn't he have taken it off, though, if he thought he had to move quickly, and it was too bulky?"

"What a dumb thing to do!"

"But if he'd gotten … confused…" Rex was grasping at possibilities, and Jo felt a swell of sympathy and affection for them. She desperately wanted to believe Rex was right. She racked her brain for more ideas—and then remembered the envelopes she'd found in the porch. She'd assumed they were a joke, and then forgotten them while out getting bagels.

"Not to change the subject, and I'm not trying to make fun of something while there's this serious thing …" Jo slipped out into the porch, returning with the stack of very cold mail. "… But what the hell is a 'Clone Collection Agency?'"

"What!" Rex snorted gloomily. "I don't know. We don't read the mail. It's all for our mom, or it's old-people magazines that don't know our grandparents moved twenty years ago."

"You're a mailman who doesn't read his mail?" Jo asked Jaymie incredulously. "Because these are all for *you!*"

"He opens the heating bill. You pay the heating bill, right? We do have heat …" Rex stopped and stared at Jaymie, who had gone stark white, transfixed by the letters in Jo's hands.

"Clone collection …" His brow furrowed in consternation.

Seeing his expression, Rex snatched a letter from Jo and tore it open. "… Received a number of warnings … relinquish rights to clone ownership … register and pay appropriate late fees … Duplicate will be *revoked* … What the *actual fuck*, Jaymie?"

"Oh shit. I might've seen the first one …" Jaymie mumbled, as Rex tore into the next envelope. "But that was, like, months ago. And I forgot."

"Pay at Duplicate Registration Offices … blah blah final warning blah blah please note that Offices do not have access to confiscated clones … Jaymie, there are like *six* of these!"

"Ugh, clone sharks! What do they want … I have no clone," said Jaymie dully.

"You *have no clone?* What are you, a mad scientist in a sci-fi movie? Like, denouncing an evil creation that betrayed you? What a fucking weird thing to say!" Rex's voice revved into a wavery, hysterical pitch.

Jaymie gazed down at the bagel, which was now smooshed into a neat and unappetizing noose in his hands. He took a bite, and then jumped up, looked around the floor for his jacket, instead grabbed Aaron's off Jo's arm, and said to Rex, "I'll be back later tonight. If I'm not then I probably got murdered by that murderer. There are people who will take care of you."

"I don't need taking care of," they protested, but the door slammed behind him.

Rex looked to Jo, who stood helplessly, holding the rest of Jaymie's mail. "What a lunatic," they said, and began quietly to cry.

31

Clone Affairs

Late that night Aaron woke to a tapping on the door of his room. The anxiety that had exhausted him enough to let him sleep also made it easy to shake off his drowsiness, though he was certain he hadn't been under long; he could still see only a square of darkness through the tiny window above him.

The room he'd been given was just large enough to fit a single bed and night table. The window was too small and the glass too thick for any hope of escape. A large framed photograph on the wall showed a view of an island oasis so hideously far removed from the frozen reality outside his window as to be abhorrent.

After an evening playing Mortal Kombat in the common area, he had more or less resigned himself to spending a few days cooped up. He regretted having to miss his family gathering and the tribute show they'd thoroughly rehearsed for. On the other hand, he was relieved to skip the stress of both events, especially if it was through no fault of his own; if Jaymie had wanted a clone this badly, then Jaymie could deal with the consequences.

This part of the situation was still baffling to him. Aaron hadn't kept up to date on the scientific possibilities and politics surrounding cloning, since following current events generally upscaled his anxiety from situational to existential levels. So it was with limited information that he'd come up with a few theories to explain his predicament.

In one, there really *had* been an Aaron, who'd recently died somehow—maybe at the hands of the cult—and it was *him* that Jaymie had cloned, with all *his* memories, and the agency hadn't realized the difference.

Or maybe he really was a Duplicate of Jaymie, but some cat hair had gotten mixed in, with its accompanying genetic coding, and it was he (the cat) who had grown up with a beloved brother quite unlike himself, hence his (Aaron's) confusion about not having Jaymie's memories … He was still working on this one.

Alternatively, everyone in the world was a clone of Jaymie Brzezinski, and Aaron and all of humanity lay in pods somewhere in the future, experiencing an illusory, computer-simulated time loop of false reality; the luckiest would be given a choice of variously-coloured pills so they could be freed from the cycle and assume their true form as Jaymie Brzezinski again.

Janey, the therapy cat, meowed from her spot on the bedside table. She'd spent the evening licking herself, making it clear that, as his live-in therapist, she was still entitled to self-care time. The knock came again.

He didn't say "Come in," because he didn't want whoever was knocking to come in, but he was too polite to say "Go away," so he said nothing, and the door opened anyway.

He sucked in air as a silhouette appeared in the doorway.

"Jaymie 2.0?" came a tentative voice. He released the breath and reached to turn on the desk lamp.

"It's *Aaron*," he said. "Cassie, right?"

"Cassie … Nobody's ever called me that before," said the clone woman wistfully.

"Well, Cassie the First isn't here, and neither are Cassies Two-Point-Zero-through-Two, so I'm not exactly going to get confused, am I?"

"No, you're not," she chuckled softly. "In fact, I worked—I mean, Cassie works—as a lawyer. We try to make things as un-confusing as possible, when it suits us."

"That's refreshing, considering everyone else I've met in the last day or so." Aaron suddenly imagined the weeks Cassie 2.3 had spent in this strange place, with only the company of the cynical 50117 and downtrodden Derick. Pity stirred in him. He pushed aside his blankets and shuffled to the edge of the bed, glad he hadn't felt like undressing before turning in.

"I hope I didn't disturb you," she said, sitting down beside him and smoothing her suit over her knees. "Those are very nice jeans."

"Thank you. They're my brother's."

"I haven't felt denim yet, in real life." She rubbed one of his belt loops between her fingers to appreciate the texture, and went on, "I didn't realize you were a sleeper. I've been playing cards with Derick, since he doesn't sleep either. He's a nice fellow, but he gets a little exhausting." She grimaced delicately.

Cassie 2.3 appeared to be in her early or mid-thirties. The corners of her eyes showed pretty creases of tiredness, no doubt inherited from her hyper-achieving Original.

"Yeah, I can imagine," said Aaron. "So, you're one of the … non-sleepers?"

"The design is more efficient that way," she explained. "They could've added sleep into my programming, but it would've been an extra step, and what would be the point?"

"Mercy?" Aaron joked weakly, and immediately felt bad. "Sorry, I just kind of enjoy sleeping, as long as I'm not having nightmares—but lots of people don't like it! Like my brother. He isn't really into it. People like him would love not to have to sleep!"

"I suspect I wouldn't like having to sleep either, based on Original Cassie. I do wish I could try it out, though."

"I'm sorry," said Aaron, meaning it.

"Still, there are other sleep-*related* activities I'm capable of …"

Aaron stared at her blankly. "Like, unconsciousness?"

"I might not have been alive long, but I do have all the memories from Cassie's life. I know how to do things." She smiled.

"That's nice," said Aaron, nonplussed.

"And it might be nice to *do things* one more time, in case I never make it out of here. Do you catch my drift?"

"Oh, um, *things,*" said Aaron, catching her drift. She shifted her thigh against his, and let go of his belt loop to take his hand. He tensed, utterly unprepared for such an upfront proposition. His rational brain prepared to verbally defend against an act that would surely be absurd under such circumstances, even as a tiny reptilian part of his mind exploratorily sent tendrils deep down to see whether there wasn't some shred of prurient curiosity to be dredged up. "Ah, hmm, Cassie, you're very nice. And you're *very* pretty." He wondered if she could feel his palm starting to sweat.

"Cassie got into skincare early in life," she said, pleased. "Coconut oil."

"It's just, I might not be the best choice for—the thing is—"

"I'm made out of plastic and I'm *technically* a virgin, so pregnancy and STIs are not a concern," she assured him.

"No, it's—wow, I wasn't even thinking about that—it's just sometimes, especially if I've been nervous, it's difficult to get comfortable with new people ..." His face heated under her hopeful gaze, and he drew on all the communication skills in his arsenal. "See, I get nervous in bad situations, but also in *good* situations, like playing a show, or on a date with a girl—I might feel like it would be nice to be intimate, but then I'll worry she'll be disappointed, or she's secretly a murderer, or for no reason at all ... I'm just nervous in general."

Cassie 2.3 contemplated the heinous coastal utopia on the wall and held his hand absently. He wondered if she was offended by the soft-rejection, and whether she might become upset. He continued, "Maybe, if we got to know each other ..."

"That all sounds perfectly reasonable," she said. "But allow me to present one single, low-pressure argument for not being nervous."

"Oh?"

"If we don't get sponsored right away—which we won't—we'll be dismantled. TNP-ed. Cassie worked enough corporate cases to see through the jargon, believe me. The collectors brought in another two after you went to bed, so the company is at capacity. The bullshit about getting more government money? Guaranteed it's just padding paychecks at the top. I doubt we have long. It could be tomorrow, if your notices have already been mailed out."

Her sweet voice was a mismatch with the cold facts, and it took Aaron a moment to say, "We're getting The Next Phased? Wait—mailed? *Mailed out?* They *mail* them? Oh. Shit."

"For me, dismantling equates to indefinite standby. For you, probably more like going to sleep forever. So, it's a good thing you like sleeping." She smirked, but not unkindly.

"Sleeping ..." Aaron stared straight ahead. "And this is a reason *not* to be nervous ..."

"Unless you just have an Off switch somewhere?" Her fingernails lifted the back of his T-shirt to examine him, one of her dark braids brushing against his spine. "No, you're real, alright. Nice soft skin."

"Thanks ... It's from ... being a human."

"I'm fascinated by the clones that are made like real humans," said Cassie 2.3, letting his shirt fall. "Five-O is one too, but he's insufferable … Should I not touch your clothes? I recall some humans don't like it."

"I don't mind, although if our roles were reversed, we might be in sketchy territory," said Aaron, still feeling dazed.

"Anyway, if it's all going to be over soon, Jaymie 2.0, what have you got to lose?"

She'd undone the top button on her blouse with the hand that wasn't holding his. She had long, glossy nails painted the same powder blue as her suit.

"I'm not Jaymie Two-Point …" he began, and then whispered to himself, "What Would Jaymie …?"

"Yes, fascinating," she murmured, cataloguing the freckles on his neck.

With monumental effort, Aaron pulled his shit together. He analyzed the situation. He felt around internally for whether the reptile brain had unearthed any nascent horniness. It had. He investigated whether he possessed anything like Rex's healthy hesitation toward radical intimacy in the face of traumatic injustice. He didn't. (He could almost hear his sibling's voice calling out the hypocrisy. But whatever—it wasn't like it was *Cassie* who'd "collected" him.)

"What a rollercoaster," he said. He turned to her, and she gave him a plasticky but soft kiss on the mouth, awakening a pleasant curiosity. He allowed her to pull his shirt over his head, and then, to his own surprise, he helped her undo the remaining buttons on her blouse and touched her side to feel the smooth polyurethane, which he was impressed to find very convincingly like the real thing.

He slid further back onto the bed, still holding her hand. She saw she was about to succeed in her venture, gave a frolicsome grin, and finished shedding her upper garments. He was careful not to stare, realizing this had the potential to be a fairly positive final experience before his dismembering, or whatever it was.

He'd always accepted that there was no length of dry spell that could push him to *do it* with a plastic person. He and Jaymie had been educated by their mother not to equate people with objects—and also, sex dolls, like all dolls, were creepy.

But he hadn't imagined a plastic partner with lovely smooth braids who could talk and feel and express in as many words that they wouldn't be offended if you had a panic attack in the middle of making out with them.

He didn't wonder about it any further, because by then the clone woman, who really was a go-getter, had undone his belt, unzipped his jeans, and leaned over his waist. A cascade of braids pattered against his skin, and by the time it fully registered in Aaron's mind that this was actually happening, he found he was too distracted to panic anyway.

The following evening, Jaymie showed up too late for the tribute show. Everyone had already left. The empty venue was dark except for the stage lights, which emitted a deep red ambience that drew him toward the stage even as his instincts warned him that everything was wrong. The microphone had come loose from its clip and now dangled by its cord from the mic stand, swaying in a non-existent breeze.

He hoisted himself onto the stage, his body seeming to move according to a will not his own. Stepping over a monitor, he grasped the mic and tapped it. At his touch, a thunderous heartbeat resounded from the too-many monitors onstage.

He croaked, "Check, one two—" and his voice blared back at him, all reverb and echoes and none of the genuine timbre of the dry signal. The mic was mixed too hot and improperly grounded; an electric shock snapped through his lips and a shriek of feedback assaulted him from the monitors. He realized the whole stage was monitors—just a jumble of unnecessary speakers with loops and coils of cords sliding between them, like a huge nest of garter snakes writhing through a pit of rocks. Or were they the angry, empty vines from a stripped pumpkin plant?

He began singing a song where all the words were backwards, and with each line he sang, he learned more of what had happened to his friends. The murderer had torn through his band, driving Jo away and hunting Rex into a frozen tundra desert-scape devoid of hiding spots ... He choked and stopped singing. The feedback remained, a dull ache on high C.

He ignored the voice that hissed in his head like a guy in a movie theatre issuing warnings at the screen, and threaded his way between monitors toward the back of the stage—*don't do it, buddy*—hating every step through the living, seething cables, and he didn't want to look but there was a red spill leaking from under the bass drum, and behind the hi-hat—*no don't look, turn back*—a pale, long-fingered hand reached forevermore toward a stray drumstick—

Jaymie woke up gasping. His stomach was in painful knots. He tried to curl into the fetal position but couldn't—a weight pressed hard into his chest, too heavy for a cat. Straining to see in the dark of his bedroom, he made out a wide brown eye peeking at him from under a veil of floppy hair, inches from his face.

"Jesus Christ, what the fuck!" Jaymie shouted. "Where have you—you scared the shit out of me!" He planted his palm on the forehead in front of him and sat up, pushing it away. "Where the hell have you been! I've been going crazy! I went out and—are you teaching me a lesson for going off with Daffodile? I get it. I'm sorry, OK? Motherfucker! I thought you got murdered!"

Something wasn't right.

"We've been looking, fucking, everywhere … I dreamed you died … Why did you leave me! Put the light on, for fuck's sake." Jaymie panted, losing steam. A freezing draught was coming through the window, which hung wide open. The breeze blew the curtain further aside, and in the moonlight a sliver of his brother's face was visible, eyebrow raised sardonically. Snowflakes dusted his hair.

"I had to talk to the frigging cops—not that they'll even do anything … Did you come through the *window?* … Quit screwing with me! … What's wrong with you!" Jaymie suddenly had the feeling he was about to wake up a second time, alone. He suspected he was stuck in a loop where you wake from a nightmare into another nightmare, indefinitely.

The visitor cocked his head. His freckles flashed in the light. But Aaron had always had that little pattern like Ursa Minor above his right eye, and now he didn't. His face was a little fuller, his chest had broadened almost imperceptibly—only someone who knew him very well would have noticed. Jaymie's stomach dropped. This man was more like … him.

"I heard you were looking for me," grinned the creature.

32

Jymmy

Jaymie had fully intended to register his clone. It wasn't like he planned to hide the poor guy in the basement for the rest of their lives. He could afford the fees; he had a day job and didn't pay rent. What he hadn't expected was for the clone to disappear within an hour of its creation. Having shown such a complete lack of gratitude, Jaymie reasoned that it could go ahead and register itself.

He'd shrugged off the first notice from the agency. If *he* hadn't been able to track down his clone, what luck would the government have? He left the subsequent letters unopened.

The doppelganger perched on his bed was correct—Jaymie had been out searching for him several hours earlier. As soon as Jo had shown him his mail, he'd begun to suspect that Aaron's disappearance was somehow related.

He'd headed downtown, trying to think of a strategy for finding the second Jaymie, whom he hadn't seen since its invention almost six months ago. Finally, he'd asked himself: if he had no band and no family, where would he go? What Would Jaymie Do?

He looked for the seediest dive he could find. At the first place he tried, the patrons gave him the type of stares that served as a lenient first and final warning that they weren't taken by his thrift-store fashion sense and scruffy-on-purpose hair. He pretended he was looking for the cellphone repair shop two doors down.

At his second stop, he was instantly rewarded.

"Jaymie! There he is, a whole day late!"

"Oh, you know, uh, Jaymie? Good! Great!" said Jaymie.

"Very funny!" The jovial middle-aged man behind the bar spoke with a rich Eastern European accent. "You forget to come to work yesterday? I should fire you."

"Ha! I know it sounds funny, but I'm not Jaymie," said Jaymie. "I'm his twin brother. Aaron. I'm trying to find him, because … we're supposed to Skype our dad today." As soon as Jaymie committed himself to lying for the entirety of the conversation, it became very easy to do.

"This guy, he's full of jokes! I like you, Jaymie. OK, you're not fired. Come on then, help Big Niki with Happy Hour," said the man, who was clearly Big Niki.

"No, seriously. I'm looking for Jaymie. Can you tell me if he'll be in tonight?"

"What! He never mentioned this twin brother!"

"We're not very close."

"Jaymie, Jaymie, always the trickster, aren't you …" This exchange continued for some minutes until Jaymie finally convinced the barkeep that he really wasn't the awaited employee. Big Niki revealed that the man he knew as "Jaymie" was scheduled for a shift the following day at 4 p.m. "*If the joker decides to show up*," he grumbled, wiping the counter with an enthusiasm that real-Jaymie suspected would soon strip it of its finish.

"I lost my phone and all my contacts. Could you give me his number?" Jaymie asked.

"Haha! No, he doesn't have a phone, that clown. You sure you're brothers?"

"I don't blame him—so distracting. I wouldn't bother with one either if I didn't have …" Jaymie forced himself to stay on track. "And you don't happen to know where he's living?"

"*You* don't know? And you're the twin brother, is what you're telling me!" The man chuckled again. "You weren't fooling about 'not close.' You sure you're not playing a big joke, here, Jaym—what's your name again?"

"Don't worry about it. So you definitely don't know?"

"Does anybody know?" He shrugged. "No, he didn't tell me, and I don't ask. A man is entitled to his privacy. What else has he got?"

A second bartender appeared behind the counter in time to catch the end of their conversation, and Jaymie repeated his question. She only shook her head and frowned.

"Hey, you know how to pour a drink, Jaymie's Twin?" asked Big Niki. There was something about the man Jaymie found comforting, and he briefly wondered how long it would take him to learn to bartend—probably more than five minutes but less than twenty.

"Thanks, but this is pressing. And alcohol is one of those weird things for me—I'll have it every day for a week or so and then I'll *need* it every day. You know?" The bartenders knew. He thanked them and said goodnight.

"A twin brother—what a funny family!" Big Niki poured a foamy beer for a patron who'd just finished his last sip, the new drink smoothly replacing the old one in his grip the moment it was empty. The customer blinked at the glass, startled, and continued drinking.

Jaymie wandered for another hour, asking at two more places, but nobody recognized him. Then he went home—it was getting late and he wanted to check on Rex. As it turned out, Jo had walked them to Maggie's house to be comforted by their best friend, so he assured them over the phone that he was on track and would explain everything soon, and then he sat on his bed rereading his mail, and, somehow, he fell asleep.

"What are you doing in my bed!"

The clone gazed at Jaymie with aggressive jubilance, like the sort of fan whose devotion inspires you to Google yourself and confirm your address isn't listed anywhere on the internet.

"My friend at work said you were asking for me!" it replied. "She came and told me right away—she was mad I never told her I had a twin. She got suspicious that maybe it was a conspiracy. She worried she'd been sleeping with *you* some of the time when she thought she'd been sleeping with me! I had to explain that I was a *clone*, not a twin! We had a good laugh."

"That's insane," said Jaymie. He backed up against the headboard, as far as possible from where the other Jaymie crouched, grinning, at the end of the bed. He turned on the bedside light and looked the clone over.

He was, of course, quite handsome. He had Jaymie's laughing brown eyes and crooked smile. He too was clean-shaven, having likely discovered by now that they couldn't grow a proper beard. He had the same wavy hair, though his had grown to his shoulders and was more unruly than Jaymie's; this was probably the result of not having someone around with whom he matched his DIY haircut at regular intervals. (People occasionally asked Jaymie and Aaron why they had done this their entire lives; they never gave a straight answer.)

To an outside observer, their hair would be the only distinguishable difference between Jaymie and his clone, and yet Jaymie was acutely aware of something off-putting and threatening about the man's animated crouch and eager scrutiny, as though he was something wild, leering at Jaymie from the shadows, ready to pounce.

"So, what can I do for you?" asked the miscreation, and Jaymie took a deep breath, tried to calm his thumping heart, and explained that his brother had disappeared the night before.

"I've been trying to find him," he finished. "I thought maybe you'd—I don't know …"

"You thought *I'd* know? I've literally never met this person," said the amused clone. "I don't even know his name!"

"It's Aaron," said Jaymie, more out of surprise that the clone didn't know than because he thought telling him would help. "… Brzezinski."

"Wait, our name is Bursinski? I thought it was Bukowski, like, this entire time!" The man let out a delighted yelp of laughter.

"It's pronounced *Brzhe*—Wait, *our* name? No. That's *my* name. What name have *you* been using?"

"Jaymie Bukowski. Like you. That's who I am, remember?"

"You're *not* me!" Jaymie snapped. "Go be your own person! *I'm* Jaymie. I was Jaymie twenty-five years before you were. You can pick your name! Literally *any* other name."

"I like 'Jaymie.'" The clone beamed at him.

Jaymie let out a string of swears triggered partly by his fury at the creature and partly by his stress over the prolonged absence of Aaron. He forced himself to take a few more deep breaths. His palms were too hot and he had a horrible constrained feeling in his legs, like when you've been running ten kilometres every day, but then today you skipped it.

"'Jaymie' is taken," he seethed. "You can be … Fuck it, you can have 'James'—you can even throw in a 'y,' if you like it that much—or be 'Jimmy' if you really want!"

The other Jaymie stretched out comfortably on the bed, leaned back on his elbows, and thought. Jaymie wondered if the clone was intentionally tormenting him.

"Ok, I'll be Jimmy," he said carelessly, as though the identity change caused him no more inconvenience than if he'd agreed to play a different character in Mario Kart so Jaymie could be his favourite one. "But I want that stupid 'y' too. Jymmy." Jymmy nodded, satisfied.

"Sure, have your 'y'. Jymmy. Shit. What have you even been doing all this time?"

"I make poems and play the piano—like you! And I watch porn," said Jymmy happily.

"Of course you do," Jaymie muttered.

"Did you know there's a growing niche for clone porn? Could be lucrative, if you ever need to make some cash—I know I could use a side hustle—"

"Ohmygod no!" Jaymie spluttered.

"It's not like we're related—"

"What the fuck is wrong with you!"

Jymmy shrugged. "I'm a six-month-old baby genius prodigy who's been exposed to the full depravity of internet culture without having learned societal norms and taboos yet?"

"This is all new to you? You have none of my memories?"

"None! It's funny, because I have *all* your skills, but then, like, no idea how I got them. This week I found out I can play all the barre chords on guitar! Or, like, how did you learn that if there's a lady you want to sleep with, you shouldn't say unkind things about the other ladies you've slept with? Because I instinctively knew that if I made sure not to do that, then girls would probably like to sleep with me. And they do!"

"Of course you're a horny psychopath … I realize I'm partially responsible for this …"

"You *made* me! Like, I've looked up how human babies get made, but I don't know what kind of crazy carnal stunt you had to put yourself through to conceive *me!*"

"You were made in a *lab*," said Jaymie through gritted teeth.

Six months ago, Jaymie had volunteered to be cloned. It wasn't the sort of procedure he'd normally be interested in—unless he was drunk, or someone dared him to, or one of his dear siblings died and he needed a new one, etc.—but it just so happened that he and Aaron had had a major falling out only days earlier, and he wasn't in his usual state of mind.

In May, the *Bukowski Brothers* had been invited on a one-month tour of Canada opening for a band of post-punk environmentalists called *Dead Zebra Beach*.

DZB (not to be confused with the hallucinogenic substance dipsilozylazine, or DPZ, which their fans were also excited about) had, upon the release of their debut album, gained the type of internet following destined to emerge, proliferate, and die out within a short period—in contrast to the pernicious zebra mussels and other invasive species that were the subject of many of their songs. (These songs were hailed as "musically ambitious, lyrically complex, and angsty enough to send your inner teen into an eargasm of self-pity," by reviewer Lucas Yarbrough.)

Jaymie calculated that, timing-wise, they just might hit the sweet spot in the middle of *DZB*'s fame cycle: hundreds or thousands of young people would be exposed to the brilliance of the *BBBFB*. Also, saving the environment was important. He'd enthusiastically signed on.

The Brzezinskis had been writing music and recording demos for almost three years. Though they'd always jammed together, it had taken most of their lives to renounce their destiny as backing musicians and take more artistic roles, and that spring was the first time Jaymie had a full set of original music and the recently acquired belief that it was actually good.

Only ten days before the tour, Aaron pulled out under the pretense of needing summer classes to graduate. Jaymie knew he was just anxious. He was sure that if Aaron gave it a chance, they'd have the best time of their lives, but there was no budging Aaron when he'd gotten the idea in his mind that something was going to be unbearably nerve-wracking.

Aaron offered to help find a replacement, which Jaymie obstinately refused, arguing that they were a *family* band—but really he'd been nervous too, and it was hard to picture undertaking an exhausting and potentially unrewarding working-trip without his best friend. He'd cancelled on the tour. (If this seems uncharacteristic of the gung-ho Jaymie Brzezinski, it's helpful to consider that he'd toured briefly as a backing keyboardist, and so knew the cocktail of anxiety and fatigue that persists chronically on any indie tour longer than a few days. He was also still in the painful and histrionic beginning-artist mindset, when one vacillates over whether their work is any good and relishes excuses to give up on themselves.)

He was livid at Aaron's inconsiderate departure; he called off the band and moved away for his infamous Adderall Couch Stint. During this time, some racketeering acquaintances of his began a clone lab in their basement and asked if he'd be a beta subject for the enterprise, free of charge. He hadn't slept in five days and he had an idea for a harmony line on one of the new songs and he needed to hear it with two voices to see if it would work. He agreed.

He spent half an hour trying to teach his clone the drums, explaining that the other instruments were taken (except lead guitar, but he didn't want any of his own style of pentatonic wankery on his songs, so that was off limits too). He'd left the clone banging at the kit, gone for a cat-nap, and never seen the man again. Two notebooks and a fifty-dollar bill were also missing.

Jaymie was understandably annoyed, but he reacted in what he believed to be the only reasonable and mature way, which was to move on and forget about the whole thing.

The twins had gotten lonely; Aaron had rejoined the band and begun to see a cognitive behavioural therapist to work on his anxiety, and peace had a short reign. The next time Aaron quit—alarmed by the murders—Jaymie was too tired to hate him, Anika supplied them Garrett, the internet gifted them Jo, and that had been that.

But the government did not forget. Human cloning had first been accomplished by scientists in 2018; within months the service was accessible to billionaires and, by a year later, almost-affordable businesses both lawful and otherwise were popping up at the same rate as craft breweries, just ahead of the laws restricting them. After several scandals of the kind imaginable to anyone familiar with the processes of exploitation of vulnerable populations (the clones, in this case), authorities were cracking down. Investigations led to Jaymie's loud-mouthed friends' lab, which was raided. The investigators procured a list of client names via hints of lower fines and less jail time for the young entrepreneurs. Jaymie was on that list.

Jymmy stood up and perused the stack of books by the bed. "Do you read these? I doubt it. It's funny—back when I was born, I thought you seemed kind of weird and grumpy, but the more I find out all the cool stuff we know how to do, the more I think, Maybe that guy's alright!" He regarded Jaymie fondly as he slipped one of the smaller books into his jacket pocket.

"I need to find Aaron," said Jaymie, grabbing his wallet from the bedside table before the clone's interest could shift to it. "He could be lost or trapped somewhere. Injured. In pain. Or worse—bored!"

"So. You thought I took your brother?" the clone snickered. "Why would *I* want him? Does he look like me and he wants to do clone porn?"

"No, he definitely doesn't!" Jaymie said angrily. "I don't know. I thought … maybe because … you haven't got one?"

"Interesting. And I'd want one, why?"

"Because you—you're alone."

"I see," said Jymmy, who'd grown still, and now seemed to be carefully considering Jaymie. "Go on."

"No, that was the whole theory. ... I mean, I've always had siblings around. Who do you care about? What do you even do all day? —Please don't answer that."

"I hadn't even thought of getting some siblings, honestly. And I know how to have company, when I need it." He winked, and Jaymie wondered if his own winking came across as predatory as this, and resolved never to do it again.

"OK. So you didn't take him. You haven't seen him."

"I definitely didn't, although you've started to sell me on this whole sibling thing. Maybe it'd be neat to have company that *isn't* trying to sleep with me. ... I do have Big Niki, though."

Jaymie looked at the mail strewn across his bed. Dick Dale had tiptoed in and attempted to recline in such a way as to enshroud as many envelopes as possible in his long '60s hair.

"I think I know what happened."

"Hmm? What happened where? Oh, your brother." Jymmy scritched the cat's chin with a long finger.

"I need your help," Jaymie told him. "The collection agency came, but they couldn't find you. I think they took him as collateral." His stomach twinged and did a queasy turn just thinking about it. Then he noticed one final oddity, and asked, "Are you wearing my pants?"

33
Jym and Jay

Jymmy liked everything about being alive. He liked eating and drinking and playing music and all the other grand material pursuits that made him come *alive*—something he understood to be different than just being "alive" in the literal sense—and he liked writing poetry and making love and having conversations with people who knew more about the world than he did, which was everyone, and he even liked sleeping, though he preferred not to do it at regular hours or for very long—but then occasionally all day for hours and hours at a time!

He also liked the internet and, like anyone exploring adulthood without having had the advantage of a lengthy teenagehood to mull it over, he'd become curious about his place in the world. He decided to put that miraculous omniscient God-phantasm to work researching the big questions. He Googled "clones." The results were alarming.

He learned of recent demonstrations by human rights activists calling for clones to be recognized not only as human and protected by the Charter of Rights, but as a vulnerable sector, since many had no access to lawful income or even memories, and were liable to end up in Original-Duplicate relationships that were at worst exploitative (e.g., involving organ extractions) and more often just kind of icky, not unlike the circumstances of newly-invented robot women in sci-fi romances.

Still, during the months he'd spent on his own, he'd become curious about his Original. When he heard Jaymie was looking for him, he decided the time had come to meet his maker.

He found his way to the house on Pandora Street where, six months earlier, he'd been secretly brought by Jaymie to learn the drums. At that time, he'd studied for half an hour, without success or enthusiasm—or any idea where he was or who he was or what was going on or what elbows were for or what the weird bad feeling in his brain was from (it was from prescription-grade amphetamine withdrawal)—and he'd quickly discovered he had no desire to be used by his Original; he wanted to make his own songs and start his own band, just as soon as he'd figured out how far the universe continued beyond the top of the basement stairs.

Now, Jymmy stood on the sidewalk and beheld the house where he'd made those early, bitter-sweet memories. He knew from past encounters with front doors at nighttime that the home would be locked and that humans with regular sleep cycles would be in bed. Proud of this knowledge, yet undeterred by it, he gained access through Jaymie's second-floor bedroom window. It was a lengthier process than he first estimated, but proved a delightful challenge.

The method involved breaking into the garden shed for a ladder, propping it against the house, taking a fantastic tumble back to earth, ladder and all, using it to instead climb the maple tree in the yard, shimmying along a mid-level branch to the low porch roof—the ice on which resulted in another comical spill back to the snow-padded lawn—making a second, more cautious vault to the porch roof, and traversing it to the pine trees at the other end, which couldn't be climbed from the ground because their lowest branches were shorn.

The next stunt was to scale the pines, jump, and grab onto the window (a maneuver which was more difficult than it looked and took two tries and one more exhilarating plunge to the ground [briefly interrupted by the porch roof]), which was not only unlocked but open the tiniest crack at the bottom—careless humans! He slid it up without difficulty, somewhat disappointed at this anti-climactic finale to his caper.

Once inside, he explored Original Jaymie's bedroom and found surprisingly little of interest, besides an excellent pair of pants slung over the back of a chair—he immediately tried them on—and Jaymie's wallet, which he relieved of its thirty-one dollars and eighty-five cents and then lovingly returned to the bedside table. He didn't even steal the driver's license (Big Niki would never ID him) or debit card (a mysterious item that people tapped on the thingy when they didn't have money for their drinks; any time he tried to ask, in a casual roundabout way, what the penalty was for having to tap the card, they seemed to think he was just being charming. Anyway, Big Niki never charged him for drinks).

Then he began a curious and careful examination of his Original, which culminated in Jaymie waking up with Jymmy sitting on his ribs.

"You know, I think I'd help you out even if you weren't letting me keep these pants. I've been sort of bored lately. I keep meaning to make a band but then I get preoccupied by things that aren't even interesting and I don't really care about—they're just, I don't know, they're colourful and the words hook me in a certain way. And my brain feels kind of strange after, like I'm agitated and I want to do stuff, but I forget what I was about to do. Do you ever get that?"

"Totally normal," Jaymie assured him distractedly. "I don't have time to explain capitalism and how everyone is preying on your attention span, but it's probably good you don't have a smartphone ..." He scanned Garry Street, looking for the address on his letters. It was still early morning and downtown was quiet; it had taken the two Jaymies very little time to negotiate an exchange of pants-ownership for backup at the Clone Office.

"These are amazing—they show just enough of my socks at the bottom! Do you have a girlfriend who buys your pants for you?"

"You can't ask people that. That's sexist."

"Really? I thought 'sexist' was when you tell a girl to smile, but she doesn't like that, and you just wanted to make her happy and start a conversation that might lead to her sleeping with you, but she says it's sexist and she doesn't like it, and then sometimes she sleeps with you anyway, and she wants you to say things that are way worse than telling her to smile, which seems bizarre after she was so offended, but what are you going to do, complain?"

"It's complicated," said Jaymie, who suspected that not even Rex was equipped with the rhetorical skills necessary to tackle this particular doozy. "By the way, you do know you have to get permission, right? Before you kiss anybody or try to sleep with them or whatever?"

"What?"

"You have to ask them! I hate this conversation, but I can't tell if you're a creep."

"I just go home with them and I tell them about music and I wait for them to put their face at my face. And if they don't, I go look for somebody else, but that only happened once."

"… Close enough for now."

"I never thought of the option of—"

"Well don't ever think about it."

"OK, Jaymie." Jymmy rubbed the soft pockets on his new pants in appreciation and smiled at a fat pigeon across the street.

"OK, glad that's over with." Jaymie stopped outside an unassuming office building. "And you know, I happen to be pretty good at finding clothes that are cheap and fit me right."

The sickly winter sun clawed its way over the prairie horizon and smeared anemic light directly onto the number they were looking for. Jaymie let out a relieved puff of frost, glad the place existed, and tried the door, which was locked.

The two men finished their cigarettes, preparing for the next step. Jaymie had known his chances of finding someone at the office on a Sunday morning were slim, and had decided his best hope was to break in and see if he could figure out where the "confiscated clones" were kept.

Something moved on the other side of the door. He peered in and knocked on the glass. A man turned the bolt, said with some uncertainty, "Are you here about clones?" and let them in.

"I'm new here," he told them. "I'm starting the weekend shift, which exists as of eleven a.m. today. It's for people who can't pay their fees during regular office hours. You're early, but that's alright." His expression brightened as they pulled away hoods and scarves. "Oh, it's you! I have to say I'm relieved. Oh my god, how many clones did you make?"

Jaymie, who had never met the man before, felt a rush of hope at having been recognized. "Just this one," he said, motioning toward his One True Clone. "I need to register him and get my brother back. Like, today."

"Hang on, *register*?" said Jymmy.

"OK, it takes a couple of business days to process—"

"Today," Jaymie reiterated. The man looked uncomfortable, and Jaymie glanced around uneasily for signs of an alarm system or security guard.

"I'm Jaymie! No—I mean I'm Jymmy!" said Jymmy, offering his hand.

"Oh, uh, Spencer," said the man. Jaymie wondered if Spencer found Jymmy as subtly unnerving as he did, but if Spencer did, he was too polite to let on.

"Spence, that's a great tie—it really compliments your shirt," said Jymmy.

"Thank you!"

"Did you pick them out by yourself?"

"I did," Spencer replied. "I like men's fashion, although I told my colleague that the other day, and she laughed and implied that I was also into men themselves—which seemed like an unfair assumption, since I happen not to be. She's a bit of a thug, I think."

"I might have done that before today, just like her! See, I get all my politics from sitcoms and the internet. But now I've been re-educated about sexism!" Jymmy affectionately patted Jaymie, who was dumbstruck with horror at his clone's diluted but nonetheless Jaymie-brand social skills. "Would you like to be friends with me?" He grinned wolfishly.

"What? Oh—OK, sure! Uh, maybe once you're registered we can watch a game or something," suggested Spencer, clearly taken aback at the forthright offer of friendship.

"Like the ones on the TV at the bar," nodded Jymmy, keen to demonstrate his knowledge of games. "The thing is, Spencer, I prefer being off the grid. I'm not sure I'm ready to think about registration just yet."

"Well, then they'd come collect you," said Spencer, regret evident on his face.

"I don't like that," said Jymmy.

"Well … maybe we can work something out." He turned to Jaymie. "What did you say about your other clone? —And I do feel bad about having to collect him the other night. Did not relish that experience."

"That's my *brother*," said Jaymie, and he briefly explained his theory that Aaron had been taken as a security deposit for his unpaid fees.

Spencer gave a startled laugh. "Oh god, no, they would never take a human! Wow, let me think. I hate to tell you this, but we thought *he* was the clone! We knew you'd had one made."

"What! They're nothing alike!" Jaymie exclaimed.

"And here's this guy who looks like you but showing sign of expiration …"

"*Expiration*? What the fuck! We're twenty-five!"

"What a hilarious misunderstanding!" said Jymmy, which was enough to ease Spencer past his guilt and into seeing the humour of the situation. The two new friends chortled to each other while Jaymie fumed at the clerical error that had caused him such grief.

"Wow, that's too funny—I'm texting my co-worker, she's going to feel so stupid … I can't believe one of them really *was* a twin!" Spencer tapped at his phone, still chuckling.

"So you're letting him out?" Jaymie demanded. "Because we have a show tonight *and* family dinner, and I'm guessing he's not a happy camper at the moment."

"I'll drive over and see what we can do about Jymmy's registration situation. Things are a little up in the air because of the policy changes. And yes—your brother. We'll work it out."

"Great. We'll come with you." said Jaymie.

"Not me," said Jymmy. "Don't want to get collected, lol!"

Jaymie began to retort, but Spencer was already explaining that Originals weren't permitted at the holding facility. He promised to go there immediately and to be in touch ASAP. Then he exchanged contact info with Jymmy and, at Jaymie's insistence, with him as well.

"You didn't tell me about registration," Jymmy lightly admonished him. "No way I'm getting taken by the government, like—what's his name? Alan. No …"

Powerless to do anything more, they went home, where Jymmy noticed that the front door was unlocked—and had been since Friday, Jaymie explained, in case Aaron had lost his key. Jaymie called Rex to fill them in while Jymmy put the toppled ladder back in the shed, shaking with amusement at his own miscalculation.

Jo couldn't decide whether to practice guitar. She sat on her bed staring at the instrument. The tribute show was twelve hours away, and normally she'd be sleeping in, in preparation for a late night, making a leisurely breakfast, and settling in to run warm-ups and go over the songs.

Instead, she'd woken before dawn and been unable to fall back asleep. She had no appetite and a headache. She'd called Big Brother Coffee to check when it opened, gotten dressed, and walked to collect her gear, trying not to think about her missing bandmate.

She called a cab to drive her home with her guitar, amp, and pedalboard. Her car was a lost cause for the time being; she'd get it towed tomorrow. She'd no-showed at work the day before and was probably fired and unable to afford vehicle upkeep for a while anyway.

When she got home the ache had eased but there was an awful, anxious knot somewhere deep in her chest, like when she'd thought they were going to get killed by the cult, but quieter, and drawn out, and with nobody around she could hit.

She knew she wouldn't be able to focus on scales.

She checked her email as a diversion and saw that a surf-rock cover band had contacted her to ask if she could sub at their next show. Their lead guitarist had been murdered in November. She was never offered paying gigs, but the circumstances voided any sense of long-awaited career victory; a surge of rage punched through the fog of her wake-and-bake habit. She thought again of Alexandre—she'd *known* him!—who'd done nothing wrong and ended up dead.

Suddenly she was seventeen and playing her first *Ballet Llama* show and she was in an ecstatic fury because of corporate greed and rich people and corruption and etc., and she was ready to fuck shit up—as she would've crowed to the rioting audience back then—before she'd grown up and realized that no matter how good she got at the guitar, nobody was going to care much or pay her enough to afford even her little basement apartment, and somehow that had become more disappointing than all the major injustices in the world. Embarrassing.

She looked around the tiny, box-cluttered space—was it getting tinier? She wondered if her life had been shrinking, but slowly enough that she wouldn't notice until she was suffocating.

Anyway, now it didn't matter whether she was broke or gigging or both because she'd lost a much more important drummer—no offense, Alexandre—and music was over.

I don't have enough friends that I can afford any getting murdered, she thought.

She found a sharpie and a late-rent warning from her landlord, and attached the paper blank-side-out to the fridge with a kitschy Les Paul magnet given to her by someone who didn't know she preferred Fender.

She wrote down "house show" and "*BL* show," and beneath the first heading she wrote "Lo Wave promoter couple" and "leopard print person" and "Garrett" and "Anika" and beneath the second she wrote "Michaud" and "Jake and Oli" and "Anika" and "Casio Bob" and "drunk teenagers," and then she realized how ridiculous this was, and how few names she actually knew out of all the people at each show, and that she didn't actually suspect any of them of murder anyway, and she threw her marker at the wall in abject misery.

Her phone buzzed. It was Rex, texting to tell her their brother was "a shitbag who I guess got high and cloned himself," (poomoji), and it was hard to explain, but they would likely have Aaron back by suppertime—and then a "Fingers crossed!" gif of Lindsay Lohan as twins in The Parent Trap—and would Jo mind doing the soundcheck while they had dinner with their family? No drums or amps to haul, since backline was provided. Rex also promised that Jaymie would provide her with beer in return, "or whatever your BEER is," and then there were some emojis of a whiskey bottle and a weed leaf and an eggplant as suggestions.

It was as though Rex had clipped free a thin guitar string that had been tightening around Jo's throat. She assured them she'd pick up their instruments in the late afternoon.

She took up her Jaguar. She glanced at her murder list. Then she wondered if any of the people on it had also been at the last *Tornado Tornahdo* show, and whether the members of the surf-rock band might have any insights. She returned to the email and wrote that she'd been tremolo picking since before she could walk and would be happy to take the gig.

34

McLeod Family Dinner Part I

Leonora arrived home on Sunday evening, shortly before dinner time, eager to reunite with her children. She was a petite woman in her early fifties with a pointy freckled face and the sort of mouth that appeared very small when closed and then revealed itself in blinding rays of glory when she opened it to share an anecdote, real or fabricated, from life on the road.

She was pleased to see that the lights were on and someone had salted the front steps so she wouldn't slip. She let herself in, balancing a couple of pie tins in one hand and pulling her suitcase behind her, two saxophones slung across her back.

She hadn't seen her brood in months; a long run of shows had transitioned seamlessly into a cross-country tour, and though she knew not to worry, because Jaymie and Aaron were now responsible adults and Rex was very mature for their age, she did miss them terribly.

"Hello, anyone home?" she called. And they were.

She hugged Rex first and longest, knowing they were going through a sensitive phase and might read anything as a rejection. She couldn't blame them, since she'd been away so long—it was funny, when she was a teenager all she'd wanted was to escape the watchful eyes of her parents for long enough to play her sax without someone breathing down her neck and asking if she was done her homework. Then she remembered Rex was already seventeen, and she recalculated. Leonora had hit the road by seventeen.

She experienced a small jolt of alarm as she greeted her sons. Had they grown even more alike? She glanced hastily back and forth between them, hoping they wouldn't notice, wishing they'd just move the hair out of their faces …

Then one grinned brilliantly and cried "You're my mom!" which seemed to perturb the other intensely, and she knew immediately who was who. She embraced them both, saying their names so they'd know that she knew, and kissing their cheeks, making a mental note that it was Jaymie who had grown his hair out, in case they changed positions. Still, it puzzled her. She'd rarely had trouble identifying them, and never when they were together and close-up.

But there was no time to dwell on it, because her sister and sister-in-law had just pulled up outside, with her niece and a tall punk who she could already tell was going to be a lot of fun.

Aaron woke to the mousy light of day. The solid black outside his window had been replaced by an equally solid grey, as though someone had decided sunshine was entirely inappropriate, considering the current social and political and literal climate, and blushingly thrown a sheet over the whole mess.

He was alone; Cassie 2.3 must have grown bored watching him sleep and resumed her card game with Derick at some point in the night. He was tempted to lie in bed avoiding his problems, but knew he'd think too much and get worked up again, and his cognitive behavioural therapist had encouraged him to focus on active solutions rather than imagined disasters.

Thinking about Cassie 2.3 felt like a healthy distraction, and he allowed himself to mentally replay their interaction, and even to feel some amount of accomplishment about it. Someone pretty and nice wanted to sleep with him! He was on an adventure! An occasionally sexy adventure! The island painting sneered at him from across the room and his chest tightened. He did a breathing exercise and promised himself he'd revisit the memory and celebrate once he was free.

He was glad to find fresh clothes laid out, since his own had been sweat-drenched in Friday's chase. He dressed in them, except for the shapeless, scrubs-like pants. He retrieved his jeans from the heap Cassie 2.3 had made on the floor and pulled them on, not wanting to feel too much like a hospital patient.

His therapist posed like a shlumpy sphynx at the end of the bed. Her only input so far had been to systematically prod his half-full/half-empty water glass off the nightstand while he'd slept, as a metaphor for the precariousness of subjective reality. He picked her up and went to join the other clones in the common area.

Cassie 2.3 was back in her tidy suit with her braids gathered in a smooth knot at the base of her neck. She greeted him in a warm but platonic manner and informed him it was already late in the afternoon.

"You weren't kidding about liking to sleep!" she said, crinkling her eyes. "You must have been tired." She sat with her legs folded under her on the corner of the lawn with Derick and Five-O, who were absorbed by something that sat on the fake grass in front of Derick. Aaron looked around for the new arrivals Cassie 2.3 had mentioned, and estimated that the number of clones lounging in the alcove across the room might have increased. He hadn't introduced himself to that group, not having need of more friends, and none had approached him, so he assumed the feeling was mutual.

(Actually, most of these clones were in a more palliative phase, having been made using cruder methods than Aaron's friends had been; they were low-functioning, or were nearer to expiration and were winding down. It's fortunate he never went to say hello, or he might have been severely creeped out.)

50117 looked up and announced, "He's got it!" and Derick hissed at him to quiet down, peering over his shoulders in suspicion. Two people had overheard, and they detached themselves from the alcove group and began an unhurried walk toward them across the lawn.

***

For once, Anika's entrance had not gone unnoticed. She was certain Michaud's appearance alone was enough to raise alarm bells in the hearts of her older family members. Even her normally supportive mothers had misgivings about him—and rightly so!

She and Michaud had made a seafoam salad with marshmallows instead of cream cheese, which was the most ridiculous item she could think to bring. Her grandmother's only instruction had been to prepare a side, and she was delighted to discover that her cousins had also contributed a seafoam salad; they couldn't have botched a potluck better if they'd planned it.

Every time she'd seen her grandparents in the past decade, she'd gotten the verbal equivalent of a pat on the head before her grandma moved on to direct toward her mothers the type of suspiciously polite comments that betrayed great judgement.

It wasn't that Anika liked stirring up drama—she was approaching thirty, and she'd never been one to act out. But if Grandma was going to spend the evening doling out admonishments, she wanted to bear her fair portion of the castigation. And maybe, if she was being honest, she wanted in on the family bonding experience. Her mother and Auntie Leonora always managed to do something disappointing in between gatherings, and the older Brzezinskis had long since failed to meet a list of expectations that had never been placed on Anika in equal measure—though their shortcomings didn't seem to hurt the hopeful attention their grandparents bestowed on them. And it could only help Rex, who was yet to fall from grace, for her to take some of the pressure off them.

Speaking of the Brzezinskis, there was definitely something shady going on. Jaymie had let her know they'd located Aaron and everyone would be present at dinner. Not that she'd had time to get worried; a Brzezinski disappearing for a day wasn't unusual.

But as she stood across the table from the two of them, she had the distinct impression that something was off. For one thing, one of them had grown his hair out in the month or two since she'd last hung out with them, which was unheard of if the other hadn't as well.

"Where'd you disappear to on Friday, Aar?" she asked. "I thought you'd be at the show."

Jaymie beamed at her. Aaron prodded their green food offering to check its consistency. Neither responded. Anika tugged the wrapping off her salad bowl and narrowed her eyes.

"Me! Right. I ran into Daffodile and … we had a nice chat," said Aaron.

Anika raised her eyebrows. "*You* talked to Daffodile? And then just went home to …?"

"Went home to drink with the cats, yeah." He placed the siblings' seafoam salad at the opposite end of the table from hers. Leonora could be heard exchanging joyous updates with Anika's mothers in the living room.

"But then yesterday you were …?"

"Left early for groceries and my phone died. Poor guys thought I'd never made it home."

He nodded in sympathy toward Rex, who glared silently back at him. This wasn't standard Rex behaviour, but Rex had some late-onset teen angst, and you could never tell what kind of mood they were going to be in these days.

"Two identical salads!" laughed Leonora, joining them at the table. "We'll have a whole dinner of mini marshmallows! This reminds me of the time our tour bus broke down by a field in Indiana and all we had to eat were smores ingredients for a day and a half. You might be wondering why we had only smores ingredients, and it's a good question—see, our driver, Brian, loves camping, and sometimes once everybody else is checked in at the hotel, we go out—"

"Mom, Grandma and Grandpa are here," Rex interrupted, looking out the window.

"Oh. Fabulous."

"Sarcasm?" asked Rex in the monotone that Anika recognized as their tired and/or nervous and/or angry voice.

"Would I ever be sarcastic about—what I meant was: How wonderful! … But should we hide one of the salads?"

The two new clones turned out to also be 50117.

"It's you, you lowlife!" said one.

"Scum! I'll kill him!" cried the other. They'd approached Aaron's friend group for a meet and greet, seeking potential business networking opportunities. Neither was thrilled at the sight of their look-alike.

"Kill me? I'll kill you! Just like I killed my—our—Original!" shouted 50117, not about to take abuse from these ignorant newcomers.

One was identical to Five-O, down to his bright black eyes and neat silver beard. The other was in his mid-teens and could have been mistaken for a son who'd fallen very close to the tree. He was dressed in expensive jeans and a skater-brand shirt and his face looked on the verge of sprouting its own neat silver beard.

"*Our* Original? It's not you, then?" asked the elder clone suspiciously.

"Did you make me? Tell me the truth!" cried the boy, clearly about to unleash a level of drama similar to that of a young jedi learning that his least favourite jedi was, in fact, his dad.

"I don't know how to make a *half-grown* one. Must be one of our Original's projects." Five-O told him offhandedly. "I get it, now that I think about it—clone yourself at your own age, and it has your health issues. But an infant requires a major financial investment. Smart." Then he pointed to the children's area, where the two pudgy toddlers were wrestling in a pile of plushies and chuckling to themselves, on a single-minded venture to entice someone to pull out a phone camera and win them the Pinterest award for Cutest Babies 2019. "I made those ones."

The teenager squinted in mistrust, but was appeased enough not to take up arms.

"Hm, lucky," said the other. "I didn't have the opportunity to create any of my own."

"How do you think *I* feel?" whined the boy. "I never even had a chance to take Julia out in my convertible before—" Everyone stopped listening to him. Five-O and the other clone—50119—were already bonding over their opinions on cloning techniques and the benefits of growing GFIs from scratch using ARG, for fresh young organs, rather than using some kind of 3D printer like the idiots who'd crafted these three pathetic SMCs and their awkward OMIs.

The three OMI-tormented idiot-copies in question huddled around Derick's project, with no time to waste on this family gathering. They knew the arrival of the newcomers could signal the departure of two of their company.

"Any luck with the 4G LTE?" asked Cassie 2.3. "The collectors will be in soon for the evening shift." She glanced around nervously.

"I can't believe two of *us* are going to get dismembered so there can be more of *him*," Aaron muttered. He dragged his loaner-cat away from Derick's contraption; she was attempting to rub her facial glands on it to remind him of the therapeutic value of physical stimulation.

"Dismantled," Derick corrected. "TNP."

"Go commiserate with that kid," said Cassie 2.3, with her gentle smirk. "Perhaps you can both take your complaints to the government." She ruffled the back of his hair, and he felt a strange mix of feelings that were mostly—but not entirely—anxiety-related.

While Derick fussed with his machine, Aaron ruminated. He was probably an anxiety expert by now. An anxiety hipster; he could identify its genres and subgenres and which anxious moments were new and inspired and which ones were cleverly referencing experiences long past.

He could parse the bad anxieties from the happy anxieties, and maybe one day he'd even have the patience to hold them to the light and determine which ones were a passing trend in his brain (PTB) and which signalled a game-changing threat (GCT) to his life. And wasn't that the final goal laid out by his CBT? Maybe he was making progress after all.

***

Jymmy had been looking forward to experiencing his first family dinner and telling everybody about his life and about Big Niki, whom he considered the closest thing to family that he had. Instead, he found himself fascinated by the people and activities around him, and was content, for the time being, in the role of an observer.

For instance, Grandma McLeod was now greeting Jymmy's fake-cousin's boyfriend and making a nice comment about how many tattoos he had, but it was one of those nice comments which Jymmy understood to somehow be a not-nice comment.

Anika and Michaud either missed or ignored the not-nice element, but then smiled secretively to each other for some reason, and Anika said, "I like how permanent tattoos are—I'm really into long-term things right now," and then she looked at Michaud with the sort of admiration Jymmy had only seen in partners of his who hadn't understood his independent lifestyle and turned out to be very hard to shake off.

"That's so fucking romantic," said Michaud, and then apologized to Grandma for the swear, but didn't look sorry at all, and Anika whispered, "Tu es magnifique," which may as well have been a different language as far as poor Jymmy was concerned.

Besides these intrigues, there was the fact that Anika looked like her mom, Dorothea, but *also* looked like her other mom, Farida, and Jymmy wished dearly to bring it up and hear how it all worked, but understood from his ingrained Jaymie-instincts that that would be inappropriate.

Dorothea—Dory—Leonora's younger sister, was trying to talk about some accomplishment of Anika's on the classical music scene, and was promptly shut down by Grandma McLeod asking how Anika's boring contract job was going, and whether there was a permanent position in sight for her, since she was so into long-term things now.

Jaymie had warned Jymmy not to reveal what he was, at least until Aaron was home safe. (Rex had sarcastically commented that their sweet grandma was already forced to repress a lot of prejudice for the sake of the family, and adding a clone to the mix might give her a heart attack.) Jymmy was instructed to be quiet and not draw attention to himself, but Jaymie needn't have worried; there was far too much going on for anyone to be concerned by his delighted little comments or the fact that his hair was longer than his fake-twin's.

His brain struggled to properly balance Grandma McLeod's complaints; for instance, it seemed to be a big deal that Leonora had only managed to visit her kids three times in the past year, which was apparently much less than most years—yet it was an equally big deal that there were two salads made out of marshmallows? *He* sure didn't mind.

Cassie 2.3 watched Derick struggle with his communication device until it clicked and beeped to life. The three friends sat around a silver box with a miniature screen, which was attached to an ancient-looking telephone receiver.

"I've done it!" he quietly proclaimed, looking like he couldn't believe it himself.

"Excellent work," said Cassie 2.3, who wasn't sure what he'd done but had been captive far too long not to be enthralled by any change in routine.

"Cool. What is it?" asked Jaymie 2.0, scrunching up his adorable anxious freckly face and drumming on his knees. Cassie 2.3 didn't think he'd stopped drumming on things the entire time he'd been there. She wondered if his friends found it maddening. Still, she could confirm that he kept steady time, if you caught her drift.

"It's a rudimentary cellphone!" whispered Derick. "I thought, if Erick could invent *me*—a *person*—out of rubber and dye and a handful of chemical elements, *I* could make a basic signal transmitter out of odds and ends!"

"Brilliant!" said Cassie 2.3. She'd never had opportunity to use a phone, but she knew from her robust reserve of memories that she loved phones very much. "Who should we call?"

Derick was already entering a number using an agonizingly slow selection system on the little screen. Cassie 2.3 and Jaymie 2.0 leaned in as a voice identical to Derick's, but tinny and faint, chirped out a response from the receiver.

"Hey, you've reached Erick and Ericka. Leave your number and we'll get back atcha!"

35

McLeod Family Dinner Part II

Jaymie could hardly believe his family hadn't recognized Jymmy for what he was. He only hoped the ploy would last until Aaron was returned to them, and they could surreptitiously swap Jymmy out. So far, he'd heard nothing from Spencer.

"How's your new music coming, sweetheart?" Leonora asked Jymmy.

"I made a poem about a drunk lady who hit on me at work, and I can play barre chords on the guitar!" Jymmy said without hesitation. Jaymie cringed and hid it just as quickly.

"How very Charles Bukowski of you." Leonora winked. Leonora's wink, like Jaymie's wink, was a singular gem—a non-creepy, non-awkward wink—that could only be produced through years of practice or a by rare natural magic residing deep in the soul. Leonora had never revealed the source of hers; Jaymie had practiced relentlessly.

"*Who* Bukowski?" said Jymmy.

"How's the circus, Mom!" Jaymie interjected. His phone gave two quick vibrations in his pocket, and he nearly dropped his wine glass. His leg began a steady sympathy-vibration in response.

"Oh, endless fun!" Leonora glanced at Grandma McLeod. "—*And* it's a decent salary which will help one or more of the kids with university, should they desire to go." Jaymie glanced at his new message under the table and breathed a sigh of relief. Spencer had gotten tied up at work, but had decided he felt bad enough about the situation that he personally would pick Jaymie up and take him to fill out the paperwork.

"It sounds like a musician's ideal—" Auntie Dory attempted.

"—I'm sure Becca will appreciate that, in lieu of having your presence in her life," said their grandmother.

Grandma McLeod was tiny and imposing. She had a voice both delicate and severe. She was usually more subtle in conveying her high standards, but she'd prepared her famous version of perfection salad that afternoon at the hotel, and had been more than a little alarmed to find that her grandchildren had supplied not one, but two, additional Jell-O-based side dishes.

"I'm only a phone call away," said Leonora, smiling fondly at Rex and mashing her gelatin into a yellowy pulp with her fork.

Jaymie noted that his grandma was snippier than usual, and felt both glad to be leaving and guilty for abandoning Rex to suffer through it. "So, I'm going to have to go really soon. It's … music-related." He tried to sound apologetic, but wasn't sure how convincing he was; somehow, he'd gone off his game again.

"Setting up your drums for the show?" asked Leonora. "I'll be there!"

Jaymie had almost forgotten the show. "Yes! That." He realized Leonora was clarifying so his grandparents would know he wasn't just trying to escape. It was clear she was working hard to keep the mood positive and her sarcasm to a minimum.

"They can't sit still through one family meal …" complained Grandma.

"If it's for a show, it's worthwhile," said his mother. "It's their *careers.*"

Jaymie drained his wine and gripped his phone, waiting for his ride. He thought he'd felt the phone buzz again, but he'd imagined it. His knees were jittering under the table. He poured another glass, starting to feel another type of buzz, different but equally comforting.

Grandma directed a probing question at Anika and Michaud, to their great pleasure, and Leonora took the opportunity to lean in and touch his arm. "Honey, you're not big into drinking again, are you?"

"What? Oh—no, Mom," Jaymie croaked, taken off guard. He tried to remember—what were Aaron's rules for himself these days? "Only at shows," he said. "Always stop at three. Four max. All under control."

"Have you gone to a psychiatrist yet?" asked his grandmother, overhearing. "You know I said I'd pay for it."

"A psychiatrist …" said Jaymie. Jymmy was exuberantly spooning a mountain of seafoam salad onto his plate, and Jaymie felt another bullet of panic, thinking he'd betray himself before they could leave with Spencer.

"He likes the CBT he was seeing," Leonora gently answered for him. "But he might look into medication. We've talked about it a few times."

"Meds? No, I'm fine how I am, thanks," Jaymie mumbled. Then he realized, with another sick jolt, that he was totally killing it. He probably couldn't do a better impression of Aaron-at-family-dinner if he'd scripted it. The knowledge that he was better off having no idea what to say awakened in him a kind of social helplessness that he hadn't experienced since high school.

"Maybe it'd help you feel a little calmer, honey. Make performing less of a struggle. Make you a bit happier," said Leonora.

"He's not—I mean, I'm not unhappy." Jaymie was fairly sure this was true.

"We're just trying to help, sweetheart," said his grandmother, smiling blandly. "Since this band of your brother's obviously hasn't." She reached to pat Jymmy's hand in a truly grandmotherly way. "Not that it's *your* fault, dear," she told the clone.

"I don't know what you're talking about!" said Jymmy happily. Jaymie waited for someone to chastise the fake-Jaymie for his lack of empathy, and when no one did he felt his face flush with something like shame, which had also hardly happened since high school.

"You might have more energy for music!" Leonora said. "Like Jaymie does—" She stopped, and he knew she was wondering if she'd gone too far. He'd always suspected he was her favourite, but he'd never seen her do anything that would cause the other two to feel left out or less-than. If Aaron had ever felt that way, he'd never mentioned it.

"I don't need to be like Jaymie!" he snapped.

"I hate to say it again, sweetie," said Grandma, "But maybe you two need some time apart. You could take a break. You don't *have* to be a professional musician, you know."

"What!" Jaymie dropped his fork. Say it *again*? Aaron had *conversations* with these people? With no Jaymie around to defend him? Or to defend himself?

"Mom, stop!" said Leonora. "He likes playing music … And you know it was far worse when Jaymie was away on tour."

"Don't leave me, Adam!" cried Jymmy, in an act of jubilant participation. He eyed his next forkful of marshmallows like it was the beating heart of a vanquished enemy.

Is this what it was like to be Aaron?

"Becca! How are your studies?" boomed his grandfather. "Any boyfriends yet?"

The greeting from Erick's answering machine landed dully among the shocked clones. There was a cruel beep just flat of A5, which was, incidentally, the same pitch as the tinnitus in Aaron's left ear. He looked at Derick, wondering how to reassure him. Perhaps there is no adequate reassurance for someone whose creator has replaced them with an updated version.

"Oh, sweetie," said Cassie 2.3. "Forget Erick! Who needs him?" She made a move to comfort the inventor, but then grabbed Aaron's arm and pointed across the room. Two collectors stood by the hallway conferring over a clipboard.

Aaron and Cassie 2.3 remained quiet as Derick worked himself through what appeared to be his own style of panic attack. The answering machine rolled, recording only his laboured and burbly breathing and perhaps the A-flat from Aaron's left ear, which seemed to have doubled in amplitude for no reason at all.

Leonora was set ill at ease by her mother's comments. She was used to it, and her kids were too, but she didn't like to think of it affecting their confidence. Thankfully, Anika—bless her!—redirected the family with a fun fact about how the guitar player from Michaud's old punk band now played in the *BBBFB*.

"Small world!" said Leonora, grasping desperately on to the new topic. "I've always loved the music scene here. It's a jumble of Venn diagrams!" She winked her gratitude at Anika. "The kids speak very highly of their guitarist."

"She's goddamn brilliant," Michaud contributed. "Big fucking burnout though, too bad. Pardon my French!"

"Don't worry, dear, my parents have heard every swear under the sun," said Leonora, suppressing an urge to thank him as well, for his attention-stealing existence in her dining room.

"Yes, well, it's a common story," said Grandma. "So many musicians go that way."

"They can't all turn out as accomplished as our Nora!" said Grandpa McLeod, who was not technically a McLeod, or their grandpa, but had been married to their grandmother for long enough that he might as well have been. He'd been a stepdad for decades, and had always been the type intent on winning affection, rather than the type intent on asserting dominance or the type who was perfectly well-adjusted.

"Drinking, drugs ... It's not their fault, necessarily—it's the lifestyle," said Grandma. "It's the people they're around. Don't you think?" she directed the question at Michaud, who was more than happy to take a stab at it.

"Oh yeah, I probably was a shitty influence on Jo, back then. We were kids! We had fun, we got riled up. What can you do?" He grinned through a mouthful of seafoam salad.

"I was thinking of making a punk band, and it's called *Bukowski One-Eight-Two*. No, *Bukowski Kill*. No, the *Buzz-kowski-cocks*. *Fugkowski*—" Jymmy was silenced by looks from Rex and Jaymie.

"Well, Mich just got an offer from a new band. He's backburnered everything else, to focus on his solo project, but if he's considering this, then it must be exciting. But I don't know, because he won't even tell me the details," Anika delicately cajoled. "But *I* think the *Llama* should try again. They only just got back together, and the show was such a hit!"

"I wish you hadn't broken up in the first place," said Rex quietly. "You must have had a really important reason ..." Jaymie was not so distraught that he didn't roll his eyes at this feeble attempt. If they hadn't gotten the story out of Jo, they sure wouldn't get it out of Michaud.

"Oh, we were falling apart. Like your grand-mère said—too much fun, eh!"

"I just hate to think of that happening to our Becca, when she has such a bright future ahead of her," said Grandma. "And these two don't set the best example—you know, dear, just because your brothers want to spend time with underachiever-types like that guitar player—"

Rex had never been first to break at family visits, but tonight was an exceptional night.

"That's not my name! Those aren't my pronouns! That's not my brother! This isn't how you make a fucking seafoam salad!" They slammed their cutlery down, and they left.

"He replaced me ..."

"We need to think of a new option," said Cassie 2.3, eyeing the collectors.

"He replaced me with a girl ... *Ericka* ..."

"I hate to say I told you so," said Five-O, who had been drawn back to them by the opportunity to say, "I told you so."

"Let me call my brother," Aaron pleaded. "He'll find a way to help us!"

50117 sneered. "If he didn't care enough to answer his notices, I doubt he'll be pleased to hear from you. And besides, how does that help *us?*" He motioned at Cassie 2.3 and Derick.

"I didn't invent this machine so *you* could get home to bed," Derick bitterly agreed.

"Seriously? Guys, I'm trying to help!" But it was true. If he found any way to get back to his family, he'd take it, even if it meant spinelessly leaving the other clones to their fates.

"Who else do you know, Derick?" said Cassie 2.3, shaking the grieving man's shoulder.

"I have no one else."

"Well, I don't either! Cassie knows I'm here. But if she hasn't come by now …"

Five-O tried, "I could call my contacts—"

"Not you!" said Derick and Cassie 2.3 in unison.

"It's true, I'd leave you here to die," he admitted.

"OK, the police!" Aaron suggested desperately. "They might be able to get us out! Dismembering people is for sure a crime—"

"We're not 'people,' and *dismantling* is not a crime," Cassie 2.3 reminded him grimly.

"The police know all about us," scoffed Five-O. "They're more concerned about busting clone labs than they are about our actual welfare. More fun, less morally swampy."

"But we're going to die!" protested Aaron. "The police could at least tell my brother where we are—he'd never want us dismem—dismantled, he'd want us all freed—"

"Unless your brother has a high-up contact in the police force who's indebted to him and could be bribed to use his power to get us out of here—" Five-O began.

"Oh my god, I *do* have—I know who to call. I can get us out of here. You have to trust me—I have a police—I mean, not police, but like, sort of. He'd never let this happen."

Derick stared at his device and then, unable to think of a better idea, handed it to Aaron, who took a deep breath and began the slow process of entering a fourteen-digit number he'd known by heart for as long as he could remember.

Jaymie excused himself and followed Rex, but Leonora caught him in the hall.

"Are they alright? Do you think they'd talk to me?" she asked hesitantly, and Jaymie realized he wasn't the only one out of his comfort zone. He wished he could reassure her and explain the situation, but knew the truth was too upsetting.

"They're just on edge. The dinner, the show—it's a lot for one evening," he said. "Uh, any other time, they'd probably like to talk, but right now … Um, I think I better …"

"I understand. You've always been best with Rex." She squeezed his shoulder.

"I have?"

"I'll try to keep everything under control in there." She winked. "Good luck, Aaron."

Rex was angry at themself for losing their cool, but too angry at everyone else to go back and apologize. They were mad at their grandparents for being what Rex considered "Florida People," and at their mom for being objectively the coolest person ever and not passing any of it along to themself, and at Anika for trying to make a mess while oblivious to the much more dire mess happening right in front of her, and at Jaymie for Literally Everything, and at the Aunties for … actually, the Aunties were OK.

The weather had gotten bored of being minus-forty and was warming up in the least mature ways it could think of. Rex opened their window to cool off and was immediately whacked in the face by a bawdy gust of sleet, which they estimated was only half as glacial as the atmosphere in the dining room they'd just left. They began penning a letter to their dad, of the variety that would go in a drawer and never be sent.

An urgent knock came at their door, and Jaymie entered. "I have to leave and get Aar, like, any second," he said. "You can't let Grandma get to you like that."

Rex shuddered at the thought of rejoining dinner and having to look at the weird clone-Jaymie across the table. "I'm stressed, Jay! And Anika's trying to piss her off on purpose!"

"She's doing it for *you*, bud! Would you rather she sit quietly while you get interrogated and misgendered all evening? Plus, it's the only reason nobody's noticed there's something seriously wrong about *Jaymie*."

"I can't handle it."

"It's not ideal."

Rex's rage surged. "*Not ideal?* This is your fault! Stop acting like you know exactly what to do! You have no idea!"

"Rex, I'm sorry, but you've got to keep an eye on him while I'm gone—if they figure out what Jymmy is—"

But Rex couldn't stop. "You're not sorry! You're never sorry. I almost got killed by a cult last month and you don't even care!"

"What! I'd never let you get killed, it'd destroy me—"

"Yes you would, if it meant you got a good story out of it. You think you're invincible, but we only got away by luck! You don't give a shit about us!"

Jaymie's face twisted in anguish. "Rex, you know I care about you more than any—"

"No you don't! Aar's gone and it's all because of you—I hate you!" A wrenching sob escaped from somewhere in their chest, like a prisoner you've had locked up for so long you're pretty sure they've come to prefer captivity, but then one day they go "What's that!" and make a break for it when you turn to look.

They wiped away their tears, and then kicked the leg of their desk, and then let Jaymie hug them to his chest and pet the top of their head.

"I'm sorry, Rex."

"I don't care."

"OK."

From downstairs, Leonora could be heard telling the story of a violist she'd met in Vegas who turned out to be a spy for the NSA investigating possible Canadian enemies hidden undercover as circus performers, or so he'd told her once she'd gotten a few drinks in him.

"Why did you make a seafoam salad?" Rex murmured wetly into Jaymie's sweater.

"That's just what ingredients we had in the house."

"We didn't even have any pineapple."

"Hence marshmallows."

Rex let out a few involuntary cry-gasps, and reminded themself that Western society has taught people to be ashamed of showing emotion, but actually it's healthy, but they still felt awkward and embarrassed, and they wished they could go tell Leonora about it, but they knew they never would.

"Anika's has pineapple," Jaymie pointed out. "No cream cheese, though."

"What was she thinking?" Rex sniffled.

"How about Michaud, though, right?"

"I like him. I'm going to make sure I become just like him." Rex unwrapped their arms from Jaymie's waist and wiped their eyes one more time on his sweater.

"Please, please, go tell him that in front of Grandma," said Jaymie.

Rex laughed shakily. "Jaymie, should we stop hanging out with Grandma?"

"I … It's your call. Mom needs the house, and the Aunties put up with her for Mom's sake, but that doesn't mean *you* have to. Except for tonight."

"OK. OK, we should go. Jymmy might be making a scene by now."

"Oh my god. Jymmy. OK, let's go, Rex! You've got this." He gave their shoulders a last squeeze and they went to join the family.

A man sat at a sparsely decorated desk, eating a microwaveable dinner and making a list of names not unlike Jo's fridge list, though none of them were names we'd recognize. A glass of clear alcohol three-eighths full (though he saw it as five-eighths empty) sparkled near at hand. It was 1:45 a.m., which was often the time he ate dinner, alone at his office.

An old CD player had been quietly masticating on the same album for the last six months. A tenor with an improbably wide vocal range yelped about the sort of complex millennial emotional problems that Poland's most celebrated private investigator didn't quite relate to, and not just because the words were sung very quickly and in English.

The desk held three pictures of his children, posed with their arms draped around each other, from sixteen, ten, and two years ago, respectively, although the last one was actually a band photo he'd printed from the internet, and his youngest cub's attire looked unsettlingly similar to that of the shoplifters he used to chase down early in his career. Appearances weren't everything, though; he was pretty sure his kid was a good kid.

In front of the pictures sat a stapler, an unloaded gun, and a fully tricked-out telephone, which rang presently.

"Brzezinski," he answered, rotating the volume down on the CD player. The singer's voice was replaced by an equally familiar keening tenor, delayed a few seconds by a long-distance connection, pleading, "Tato, you have to help me! I got kidnapped by a collection agency and I'm going to get dismembered!"

With the swift, calm motion of someone who has been coping with alarming situations on a frequent basis for decades, the detective set his phone to record and trace the call, and said, with only a brief stammer as he switched to English, "OK—OK, tell me of the situation."

And then there was a clunk and some indecipherable shouting and someone cried out in pain and the signal was lost.

36

Brzezinski Family Dinner

As a very young man, Detective Brzezinski had occasionally pictured the family he would one day preside over as benevolent patriarch. These visions were never particularly detailed, as he was a practical person and daydreaming was not his specialty.

He'd imagined that he'd one day marry, and he'd have a son who'd grow tall and strong like him, and who'd look up to him and follow in his footsteps and strive to make the world a better place.

Eventually, he'd retire from being a great police detective, he'd cede his mantle to Brzezinski Jr., and the legacy would continue, and Jr.'d have a brave, strapping son of his own, and his line would be known throughout the land for courage and heroism, and so on and so forth. What Brzezinski lacked in imagination he made up for in ambition.

By the time he was six years into his police career, he'd been shot at seven times, hit two of those times, hospitalized three times, had lost a trusted colleague, seen several other trusted colleagues do very untrustworthy things, realized everyone more than a tier up from him was potentially corrupt, and had two bright, healthy children who he prayed would take after their mother and grow up gentle and willowy and with zero interest in upholding the law.

His elder sons had exceeded their father's hopes. In fact, they weren't even particularly upstanding people, and he couldn't be more relieved. They weren't devious enough to consider seriously breaking the law, nor did they have high enough moral standards to make enemies who were. As far as he could tell, they were pretty nice guys content to focus on their hobbies. A musician child, he'd concluded, is a child you don't have to worry much about.

But nobody's children are perfect, and occasionally one must worry. Brzezinski dialed in the "call back" command. A recorded voice told him the number was disconnected and he was already getting exorbitant distance charges just for trying. Next, he called his son's phone, which went to voicemail, and then he called another son, who answered "Yes!" on the first ring.

"Syn, your brother calls me and he says someone is going to dismember him. Please tell me he is only having one of his upsets?"

"Dad! Tato, hey, don't worry—dismember? I would never let that—but did you happen to trace the call, though?" Jaymie sounded a bit frenzied, but that wasn't unusual for Jaymie.

Detective B. looked at his computer and read off the coordinates obtained by his complicated triangulation system. "It is not precise, this tracking," he added. "Let us check the map ..." He pulled one up, muttering soothing technical jargon until he could relay to Jaymie the general area the call had come from.

"I'll go pick him up now. Everything's under control! I'll text you later." Jaymie hung up. The detective took another bite of cold chicken linguine.

Dominik missed his kids considerably, which he hadn't fully expected when he'd "bailed hard" (- Rex Brzezinski, age thirteen) twenty-three years ago. He wished he knew them better, especially Rex, who was reluctant to even talk on the phone with him.

He felt fortunate that his older sons hadn't resented him enough to cut him out of their lives—he had the impression that it hadn't crossed their minds at an early enough age that a parent of theirs could have any reason not to desire their constant presence, and so they'd accepted it was circumstance that had torn him away, rather than lack of affection. His youngest was either less trusting of family bonds or didn't have the same ingrained self-esteem.

In truth, he hadn't realized Rex was his child until they were about a year old. He'd gathered, from the twins' semi-sensical kid-ramblings over the phone, that there was a baby around in some capacity, but at that age they'd enjoyed talking to him in a Polish-English hybrid language of their own invention, and neither ever spoke without the other saying something different at the exact same time.

It wasn't until video calling caught on, and they'd presented Rex, held up Simba-style on his computer screen, that he'd been charmed enough to look into it. He launched a serious investigation into their date of birth, dug around the shady underbelly of his 2001 date book, made a bulletin-board map replete with photographs, push pins, and a few metres-worth of red yarn, and put it all together. He'd solved that case more thoroughly than some of the murders he'd put offenders behind bars for life over. The man was undeniably an exceptional detective.

For her part, Leonora had never meant to keep Rex from him; she was having a busy year gigging and had simply assumed that J and A had filled him in.

"So we're in Atlanta—thriving indie rock scene, by the way—and we'd gotten suited up for the show before we realized the arena had booked the wrong week—no idea what they did about all the tickets—and they couldn't fit us in because those Lipizzaner horses were doing *their* shows, and try rescheduling with a bunch of abused stallions—they're divas. Ha!

"So anyway, it turns out our bus driver, Brian, had family there, and they'd planned a gathering while he was in town. You can bet they weren't expecting a troupe of fully-costumed acrobats and musicians and etcetera to show up at their backyard barbecue!"

Rex and Jaymie's return had garnered concerned smiles from most of the dinner attendees, and no reaction from Grandma, who was sharing a parable she'd made up to illustrate her tough-love vision for country-wide poverty-reduction. Leonora managed to change the subject, and Rex stoically resumed glowering away in their seat. Jaymie had reassured them that as soon as G and G had gone back to the hotel, everyone would relax and start chatting about whatever pop psychology tidbits they'd enjoyed that year, like regular people.

"That's lovely, dear," Grandma drawled emotionlessly to Leonora.

"The adventures this one has!" chuckled Grandpa.

"Auntie Nora, every time you come visit, we hear more stories about Brian. Is Brian a special guy or something?" asked Anika, who was almost definitely holding hands (or more) under the table with the heavily tattooed arts administrator.

"Anika, darling, you and your teasing!"

Rex bristled, not having developed any suspicions about Brian (probably a sketchbag), and angry at themself for not paying closer attention.

"Hey, Mom, so did you and Brian really catch a serial killer in Louisiana, or did you just watch a ton of detective shows together on the bus?" they asked.

"Rex, honey, would I lie to you?" Leonora winked.

"Would you? I literally have no idea," said Rex.

"My girls wouldn't have spoken to *me* that way—" their grandmother began.

"Have you talked to your dad lately? He loves to hear from you," Leonora broke in.

"I write him a letter every month, so."

"It's true, I mail it for them," said Jaymie. "I mean, Jaymie does."

"I do? I do!" said Jymmy. He cast a look of rabid affection at Rex, who shrunk in their chair.

"As in *snail mail*?" asked Leonora dubiously.

"You could Skype him once in a blue moon, Rex—or join in when Jaymie and I do." Jaymie was very obviously being careful not to sound reprimanding now that Rex hated him.

"I like old-school. It's like having a diary I write in about my life and it responds in broken English," said Rex. "Like Tom Riddle."

"He's self-conscious about his written English," said Jaymie.

"I know," said Rex.

"How was your final course, sweetheart?" Leonora asked Jaymie, probably wanting to make up for their earlier conversation. "You finished last month, right?"

"Ah, yes, got the old GED?" asked Grandpa. "How were your grades!"

"Uh, yes ... and ... good," said Jaymie, who Rex suspected had no idea whether either answer was true. He audibly knocked his empty wine glass against his teeth and winced.

"You've put on some weight," said Grandma. "Good."

"They're more alike than ever!" said Grandpa.

"He looks just like me!" said Jymmy.

"No I don't."

"I'm going to cut my hair to look just like his!"

"Don't you dare."

"Is something going on?" asked Leonora. "I thought you two liked having your hair the same?"

"It could use a cut," said Grandma. "Yours too, Anika—how do you get a brush through it?"

"I keep telling her she should grow a 'fro again!" said Michaud. "I've seen the pictures—so badass! I mean, it's up to you, Nik. It's great how it is," he added. Anika appeared unsure whether this was the sort of attention she was seeking. Jaymie opened his mouth and closed it again. Rex looked between them with anxiety throbbing like a physical pain, wishing the two could have communicated earlier about their collaboration on managing the evening.

Jymmy rubbed the side of Jaymie's head. "I think his looks like Posh Spice, but fluffier. Like, kind of crooked on the one side—I know because Big Niki listens to the Spice—"

"We need a word." Jaymie grasped Jymmy by the arm and tugged him out of his seat. The clone obediently followed him into the hall.

"Are they fighting again?" Leonora asked Rex under her breath. Rex grunted in distress.

"My two girls—you two never fought. We made sure of that!" said their grandmother. "Their father and I disciplined them very effectively," she added, for no acceptable reason, to Auntie Farida, who had completely tuned her out.

The unfortunate woman looked up, startled, from her plate of gelatin and marshmallows. The aunts had cooked a chicken, but it wasn't their best work. It seemed everyone had noticed its dryness and opted to fill up on the sides and whatever dessert Leonora had picked up.

"Is that so," she coughed. Dory rolled her eyes at Farida.

It had been years since Farida had attempted actual conversation with her in-laws, but she tolerated them—they never said anything overtly racist or transphobic to her and always left subtext just sub- enough. She smiled painfully and sipped her drink, waiting for the moment when they'd leave and she and Dory and Leonora could stay up late into the night drinking wine and catching up, and then they'd retreat back into their quiet life until the next time Leonora visited. One evening with Leonora could hold you for quite some time.

"Well, I've had about enough *salad* for one evening," said Grandma. "Nora dear, what kind of pies did you get for dessert?"

"Oh, um, chocolate," said Leonora. "That chocolate filling the kids like so much …?"

Rex glanced painfully at Anika, who had also seen the pies and was trying to catch their eye to share a look of scandalized mirth.

Leonora cleared her throat self-consciously. "With a marshmallow topping." She shrugged her defeat. "Since obviously the answer to all our shortcomings is more marshmallows."

50117 writhed melodramatically on the plastic grass, clutching his side.

"You little beast!" he growled. "That's my *kidney!* Do you realize what you've done? This was my insurance policy! I swear to god I'll murder you! I'll murder you like I murdered the man who made me! I'll murder you worse, because you're the man who ruined me!"

"It was an accident!" Jaymie 2.0 objected. (*Aaron*, Cassie 2.3 reminded herself.) "Why did you sneak up behind me like that? I was trying to talk to my dad. He's a detective!"

"I can't believe you punched me in the kidney!"

"I *elbowed* you. I didn't mean to! You startled me!"

"It's broken," said Cassie 2.3, feeling the weight of the tragedy as she examined the silent receiver and blank screen of the apparatus. She'd been longing to try entering in some numbers for fun once Aaron was finished with it. "Well done, Five-O."

"Me? It's his fault!" Five-O pushed himself onto a forearm and glared at Aaron.

"*You* saw the collectors coming and tried to take it from him!" She looked across the field. "Doesn't matter now. We're out of time."

"What's going on there?" The collectors had noticed the scuffle and begun to jog over. Soon the tall woman who'd brought Aaron in and a new, equally tall man converged on them.

"He attacked me," groaned Five-O, pointing at Aaron and collapsing back to the AstroTurf.

The woman took hold of Aaron's arm and pulled him to his feet. "Not surprised. This one is spirited."

"He's not—he's faking! I didn't mean—I said I was sorry!" Aaron stammered.

Cassie 2.3 turned on Five-O in anger. "You're trying to sabotage him so you won't get TNP-ed!" she accused. "You frightened him on purpose! Of course he was going to lash out! He's obviously a drummer!"

"I only wanted to see the nifty machine!" said Five-O, in feigned innocence. She recognized his expression as that of a man who's been called out on his ruse and knows he's going to get away with it anyway—usually because he has expensive representation.

"Let me guess. You needed to buy some time for your 'contacts' to come through ..." Cassie 2.3 took a step toward him like she intended to cause further bruising, but then she looked helplessly at her clean suit and her manicured nails and she felt fragile and plasticky, and she finished with, "I'm going to see you in court one day."

The collectors, still holding Aaron, looked at their clipboard and conferred quietly.

"I don't *know* that I'm next," muttered Five-O. "But you can't be too safe."

The tall man tapped Derick's shoulder and said, "Alright, you've got an appointment."

The woman nodded toward Five-O. "Actually, it *was* his turn," she said. "But this one's Original has gone months without responding to his notices. And we have to keep the place safe. Come along." She followed the man and Derick, leading Aaron away by the arm.

He looked back at Cassie 2.3 with wide, disbelieving eyes, and she wished she'd been made out of titanium instead of super-light, flexible polyurethane purchased wholesale by the company Original Cassie had hired and probably overpaid to make her.

She sadly picked up the telephone, now a useless toy. Cradling it to her chest like one of the children she remembered having but had never seen or touched IRL, she went to curl up in the alcove, giving Five-O a light kick in the other kidney with her flimsy plastic foot.

"I've been going crazy in there. *You* were supposed to be Aaron!" Jaymie hissed.

"I tried!" Jymmy protested. "She labeled me a 'Jaymie' as soon as she walked in the door! How's that for open-minded?"

"I told you to just be quiet and not act so happy!" said Jaymie. "Is it that hard to not be, like, brimming with evil joy all the time?"

"I'm not evil! I just want to be loved!" said Jymmy, with such a gleeful, conniving leer that Jaymie considered giving up the act that very moment and taking Rex away to Florida to start a new life with their grandparents. "I'm actually pretty good at doing impressions," Jymmy continued. "At least, Big Niki says so. But I told you, I have literally never met this person."

"Huh. That's right. You don't know Aaron." Jaymie quelled his panicky Florida reverie. Nobody would like his music down there. "You're me, without a twin. Maybe that's what's really wrong with you. You're just a poor twin-less sucker."

"Look, dear brother," said Jymmy, with the tender animosity of a movie villain psyching up the protagonist for a series of cruel and unusual punishments. "*I'm* having a great time, and *you're* a complete mess right now, no offense, so your theory on the benefits of twin-hood is going to need a lot more supporting evidence before—"

Jaymie's phone rang and he answered "Yes!" instantly, hoping it was Spencer, before recognizing the string of digits on his screen as his father's work number. Jymmy flashed his tiger grin and went back to the dining room.

"Dad! Tato, hey, don't worry ..." Jaymie listened to the familiar voice as his father checked coordinates. Aaron's call had come from a location outside the city, which was fortunate, his father told him, because the system was imprecise and it was easier to find a lone building in the country than to search through a whole city block. Jaymie hoped he wouldn't need the GPS numbers, but was glad to have a backup plan in case Spencer flaked again.

"You're sure he is alright out there, Jaymie?"

"He probably took a drive with some friends and got a little stoned— I'll take care of it. YouknowmeI'mveryresponsible!"

"Follow up, OK, Jaymie?"

"I'll just go pick him up ..."

Jaymie was soothed by his father's gravelly bass, but also aware of that weird feeling he only ever got talking to his dad, like suddenly he wanted to do A Very Good Job at all these random things that weren't even similar to the usual things he put his countless watts of energy into every day.

His dad had never expressed a wish for him to become a PI or have a fancy or heroic professional career. Yet when they spoke, he felt vaguely compelled to serve humanity in a more tangible way than creating clever arty music allowed for. He wasn't sure how. Was delivering the mail not enough? Anyway, he could at least track down Aaron—whom he knew his dad to be disproportionately fond of—and thus save the day!

Both feelings drained away the moment he returned to the dinner table. Jymmy was absent and Rex's face became a mask of alarm when they saw him. Michaud was telling Leonora, "—new project, but I can't decide if the concept is genius or cringe—I've compromised a few creative values for that guy, but there's a line—"

"Where's Jym—Aar—Jaymie?" he interrupted.

"He said there was a ride here for you guys," said Rex, who had swiftly lost all colour. "I thought you went with him."

Jaymie delivered some phrases that his grandparents would probably never forgive Aaron for, fled back into the hall, grabbed his coat and boots, and followed his clone into the night. The street was empty; their ride had left.

37
TNP

Aaron and Derick were led to a comfortable-looking waiting room further down the hallway from the director's office, the tall woman monotoning to them that their patience was appreciated until it was time for their appointments. As soon as the collectors left, Aaron turned to the devastated clone.

"I don't know about you, but I'm sure as hell not waiting around to get dismantled."

"It doesn't matter anymore," Derick moaned. "I knew the process he used was imperfect. I'm just a … a rough draft." His chest shook with the beginnings of a second panic attack, and he gasped, "It's all ending!"

"No, it's not. It helps to remind yourself that it's not a heart attack, and it can't actually kill you, and it'll pass in a few minutes," said Aaron, who had been about to have a panic attack himself but managed to forestall it to tend to the inventor.

"I thought he'd try to fix me—we were researching better techniques! Instead, what does he do? Makes himself a new one and lets them put me away, where he'll never have to think about how he failed!" Derick wheezed and coughed into his sleeve. "Five-O was right."

"It's easy to lose hope in the moment, but if you try to deepen your breath and focus on something simple, like your feet on the floor or how your shirt feels or whatever, it can help calm you down. Like, mindfulness, you know? Also, telling yourself that nothing about this defines you, and there are people who love you—or, I mean, it seems like you have some really nice friends here—"

"He probably couldn't bear to watch it happening, so he used our money to make *her* instead ... And he let me disappear here, and f—forgot about me ..."

"See, what makes it spiral out of control, is that you get anxious *about* being anxious. You try to stop it and it makes it worse. If you can pause and examine your thoughts, and ask yourself: Is this actually as bad as I think it is?" Aaron watched the clone for some sign that the attack was dying down. "OK, I don't know if what you're saying about Erick is true, and as for our situation right now, yeah, we're maybe about to die ..."

"There's no point trying."

"But *most* of the time, it's something much less significant, like some socially awkward thing happened, or there was some miscommunication—"

The clone finally sucked in a deep breath and looked him in the eye, his expression one of desolate annoyance. "OK, kid. Please shut up. Let's get out of here."

Aaron nodded, re-postponed his panic attack, and went to check the door to the hall. He saw the tall woman's leather sleeve brushing against the window, and carefully angled himself out of her sight. She slouched over her phone. Something on the screen made her raise her eyebrows, and she glanced around, looked at the door she was guarding (Aaron ducked), and then swore under her breath and strode off down the hall.

Aaron didn't know it, but this was the first time she'd checked her phone all day. She'd worked late the previous evening collecting the new 50117s, stayed up for a few Saturday night beers, slept in until her shift, hurried to work, and left the phone charging in the office. She'd finally found the message from her co-worker telling her they'd made a mistake and the clone that said he was a twin *really was* a twin.

Unfortunately, Spencer had failed to remember that literally every clone in the building had at some point insisted to her that it was a twin.

And what had become of Spencer, anyway?

As it turned out, many citizens were eager to take advantage of the agency's new weekend hours. As soon as Jaymie and Jymmy had left, a woman came in to inquire about the status of a payment plan application she'd submitted ages ago; four separate people phoned to ask questions about the penalties of illegal cloning in a way that led Spencer to believe they had either made an illegal clone or were planning to do so very soon; a man registered a clone he insisted he'd invented before the laws against home-cloning were set in place—the clone was, remarkably, female. Spencer didn't ask how he'd done it.

It was past dinnertime when he got out, and by then he'd decided he'd take Jaymie to get his brother himself, and if the agency had a problem with it, he'd remind them that they'd accidentally collected someone's innocent human family member. He parked on Pandora Street just before 7 p.m. to pick up the man he thought was Jaymie.

When the woman guarding Aaron and Derick saw the message telling her she got the wrong guy, she sent a reply reading, "Which one?????" and went to consult the other collector on duty about whether it might be a prank.

But Aaron didn't know any of these developments, so he and Derick seized their opportunity as soon as her back was turned, sprinting down the hall toward the office of the director, who didn't work Sundays, and who had the one large window Aaron had seen in the building. He cranked it open and kicked the screen out and prepared to jump toward a new, terrible, grinning danger.

Jaymie lurched down the front steps and into the garage, fumbling in his coat pocket for keys and cigarettes. He flicked his lighter, swore when it didn't catch, and swore again as he stopped short to avoid kicking an unexpected mound on the garage floor. He stumbled, bashed his funny bone against the side of the van, and landed hard on his knees. His lighter skittered beneath the vehicle.

"Motherfrugger! Sonofabirch—" He lay on the dirty concrete floor, groping under the van, only to feel his keys snatched out of his other hand.

"You're *not* driving," said Rex.

"Have to save Aaron! Goddammit! Jymmy, that bastard!" he panted, scrambling to his feet, his sleeve grimy and his hands lighter-less.

"You're drunk, you wino!"

"I tripped!"

The heap he'd nearly bulldozed turned out to be the three elderly cats, who'd decided that a few hours in the chilly garage would be preferable to a reunion with the Brzezinskis' grandmother, who always greeted them with cold, closed-fingered strokes that made them feel icky deep down.

"Passenger side." Rex stood stony-faced, pointing to the other side of the van. The sleet-filled squall had sculpted their clean, combed hair back into its spiky halo, and their unzipped, too-large winter coat winged around their skinny frame as the wind hit them. Light from the porch gleamed off their septum ring. Three shadows prowled around their planted boots.

"Dropped my lighter ..." he said feebly.

"You can use mine. Go."

"Why'd you have a lighter!" He took it from Rex. "God, thank you—we're gonna talk about this later, though. I'm keeping this! Fuck, my stomach hurts."

Jaymie nearly tripped over the cats a second time as they braided themselves around his boots. He clumsily moved them away from the van and got in, pulling a cigarette from his pack with shaky hands.

"Rex, you have no idea how bad I needed one of these. Didn' even realize it, I was so distracted in there—I was thinking about Aar, and I was sure Jymmy's going to fuck everything up—ohmygod—how could they all go on thinking he's was me? This—" he waved the cigarette, "—is what I wanted the whole time, and I just forget it's what I wanted—"

"Are you wasted? How would you forget? You were chain smoking all afternoon!" Rex snapped, carefully backing them out of the garage. Jaymie cracked his window and blew out a stream of smoke, which was immediately regurgitated back into his mouth by the storm.

The door to the house opened with a warm flash of light, and Jaymie flinched as though caught by a paparazzi photographer. Their mother leaned out and called, "Are the cats out here? It's too cold—they're as old as you are, Rex!" She padded down the steps to collect them, hunched against the wind, hair blowing across her face, rubbing her arms and trying to smile, and it occurred to Jaymie that she'd been enjoying the soft, southern, early winter sunshine until that afternoon, and she'd just voluntarily deposited herself into the middle of a nightmare.

"It starts at ten, right? You're on first?" she asked.

"You got it, Ma!" he yelled out the window. "We'll see you there!"

"It's too far to jump," said Derick, still short of breath. "And it's freezing." Outside the window an empty parking lot was dimly visible under a light perched high on a pole. Colossal pine tree silhouettes swayed like tipsy sentinels at the other end of the lot.

"We're better off against the cold than against *them*," said Aaron. He peered into the darkness, gauging the distance to the ground. It was the kind of jump that wouldn't kill you, but might casually break an ankle before sending you on your way. "I'm gonna go for it."

A voice shouted from down the hallway. Derick clasped his shoulder and began to gasp.

"Keep calm," Aaron whispered, as hysteria welled in his own chest. A tiny mewl sounded behind them—his therapist had abandoned professionality and followed him to provide moral support in his time of need. He scooped her up without thinking and stuffed her into his shirt, tucking the bottom firmly into his jeans.

He swung his legs over the sill. Heavy wind pummelled him. He twisted around, dangling by his elbows and then his fingertips. The cat complained half-heartedly against his abdomen. He dropped.

The impact was jarring but not painful; his feet hit wet snow on a bed of pine chips, from which the remains of some brambly plants sprouted, leftover from summer months.

"It's safe," he hissed up to Derick. "Not even concrete."

Derick was panting again. "They're coming," he rasped.

"Hurry up!" said Aaron, already shivering. "We've got to keep moving!"

"Can't ..." Derick breathlessly lowered a leg over the edge and pulled it back again.

"Derick for christsake they're going to take you apart!"

The scientist edged his feet over the sill, gasping.

"Look, hang by your hands, like I did, and as soon as you drop, I'll grab your legs and help you down. I'll basically catch you!" Aaron removed the cat and put her in the snow, where she crouched sadly. He pushed his sleet-soaked hair out of his face, wondering for how much longer he'd be able to feel his arms, and reached up in encouragement.

"*It's over!*" Derick suddenly howled, toppling forward from his seat on the ledge all at once and without warning, so that Aaron was forced to throw himself out of the way or be struck by a pair of pointy-toed brown shoes. Derick fell as a dead weight and landed in a formless jumble on the ground.

"Aahhh that's not what I said to do!" Aaron cried. He scrambled to Derick's side and rolled him, as carefully as possible, onto his back. There was little he could have done; the clone was dead—as they say—before he hit the ground. He'd reached expiration, having lived the usual, healthy lifespan for a being crafted of rubber and dye and a handful of chemical elements.

He had no visible broken bones, but the rubber mask of his face had been knocked off-kilter by the fall, skewing his features one notch away from human, like one of your action figures after your toddler sibling has gone unsupervised for thirty seconds and put it in the oven with some baking cookies to see what would happen.

In the weak light, the folds of his mouth had odd, asymmetrical shadows. One of the open eyeholes was slightly misaligned with where his actual eye was, catching him in a wink that was neither the non-creepy nor the non-awkward type. He looked like a reflection in a fun house mirror—not the skinny or fat ones but the one at the end that just makes the subject look vaguely wrong. A rivulet of sleet ran down his forehead and melted into the eye socket. Aaron heard himself let out a whimper. He gripped his wet cat and began shivering in earnest.

He realized the truth about his friend's demise; what he'd thought were panic attacks were possibly a signal that Derick's hand-crafted form was failing. He wondered if he'd have caught on sooner, had he been a better listener.

A shadow fell over him. "Oh, shit," said the collector.

Aaron looked up and made eye contact with her for a split second before they both bolted—she to a safer exit and he to wherever she was not.

He stepped on a stone, cursed, and turned back to tug the shabby dress shoes from the feet of the deceased clone, mumbling, "I'm a terrible person." He tucked them under his arm and the cat back into his shirt, promising his panic attack one final rain check. The gale blew him toward the towering pines, and he ran sock-footed for their cover.

He could have perished of exposure had it still been minus forty, but the weather had broken its days-long cold spell and decided to have one last wild night before really committing to the bitter-arctic-winter thing. Unfortunately, it no longer knew its limits. It had overdone it, and it spewed freezing rain down on the escaping drummer in a way that made you seriously hope it had someone holding its hair back.

38

The Jo Connors Guide to Soundcheck Etiquette

Aaron pelted toward the trees, trying not to think about the health ramifications of hiding jacketless in the woods; he'd quickly realized he was far from the lights of the city. He wondered how much time it took to catch hypothermia. Not to mention the outer extremities—how long could an appendage stay frozen before you had to amputate?

Fortunately, the pines did not mark the entrance to a dense forest, as he'd imagined, but the edge of a ditch, beyond which lay the highway. The trees stood in an even row, blocking the looming facility from sight of the road and sparing travellers the feeling that the squatting building lay in wait to lean over and crunch them up as they drove past.

As he stopped to tug Derick's shoes onto his feet, Aaron spied a flash of headlights between the branches. He sprinted for the road, knowing that the longer it took to find a ride, the more likely he was to catch a lift from collectors who'd been called in to find him. He had no idea how far he was from home.

Aaron had never liked being outside the city. The countryside was home to all kinds of frightening wild animals, and rural dwellers seemed to have decided that this was a good reason to let their own animals (read: dogs) run wild as well.

Besides these hazards, country residences were an obvious choice for drug dealers and other criminals wanting to hide in anonymity. And what did all kinds of villains have in common—as if their own felonious natures didn't provide enough defence against the world?

Dogs.

He scrambled through the snowy ditch, soaking any patches of his clothing that weren't already drenched from the rain. His therapist loudly reminded him that such activities were not good self-care, but was fortunately not the type to rip up his abdomen in protest. He climbed up to the road and waved frantically at the approaching car, squinting into the high beams as the vehicle slowed. It was sleek, black, and inconspicuous.

The driver reached to open the passenger-side door, and Aaron was about to gasp out his thanks when he saw that it was none other than his own brother, wearing Aaron's jacket, undone, with the hood pulled over his hair. Aaron leapt inside and wrapped him in a soaking embrace.

It was only a few weeks since he'd been picked up on the side of the highway by Stan, narrowly avoiding being sacrificed by a cult. He was having a lucky run, that autumn, for desperate roadside rescues. Or so he thought.

"Kick … Kick drum … Big one with the—"

"Oh, sorry, distracted." Jo thumped the pedal, generating a lethargic heartbeat for the sound guy to doctor. She'd already set up and line checked the guitars, bass, and synthesizers to the best of her abilities, and now sat behind the drumkit, pawing through Aaron's stick bag.

"OK, snare?"

She selected two ragged-looking sticks.

"It's the one on the left with the—"

"No, I know, thanks," she said, striking the drum.

Lucas, who drove a hip, worn-down beater of a car, had taken her to pick up the Brzezinskis' instruments earlier that evening. Rex had told her they didn't have Aaron back yet, but that Jaymie was expecting the "clone office guy" (?!) to contact him at any moment. Perplexed, Jo had no choice but to trust she'd be filled in later. Rex seemed as calm as always, but Jo knew them well enough to intuit that they were aggravated.

The venue had provided most of the kit; she'd fitted Aaron's snare drum onto the stand and placed his cymbals close by so he could install them when he got there. If he got there.

Lucas sat at a nearby table, typing in his phone. He looked to the stage and gave her a thumbs-up. She returned a tight smile and he went back to his work.

"Floor tom … That's the one on the fl—"

"I hear you!" She gave it a reverberant pounding.

She ran her thumbs over the chipped wood of the sticks, feeling their furrowed surface. They were very light—it was no wonder he was accidentally always letting go and flinging them around. She tried to imitate his relaxed grip, which always seemed so incongruous compared with the rest of him. She pictured the motion of his wrists eliciting low, jungle timbres from the toms, or sliding a stick across the edge of a cymbal with a soft, golden hiss.

"What?" Jo forced herself back to attention.

"I said, what all does he want in the drum monitor? I'll just put everything." The sound tech was probably losing patience, and to his credit hadn't tried to occupy himself explaining her own setup to her or informing her how incompetent every other sound guy in the city was.

"Yes, please. But more guitar than keyboard, more backup than lead vocal." She remembered her bandmates' usual requests by now.

"He probably wants them equal. I'll make it equal."

"OK then." She rose from the stool.

"And the vocal mic back there?"

"Oh, right. Check. One two. Cheeeeeck. One two three testing testiiiiing. What's even a song I know, *we're just two lost souls swimming in a fish bowl ...*"

"Hear it in the monitor? You should sing louder."

"THE SAME OLD FEARS, WISH YOU WERE—"

"You've got to eat the mic. You need to project. From the sternum."

"It's OK, I'm not even a singer—"

"Hang on, I'll come show you."

"There it is," she muttered, and left the stage.

"Am I a clone?" Aaron asked, between exhausted breaths. "Did you somehow, by some unfathomable method, for some unfathomable reason, create me? Like, earlier this year? —And I don't want to know how, or what material you used, or what my life expectancy is."

"Yes. I did that. That's what happened," replied Jaymie, peering through the rain-spattered windshield and U-turning back toward the city. "You're a clone. Sorry."

"You know I could've gotten killed in there?" he said, letting his brother's confession sink in.

"That would've been so unlucky and inconvenient! Good thing you didn't!" said Jaymie. Whatever pain Aaron felt at this response he stored away in the same place he'd stashed his future panic attack. The two agonies could gossip together about what a procrastinator he was until he got around to addressing them.

"It's freezing. Why isn't the heat on?" Aaron fumbled at the dial with numb hands.

"I'm just learning how to dri—I was so worried about you I forgot all about the heat," said Jaymie. Aaron sighed and held his hands against a vent, waiting for his breath to return to normal. Then he looked around.

"Whose car is this?"

Jymmy was starting to have second thoughts about the whole twin thing.

First, he'd been hugged—without prior consent—by the wet, hysterical guy. Exploring the driving skills he'd inherited from Jaymie was hard enough without such a distraction. It didn't faze him that his new twin had cold skin, because he didn't notice that kind of thing, but he minded that Aaron was completely sodden, because he'd stolen a very nice shirt from Spencer whilst expunging him, and now it was sticking to his chest.

"Unfortunately, the government is not happy about me having a clone, so we may have to hide away for a little while," he told his new brother.

Aaron (Jymmy was proud of remembering his name) did not look pleased at this prospect. He shuddered and stared into the darkness ahead of them. Jymmy tried again.

"I'm happy you didn't die, because there's a lot of fun things left for us to do together!"

He received a dull, cynical look.

"For example, the band! We'll make so much amazing music. Isn't that great?"

Aaron's expression told him it was not great.

"Also, there are these exciting new things people can have, and they make everything fun, even when what's actually going on in reality is normal and boring ..." He struggled to explain it the way he'd heard about it. "It's like having a few drinks, but more so."

Aaron's forehead creased with incredulity. "Are you fucking with me right now? You're talking about *drugs*?" he said. "Because I've put up with your little streaks of not sleeping for three days and making me record thirty drum takes per night, but if you're going any further than that, I'm, fucking—I'm out. If you want to get into coke or designer pills or whatever the fuck else, I'm taking Rex and—hang on. Are you ...? It would explain some things …" Aaron leaned over, grabbed Jymmy's chin with his cold fingers, and looked with suspicion into Jymmy's pupils, which Jymmy was fairly certain were their usual shape and size and were focusing intently on the challenging task of making a car move in a straight line.

He shook his head free and tried again. "OK, but I heard about this one, it's called TwiLite—it gives you pictures but it makes you happy at the same time—"

"What, like when we tried acid? Shrooms? We just freaked out for most it! All of it, in my case. Remember how we're basket cases?"

"—Which, I'm happy anyway, even without it, to be honest, but people I've talked to who took Twi seemed to really like it—"

"Are you out of your fucking mind? That stuff makes you crazy! You'll fry your brain!" Aaron's emotions, which weren't used to being suppressed this long, were creeping into the upper tones of his voice and threatening to commandeer his tear glands.

Jymmy had little patience for other people's emotions, and was fast becoming irritated at his new twin for being such a poor sport about all the nice, light adventures he had planned.

(TwiLite, incidentally, was anything but "lite." It was a synthetic substance first concocted—legend had it—late at night in a university chemistry lab in Edmonton by a grad student in a Bio-Medical Ethics class who incorrectly completed an experiment involving some kind of molecular alteration, an adequate description of which would cause most of the type of people who bought Twi to zone out after the words "molecular alteration." This student was very open-minded about his failures. As they say, make lemonade—or rather, party drugs.

It was named not after the Mormon vampire stories, but for the fact that ingesting it in any kind of high-dosage or chronic way would put a person in the twilight phase of their existence in short order. [There may also have been a Twilight Zone connection, in reference to the bizarre mental effects it generated.] It was, admittedly, a very good time.)

"Why are we talking about this! I've been stuck in a weird playground with a bunch of clones, about to get TNP-ed—"

"I'm trying to use positive thinking! There's this other one, DPZ—"

"*What the fuck is wrong with you!* That stuff can kill you! Or make you stupid! No. You're not doing DPZ. Got it? The only people who do it are teenage crusties who are already perma-fried." Aaron appeared to be wrestling with his hysteria, but then swore and started playing with the radio dials, muttering, "Put some fucking music on ... Jesus, you sure haven't gotten any better at driving, have you?"

Jymmy sulked. Having a sibling was not as exciting as Jaymie had made it out to be. This man was not only No Fun At All, he also struck Jymmy as being extremely high maintenance.

His initial plan, obviously, had been to convince Aaron that they needed to hide out, away from the collectors, and then to keep him as a drummer in his own band, which would be much more successful and revered than the *Bukowskis*. He'd developed the scheme over the course of that day; it didn't seem fair that Jaymie should get two siblings and he get none.

But as he drove down the murky highway next to a guy who looked very much like himself but skinny and wet and tangly-haired, Jymmy was forced to reassess. It was an unsettling experience—like looking at his own face in the mirror but with the features subtly distorted. It was much different from looking at Jaymie, which was like seeing his own beloved reflection, period. There was something off about Aaron, that was for sure.

Aaron finally failed at suppressing his panic attack. He turned away from Jymmy, whacked the dashboard in frustration, and curled up against the window to let it run its course.

No, Jymmy thought. This would never do. Having a twin was not for him.

He could get rid of Aaron the same way he had Spencer, after the collector tried to convince him to register his clone (thinking, of course, that he was Jaymie). Spence had even gone so far as to suggest he do it without the clone (meaning himself, Jymmy!) knowing about it, so Jymmy could "live his life without trouble from the authorities." *Actually* meaning: he'd no longer be off-grid and anonymous, and wouldn't even know it until it came back to bite him. What fraudulence! What an insidious display of false friendship! The internet had warned him about the government playing these kinds of tricks. Jymmy did what he had to do.

But he realized that leaving Aaron at the side of the highway would be risky, because he'd just noticed his new car had a mirror—to see behind you with—and in the mirror had appeared two headlights, growing brighter.

Besides, he'd gone to all this trouble. Perhaps it was fair to give Aaron a few more minutes to prove he was worth keeping around. Jymmy drove on in the night, toward comforting city lights—and toward discreet alleys and dark hidden corners, if it came to that.

39
Roadkill

Jaymie and Rex almost drove right past the facility; Jaymie was transfixed by the blue GPS dot traversing the map in his phone, willing it to crawl faster into the area encompassed by the coordinates from his father. As they passed, the wind bent one of the pine trees almost in half, and light from the tall lamppost behind it cast a furry halo over its creaking branches.

"There!" Jaymie lunged against the dash and yelled so suddenly that Rex stomped on the breaks, sending them into a wobbly skid. Rex nervously steadied the van, reversed, and turned down the drive into the parking lot.

"Will anybody let us in, do you think?" they asked.

"They were bringing Jymmy here, so somebody's have to, I mean somebody must be around, right?" Jaymie replied. They stepped out of the van, Jaymie leaning on his door to get his balance. Rex hugged their jacket closed against the wind and looked around. Theirs was the only vehicle in front of the building; a single black SUV sat in a reserved parking area to one side.

"Well, we may's well just ..." Jaymie nodded toward the main entrance, and Rex followed him through the unlocked glass doors.

Up close, the building was unassuming. It had been built some decades ago to house a school or institution, then repurposed by the agency after it had closed. The front entrance was nondescript, neither welcoming nor threatening. A few black mats inside the doors suggested it would be proper to wipe their boots, and both of them did so, out of habit. A security guard watching over the foyer stepped forward to meet them.

"Did you find him? —Oh, you're not ... Who are you?" asked the guard.

"We're here for our brother," said Jaymie, too quickly. "There's a misunnerstanding and we need to take him home right away—"

"Your brother? Is this a *clone* you're referring to? You need to go to the main office ..." The man looked them over, his gaze hovering over Rex's partially shaved head until they pulled their hood up resentfully. He was clearly not expecting civilians to walk off the street into the secret facility he watched over, especially young ones, especially on a Sunday evening.

"Yeah, we went to the office, and the guy—Spencer—he says we should come and—uh, he says he'd ... meet us here. Did he not get here? He can explain—sort of a funny story, actually." Jaymie gave a clipped, insincere laugh.

"I don't know about that," said the guard unhelpfully. "Actually, we're taking care of some escaped clones right now, and it could be dangerous, so I need to ask you to leave immediately."

"Excaped? Just now?"

"All queries are dealt with through the main office. Your confiscated clone will be returned after the paperwork has gone through."

"But I need my confisclated phone *now!*" Jaymie objected.

"Sir, are you drunk?" The guard ushered them back to the door without waiting for a response. Rex was ready to resist, but Jaymie's expression had became calculating, and he seemed to lose his gusto. He put a hand on their shoulder to stop them—or perhaps to steady himself—and gave them a look indicating they should cooperate. The lock clicked behind them.

"We're leaving? Just because that tool says so?" Rex protested.

"Listen, Rex, listen. Rex. Listen. Think about it. Jymmy left before us, so he should've got here before us. And some clones are missing! Jymmy is *not* here—and if had been, like, if he'd gone inside, the security guy would've reconnized me." Jaymie raised his eyebrows.

"You think Jymmy broke Aaron out? What about the guy who was driving him?"

"Spencer? I dunno. Might've helped him—maybe he—Jym's persuasive, you know? And they were pals, or something. Fits, though, right?"

"Maybe ... But why sneak him out of there, when Jymmy and Spencer could just explain what happened?"

"You met Jymmy! He's—d'you really think he's into, like, paperwork and exclaiming what happened? Plus, he didn't want to be registered, so his options is either are he admits he's a clone and gets trapped here, or to keep posing as *me*—and *I* have a bunch of fees to pay, and whatever other paperwork to register *him*. Too complicated."

Rex looked back doubtfully, evaluating Jaymie's theory. It wasn't implausible, considering the events of the weekend thus far. Still, they couldn't bear the thought of being wrong and leaving Aaron locked up; the building looked like a giant lethargic toad digesting the contents of its great, grey belly.

Rex didn't have to waver for long.

"There!" A tall woman rounded the side of the building and shouted in their direction. "You, stop!" She thrust her index finger at Jaymie, who pointed to his own chest and then looked around and behind himself, as though to confirm the instruction wasn't aimed at someone else.

A tall man stepped out of the trees on their other side, shouting back, "What? Any sign of—oh, is that him?"

"Stop them!" cried the woman, picking up speed.

The man rushed to head them off, calling to stay still, spouting threats. Alerted by the commotion, the guard popped his head out of the door.

"That's him! The one that got away!" the woman yelled at him. "Don't let him go!"

Jaymie and Rex ran for the van. Rex jumped in, reached to pull Jaymie gracelessly through his door and into a jumble across the passenger seat, and pulled out of the lot as smoothly as their one year's worth of driving experience allowed.

"I get that a lot," said Jaymie, once he'd straightened himself out and they were back on the highway. "From women."

"Give me a fucking break," said Rex.

Safely back within city limits, Jymmy drove the stolen car toward downtown, trying to decide on the best place for Aaron and him to live in the timespan between the escape they'd just executed and becoming famous rock stars.

Jymmy made friends even more easily than Jaymie, not having his Original's solitary day job, haven in the suburbs, and steady musical commitment. Even in the beginning, Jymmy had never had trouble finding couches or guest rooms or girlfriends' beds where he could spend the night.

He'd often secretly slept in the basement at Big Niki's bar, which was his favourite place anyway, and was where he'd first begun practicing his instruments.

More recently, he'd learned that the money he received at the bar could be used to obtain space of his own, to put his acoustic guitar and his Casio keyboard and his clothes in. The apartment he found was small, though, and he had an odd older roommate to whom he didn't want to explain Aaron's sudden appearance—and possible subsequent disappearance. Besides, he couldn't tell Aaron he had his own place when, as far as Aaron knew, they'd been living together at their mom's house their whole life. The bar, he concluded, would be simpler.

"I know a safe place we can go," Jymmy said carefully. "Where the government people won't find us."

"Fine," said Aaron. And there was more silence.

"So, what were the collectors like?" Jymmy asked it in an effort to make conversation, but Aaron interpreted it as a tactical question.

"A man and a woman. Really tall. Black jackets. They carry chloroform and they're good at sneaking up on you, so watch out for that," he replied, staring out the window and holding his stomach, which Jymmy now noticed was bloated and lumpy-looking. He wondered if Aaron had caught some kind of fast-acting disease while in captivity. If it were fast-acting enough, Jymmy speculated, perhaps he'd be saved a moral dilemma down the line.

"Do you trust me?" Jymmy asked, not sure himself why he cared or whether the answer was important.

"Sure, whatever." Aaron appeared to be irritated by something on Randy Bachman's Sunday evening CBC show; he switched to a college station and turned the volume up. Jymmy pursed his lips; he'd liked the CBC show. The theme that week was Songs with Women's Names, and it was the last of a three-part series he'd been enjoying for a few consecutive Sundays, though he couldn't remember the names of any of the songs the host had played.

If Jymmy had had more experience over the course of his short life with close relationships and/or compromise and/or negative emotions, he might have been able to identify the feeling he had as a kind of calculating resentment that built on past resentments and half-hearted score-keeping, and in a normal long-term friendship might be combined with enough familiarity and comfort to temper it into a gentle annoyance. Jymmy could not identify or temper it, and it instead bothered him deeply.

"It's a very safe place," he reiterated quietly. "Nobody will ever know we were there."

"What now?" Rex asked, gripping the wheel. "Do we know where Jymmy lives?"

"We do not," said Jaymie. "Think think think let me think ..." he mumbled feverishly. He'd found a water bottle of Rex's between the seats and chugged its contents to clear his head. Still, it was difficult to focus.

Rex aimed them toward home. The storm had blocked out the city lights, and they drove blindly. "Aaron would contact us right away, right?" they said, fear shrinking their voice.

"'Course he would. But if Jymmy wanted him to be with us, he wouldn't have left without me and gone all by his self with Spencer in the first place ..." Jaymie hunched forward in his seat, compulsively tugging a corner of his phone case on and off the phone. "Scenario: Jymmy wants to make a band. Of course he does—I know how this guy thinks! He's me, Rex! What I wanted most in the world was to make a band, and so which means what Jymmy wants most in the world is a make a band, right? Right!"

"You sound like a crazy person."

"So, he needs a drummer-slash-backup-vocals, and who better than the guy who's been doing it in *my* band for years—a band which is, stylistically spleaking, similar to *his* future band, you can, one can, obviously assume. Jymmy thinks Aaron will be mad at me because I replaced him with Jymmy, and could be convinced to choose him—Jymmy—over me! He's arrogant, Rex. He'll tell him some lies and rumours and some lies about me—and some truths. For insistance, how I'm careless and I drive my siblings to hate me." He looked pointedly at Rex.

Rex ignored the nudge and suggested, "*Or* he's still pretending to *be* you, and hoping Aaron won't know the difference. He could tell Aar that he nearly got caught busting him out, and that the two of them have to go on the lam. He could say they need to not contact me, to keep me safe."

"That's crazy, Rex. Aaron has known me our entire life—I'm pretty sure he'd know the difference! To continue my hippophagy—"

"Your what?"

"—my hypoxesis: Jymmy—in his vanity!—thinks Aaron will like him better and choose *him*, but obvioulsly Aaron will be as creeped out by him as we are, and he'll want to come home to us! Which leaves Jymmy with a choice to make: let him go home? Or no?"

"He'd ... He'd let him go ... Right?" Rex squeezed the wheel tighter. "That's what *you* would do, if you'd captured somebody to make a band."

Jaymie looked at them helplessly. "Of course I would! I mean, I'd've never have captured someone in the first place to make—can you even imagine?"

"None of this is stuff I've ever imagined."

"Aaron and Jymmy, though ... Rex, picture it! No, don't. That is two people who are *not* going to get along. Talk about opposing personalities ... I don't like it, Rex. Is not good..." He rested his elbows on the dashboard and put his head in his hands, and immediately smacked his forehead against the dash as Rex drove over a chunk of animal matter, the original size and species of which had been rendered a mystery by time and the weather's bored prodding.

"Oh my god," said Rex, slowing. "Oh my god, what did I hit!"

"Already dead. Wasn't moving," Jaymie reassured them.

Rex jumped out of the van, intent on making sure they hadn't injured an innocent animal, and Jaymie rubbed his forehead and tried to come up with a plan. The components of his brain responsible for confidence and composure had hidden away somewhere, like a box of two hundred of your band's EPs that you got pressed a week before computers were redesigned without CD drives, and have been sitting in your basement ever since, and now finally an older relative wants to buy one and you can't for the life of you remember what the box looked like.

Rex screamed.

Jaymie tumbled out of his seat and ran back down the highway, the wind nearly buffeting him over as he shielded his face from it and sought his sibling in the darkness.

Skid marks on the asphalt indicated they weren't the first to run over the ambiguous smear. Someone swerving to avoid the long-dead creature had gone off the road, then left a path of tire tracks in the tall grass as they drove back onto the highway. Rex stood by the ditch, staring in terror at something half-hidden in the weeds—something much fresher than the roadkill they'd hit.

It was the body of Spencer, white and lifeless and, for some reason, partly covered by Jymmy's shirt.

"B-backup," Jaymie stuttered. "Need backup."

Rex grabbed his arm and the two of them struggled back to the van, the gale thrashing away at them like a band too terrible and too loud to bear, in a venue too packed to find the exit.

"We have to find out where he lives!" Rex wiped rain out of their eyes and shifted the vehicle into gear.

"Yes. Lives," Jaymie panted.

"Do you know anybody who knows?"

"I know his bar is where what bar he's work. I mean, I know where he works, and he has coworkers …"

"You think they'd tell us?" At Jaymie's paralyzed expression, they frantically continued, "Or you could, I don't know … charm it out of them? Or whatever it is you do?" Rex reached the speed limit suggested by the highway signs and continued to accelerate.

"Don't think I have any charm left in me. We'll have to beat it out of them." He chose a contact in his phone and heard the dull A5 dial tone, like the tinnitus your twin is always complaining about that you know he could alleviate if he'd just wear earplugs to shows.

Rex emitted a derisive snort that sounded more like a hiccough of dread. "Yeah, right. Dramatic enough. Have you *ever* been in a fight?"

"No, but hopefully we won't have to. Intimidation tictacs, Rex! The last resort, when charm finally flails."

Jo slumped at a back table, one foot jittering. A crowd was beginning to gather. One of the other bands was loudly sharing a pizza at the next table. She considered going for a brief walk behind the bar, but then looked at Lucas gazing into his screen with endearing focus and little crinkles in his forehead, and then felt self-conscious at the thought of returning smelling like weed, and then felt annoyed about feeling that way.

"I'm not a singer," she mumbled.

"What's that?" said Lucas, typing.

"I know the parts of a drumkit."

"… 'Course you do."

"Eat the fucking mic? Fucking ew."

"Oh, that. Guess he was trying to be helpful … Sorry, I swear I'm almost done here. Just prepping Allene's interview for tomorrow, so I can enjoy you guys tonight. I really should be at her show—I probably won't get there unless this starts right on time, but I'm going to use the old trick where you look at the posts the next day and say you were there. Is that bad?"

Jo's phone buzzed, and she picked it up, listened, and said, "Hang tight, I'm coming."

40

Ramen High

"Here we are!" said Jymmy. He steered the car onto the curb and off again with a bounce. They were a few blocks off Main Street, not far from downtown. Aaron surveyed their surroundings, his expression conveying extreme reluctance.

"This looks like the last place I'd ever want to hang around at night," he said.

"It's my favourite place in the whole—" Jymmy began, before remembering that he was Jaymie. "I enjoy coming here occasionally, though of course if I truly loved it, I'd have shown it to you before now." He exited the vehicle and waited for Aaron to follow.

"You're parked halfway into the street. You're going to get towed," Aaron pointed out.

"It's not my car," said Jymmy.

"If you leave those loonies in the cupholder the windshield will get smashed even before it gets towed," said Aaron.

"How do they tolerate you?" muttered Jymmy.

"Whatsat?" said Aaron.

"I said, it's not my car."

"Where are we going? I'm cold."

"We could be inside by now, if you weren't taking a fucking million years to get out of the car!" Jymmy's loss of temper surprised himself more than it did Aaron, who just shrugged in resignation.

Though Jymmy was not a patient person, he was rarely angry at others, because he was rarely directly affected by other people's actions. If he didn't like the way a friend was behaving, he removed himself from their proximity. If pursued by a girlfriend whose companionship he no longer desired, he used his words to make sure she desisted.

No one had ever looked to Jymmy to take responsibility or give directions. He'd never had to question whether he'd succeed or fail in such a role. Before his short time in the car with Aaron, no person had evoked in him such prolonged feelings of frustration and disappointment, toward either that person or himself. It was confusing and upsetting.

"This way," he said.

"Tell me we're not going in this sketchy bar. It looks like a total shithole."

"We'll go around back. I promise you won't have to make any friends."

"OK, good."

If there had ever been a point at which Jymmy could have explained to Aaron who he really was and the miscalculation he'd made in trying to enlist Aaron in his band, and then dropped him off at home and laughed it all off, Aaron had infuriated him well past that point, and now it seemed like too much energy to be worth it.

Besides, this situation was Jaymie's fault, and it wasn't his job to deal with Jaymie's blunders. Best to extricate himself and forget about it as fast as possible. He unlocked the back door and held it open for Aaron.

"Yup, a total shithole," said Aaron.

Jymmy could've reminded him that the bar served as a community hub and a source of affordable food and drink in an area being slowly devoured by gentrification, but he didn't have the motivation, so he just muttered to himself, "What a fucking snob," and locked the door behind them.

The overhead light in the basement had burned out. In the center of the room was a tight oval of illumination cast by two lamps procured in the early seventies; both had deep burgundy lampshades and metal stands that wavered as though they stood behind a heatwave. Apart from the hellish glow of the lighting it was a nice place to hang out, and many bands had done so in the days when the bar hosted live music five nights a week.

There was an old couch which was mostly used by Jymmy for napping and practicing, and otherwise sat gathering dust. Along the shadowy perimeter of the room were counters with cupboards and drawers full of arbitrary supplies and snacks of unknown age and origin. Jymmy motioned to Aaron to have a seat and began rifling through one of the drawers.

Aaron joined him at the counter. "You hang out here? Weird. But like, I can see it."

"Do you ever stop drumming on things? It was, like, the whole car ride here …"

"Am I? I didn't notice." Aaron bounced restlessly on the balls of his feet.

Jymmy forced himself to remain composed. "You can chill out, if you need a rest." He gestured again at the couch and put a few feet between the two of them.

"It's OK," said Aaron, following him. "What's in there?"

"Wow, you're, like, *really* up in my personal space, man." Jymmy gave a strained laugh.

"What do you mean?"

"Like, are you always this close in my bubble?"

"Uh … yes?" Aaron looked perturbed. "Since when have you had a bubble?"

"Never mind. Lol." Jymmy thrust open the next drawer and dug through it with frenetic, desperate motions.

"I need some dry clothes or I'm gonna die of pneumonia."

"Noted."

"Seriously, I'm so cold."

"Ok, yes, I'm on it! There's some in here somewhere … Jeez. Demanding, much."

"You have to take care of your clone if you wanna enjoy your clone, dude," Aaron deadpanned. It appeared the revelation of his clonehood had defeated him, leaving him content to let Jymmy take the lead on all life plans henceforth. He found an old radio on a shelf, turned it on, and clicked to the university station again. "Hey, it's us," he said.

"Us?" said Jymmy. Then he recognized the voice. "What! How is it—how did you—"

"It's CKUW. You were right—they play a ton of local stuff. I dropped our CD off a couple months ago, remember?"

Jymmy was so amazed by the phenomenon that was local campus radio that he forgot his irritation. Not only was he astounded that Jaymie was famous enough to be on the airwaves, but this was a song Jymmy knew! It was on the *Bukowskis'* EP, which he listened to religiously!

"*Ramen high, I'm just trying to get by,*" he sang in giddy unison with Jaymie. "*Live like this, you'll be so happy you could die* … Hey, speaking of, you hungry?"

He reached into a cupboard and handed Aaron a package of microwave noodles, which Aaron broke open, dumped the flavour packet into, and began to eat dry, despite the presence of a microwave in the room. Jymmy wrinkled his nose in disgust.

Aaron poked at the dingy couch and apparently decided it was safe to sit on. He settled among the dusty cushions and gazed around his new hideout, idly joining in on the upper harmony under his breath, *"Why do these poisons make me feel like I could fly … Throw some hoisin in your deadliest stir-fry …"*

"If it's the end, is there a new beginning nigh?" Jymmy warbled.

The song's bridge described the time in their late teens that the twins had gotten scurvy from living off carb-heavy microwave dinners and beer. Jymmy sang the first lines of it along with Aaron, but stopped when he realized they were on the same vocal part.

"Oh, I forgot you sing the melody on the bridge," he said quickly.

"I don't. That was the harmony," said Aaron.

"Obviously the upper line is the harmony. It has been the entire time."

"Yeah, that's what I spent, like, *an hour* trying to convince you when we wrote this. I don't know why you *always* have to have the more interesting part. You're all, 'The melody changes to the top line so everybody will notice what a good singer I am, look at me I can sing anything, never mind that Aaron's jumping down a whole octave in the space of one beat …'"

Aaron's tone had lightened now that he was warmer and fed, but Jymmy's annoyance flooded back, and he resumed his search for "dry clothes."

"Did you seriously forget that argument?" Aaron persisted.

"No. I just changed my opinion. The melody is always lower in this song. Obviously." Jymmy slid open another drawer and felt among some rusty tools.

"So, you admit I was right." Aaron stopped drumming, and Jymmy tensed, detecting real wariness on his face for the first time.

"Yup, you were right." He wondered if he'd made a mistake, but wasn't willing to argue about a vocal line that was *definitely* a harmony, just for the sake of his disguise.

"I'm right! Ha. Just like that." Aaron's mistrust appeared to ease away again. He tapped a rhythm on the arm of the couch. Jymmy relaxed.

"Just like that." Jymmy's fingers closed on what he was looking for.

"OK, well, good." Aaron crunched his noodles.

"Good," said Jymmy.

"Good," said Aaron.

"Let's order real food! I'll come sit with you."

"Sure."

Jymmy pulled his sleeve over the end of the tool and let a reassuring grin melt over his features. He stepped toward Aaron. In the same instant, Aaron launched himself off the cushions, vaulted over the back of the couch, and dashed for the stairs.

It hadn't taken the collectors long to start gaining on Jaymie and Rex. Rex had little experience driving in winter storms, and they'd been slowed by poor visibility and rain freezing to ice on the highway. Headlights shone behind them the same way their own, unbeknownst to them, had flickered in Jymmy's rear-view mirror before they'd stopped to check on the roadkill.

Rex drove through the outskirts of the city toward brighter lights. They chose a twisting, circuitous route in hopes of losing their pursuers amongst the one-way streets of downtown, and they succeeded—temporarily.

Unfortunately, Jaymie had been on foot when he'd found Big Niki's bar the previous day, and he couldn't recall the route he'd taken. They ended up wandering in circles for fifteen minutes, during which time the black SUV stealthily caught up and trailed them, from an unnoticeable, professional distance.

Jymmy took the basement steps three at a time with easy catlike leaps. He caught up to Aaron, who struggled with the stiff lock on the back door and dodged aside just in time as the clone slammed against the door beside him. Jymmy's hood fell back. His waves of shoulder-length brown hair spilled loose.

"Who are you what did you do to my brother!" Aaron yelled. He hurled the pack of ramen at Jymmy's head to distract him, but the creature raised a hand with impossible speed, caught it, and crunched its contents to dust in his fist.

Jymmy widened his eyes and purred, "What did *you* do to *my* brother?" for no reason other than to mess with Aaron. He grinned and let the plastic package flutter to the floor. Aaron bolted in the only remaining direction, down an unlit hallway toward the kitchen and bar.

Aaron was fast for a human, but Jymmy was not quite a human. He caught up halfway down the hall and tackled him, wrapping his wiry arms around Aaron's ribcage. The two crashed to the floor, Aaron twisting sideways and letting out a sharp breath as he took the impact on his hip and elbow, and Jymmy careening overtop of him, his momentum rolling him a few extra feet across the floor. A flash of rusty silver glinted from his sleeve, and he immediately looked to Aaron to see if he'd glimpsed it.

Aaron wasn't looking; he was nearly on his feet. Jymmy sheathed the jagged screwdriver and grappled him around the waist, intending to get him firmly pinned before revealing the weapon. Suddenly, a stinging pain lanced through his arm.

Jymmy was not used to pain. He cried out and cradled the wound—three parallel scratches running the length of his forearm, violent red, though not quite bleeding. Aaron's tummy-disease-lump, as it turned out, was sharp and pointy.

Aaron was already fleeing down the hall, his soggy stolen dress shoes hitting soundlessly on the cement floor. Jymmy made swift pursuit.

Sunday was a slow night. The bar's regulars sat relaxing, watching the two TVs, looking at their phones if they had them, or making slow, drawn-out conversation. They raised their heads listlessly as Aaron burst into the room, wondering if they were about to witness a hipster bar fight, and whether it could possibly be worth watching.

The exit lay at the other end of a long counter against which two men chatted lazily and another two nursed drinks alone. Big Niki wiped its surface with his usual aggressive devotion.

Whether it was a stupid attempt to deter Jymmy or just a need Aaron had to find the most direct route possible, Jymmy would never know—Aaron leapt onto the bar, sprinted the length of it (kicking over a full beer glass that Jymmy knew Big Niki would replace at no extra charge) and jumped off the other end, landing lightly in a crouch in front of the door.

Jymmy sprang onto the counter after him, but stopped short when he saw tall, black-jacketed figures looming fuzzily on the other side of the rain-streaked glass door. Remembering Aaron's description, he made a guess as to who they might be, and the sight of a common enemy threw him for a moment; he called, "Aaron! Collec—" Then he shook his head and retreated, vanishing into the shadows of the back hallway.

Aaron rose and reached for the door. At Jymmy's shout, he looked back for a split second—the time it took for the door to swing open and a tall woman to step inside. By the time he was facing forward again, his motion brought him colliding head-on with the front of her coat.

***

Jaymie finally saw a landmark he recognized. He signalled Rex to stop, knowing the bar was nearby and that he could find it on foot. Rex parked and jogged after him down the empty, icy street.

The collectors had given up trying to follow the van's confused circling. They'd already concluded that Jaymie—who'd been wearing outdoor civilian attire—was not the escapee they sought, but an Original who'd shown up to help with the getaway.

At first, they'd theorized that the missing clone was hidden in the van with him, but they changed their minds when they caught sight of the sleek black car Jymmy had stolen from Spencer, now conspicuously parked halfway into the middle of the street. They deduced that it was Aaron who'd somehow stolen it, and that its presence indicated a previously determined meeting place that the Original in the van was also heading toward. All they had to do was wait.

The woman caught Aaron's shoulders to steady him, and he threw his arms around her in relief. Someone meowed irritably. The bar's clientele instantly became bored and went back to their drinks and/or hockey game. Lucas entered behind her and said, "The fuck's going on?"

"Jo, I'm the real Aaron! You have to believe me! Whatever anyone else says!"

"Sure, Aaron, I believe you," said Jo. "You're pretty distinctive. Was that Jaymie?"

"No!" Aaron pointed toward the back hall. "That guy's nuts—*he's* the clone! Oh my god, did he kill Jaymie? Is Jaymie OK? And Rex?"

"They're fine. Jaymie called fifteen minutes ago and told me to find this place and hassle the employees until they gave me the address of a guy who's also named 'Jaymie.' He said they'd meet me here and then we'd go find … you." She smiled at the bartender in acknowledgement that she'd confessed a plan to make a fuss in his establishment. "I actually have no idea what's happening. Sure am happy to see you, though!"

Big Niki kept an eye on them in case they meant trouble, but didn't intervene. He mistakenly recognized Aaron as Jaymie's (Jymmy's) unstable twin brother, whom he mistakenly thought he'd met the day before, looking for Jaymie (Jymmy).

"They're alive? Thank god! You saw him too, right? For a second I thought maybe I hallucinated him—that stuff happens when I'm stressed. Shit, is he getting away? Oh my god, do you think he'll go after Jaymie?"

Jo wasn't sure how much faith to put in Aaron's theories, but she didn't think he'd invented the clone story. Remembering the strange snippets of plotline she'd gleaned from Rex and Jaymie, and wanting to be useful, she made a quick decision.

"Let's not risk it. Go around the building," she directed Lucas. "We'll cut him off." Lucas gave her a dubious look but went back outside. "Wow, you're soaking wet. Stay here," she told Aaron, who glanced at the intimidating form of Big Niki and nodded. "Jaymie will be here in a sec," she assured him, and pushed her way through the room.

In the minute that followed, Jo would find the back door of the bar hanging open on squealing hinges and race into the night after Jymmy's retreating shadow; Lucas would be delayed—and thus spared an encounter with Jymmy's rusty screwdriver—by an inebriated older person who needed assistance getting situated at a bus stop; Jaymie and Rex would throw open the bar door and find that it wasn't Big Niki's at all, but rather the *first* place Jaymie had tried the day before, beside the cell phone repair shop; the two collectors would tire of waiting by the stolen vehicle and decide to investigate the neon signs of the nearby watering hole, where they'd find Aaron shivering inside the entrance, seize him by the arms, and drag him kicking and swearing back to a black SUV equipped with infallible child-protection locks and the kind of substances that made their chloroform look like a spritz of perfume; and they'd syphon out enough mystery-liquid to dismantle a small army of superhuman Jaymies struggling for their lives, never mind one defenseless mortal brought past the brink of exhaustion by a full weekend of one fucking thing after another.

41
Reunion, Part I

Jymmy pelted down back alleys, the bootsteps of his pursuer ringing in his wake. The black-jacketed woman had very long legs, but she was no match for Jymmy's extra-human speed. He slowed to an easier pace, looking over his shoulder every few seconds to determine his adversary's strengths and weaknesses—or to be perfectly honest, checking her out.

She was tall and ran with a heavy grace, like a big tall muscly gazelle, Jymmy thought. Rake-straight, raven-black hair streamed from under her toque as she slid on the ice to make a tight, agile turn down a narrower alley after him, hunting him like a dauntless comic book heroine. Her breath plumed in front of her determined visage in a misty dewy cloud of danger, to be swept from her fearsome cherry lips by the rain. He sure wouldn't like to get collected by *her*.

Or *would* he?

He paused. Then he remembered Aaron's traumatized rambling and the freaky lump in the front of his shirt. He dialed his male gaze down to a male gander and played it safe.

He swerved into a cramped opening between a garage and tool shed, edged through sideways, and climbed over a wire fence into a backyard. From there he shimmied up a telephone pole, lost his grip, slid back down, bounced off the top metal bar of the fence he'd just climbed, fell five feet, belly flopped into a snow-filled garden box with an echoey *poof*, stifled a snicker at his own clumsiness, clambered back up the pole, scaled a garage, and leapt to the roof of a house, where he lay flat against the shingles, invisible in the darkness.

Jo slowed to a halt in the middle of the alley, breathing hard.

"Ohmigod," she panted. "So out of shape." She hunched over, bracing herself with her hands on her thighs for a few breaths, then turned in a slow circle, scanning the alley. Jymmy lay in fidgety silence, torn between competing desires to win at hide-and-seek or go say hi and ask if she'd met Big Niki and would she like to hear a poem he'd made up about her just now.

Jo apparently accepted she'd lost the trail, swore to herself, and headed back in the direction of the bar at a slow jog.

He watched her depart. Then he sat up and picked idly at the shingles, wondering what to do next. He considered walking home to his apartment, as he usually did after a night of bartending, but he was curious about what had become of Aaron, and about where Jaymie was and whether he was mad at him about all this. He was already getting a case of FOMO, and he thought the giant girl chasing him was actually really pretty, so after another minute he dropped to the ground and began cautiously to follow her back.

Despite the woeful cliff-hanger, Aaron was still alive and conscious. With flight off the table and fight resources depleted past hope, his sympathetic nervous system activated its final defence, which was to hand over the reigns to its peacefully defeatist parasympathetic twin, stop yelling, and freeze.

He allowed himself to be led to the vehicle. He waited in quiet anticipation for a mental slideshow of his life, as promised by all the media he'd ever consumed. He hoped he'd get as far in as Rex being around, but not as far as all the dog stuff. But instead, the face of the clone flooded his mind. Beside him, the tall woman manipulated a container he didn't want to look closely at. He shut his eyes. On the screen behind his eyelids, the fake Jaymie said, "It's like having a few drinks, but more so." He hugged the cat in his shirt.

The tall man guided his head under the top of the car door and he settled numbly into the back seat. It had the same leather smell as Other Jaymie's stolen car. Janey was shivering now—he could feel her little ribs through her fur—or maybe she had sympathy shakes, having accidentally gotten too close with her client and begun to mirror the shivering he himself was no longer aware of. *What a stupid name for a cat*, he thought. He heard yelling, which mingled with the intrusive recent memories currently denying him his well-deserved life summary—*"What did YOU do to MY brother ...*"—and he remembered how close behind him the creature had been, and he sighed in gratitude, for this was surely a better end than that.

But the voice was coming from outside. Someone very familiar was calling for him.

Jaymie and Rex, again lost and wandering, had overheard several desperate poetical insults they recognized as personal inventions of their dear brother's, and they'd followed the cries through the night streets. They finally intervened, shouting with such rage and relief that the bewildered collectors released their hold on Aaron and allowed him to be pulled from the vehicle, embraced by his siblings, and wrapped in Jaymie's warm, almost entirely dry jacket.

Jymmy skated his way down the sidewalk, nerves atingle with confusion and glee at the strange day he'd been having. The weather was grudgingly wearing itself out and sending its last few acidic chunks of precipitation gurgling down from the sky to solidify in the gutters. Jymmy tapped his heels and whistled his version of "Singin' in the Freezin' Rain."

Side note: Jymmy is obviously the killer, right? He'd come to life without any understanding of what life was—or knowledge that life had a dire opposite—about six months ago, shortly after the first murder, and before the subsequent four more. That first one could have been a fluke. Plus, Spencer's death was, without a doubt, his fault. Even without real motives for the others, this evidence was against him.

But whether Spencer was a one-off or part of a serial endeavour, it was not murder on his mind as he followed Jo back to Big Niki's. He wheezed with laughter at the irony—the pursuer becomes the pursued!

It was good he went back, because his desire for some light flirting (with the possibility of obtaining a kiss or maybe a guitar player for his band) would send him down a Jo Connors internet rabbit-hole on Big Niki's phone until quite late, and culminate in him listening to—and commenting aloud on—everything the *Ballet Llama* had ever recorded, while the bartender chuckled fondly at him, thus providing an alibi for what was to happen later that night, should he ever need it.

The Brzezinskis' joyous reunion was short lived. As soon as Aaron had gotten his arms through the sleeves of the jacket, he turned on Jaymie.

"Who is that clone?"

"I sure missed you, buddy—"

"Why does that clone exist?"

Jaymie was evasive. "Why does *anything* exist, Aar-bear? What curious ways life has of—"

"Did you try to replace me with a clone of *yourself*?"

"OK, *replace* is a strong word—and it was when I was living on that shitty couch and not sleeping—I think any important decisions I might have made in that difficult period—and *you* had just broken up the band, like, a week before the tour that would've made us famous, so yeah I might have done it but it's not like I didn't have *some* reason—"

"I can't *believe* you!" said Aaron, his voice rising. "I'm sorry, but I only had one happy tearful reunion in me, and I wasted it on that creepy monster that looks like you and picked me up in his creepy car and chased me through that creepy bar—"

"That's a lot of creepy, Aar." Jaymie patted his shoulders. "If you're unsettled, it's perfectly understandable—I was too, when I met him. Celebrations can wait, it's no problem. I know you're probably miffed at me—"

"*Miffed* at you? *Perfectly underst*—I don't even know what to—you're fucking—this is just—"

"If you're about to have a panic attack that's totally fine and I'll sit with you and find you some water and anything else you need, and I am *really* sorry about the clone fliasco—"

"Are you slurring? Are you *drunk* right now?"

"No! I just got very stressed out that you were gone so long, and I had some wine at dinner and forgot to eat all day but I'm practically sobered up—"

Aaron was gripped by a new energy that came from somewhere deeper and darker than either the para- or sympathetic systems could account for. He seized Jaymie by the front of his sweater and threw him against the brick wall of the bar. "I don't even know how to deal with you!" he yelled.

Jaymie blocked Aaron's fist before it could connect with side of his head, then ducked under the arm pinning him. He caught his balance as Aaron tried to kick his legs out from under him, and shoved Aaron away with a forearm to the chest. "Hey, you quit the band like five times! Why do you have to be so fucking unpredictable!"

"*I'm* unpredictable?" Aaron refused to be fended off, jabbing Jaymie's shoulders with his palms and sending Jaymie staggering off the sidewalk into the space between two parked cars.

"Why can't you just *like* our music?" Jaymie shouted. "Everybody else does! What do I have to do? I got us the guitarist from the fucking *Ballet Llama*!" Aaron lunged. Jaymie dodged, grabbed his arm, and threw him past, letting his momentum propel him into the street.

"I do like—I *would* like it—" Aaron gained his footing on the icy road and intercepted a half-hearted swing from Jaymie. "If it didn't keep almost getting us murdered! If you didn't care about your stupid music more than everybody else—" Aaron's knuckles skimmed over Jaymie's jaw with not quite enough force to leave a bruise.

"You never believe in us!" Jaymie wrestled Aaron into a loose headlock.

"You never care when I think something's a bad idea! And sometimes it's legit bad stuff like that cult!" Aaron twisted free and kicked Jaymie in the shin without much force.

A car made a too-quick turn onto the street. It skidded sideways on the pavement, straightened out, and accelerated toward them.

"*Don't care?* I'm constantly trying to reassure you! Why do you think I'm so goddamn positive all the time?" He struck Aaron's shoulder. Aaron leaned into it and body checked him, sending him staggering further into the road.

Rex waited out the storm slouched under the building's shallow awning, coolly filming the fight for future lols. Suddenly they cried out in warning. The car shrieked past the bar in a zigzaggy blur, its driver speeding and almost definitely drunk.

Both brothers grabbed each other's arms, stumbled to safety, and hollered a handful of profanities after it. Then Jaymie shoved Aaron into the side of a parked car, Aaron grappled him around the chest, and the altercation resumed.

"Fuck you, I hope your clone steals your identity and ruins your credit!" gasped Aaron. "—Hey just don't punch me in the stomach, OK?"

"Fine! Why, did you get hurt?" grunted Jaymie, elbowing his brother in the bicep.

Aaron kneed Jaymie in the gut, not particularly hard. "No, I just don't want you too!"

"Fine, I won't, you fucking hypocrite!" Jaymie's mental choreography dictated punching Aaron in the stomach next, but he compromised by tripping him so that he sprawled against the hood of the car.

Lucas returned from behind the building. He wiped the rain off his glasses with the end of his scarf and squinted at the brawl. "Hey," he greeted the collectors, who were pretending they had protocol for dealing with this exact situation and were about to leap into action to enact it. "Should I try to ... intervene ...?" he asked Rex.

"Don't bother," said Rex, looking up from their phone. "They know how to do it without actually hurting each other."

Sure enough, Jaymie and Aaron soon worked past trying to kill each other and moved on to holding each other's shoulders and tussling each other's hair and saying things like, "I promise I'll do a better job from now on," and "It could've gone a lot worse, now that I think about it," and Rex knew it was safe to put them in the van.

"OK, you walking gender stereotypes, are you done processing your emotions? We have a show tonight," they said.

"How quick did you figure out it wasn't me, though?" asked Jaymie, his arm slung around Aaron and his thirty-six hours' worth of stress finally easing away.

"What do you mean?" said Aaron, examining Jaymie's jaw to make sure his punch hadn't left a mark.

"I mean, you've known me since we were born, you must've noticed right away that clone was a total psycho," said Jaymie.

"Oh, right," said Aaron. "Yeah."

"Good," said Jaymie. "I bet you were just biding your time till you could get away from him—so smart!"

"Yeah ... Of course I noticed," said Aaron.

"Right away?"

"Of course I noticed right away."

A stage full of unattended instruments awaited. It was time for the *Bukowskis'* tribute show to start. Anika arrived and, seeing they'd been delayed, invented to the soundperson a story about a family emergency, since she didn't know the story of the real family emergency. A big crowd had gathered—people loved cover acts—so Band #2 finished their pizza, moved the gear to the back of the stage, set up in front, and kicked off the night. No harm done.

But in the lands west of Downtown, another Sunday evening show was taking place. The headliner was bigger than any of the cover bands, so the West End show was the most popular event of the day, unless we count a vastly better-attended matinee hockey game, which we will not. Despite its draw, there were two guests who judged it inferior to the reunion show they'd been at on Friday.

"It's like if you took real a punk band and slowed it down to half speed on YouTube," said one. "It's like if you put a microphone up to a dishwasher and ran it through every possible effects pedal and left it there."

"Harsh," said the other, smiling.

"There's no depth to it."

"Hmm. Could use more low end. Synth bass is never the same."

"It's like they wrote some songs but forgot to have an idea first." She finished the last sip of her drink. "It's like nihilism that cares too hard that it's nihilism and cancels itself out."

"Wouldn't go that far. But it is a little embarrassing when your opener is better than you."

The opener, who had a day job to be at in the morning, was at that moment packing her instrument into its case. She pulled on the many bracelets she'd removed in order to play that instrument, settled a hobbitish hood over her hair, and slipped out before the main act finished, which the two churlish attendees knew was an extremely rude thing for an opener to do. It helped ease any ethical struggles they might have had about what they were planning next. They crumpled their plastic cups into the garbage and followed her out.

The collectors eyed Jaymie with disdain. They'd opted not to intervene in the fight, but they certainly weren't going to let him off without consequences for this stressful and inconvenient episode.

"You think you could be approved for clone ownership after *this?*" said the woman.

"I'll pay all Jymmy's registration and late fees and whatever—" Jaymie tried.

"You helped a clone break out of a top-secret private facility—you'll be lucky if they don't press serious charges!"

"No, that was *my clone* that broke in there, not me—I just got here!"

"You expect me to believe that, when I just watched your clone *break out?*"

"That was my twin! The clone broke him out!"

"I broke *myself* out!"

"So where's the clone?" challenged the collector.

"I thought he would be here, with Aaron!" Jaymie looked around desperately.

"He ran away!" said Aaron.

"You didn't see—? He looks just like me!" said Jaymie.

"Kind of like this guy?" The man took hold of Aaron's arm.

"Didn't Spencer tell you—" tried Jaymie.

"Spencer sent me one text and went quiet, and I'm thinking it was a joke."

"Just give me time to find him!" Jaymie begged.

"You've had six months' worth of time. And I don't."

"No!" Rex objected shrilly, grabbing Aaron's other arm.

"A sponsor!" said Aaron suddenly. "I can find a sponsor, right?"

"That's set up by the administrative staff, not the clones themselves …" said the woman, but there was doubt in her voice, and Aaron remembered that they had little by way of established procedure for clone sponsorship.

"I'll do it!" said Rex. "Just tell me how much—I have money!" They glanced at Jaymie, certain where the funds would come from.

"What are you, fifteen? No can do, kid."

"What's going on?" Jo had arrived in time to hear the end of their conversation. Identifying the tall woman as the primary foe, she engaged her in a stare-down to determine who was more frightening; the collector eventually looked away. Rex filled her in.

"I'll sponsor him," she said quickly.

The woman looked Jo over, taking in the tattoos peeking over the top of her scarf and decorating the backs of her hands. "You can prove your employment? And steady income?"

"Well, when you use those words, 'employment,' and 'steady'…"

"Or a spouse who can co-sponsor?"

"Yeah, right here," she said, grasping a surprised Lucas by the elbow. "Lucas, will you adopt a drummer with me?"

"Um, I'm not sure we're there yet …" he said, half-joking, but when he saw her expression he finished, "But how could I say no to you?"

Jaymie would, of course, cover all their expenses later—it was the least he could do, he assured them, once the collectors had taken their information and been on their way, "Since at least a small part of this is partially my fault."

42
Reunion, Part II, Part I

A young woman walked through the spitting rain toward West Broadway. She had a forest green hood over her face and a mandolin on her back. The instrument case was wrapped in a light tarp, because she frequently spent time in nature and had actually established a shaky accord with the mercurial and much-maligned weather—she'd be granted unimpeded passage home on foot in exchange for displaying proper preparation and respect. She wore high leather boots in which it should have been impossible to stay upright on the uneven layers of ice coating the sidewalk, and yet she dug her pointy heels in effortlessly, like a climber swinging an ice pick into a cliff face. She munched a granola bar for bedtime snack.

A small-town folk star since her teens, she'd planned for tonight to be her last solo show before beginning rehearsals with the band she'd put together for the release of her full-length album. Unfortunately, it was to be her last show, period.

The rain had melted the buildings on either side of the street into a bluish blur, and made the girl into an otherworldly traveller navigating a stormy mountain pass with only her odd-shaped pack and some elven bread. And from one craggy perimeter, two figures emerged, like frost giants crafting solid forms for themselves from the mist.

Sensing something amiss in her environment, the mandolinist turned around. A man in a snowsuit stood a few feet back, taking up the entire sidewalk. She looked back over her shoulder, gauging the distance to home—but down the block, a crooked, wiry figure now wobbled in her path, the tassels of its scarf smudging into blowing rain.

"Allene," rasped the man behind her.

At the sound of her name, she whispered a spell to summon kindly elemental spirits, called out in a lost tongue to the local boreal animals to come forth from winter dens and bare their jagged little teeth in her defence, and drew in the air in front of her the mystic runes that would send a gush of fyre magic cascading forth from the ruby gemstone in her necklace, to engulf the evil being.

But actually, she crossed her arms and monotoned, "Hey, didn't you get my DM? What do you want now?"

"Just send me the bill!" Jaymie told Jo, waving with fake geniality after the departing SUV. "Jesus, what terrifying people … Aaron! Did they treat you OK? Were you OK in there?"

"I punched a guy in the kidney, had sex with a plastic woman, and stole the therapy cat," said Aaron, producing the squashed and bedraggled animal from under his jacket.

"That's my boy!" said Jaymie.

"God, I try so hard to respect you guys," said Rex.

"It wasn't a brag," said Aaron. "You know," he confessed, "there was a little while when I thought maybe I really was a clone." He looked down in embarrassment at the shabby tapered shoes he'd borrowed from Derick.

"Aaron," said Jaymie gently, "If you were a clone, I'd have milked it our entire life."

"I thought maybe there's a reason I'm such a mess, maybe it's a sign something went wrong. That I'm defective, or like, it seems like I'm shutting down, just when everybody else is gaining speed. I know that's not how it works, but for a minute it seemed like it could explain some things. And then I wondered if maybe I'll expire, like the other clones," said Aaron.

"What! You're not defective—lots of people have anxiety! And thinking some outrageous terrible thing is about to happen, like expiring or whatever, that's just part of it. It's just, like, a project. We're working on it. We'll get better at it," said Jaymie.

Aaron nodded. "So, for sure not a clone?"

"I would never have invented you and not told you about it. You're not a clone," said Jaymie firmly. "… You're *me* from another dimension! See, when I was little, I was so lonely. But I found an interdimensional portal! I stepped in and found a parallel world where Mom had drowned whilst on a bender on tour—I know that's dark, but there's a happy ending! The Jaymie in that universe was all alone (she drowned pre-Rex), so I rescued me—you—from an orphan life and brought you—me—back here to be my best friend forever! Am I cheering you up?"

"That never happened," said Aaron. "It took me years to even figure out who you were! I thought you were just this loud guy that lived with me and Mom. Like a weird roommate that climbs in your bed uninvited every night and sings until late for no fathomable reason. Then when I was four or five, I was like, OK, this guy looks *a lot* like me, and then I put it all together about the zygote splitting post-fertilization and making two people instead of one."

"It's funny, because in some of those alternate dimensions, I actually *did* have a twin brother, and his name was Josh and he was an OK person, but I never would have separated him from his Jaymie because what kind of a *complete psychopath takes somebody's twin?*" He projected this last question toward Jymmy, who'd reappeared a little way down the block, smoking a cigarette and lurking.

"It's him!" Aaron exclaimed. "He tried to—I don't know what he was trying to do but he came after me and it was really fucking scary!"

"I wouldn't have hurt you, Aaron! I just didn't want you to go out and get caught by the collectors," Jymmy lied, cautiously approaching. "And I needed a drummer!" This was true.

"What about Spencer, then!" demanded Jaymie. "You killed him!"

"We ran over something dead and he hit his head on the steering wheel!" Jymmy did not add that he had helped facilitate the meeting (and several more meetings, shortly thereafter) between Spencer's head and the steering wheel.

"So you just put him in the ditch?" Jaymie asked incredulously.

"I'd have dealt with it better, but I had to go save Aaron!"

"You're insane." Jaymie's expression was withering but uncertain, and Jymmy picked up on the uncertainty and smiled endearingly.

"Should I … Do we need to catch him?" asked Jo, also clearly unsure what to do about the rogue and impossibly fast clone.

Jymmy began, "If you would smile more—"

"Jymmy!" said Jaymie sharply.

"I meant, it's nice to meet you, nice girl—nice *adult person*. How do your feelings feel today?" Jymmy corrected himself.

"They're fine now, thank you," said Jo.

"'Jymmy?' *Really?* OK, so what's up with this guy?" said Aaron.

"Aaron, this is my clone, Jymmy," said Jaymie. "With a 'y.' Two 'y's. I understand you're already acquainted."

Aaron avoided Jymmy's proffered hand. "Did Jaymie name you that? Our mom tried to spell my name like that—Ayryn with y's—but I dropped it ... Jymmy with a 'y.' Jesus."

"Jysys ..." Jaymie whispered, spelling it in the air behind Aaron. Jymmy yipped with mirth.

"Aaron, I'm happy you're back," said Jo. She squeezed his shoulder.

"Yeah, thanks for ..." Aaron glanced at Jymmy, "... helping me out."

"I'll let you do your band stuff," said Lucas, who'd been watching this exchange with bewilderment and the disappointing instinct that, for the safety of those involved, he wouldn't be allowed to use any real names writing about it later. "I'm meeting some folks at the show. See you there?" He waved and headed to his car, calling back, "And later you'll explain ...?"

"I'll explain everything," Jo promised. "Once I know what the hell is going on."

"Jo! You've got a new romance! —Or something!" Jaymie observed with excitement.

"Or something," she agreed.

"I'm not so sure about that guy," said Aaron, pulling Jaymie's jacket tighter around himself and the cat.

"Just remember, Jo," lectured Jaymie, "Our culture over-emphasizes the importance of romantic love—no need to beat yourself up if you find you're not as into your BF as your *BBBFB*. There are many things in life just as meaningful as romantic relationships—"

"*I* told *you* that!" Rex cut in. "You couldn't understand why some ex was stalking you and I had to explain that girls get inundated with messages since childhood saying they need a guy in order to feel validated—"

"And they were truly wise words, Rex. I felt I should pass it on so Jo won't fall victim to being 'inundated with messages,' and so forth. I really took it to heart."

"No doubt," said Rex scornfully.

"All I'm saying, dear Josephine, is don't make any hasty decisions re: marriage and/or children, because we adore you, and your skills are vital to the success of our enterpr—"

"My name is Joanna."

"What!" Jaymie yelped. "How did I not know that! Did you all know that?"

Aaron and Rex gave an affirmative "Yes," and "Duh," respectively.

"I'm just thinking," said Aaron. "What do all the shows where somebody died have in common? … *That guy*." He raised his eyebrows.

"Ah—that's the Aaron we know and love!" said Jaymie happily. "You know I love you more than anything, right?"

"Still drunk, huh?"

"Except Rex, of course—our little Buddha-punk! You know we love you more than anything, right Rex?"

"I'm still mad at you, Jaymie," said Rex.

"Right, Aaron?"

"That's right," said Aaron. "I love you, Rex, but I was thinking about it while I was locked up—you're going to get, like, *a lot* of botulism in your lifetime. Sometimes I have to put up some walls, you know? I foresee many punk houses in your future, Rex—don't eat any rice you find in the fridge!"

"Aaron, quit stressing about things that haven't happened yet. You guys *are* my punk house," said Rex, as Aaron shifted his cat into the crook of his arm and hugged them tightly. "And I got food poisoning just last week from a casserole you left."

"Rex, that was there for like a month!"

"I know, but I was hungry and I don't know how to cook like you guys do," said Rex, blinking balefully.

"Poor little guy," said Aaron. "Did Jaymie remember to feed you while I was gone?"

"Rex, you only ate a scoop of marshmallows all weekend!" Jaymie exclaimed.

"I was stressed, and don't try to distract me!" Rex scowled. "If Aaron's not going to hold you accountable, *I am*."

"I'll make it up to you!" vowed Jaymie. "I'll do anything—say the word! I'll make your favourite supper every night for two weeks!"

"Two weeks is a lot of plain macaroni with vegan butter and salt," Aaron muttered.

Rex gave Jaymie one of their indescribable teenager expressions, and Jaymie knew he'd made a mistake.

"Quit smoking," said Rex.

"Perhaps I was too hasty in my offer," he said. "A few stipulations—"

"Quit smoking or I'll never forgive you for cloning yourself and getting Aaron kidnapped."

"Rex!" Jaymie pleaded. "You know cigarettes are my third or fourth favourite thing in the world—after you guys, of course, and the wholesome joys of music-making!"

Rex crossed their arms.

"OK, fine. I'll quit after this pack—"

"Give me them."

"They're very expensive and I don't want them to go to waste—"

"I'm always afraid one or both of you is going to die and I'll be alone," Rex complained, and Jaymie finally handed the box over, with great tragic ceremony and many curses. Rex immediately pulled out three cigarettes, put them all in their mouth, and mimed playing their bass, pleased with themself.

"Rex, cigarettes aren't cool," Aaron said sternly, even though he knew deep in his heart that they were.

"I hate it. Somebody take them away from them," Jaymie moaned.

"Give them to Jymmy," Aaron suggested. "As a truce—so he doesn't murder us in our sleep." He turned toward their clone-triplet, who stood chain smoking and observing them intently, the way a child watches adults discuss something they believe is beyond the child's ken.

"Hey! Jymmy," Jaymie grimaced at what he was about to do. "I'm sorry. I'm sorry I made you and then never explained the world to you, and let you go off on your own to figure things out. I don't know if you're a psycho-killer or not ... but I shouldn't have done that."

"OK, Jaymie," said Jymmy, grinning like an overexcited dog that you're not sure is about to lick you all over or rip your face off. "I won't psycho-kill you guys."

"Or *anyone*. OK?" At Jymmy's vigorous nod, he continued, "Would you like me to help you get a job at the post office? I have some leverage with one of my bosses."

"What does 'leverage' mean? Can I get some?"

"It means she sent me really inappropriate messages and I complained enough to probably get her fired."

"Oh. Are you OK?" asked Jymmy unexpectedly.

"Yeah, because it wasn't scary, and I got funny stories out of it. Still, it feels better when people respect your wishes to keep things professional," said Jaymie.

"So then it's not super bad? But if *I* were to do that same thing with the ladies at the bar, *that* would be bad, right?"

"That's right. Don't ever do that."

"OK. How come it's worse if *I* do it? Is *that* sexism?"

"It's a good question. Rex?" But Rex was too busy trying to light a cigarette in the wind to be interested in explaining power dynamics.

Jymmy internalized the lesson and made up his mind. "I couldn't leave Big Niki. He really cares about me. So much that he gives me money just for hanging out behind the counter and pouring people's drinks."

"That's a *job*, Jymmy."

"And there's something about him that makes me feel comfortable. If I was worrying about something beforehand, like whether my landlady will be upset when I pay my whole rent in toonies again, it goes away for a little while. I don't know why."

"Ah." For the first time, Jaymie felt actual compassion for the clone. "I think it's his accent. And he's big and confident. He reminds you of our dad. Even though you don't know our dad."

"If you think so, Jaymie!" trilled Jymmy. "What's that about cigarettes?"

Rex tossed the package to the clone, who merrily pocketed the offering, said again, "OK, Jaymie, I won't murder you, I guess," and bounded away into the night.

"Good solution, Aar," said Jaymie, still looking sore. "I'm glad to have you back … Hey, you were bluffing before about moving out, right?"

"Yeah, I was just trying to make you mad," Aaron admitted, adjusting his cat so her head poked above the collar of his jacket. "Can't leave Rex. Kid deserves a two-parent household."

"Again, basically an adult," said Rex.

"Come back to me when you can eat three meals a day that aren't rotten casserole."

"I figured you weren't serious," said Jaymie. "Give it a few more years, you know? Go see your CBT. Make sure you're equipped, right?" Then he noticed something. He narrowed his eyes at his brother. "Are those my jeans?"

"What? Oh, yeah, I wore them to go see Jo's show, because I wanted to look nice—"

"Without even asking."

"—And my good ones were in the wash. But then I got *collected*, so I've been wearing them all weekend, and now they're all wet and dirty ... Can I borrow another pair for tonight?"

"Unbelievable."

Jo drove the van to the venue, with a stop at the Brzezinskis' to drop off their new pet and get dry pants. Rex was fed sweet potato fries from a drive-through on the way.

As they pulled up behind the bar, the exhaustion began to set in. Jaymie wrote setlists. Rex ate quietly. Jo waited a few beats and said, "Guess I'll go let them know we're—" and was met with versions of "Na, just stay." Aaron sat in the back seat for ten minutes with his head against Jaymie's arm, motionless except to demand a setlist change that Jaymie carried out without complaint. Then he nodded and picked up his drumsticks and played the show.

The *Bukowskis* had made it in time to play third, which was convenient, because had they arrived earlier it might have been challenging for Jaymie not to accidentally charm a cigarette out of someone. They performed what they'd all agree afterward was a flawless set—and I could tell you what band they duplicated, or suggest that they were something on the fun side of almost-indie, like *The Strokes* or *Arcade Fire* or *The Killers,* but wouldn't you rather imagine them as *your own* favourite band? That sounds much more fun, to me.

43

Reunion, Part II, Part II

After the set, Jo's mind buzzed with giddiness and agitation. She wasn't sure what she wanted to do, but neither going home to bed nor smoking herself into oblivion seemed appealing. She packed up her guitar and pedals and wondered what the Brzezinskis' plans were.

Seated at a table nearby, Aaron was reassuring his dad over the phone that he hadn't been dismembered but had simply gotten confused, while at the same time voraciously polishing off the last of two orders of nachos his family had been sharing while the *Bukowskis* played. Jaymie sat precariously balanced on the back legs of his seat, holding Aaron's chair to keep from tipping backwards, animatedly relating to his mother and aunts a censored story of their botched tour. Rex perched lankily on the corner of Leonora's seat. They'd allowed their mother to wrap her arm around their waist; in return Leonora was pretending not to notice Rex taking disgusted but determined sips of her bourbon-based drink every few seconds.

Jo had forgotten her bandmates were in the midst of family festivities. She went to get another drink, exchanging a greeting with Anika, who was coming the other way.

Michaud slunk up beside her at the bar. "Good show," he said. "Too bad you have to tone it down so much for this band, hope your wrist isn't getting bored—"

"Hey. You still owe me from Friday," she reminded him.

"Friday?"

"Yeah, Vendredi. *Our* show?" She tried to stare down at him and immediately remembered he was an inch taller and oblivious to intimidation tactics.

"Don't look at *me,*" he said. "Jake put together that show. Didn't he pay you? I must've caught him before he was too trashed. We made one-fifty each—including Hannah! And that's after the openers' cut. Pretty good, eh? For what it was."

"Right, retired bassist Jake organized a secret show between med school lectures for all the nostalgic crusty-punks and the kids too young to see us when we were actually good," Jo said caustically. "*You're* the one trying so hard to keep your foot in the scene. Jake's moved on!"

"*Keep my foot in the scene?*" Michaud gave a surprised bark of laughter. "OK, I know you haven't kept up much with the outside world, so let me fill you in. Not to sound arrogant, but I *am* the scene. I have a sold-out album release next month. I'm touring with Daffodile. The government pays me to help bands learn to do what I'm doing—that's my literal day job." Jo opened her mouth to interject, but he raised a hand.

"Look, I know I've lied a few times in the past, I've pulled some shit. Nine *years* ago. We're grown up now—I'm not trying to swindle you out of a bit of door money. It fucking sucks about Alexandre, and I know we're both feeling it, but that show was supposed to be *fun*—forgive me for thinking it might be *nice* to hang out with you guys like we used to.

"And you! —*3BFB* aren't really my cup of tea, but it's looking like they might be the next big thing in town! And you want to act like we're has-beens? We're not even thirty! I'm sorry Jo, but get over the fucking *Ballet Llama*. It was great. Now it's done."

Jo was speechless for a moment. "Sorry, Mich," she said reluctantly. "I was out of line. It's not your fault Al's gone. I had a weird day."

"You're telling me! I just had dinner with your band's *family*—it was tense, dude! Those guys are fucking odd—I mean, they're great, I know you love them, but like, weird dudes."

Jo felt a pang she wasn't sure the meaning of, and gave a small laugh that she wasn't sure was the response she intended to give. "Another Standard, please," she told the bartender. "Hey, Mich, congrats on all that stuff. I know you moved on, but I'm glad you still played the show with us. Sorry for being a …" She wasn't sure what it was she was being.

"Pas d'problèmes, Jo. If you ever get tired of the 'Bukowski' gimmick, I might have some room for you in my backing band." He smiled slyly. "If you can learn to get along."

Jo ignored this remark. "Hang on, did you say *3BFB?*"

"That's what the kids are calling you guys—bet you didn't realize you joined a boyband," he teased.

"We are *not* a—"

"Stick with it, Jo, you'll be even more famous than I am! Finally one of the boys!"

By the time she'd finished rolling her eyes, Anika had joined them, and he looped an arm around her and vanished. Jo forgot about her beer, leaving the bartender shaking his head, and wandered to the stage to gather her things.

"Need a ride home?" asked Lucas, who'd been greeting friends in the other bands. It seemed he knew everyone.

"What are you doing after this?" she asked.

"I'm doing an interview tomorrow morning. Need a decent sleep." He shrugged in apology. "Or as decent as possible, at this point."

"Oh. OK. A ride would be great. I'm, uh, I guess I'm ready." She glanced with some regret toward her band's table and picked up her guitar.

"Great! Let me take that pedalboard."

Once Lucas had dropped her off and kissed her goodbye, she shoved her gear in the apartment door, put her one hitter in her pocket, and went back out into the night. It was balmy compared to the last two days; the sky had quit its brawling, hacked up the last of its rain, and passed out, leaving the temperature unsupervised at a perfectly neutral zero degrees Celsius. She pocketed her toque, ran a hand through her sweaty hair, and drifted down the street.

The lights of the Osborne Bridge blinked whimsically ahead, as though celebrating her having played a show where no one was murdered. She decided to go take in the view of the white-frozen river. She couldn't decide if she preferred to admire it alone, or if she wished she had company.

She was fiercely relieved that Aaron was back, and glad they'd had a good crowd, but she felt like something potentially significant had just ended abruptly, and her neurons hadn't shaken off the cortisol.

She was broken from her thoughts by a small voice that hailed her just before the bridge, chirruping shrilly out of the darkness like the distant horn of a long-awaited steam train, breaking through the ice after many months to bring supplies and medicines to a lonely winter-locked pioneer girl who'd thought herself long forgotten by civilization.

"Huh?" said Jo, looking for the source of the sound.

The demon faerie-child emerged from the depths of the under-bridge realm with her coat-full of wares and squinted at Jo from the slit in her balaclava.

"Twi?" she asked.

The next week, Cassie 2.3 was welcomed home by her Original. Cassie's payment plan had spent weeks on the wrong desk under someone's Emergency travel mug, and was finally approved the day they forgot their Favourite travel mug at home.

Cassie 2.3 renamed herself. She tossed around "Cassandra" or "Callie" or "Khaleesi," and then called herself Samantha, because she was her own person. She rented an apartment and obtained both a home phone and a cell phone, just because she could, and used them daily for long chats with the other Cassies.

Cloning became strictly prohibited, but Sam would appear soon after in a courtroom where new legislation regarding the status of existing clones was to be drafted.

In her powder blue suit and smart blue shoes, with her sleek braids coiled elegantly behind her head, she would present a moving argument for clones to be considered real people, to be recognized for the unique challenges their circumstances presented them, and to be provided government support to get their lives underway, rather than end them.

She strengthened her case using three heartbreaking examples: a scientist who'd passed away in captivity after being replaced by an updated version; a young man who suffered serious anxiety because of the uncertainty of his life situation, having been cloned as a musician through no fault of his own; and a possible act of roadside manslaughter that went tragically uninvestigated when it turned out the victim was himself a two-month-old unregistered clone who'd gotten an under-the-table job with the collection agency as a cover (friends close, enemies closer, etc.).

She captured the empathy of all those who attended or watched online afterwards. She charmed her way into policy-writers' hearts even faster than she'd charmed her way into Aaron Brzezinski's pants (which were actually Jaymie Brzezinski's pants, come to think of it).

The province's premier, a known sociopath who spent approximately four quarters of the year at his vacation home in Costa Rica, had approved the agency's TNP program as a way to cut costs, similarly to how he was dismantling the city's hospitals, labour boards, and education system in order to give some rich friends of his tax breaks. He was not swayed by Samantha's argument.

Fortunately, the federal government intervened; dismantling became obsolete and all clones were provided government IDs and a modest Basic Minimum Income for the first few months of their existence.

Many benefited from the program—including Aaron, whose official clone registration was accepted, and who'd been between jobs for a little while.

Samantha joined a law firm, launched a career, and occasionally got flack from her bosses for taking on too many pro-bono cases. She was keen to get serious and re-create the family life she remembered, but these ambitions didn't stop her from phoning her drummer friend for the occasional booty call.

Other relationships did not end on such happy terms. Ericka, the clone created by Erick—a scientist with incredible knowledge of mechanical and chemical engineering and a passion for sci-fi anime—and then tweaked to have two X chromosomes, did not retain the level of fondness for her Original that her predecessor, Derick, had.

She was initially content in her humble existence, willing to help in the lab as well as the kitchen, not to mention the bedroom, and the two lived peacefully for the first months of her life.

Unfortunately for Erick, the clone soon desired her own projects and general autonomy. She turned her vast scientific research skills toward the world around her and, realizing the possibilities open to her, she left. She discovered a city full of potential friends, colleagues, and romantic candidates whom she could collaborate with or not, as she (and they) pleased.

She held a funeral for Derick, whom she'd never met, found an esoteric university research job, and returned to Erick's lab only once to collect a few materials she felt she was entitled to and inform him he was "a sick wacko." So, at least one villain got his comeuppance!

Meanwhile, 50117 bribed his way out of captivity. A few more bribes gained him custody of the two toddlers he'd created to supply spare organs and enable him to live a hundred years or more. Seeing the benefit of a business partner, he won—through bribery—the freedom of his counterpart, 50119, and then adopted the teenager (who was numbered 80258 but called himself White Scorpion) just in case one of the babies didn't make it for whatever reason.

Having exhausted his once-plentiful riches on bribes, and discovering that his new business partner was similarly destitute, Five-O applied for the Basic Income Program for Clones. The plan backfired when the review of his application brought attention upon him and his illegal exploits, including extensive bribery and the murder of his Original.

But the murder case was tricky, considering the circumstances of his creation. He was placed under house arrest and forced to declare bankruptcy. The other Five-O scrounged enough to rent a home and then got a dull job at an office supply company.

The biggest inconvenience was that they couldn't afford to get a nanny for the children and then ship them off to boarding school until their body parts were needed, as they'd previously planned. As a result, the two adult clones were forced to cultivate some semblance of a middle-class nuclear family, co-parent both the identical babies and the sardonic teenager and, like most parents, coach all three through surviving the humilities of public school.

So it turned out that two men, who were really the same man, and their teenage son, who was him as well, and their two young children, who were *also* that same guy, became as tight-knit a unit as was ever known, sharing numerous tender moments, arguments-turned-bonding-experiences, and tearful celebrations of accomplishment at graduations, sporting events, etc.

As one might expect, this unconventional domestic arrangement nurtured a fair bit of light comedy, which didn't go unnoticed. Netflix put out a trite sitcom based on the clone family, which would run for many seasons and, due to good contract negotiation, eventually put all three children through college. White Scorpion would launch an acting career playing himself.

The younger sons would grow into pretty nice guys. They'd conceive of several business start-ups, which would fail, and then do other stuff. When Five-O suffered kidney failure much later, which he blamed on a poorly-healed blow he'd received during a strange, unsettled period in his life, the boys would argue over which of them should get the honour of donating a kidney to their beloved dad; in the end they'd flip a coin for it.

Other clones preferred to remain out of the public eye, or even completely off the map. Jymmy took his cigarettes and merged with the night, melting into legend of the sort recounted on the darkest, coldest days, when the sun was suffering from Seasonal Affective Disorder and refused to get out of bed. The grinning freckled clone was never seen again.

Just kidding. He climbed through Jaymie's bedroom window a week later with a messenger bag full of loose change; he'd found a synthesizer he wanted online and he needed Jaymie to get out his magic credit card and place the order for him.

With her adrenaline buzz finally depleted, Jo arrived home exhausted. She acknowledged to herself that it had been an unusually eventful weekend, and she felt relieved to be past both the drunken giddiness of her night with Lucas and the distress over Aaron's disappearance. She was more than ready to settle back into passivity.

She hauled her gear into the kitchen, tripping over some cardboard boxes and muttering irritably. She rinsed one of the two plates she'd been alternating eating off of. (She knew if she unpacked the rest of the dishes, she'd never wash them, and the sight of them greasy and abandoned on the counter could tip her mental scales from apathy into despondence.)

She opened the fridge and accidentally brushed her list of suspects to the floor, where she left it. Finding little worth eating, she instead carefully packed her pipe for her before-bed ritual. Her phone buzzed.

She saw with alarm that there were several missed calls and messages from the Brzezinskis. She immediately thought of Aaron and of the unpredictable clone, and her tinnitus flared. She dialed back and heard Jaymie's relieved voice: he'd called to check she'd made it home and warn her to stay inside.

A woman had been murdered one street from Jo's building. Her identity was still undisclosed, as were any details: for instance that she'd been found wrapped in her own tarp with her mandolin case clutched in frozen fists, the mandolin missing, replaced with the woman's many, many bangles, which had been removed from her cold wrists and left jangling at the bottom of the case.

Warnings were sent to the city's venues, urging audiences to return home quickly and not linger outside in Jo's area. It had all happened shortly after Jo left the show; she'd probably just been dropped off and might've already been on her walk from the time of the murder to time of discovery.

She assured the siblings she was safe, and said good show and goodnight. She read her texts: worried messages from the band, and a note from Lucas that his interview was cancelled and he'd like to take her for breakfast if she was up for it tomorrow. Then she sat at the table, too tired to feel angry or afraid, and poked at the bowl of her pipe, thinking.

She set the pipe on the counter, retrieved the paper with her two lists, and fastened it under its guitar magnet. Then she scanned the floor, spotted her sharpie lying where it had come to rest under the cupboards, and used it to write "Lucas" on the sheet, twice.

44

Interlude 3.1: The Further Laments of Jaymie Brzezinski

Voice File: WPS120719_001
Interview of Jaymes Brzezinski, 12/07/2019, 11:15 A.M.
Transcribed by Adam Glennon, Admin. Asst.
Interview concerns Ayryn Brzezinski, reported missing twelve hours.
JB = Jaymes Brzezinski
CP = Officer Carl Porter

JB: Or it's like you know when you've been invited to more than one party and one is better, but the other one is a birthday you're obligated to go to so you need someone to pretend to be you, because they're happier at the chill party and couldn't care less that three out of six members of Noble Pirogue are at the other party and maybe they'll recognize you this time. See this is why I need a teammate.

CP: Back to the matter at

JB: Or like when you have a job interview but you're working at your current shitty job and you need someone to pretend to work at a meat packing factory while you interview for the post office, and yes I should have prepared him psychologically for the duties a meat packing job entails, but I was just trying to make a better life for us all. Am I such a terrible person?

CP: OK, I can see you're upset. Is there anyone who might
JB: Oh are you recording?
CP: Please don't touch the (indecipherable)
JB: (Louder) It's like, you know when you're locked out of eBay because of a wrong password, and someone comes with his stupid notebook full of thousands of passwords, because he's totally paranoid about hackers hacking his online banking even though he only ever has like eight dollars at any given time, that's why he never leaves a tip even though it's abominable behaviour, and he has all your passwords too because you never use the same one twice because of creativity. Like what do the rest of you do? I guess you have a password book of your own, all to yourself? Oh my god that's so fucking depressing.
CP: (indecipherable)
JB: I don't think he'd get murdered like the other ones did, he's always on guard, and he's scrappy. You've never had a fight with him but I have, like sometimes I'll say something that rubs him the wrong way and he'll just take a swing at me, you know?
CP: (indecipherable)
JB: Yeah, we fight. Drummers can be physical people. Like, I'll debate an issue all day if you want but he'll just lose patience and suddenly I'm defending my life. He's got some moves up his sleeve. Underestimation, that's what gets you. I've lost like thirty percent of those fights, OK possibly more, I see that look you're giving me Rex. All I'm saying is I don't think he's dead.
CP: (indecipherable)
JB: What? No nobody is saying he's dead, I just figured you would assume. We were going to a show, which is obviously, our dad's a detective so I feel like I have a natural instinct for the type of assumptions a professional might make in this situation
CP: (indecipherable)
JB: No I wouldn't say we're aggressive people. All I meant was OK we're brothers so that's different. It's not like he
Where was I last night? It's a long story. OK I feel like you're looking at me in a weird way like I might have done something, which is frustrating. Like he might have gotten confused or seen a dog and had to hide. It's a whole thing, I don't want to get into it

but I really need you to help me because I left my paranoid brother alone in the minus 40 and I have no fucking idea where he is and if I can't find him I don't know what the fuck I'm going to do.

CP: (indecipherable)

JB: I guess he does, at least according to the self-diagnosis quiz we found on WebMD. I don't think of it that way though. But I see you're getting out what looks like a missing persons report, so OK good in fact he's deeply disturbed and, no I can't even. What? No he's not on medication. Nothing against hey I know it helps a lot of people. If that's what gets you going. I've been known to take a few supplements here and there myself. Just sometimes there's a lot to do in a day, you've got a family to look after and work and dreams and sometimes you've really got to GO FOR IT you know? Sorry didn't mean to startle you. But nothing long term, hey I'm not like a drugs guy. What are you writing down? Anyway I guess we're more like 'you are who you are' type people you know? What?

CP: (indecipherable)

JB: Oh, this. Forgot I was holding it. Here.

CP: (indecipherable) could be helpful if we do launch an investigation. Do you have

JB: The thing with him is he just needs a bit more reassurance, which usually is fine and no problem, but then sometimes I just get careless and I. I should just do a better job, shouldn't I. You know I think you have the mic pointing, here let me fix

CP: (indecipherable)

JB: That's it? Yeah we'll call if we think of anything. Thanks for your help

45

Interlude 3.2

The Ballad of the Ballet Llama
By Lucas Yarbrough. December 12, 2019.

What can be said about the once great band that was/is the Ballet Llama? Though Friday's "secret" show was appointed a Reunion, perhaps this question is better answered with a Retrospective (for by now most of their OG crowd have come to understand the toll that time can take). And what grand memories such a recollection shall comprise!

You will be happy to learn that this reporter has done his research: The BL was formed in the spring of 2009 by long-time friends Michaud Dubois, Olivier Martine, and Alexandre Valliere, in the latter's parents' garage. Their first show was held in that same garage on the third of June—an unplanned organic response to the weather finally being nice enough to spend an evening outside. There was an audience of six. I, dear readers, was twenty-one at the time, and had just finished college and moved to the big city. I was one of those six. Not to brag.

That summer saw the addition of seventeen-year-old guitar wizard Jo Connors and bassist Jake Lowes. With the full lineup and a brand-new debut album recorded DIY-style in somebody's basement, the band had found their sound—by autumn they were selling out Lo (a bar near the university that was the happening spot at the time) to hordes of seething punks, and the record was an underground sensation across the country.

The band was unofficially governed by Dubois and Connors, who became close friends (and rumoured lovers, though I have confirmed with an inside source that these rumours are false) over the band's two-year existence. However, not everything was fun and games. The group's strong personalities didn't always meld as well offstage as on.

It came to a head in 2011, during a three-week tour to Quebec, where they had an especially high concentration of fans, as one might expect of a Franco-punk band. Rumours of scandal/murder/overdose/heartbreak/bankruptcy have also been discredited by this investigative journalist (apologies to those of you who've been loving the legends) but still, too many drunken shows, unruly afterparties, and poorly planned sleeping arrangements had thrown the bandmates' tempers (some of which were already famously fiery) into disarray.

Said Connors in a recent exclusive interview, "Yeah, bit of a shitshow."

With the previously harmonious Connors and Dubois at each other's throats over the slightest disagreement, it was unclear whether the band would last the tour. According to Connors, the performance quality was deteriorating. As the only one to have learned an instrument before joining the band, Connors was annoyed that (in true punk rock fashion) the musicality came second to the band's own enjoyment of the tour. Of her bandmates' musicianship, Connors recalls, "Alexandre and Jake eventually got decent. The shows were still falling apart though." More significant were the disagreements about the direction of the band. Some members wanted to sign with an indie label, while others wanted to double down on their raw, lo-fi sensibilities and

DIY promotion tactics. A couple of members were "down to sell out, basically," and the ensuing discord spelled the premature end of the tour. Somehow, they made it home, and even went on to (separately) make more music! So, where are they now?

Dubois's debut solo album "Mon Nom" hit number one on the college charts last year, and the upcoming release show for his follow-up has sold out (not before yours truly managed to snag a spot on the guest list. Again, not bragging. Maybe a little).

Connors disappeared from the scene for a while, but now plays with local indie rockers The Bukowski Brothers (see my October post about the BBBFB), whom I suspect not only of learning their instruments before starting the band, but also of possibly being kind of a bunch of nerds, in a good way. A definite change of direction, for Connors.

Olivier Martine and Alexandre Valliere formed Shifty Principals, though Valliere took a step back from music and was frequently substituted on drums by Garrett Kliewer, who recently did a stint in the Bukowskis. (Funny little scene we live in, isn't it?) SP, who are strictly straight edge, still have a following and perform occasionally, though Martine's principal project is now The BMI Babies, who play Motown covers with an alt-rock twist.

Jake Lowes quit music and went to med school, having obviously asked himself the question: how do you follow up a band like the Ballet Llama?

But, dear readers, I promised reminiscences! Highlights of past local Llama shows include:

- The time Olivier "Three Chord Oli" Martine challenged Connors to an impromptu guitar-off that consisted of Connors ripping some kind of disjointed ingenious mayhem for about ten minutes and Martine playing the same

- drunken three-note lick repeatedly and poorly each time it was his turn, to the great amusement of the audience

- The time Michaud Dubois mosh-surfed all the way to the sound booth and accidentally knocked the sound guy out with a combat boot to the head (the difference in sound quality for the rest of the show was negligible, the BL's main mixing request being "make it loud")

- The time bassist Jake got too inebriated to stand up, sat cross-legged meditation-style on his massive bass amp, fell off, and finished the set lying on his back on the floor

- The time Casio Bob of [scrunge-rock duo Gunt](#) tottered onto the stage in a fit of incomprehensible plastered passion, tore the microphone from Dubois's sweaty grip, unleashed a trilingual (English-French-Gibberish—and maybe Low German?) tirade against the Establishment, and then proposed to his girlfriend before being escorted from the stage. Needless to say, the BL's rhythm section provided an affecting soundtrack, Connors filled the gaps when he stopped to chug his drink, and Dubois provided semi-accurate French translation. (She said yes.)

- The time I got home at 6 a.m. from a BL after-after-party that I'm not sure any of the band were even at and, deeply lamenting that I'd never learned an instrument myself, took up pen and paper to proclaim the glory of the province's punk scene—and so this blog [was born](#). Fun fact!

The Llama broke up before their third summer and left us with a one-album legacy, a handful of bootlegs and B-sides, and many fond memories. Let's not sugarcoat it: The Ballet Llama were a mess. But they gave us something that few bands can achieve: the embodiment of a feeling—robust, inflamed, alive, and very much an expression of this city. At risk of sounding like a punk rock preacher, it is this feeling that we need to hold onto in such uncertain times, when the experience of live music, once so life-giving, now brings with it life-threatening risks.

I urge you, everyone who lives and breathes and feels and especially everyone who loves local music, to take up the mantle left to us by our lost fellow show-goers, and let the scene thrive. It's what they would have wanted.

Oh yeah, and this past Friday's secret reunion show? Hell, I had fun. Before, during, and after. Especially after.

R.I.P. Alexandre Valliere

46

The Interview

"*Especially after?* Wow, dude, way to burn my band!" Jo stood in the entrance of Lucas's apartment building with her hands shoved in her coat pockets and her hair flying wild. She'd forgotten her gloves and hat.

"Oh, you finally read that," said Lucas. "I posted it three weeks ago, so I figured I was in the clear by now. Will you come in? I missed you—wow, eight whole days!"

Jo frowned but stepped in from the cold.

"It was a really fun show," he said as she followed him down the hall. "But that drummer kid only played one beat the whole time. I couldn't say it was amazing—I'd lose my credibility!"

"I know we weren't amazing! I just didn't think you'd talk about us that way. Like the show was a joke because the band has been over for so long—" She paused, trying to organize her anger into cohesive thoughts.

"I never said that! Are you projecting? You're great, and so is Michaud and the rest of them. But people are nostalgic. Most of my readers weren't even *at* the show, because you guys made it a secret for some reason." He laughed. "They just want to remember how much fun they used to have."

"You could have at least *told me* you were interviewing me! I never would've said the tour was a shitshow, or that only Jake and Al were any good!"

"I thought you knew why I was asking."

"Forgive me for thinking you might just be interested in my life!" she snapped. Lucas held open the door to his apartment for her.

"OK, but I was obviously planning to write about the show."

"You *didn't even* write about the show! And we were *in bed!*"

"Only for some of it!"

Not all the material for Lucas's article had been collected while he and Jo were in various states of undress, but it was safe to say a lot of it was, since a significant portion of their time together had been spent that way.

Jo hadn't entirely put aside the misgivings niggling at the back of her mind since the murder so close to home, but the holidays had arrived with a jolly brutality and she felt surreal even thinking about the subject. She balked at the thought of asking questions—innocently and to gain clarity ("But don't you feel weird that the murder happened right here? Where *we were?*")—and seeming paranoid, especially after recently trying to convince a few friends and family that she'd been abducted by a cult. (That *had* happened, right?) Plus, Lucas was perfectly nice, they'd had nice dates, and it felt nice to have someone to see over the holidays. Nice.

She'd tucked her murder list in a drawer and commenced job hunting and practicing for her upcoming surf-rock gig, and she'd have dismissed her reservations entirely and declared Lucas a totally normal person, except that she felt a disconnect between them more complex than simply the fact that they'd only been dating a month. It was sometimes like they were shouting into each other's ears over loud music, and each missing a few key words of what the other was saying. She sensed that they were failing to fully connect, either because he was deeply disturbed, or because he wasn't a musician. She couldn't tell, because she'd never been with a non-musician before. Maybe if she'd spent more time on dates and less time with her guitar, it'd be easier to avoid hooking up with a murderer.

She was also struck by a strange insecurity when she thought about how this man was the most respected information source on the city's music scene. Even the handful of small publications mostly overseen by musicians weren't as popular as he was, because frankly they weren't as consistent or as good. He was the main media window into what she and her friends were up to, and it clearly gave him a confidence she herself didn't feel, even as a purveyor of the music itself.

Finally, Lucas had gone to Alberta over Christmas to see his family, and Jo had had some time to get her thoughts together—and to read the blog post he'd written about the *Ballet Llama*, which she'd had open in a browser tab for a while.

Lucas kept his composure. "Maybe we *were* in bed, for part of that discussion, but I thought I played it pretty safe with those quotes—you said things about those guys that were way worse than what I wrote in there—"

"I was venting, and you took advantage of—they're good musicians, I just—I mean, do you think *I* could've joined the *BL* without knowing a B chord? I'd have to be pretty damn hot!"

"First off, you are."

"Not the point!"

"And second, I *could* remove the post if you're *really*—"

"And Michaud kicking the sound guy in the head is not some sentimental joke. He could've been concussed!"

"They poured some beer on him and he woke up right away. I remember."

"And then at the end you make this melodramatic spiel about how we should all keep going to shows even though everybody's getting murdered!" She became aware of how wildly she was gesturing, and jammed her hands back in her pockets.

"I can see you really picked it apart line by line," he sighed.

"It's kind of a weird thing to say, don't you think?"

"I know shows aren't safe now—

"Well, when you think about it, they weren't exactly safe *then* either. Like, our crowd was almost all dudes, and the girls who did come didn't all have a band of scrappy guys who had their back like I did, you know what I'm saying?"

"OK, what are we talking about? Are we talking about Safe Spaces now?"

"People are all, *Oh, back in the good old days* … Like, sure, glad *you* had a good time."

"I think you have a lot on your mind. Do you want to take off your coat?"

"No!" She stood on the doormat. He filled a kettle and plugged it in.

"I don't like that people have been killed," he said. "But this is my livelihood. And yours—even if you don't actually make a living." (Jo kindly ignored this comment.) "I know you'd go nuts if you couldn't perform. So I stand by what I said—we should stop that freak, but it's not worth losing the scene." He sat down on the couch, and she resented his calmness.

"You're right," she admitted unhappily. "But …"

"So, you accept my apology?" He leaned forward with a perfect and appropriate expression of repentance. She felt a surge of frustration.

"Also, you did a Where Are They Now and you wrote like half a sentence about Jake—classic Ignore the Bass Player," she said, not ready to let him off the hook. "And he's not even in med school—that's an inside joke and I never even told you that."

"Well, sorry I misunderstood the *Llama's* inside joke. He just wasn't in any other bands."

"OK, but he got a Master's in anarchism or something by the time he was twenty-three! And now he's getting a PhD—that's at least as impressive as us and our bands."

"Not more impressive than the BBB—"

"Don't try to flatter me!"

"Well, I didn't know! I would've written more about him. I would've written more about the band, more about the *end* of the band—?"

"Are you seriously trying that right now? You sure pretended like you knew how it ended! Way to kill the mystery, by the way."

"No, forget it, keep your secrets. But you could've at least told me about Jake."

"You could've told *me* I was being interviewed!" raged Jo.

"I thought I did! You knew about the blog, and I asked you those questions—I pretty much did everything except, you know, use that actual word, *interview* ..."

"Wow, and somehow I thought dating someone who uses words professionally might result in some decent communication," said Jo.

Lucas stood up abruptly, his face finally mirroring her anger. "OK, we've been going out for *a month*, and I didn't realize we had issues to *communicate* about yet." He moved brusquely into the kitchen to unplug the kettle, which was making an irritating hissing sound. When he returned, he was calm again. "So maybe I messed up, but also maybe there's more going on here than I realized—not saying you have baggage, just maybe there are some touchy subjects I should be careful about. And I do want to communicate. You can always ask me anything."

Are you the murderer? Jo thought, but somehow she didn't think that was the kind of communication he was looking for. Well, what the hell—

"Are you the murderer?" she asked.

***

She arrived home and found a post-it on her door notifying her that rent was due soon. Insulted, she folded it and tossed it down the hall.

Taking in her half-unpacked apartment, she suddenly felt frustrated that she hadn't been adult enough in the past few months to make a basic, pleasant home for herself. She chose a box at random and upended it onto the kitchen floor. Out fell a landslide of the smaller boxes that her effects pedals had come in and which now held safety pins, makeup, and other easily-lost items. She opened a sub-octave fuzz and discovered a pair of feather earrings her sister had given her.

She put them on and went to examine the effect. The bathroom mirror had been remounted in a ludicrous position by a previous tenant much shorter than her, and she had to bend to see her whole head.

She found an elastic and scooped her long hair into a parody of an elegant bun. The corner of her mouth twitched in displeasure. She moved closer and saw there was a very small line there that remained when she wasn't smiling. The delicate feather earrings tickled her collarbone, causing her to shrug uncomfortably at her reflection. *All grown up*, she thought.

She was leaning on the sink, ruminating, when a rap came on the window in the other room. There was only one person she knew who had the audacity to do this without even texting first. She sighed, but felt something ambivalently release within her at the thought of company. She moved to her window and slid it open.

"OK, what's in my mail today?"

"Some kind of rent threat, and some kind of death threat. Popular guy, aren't ya?" Her mail carrier slipped through the bedroom window, flailed for a second, and then twisted lithely to land on the floor without touching his snowy boots to the bed. He tugged his bag after him and handed over the mail. She scanned a postcard with a scenic view of Montreal and some newspaper-cut words half in French.

"Ha! That'll be the *Llama*," she said. "They've got a weird sense of humour … For fuck's sake, there was already a rent notice on the door …" She crumpled the other letter and tossed both missives onto her desk. "Sorry, not trying to shoot the literal messenger. You here to tell me about a new tour we're going on?"

"Never, I refuse."

"That's still where I'm at. Mostly."

"It's Aaron, by the way."

"Oh! Sorry—context—why are *you* here?"

Aaron set down the heavy bag and stretched. "Jay's got a tummy ache, so I'm filling in. My CBT wants me to try exposure therapy, and there are apparently three dogs on this route, which I'm informed are so-called 'very friendly' and so-called 'basically rat-sized' and so-called 'just want a belly rub,' so here I am, getting exposed."

"Well, you must be hours behind. Jaymie only ever stops by at six in the morning."

"I'm hours behind," Aaron confirmed. "Heard on CBC yesterday there were two more sightings of the jumbo coyotes. In St. James—have you been following that story? Anyway, I wouldn't say I crawled down here for a pep talk, per se, so much as needing a five-minute congratulatory breather after petting Dog Number Two. *Almost* petting."

Jo smiled and made a gesture offering him the end of the bed, then sat down at the head of it and pulled her feet up. "Welcome. And, since you're here, I've actually been wanting to ask your … input. On something."

"No one's ever said that to me before," Aaron said, in facetious wonderment.

"Ha. You mentioned that Lucas has been at all the shows where someone died. I keep thinking about it."

"Oh, I forgot I said that. Yeah, except for the most recent, he was at the last two. I don't know about the earlier ones." Aaron settled on the bed.

"He's at every show worth going to, so he would've been at most of them—and the mandolin girl died *in my neighbourhood*. Right when he dropped me off."

"Oh damn. That does sound sketchy."

"I keep thinking, it's so weird they're all musicians. Even if they weren't playing the show they died at, they were all in some kind of band. Except for, like, the one donut vendor. But musicians are Lucas's thing—he meets them, studies them, built a livelihood, like he said …"

"OK, now you've convinced *me* he's the murderer. But …" He took deep breath. "I am often reminded by my siblings and my CBT that I'll come up with a million reasons why something terrible must be true, and I become one hundred percent certain, and then once I've calmed down I realize that there are actually a lot of other possible explanations."

"OK. Well, since you pointed out that it could be him, I sort of asked him about it and made him pretty angry at me. And since we're in a fight anyway, maybe it's worth checking the evidence …" She stopped, realizing she'd just been called out by a guy who'd once made her play car-Twister because of an animal many metres and several fences away from them.

Aaron leaned forward, pensively rifling the contents of Jaymie's mailbag, and Jo wondered if she'd said something wrong. He finally said, "Shit. You got in a fight with your boyfriend because of something I said? You know I just *say* stuff like that, right?"

"What, so you never actually thought it could be him?" She felt a twinge of annoyance, and couldn't help but flash back to Lucas's angry-hurt face earlier that morning.

"I did, but I also thought it might've been the sound guy at the last show, or Stan, or maybe *you*—"

"Well, sorry for respecting your opinion!"

"Don't apologize. Just keep it in mind, next time." He gave a weak laugh. "Seriously though, you didn't break up over it, did you?"

"No, he just got pissed off and I left … You should come with a disclaimer, you know? Like: may come up with random theories and present them as actual insight." Jo was already planning an apology to Lucas for the things she'd said, and then an apology to Aaron for the things she was now saying and possibly had yet to say before the conversation was over. She felt an odd lump in her throat. It seemed like she'd been issuing a lot of apologies lately. Maybe she should go back to just avoiding people. She hugged her knees.

"I thought it was basically stamped on my forehead," said Aaron drily.

"Yeah well, sorry for forgetting you're—" She caught herself. Aaron's usually pale face was flushed from the cold, and she couldn't determine whether his expression was amused, offended, or simply thoughtful. She knew he'd been dealing with his issues long enough to have developed some resilience about other people's reactions to them. "I think I'm a little … off balance today," she said slowly. "Sometimes I get stressed out by …" She looked out her snow-laced window and improvised, "the holidays."

"No kidding. Our grandparents were in the city—poor Rex was at their wit's end, and Mom was scheduled back in Vegas to play for Christmas, so we were trying to think of stuff to cheer up Rex, but Jaymie quit smoking like six different times in two weeks and he was a total wreck. But we had a good x-mas lunch with Anika and our aunties. How's yours?"

"Good. Quiet," said Jo. "Sorry for … Are we practicing soon?"

"Definitely. You know Jaymie." He paused. "It's funny because I'm having a bit of a dilemma today too."

"What's going on?"

"My friend Samantha messaged me to get together, and I like her, but I'm not great at this on-a-whim stuff, in the long term. She thinks I'm a misused clone and that we therefore have a deep bond, and I don't want to be rude, but I think I've gotta call it off ... I haven't had to do this a whole lot before. It's been fun, but she needs to know the truth. And it has to be today, because she just got a Pomeranian to settle her baby-cravings."

"And I thought being in a relationship was complicated."

"I mean, that's the ideal situation, since this casual stuff is making me kind of nervous, but women seem to be OK to sleep with me but then not super keen to, like, date and hang out in public. I'm not sure why."

"Oh," said Jo.

"Kidding—I know why," said Aaron.

"You could say you need to hang at your place, no dog." Jo suggested. "Boundaries."

"It's obviously because I'm very handsome but very stressful to be around."

"I don't find you stressful to be around."

"I was kidding again. But you're right—she's not going to, like, call the government and tell them I'm not a real clone."

"You haven't told her you're not a real clone?"

"Of course I have, but nobody ever believes me! Jo, I'm living a lie!"

Jo snorted in sympathy. "I know you'll do the right thing," she said.

Aaron sighed and checked the time on his phone, then said, somewhat surprisingly to Jo, who had finally managed to forget about it for a few seconds, "Really sorry about Lucas. I hope you can work it out." He stood and shoved his bag out the window. "I'm late for Dog Three."

"OK, good luck exposing yourself?" She offered him a boost.

"Thanks, Jo. See you at practice!"

They did not practice that week; Jo cancelled because someone she knew had died the night before, and she was out of sorts. Normally her stoic enthusiasm for her craft made her happy to jam at both the best and worst of times, but something within her finally faltered.

The victim wasn't quite a friend, but a long-time acquaintance—the mastermind behind a project that was a quirky, decades-spanning staple of the scene, a producer of scads of lo-fi, experimental home recordings, often forgotten until he resurfaced with some bizarre idea for a concept album or for a show that would come off either brilliantly or disastrously but was invariably underpromoted, barely attended, and mythologized later. Casio Bob of the scrunge-rock duo *Gunt* had been murdered, and Jo was hell-bent on vengeance.

Part Four

TwiLite

47

Jo Makes a Murderer

It was a Friday in early January, and Jaymie Brzezinski had woken up early, consumed too much coffee—or whatever Jaymie Brzezinski's "coffee" was—and decided to change all the locks on the big old house on Pandora Street.

His siblings sat eating a leisurely breakfast and making occasional remarks of encouragement or skepticism while he disassembled their front doorknob.

Rex was still on winter break but had today risen hours earlier than they normally did on holiday. Aaron was wearing an uncharacteristically tidy button-down shirt and black pants, and doing nothing to dissuade Jaymie's mania; Rex was fairly certain he felt more at ease when Jaymie was in a rare paranoid funk.

"What if Mom comes for a surprise visit, and we're all out somewhere, and now her key doesn't work?" asked Rex.

"Maybe that'll encourage her to inform us of her plans," said Aaron.

"We'll hide one somewhere for her," Jaymie assured them.

"I'm just not sure this is necessary," said Rex.

"It's basic safety, Rex," said Jaymie. "We should have done this years ago. You never know who's skulking out there …"

"Basic safety," nodded Aaron. "We've given out a ton of keys over the years."

"… They break in through a loose screen door …" Jaymie murmured. "They pawn your gear, they steal your twin …"

Rex rolled their eyes.

"If you're concerned, you could check all the windows to see how easily they open from outside," Aaron suggested.

"I'm way ahead of you, Aar. I was up at five a.m. sneaking into my bedroom while you were still asleep. All I had to do was break into the shed—I changed the lock after that, I can assure you, I was at Canadian Tire the minute they opened. All I had to do was break in and get the ladder from the shed and lean it against the maple tree—not against the house, see, it looks like it'd work against the house but I tried that first and it turns out you have to use the tree, and I'm really hoping my ribs are only bruised—and you climb up and you walk across the porch roof to the pines on the other side—the ones where you can't climb from the bottom? Because the branches are gone? But if you're as high as the porch roof—"

"You're at least as high as the porch roof," muttered Rex.

"You just climb them like a ladder, and guess what! My window was open a crack—"

"We like some fresh air," Aaron clarified for the benefit of nobody.

"We do—and I just jumped over and pulled it open!" Jaymie finished ecstatically.

"You didn't!" said Aaron, setting down his spoon in dismay. "That easy?"

"That easy! … On the second try. It's actually pretty icy out there. But if you grab the windowsill—you can get a grip on it if you aren't too far when you jump—and then you kind of shimmy along … Like I said, it took a couple of tries, and we may have to repair the roof."

He finished unscrewing the doorknob and it clattered to the floor, its smaller components scurrying away under chairs and cupboards like insects streaming from under a rotten rodent carcass grabbed off the ground by a fascinated toddler intent on showing it immediately to their two older siblings.

"You fell? I thought I heard something loud outside the room this morning, but I figured I dreamt it," said Aaron.

"Are you guys sharing a room again?" Rex asked in amusement. "Because you're afraid of Jymmy?"

"It's such a big house, we'll never fill all the rooms anyway," said Jaymie. "And I'm not sure if you've noticed, but Jymmy is *extremely* off-putting. Nearly gave me a heart attack the last time he showed up. Anyway, why put in extra effort to take up space?"

"We wouldn't share if he had a lady-friend over," said Aaron. "Obviously."

"Or if *he* had a lady-friend over," said Jaymie. "Hypothetically."

"Anyway, it's been a stressful few months," said Aaron. "People shouldn't isolate themselves."

"You know, Rex, this whole room-sharing stigma, it's all part of the suburban-industrial complex. Keeping communities apart …" Jaymie dropped one of the tiny screws he'd been working into the new lock and scrabbled at the floor tiles for it. "Keeping families separated in unnecessarily large houses—for what?"

"It's usually just that I'll fall asleep watching TV before I go back to my own room—"

"It's a culture of loneliness—a *conspiracy* of loneliness! That's what it is. Human beings alone are weak! So how best to make us all feel helpless? Cut us off from one another until family members don't even know how to have a conversation with one another—don't even know how to sit down and have a G-D meal together …"

"Oh my god, I never thought of it that way," said Aaron, draining the last of his cereal milk.

Rex had had quite enough. They deposited their bowl in the sink, then seized the box of cereal and pulled the bag out to examine it. Someone had yet again picked all the marshmallows out and left only the cereal, though none of the three would ever admit to it. Rex shoved the bag back in and put the box haphazardly on top of the fridge with the others.

They briefly considered moving back in with their aunts, but decided getting out of the house for the day might suffice.

"I'm going out," they interrupted, as Jaymie ranted about the paradoxes of social media and loss of human connection.

"Wait till he gives you the new keys, Rex," Aaron advised. "You never know where he'll end up today or when he'll be back."

"Aaron! I'm driving you downtown for your job interview, on my way to work! Did you forget? You keep the van, and I'll walk the rest—I don't mind. What a nice brother I am …"

"I didn't forget," said Aaron. "I just didn't get as nervous as usual because I already know the boss isn't a mobster or a nutcase."

"Here, I don't need this right now." Jaymie put down his screwdriver and dug a key from the lock kit. He tossed it to Rex. "Make some copies, 'kay?"

"How many?" asked Rex, pulling their boots on.

"Six. Hmm, twelve. We do have a few friends, after all. And you know how fast Aaron loses them. He won't use a keychain and he'll drop it in the snow and then it's gone until springtime—"

"That's *you* that does that!" Aaron protested. "Watch, Jymmy will stop by in May and find all twelve keys scattered—"

"On second thought, only three. Better to be safe," said Jaymie.

"Better to be safe," echoed Aaron.

"Sounds Jymmy-proof to me," said Rex wryly.

"Rex, he's very clever!" Jaymie warned. "If you're out and about, and a guy who looks exactly like me comes up to you and asks for a copy of that key, don't give it to him!"

"Rex, can I have a copy of that key?" asked Aaron.

"Is this a test?" said Rex.

"Very good, Rex, you pass," said Jaymie.

"OK, I'm glad you guys are happy," said Rex, grabbing their coat from its hook. They weren't sure if their brothers had worked themselves into a neurotic feedback loop, or if this was standard early morning behaviour and Rex was usually too busy sleeping or rushing to school to witness it.

"Actually, I have a terrible stomach-ache," said Jaymie, as Rex grasped him by the shoulders and moved him out of the way of the door.

"And you smell like cigarettes," they commented.

"Savour it, Rex! I quit again twenty minutes ago, so this is the last time you'll detect that sweet, heady aroma," he said with a hint of umbrage.

"Sure it is," said Rex.

"Why are you awake?" he retorted. "Noon is still five hours away."

"I woke up because *somebody* smashed into the porch roof three times at, like, six in the morning. I thought there was a very slow gunfight happening outside. I'm glad there isn't, so I can leave—bye!" Rex stepped into the winter sunshine and loped down the steps as he rambled something behind them about the recklessness of youth.

Taking a deep breath of icy air, Rex wondered where to go. Maggie's? No, she was at a curling event with her new boyfriend in the red toque, probably living a thousand lifetimes in one afternoon. Rex walked toward the bus stop and decided to make their way downtown. They felt a surge of excitement as the Number 47 conveniently rounded the corner. It was a new year, and it felt like the kind of day when anything could happen.

***

Jo woke in a pool of rich amber sunlight, pouring through the window above the bed like the contents of many expensive bottles from your ex's whiskey collection, as you dump them one by one into the toilet.

What kind of psychopath doesn't put curtains on their bedroom window? she thought, rolling over and twisting a rope of hair across her eyes as a mask. Her movement woke Lucas, the psychopath whose bed she was sharing.

"Morning," he mumbled, from somewhere to the left and slightly on top of her. "I'm sure glad you came back."

"Likewise," she replied, trying lethargically to extricate herself from his limbs.

"Still early …" he yawned.

"You're lying on me again."

"Sorry," he said, rubbing his eyes and freeing her. "But you do tend to take up the whole bed." He gave her a sleepy smile. "Do you want to keep resting for a while?"

"Until at least eleven, ideally," she admitted. "But you don't have curtains, and it's so bright in here!" She sat up and hugged her pillow in front of her chest, resting her chin on it.

He groaned. "I know, I took them down because they had stains, and I guess I got used to waking up with the sun. Did the five-thirty a.m. thing for a while …"

"Oh. What kind of stains?" Jo asked, and then inwardly chastised herself. It was way too early to start getting suspicious.

"Uh, mold? I don't know … Or was that supposed to be a dirty joke, because they're right beside the bed?"

"What? Oh. Yep. Ha."

"Well, since we're both awake, and we have nowhere to be, and you're already making dirty jokes …" He reached around the pillow to stroke the skin of her back. Lucas's hands were large and capable-looking and weirdly devoid of music-related callouses.

"Hmm … Just need some water," she said.

Jo had never been quick to get in the mood in the morning, a time she'd come to associate with coffee-withdrawal headaches, bad breath, and, if nothing was pressing, the first hoot of the day. She reached over the side of the bed to scoop up her clothing pile.

"No need to get dressed for my sake," said Lucas, and she shrugged and dropped it again. Several guitar picks had crept from the folds of her discarded clothes, reminding her she needed to go over a few songs before the surf-rock show. She still hadn't asked Lucas if he'd been at *Tornado Tornahdo's* last performance, where the guitarist she was replacing had been killed.

"Are you coming to the show tomorrow?" she asked.

"Of course. I love surf-rock, and I heard a rumour that the guitar sub will perform in only a bathing suit."

"I assume you started that rumour and used your media mogul powers to disseminate it. Or maybe that's what their guitarist wore at the last show? Which you were at, of course …?"

"I *was* there, and that *is* what he wore. I assumed you'd honour his tradition." Lucas blinked at her raised eyebrows. "What, too soon to use the poor guy to coerce you into objectifying yourself on stage?"

"Oh god. Were you there when it happened?"

"No, I went for a burger during set break. I heard he was in the back room by himself. It's crazy, because we'd just watched them play this fun, energetic set, like, five minutes before."

"Brutal."

"Let's not think about it."

"Are you ever worried *I'll* get murdered?"

"I like to think you could hold your own." He brushed her hair behind her ear in a way that might have felt sweet if Jo weren't preoccupied.

"So you're not concerned about me? Even though I could end up like that trombonist at Jazz Fest last summer."

"So could I," he pointed out.

"Fun fact: he was in the *BMI's* horn section and he'd just finished recording on *DZB*'s latest album. Or the singer outside that shoegaze show—she had a performance art project called '*Lost, the Show, the Band.*' Real elaborate. Philosophical, conceptual. Only played out once. Did you know that?"

"I guess I did."

"Or the kid from our house concert. He was a music student—solid keyboardist, apparently. Filled in with the *BMI Babies*, I found out."

"I'm impressed. I honestly thought you were a little out of touch with the scene, for someone who used to play in it all the time."

"I looked into it a little, after Casio Bob," she tossed her head indifferently, as though she'd caught herself up on a trending political issue and not a slew of violent deaths. "He was a keyboardist too—obviously."

"Jo, I think you're psyching yourself out."

"Do I look psyched out to you?" She forced a calm smile.

"You look charmingly piqued," he said, and kissed her shoulder. "I think you should forget about it. The police are on it, and I'll be at the show, so if you're afraid, I promise not to let you out of my sight."

"The police, yeah. I always forget about them because they haven't found anything yet. I'm sure they're investigating … Hey, I wonder if they'll want to ask *you* anything, since you were at all those shows and wrote about them," she said innocently.

"Hm."

"Wait, have they?"

"I didn't have anything useful to tell them. I'm not a musician—I didn't hang out with any of those people … How'd we get on this topic?"

Jo wondered what the police had asked, but could tell he wasn't eager to discuss it. So, it was probably time to employ an age-old cinematic cliché that Rex would probably not approve of: i.e., exploiting one's God-given feminine wiles for purposes of manipulation.

She set aside the pillow she was holding, gave a slow, languorous stretch, and shed the blanket that had entirely abandoned Lucas to tangle itself greedily around her legs at some point in the night. Lucas leaned back on his pillow, smiling politely at her and neither displaying overt lust nor making an effort to avert his eyes.

"Well, you can't have been to as many shows as you have and not know Bob, at least a little. Poor Bob," she sighed.

"I'm honestly finding it difficult to focus on Casio Bob right now."

She swept her hair off her shoulders, then arced her legs gracefully over the side of the bed. There were times when one had to briefly compromise their personality for the sake of a noble investigation. Seduction was a potent tool, not to be overlooked in its power for Good—

"*Ow, fuck! Jesus!* What the hell is on your floor! Is that a *knife?*"

"Shit! Are you OK? Ah, yeah, I started carrying it when I go out." Lucas leapt out of bed in contrition. "Fuck, how'd it come open?"

"The thing's sticking right out! Goddamn, I thought I got stabbed in the foot! Fuck, that's the hugest pocketknife I've ever seen!"

"Ugh, I'm sorry! Is it bleeding? I for sure owe you breakfast at this point."

"Ahg, sonofabitch little—not you, *it*. No, it's not bleeding. But what a stupid fucking …"

"Here, lemme rub your foot."

"It's fine, I'm fine ... I mean, I guess if you ... OK, that actually feels pretty good ..."

Jo re-evaluated. Perhaps there were more effective strategies.

"Sorry, Lucas," she sighed. "I think I need to put some clothes on and get things done today. Gonna apply for jobs before the weekend, so I'm not stressed about it."

"No problem. I'm looking forward to the show tomorrow!"

"Me too," said Jo.

"Hey—dumb question—when you asked me the other day if I was the murderer, you weren't serious, were you?"

"Na. I was just pissed about the article. But also, how did you know? That you wouldn't be interviewing Allene the next morning?"

"What?"

"You asked me out for breakfast. How did you know your interview was cancelled?"

"Oh, she cancelled it first. I was supposed to call her at work but they scheduled her in meetings. Sorry Jo, the truth is always more boring and sad than you expect, right?"

"... Sure, right. Damn it, poor thing."

"Well, I have a few tasks today, too. I need to take some things to the pawn shop."

"What kind of things?" Jo asked, too quickly.

"An embarrassing typewriter from my hipster days ... An old acoustic guitar I'm too ashamed to learn now that I'm dating a super-sexy pro ..."

I'm losing it, Jo thought. *He's totally normal and I'm being crazy. Aaron was right.*

She gave Lucas an apology kiss and said goodbye. She wasn't completely ready to accept that she had no real hope of finding the murderer—Casio Bob deserved better, Alexandre deserved better!—but she was ready to acknowledge that her nerves were frayed lately, and she needed to calm down and rewire her frazzled brain. And she had the perfect thing to help her along. She'd been saving it.

48

Rex Meets a Murmurer

Rex disembarked on Main Street and took a walking path to The Forks, where the city's two rivers converged, marking a site Rex was vaguely aware had some kind of historical significance, but was best known as a tourist destination abounding with upscale boutiques and food court treasures. They stopped in at The Market—a folksy sort of shopping mall—bought a samosa, and Google searched on their phone whether any major colonial atrocities had been committed there.

The sun was enjoying a rare stint of New Year's optimism. Possessing mercifully little foresight as to what the year 2020 had in store, it shone sloppily down from the endless sky, dappling the ground with dancing shadows and making it impossible to tell the yellow snow from the white.

Rex made their way toward the river, admiring a snow sculpture of a bison and leaving a trail of curried potato crumbs. More carvings lined the path as it wended its way along the riverbank, some hewn from transparent glassy ice, others from snow packed like solid marble.

A recent sculpting competition had produced a fantastical array of pieces in all different styles. Rex strolled through a bucolic pioneer scene, turned a bend, and patted the intricately textured fur of a snarling wolf that had frozen solid a moment before eviscerating an invisible prey. They gazed up at a life-sized elven woman riding a muscular reindeer and wearing only a short woolly skirt and fur bikini top. They wondered if she felt chilly.

They wiped their greasy mitts on clean snow and rounded a bend to where a number of artists had collaborated on a Christmas-themed diorama, including a delicate ice nativity.

The scene had not remained unadulterated long; skilled vandals had graffitied it into a dance party, given Joseph innumerable piercings, and arranged two of the three kings so as to appear engaged in a shady transaction, while the third stared skyward with swirls over his eyes.

Rex smiled and took a picture for Maggie before their gaze settled on a laughing Little Drummer Girl. The snow of her body was tinted a rose-quartz hue in the shadow of the trees. Her rimy sticks were suspended in an eternal paradiddle, her head tilted back in merriment, and her hair spray-painted neon pink and lifted by a permanent breeze.

Rex still hadn't worked up the courage to ask Jo to track down the drummer from the secret show. What if she thought Rex was a stalker weirdo? Rex wasn't a creep! Rex just wanted to jam with her! —Unless she wanted to do more than just jam, in which case Rex would maybe like to do that as well.

It felt complicated. They knew gender had something to do with their apprehension, and while they understood that anyone who couldn't accept them could go suck it, they still would've preferred just to be accepted all the time and not have to worry. It had been four months since they'd mumblingly informed their people of their name and pronoun change and stoically agreed—to much all-around relief—to bear the remainder of high school, and while it felt like a weight had lifted since then, they'd begun to see and hear, or imagine they saw and heard (they weren't ever sure), a shadow in some people's expressions and tones that wasn't friendly but wasn't unfriendly enough to call anyone out on. It was worse than the opinionated idiots, who were mostly kept in check within school walls by teachers and the general culture. To detect that subtle, unnameable hostility from the new *Llama* drummer (whom Rex admittedly had met one single time and had one single conversation with) would be (melodramatically, Rex knew) unsurvivable. They lifted their phone for a snapshot of the frosty snare drummer.

A blurry form lurched though the image. Rex's head jerked up from the screen.

There was no one there. They peered through the manger.

Then the gentlest murmur came from the direction of the holy family of ice, as though the radically decorated parents were comforting their green alien baby.

"Bukowski…"

Rex looked around wildly. The graffiti artists had given leering Guy Fawkes masks to a row of shepherds. One clumsy defacer had accidentally beheaded a lamb, sutured it back to health with fresh snow, and embroidered a ring of painted stitches around its fleecy neck.

Rex looked back at their phone. The backdrop of trees moved in the wind, and the drummer was brought to life, her hair undulating on the small screen. The breeze fell, and the illusion was lost. No longer tempted by a photograph, Rex resumed walking.

Then, on a whim, they stopped, held up their phone, and moved it slowly across the diorama. Everything was in its place—the quiet anarcho-shepherds, the tranquil Mary with elaborate Celtic facial tats, the inanimate reanimated lamb. Then, behind the drug-dealing kings, the screen exposed a hunched greyish figure that should not have been there.

Rex froze, as petrified as the ice-people that surrounded them. Rex had not had Pokémon GO on their phone since 2018. They racked their mind for other explanations.

The being moved offscreen. With shaking hands, Rex tried to find it again, the picture blurring wildly as they scanned the display. There—behind the shepherds. Rex's thumb found the Capture icon.

When it came to amateur photography, Rex was no, uh, amateur.

Rex had had a smartphone since elementary school—for safety reasons, according to their father, and so they wouldn't be "literally the only kid without one," according to their mother. Rex could snap a flattering group selfie midway down a toboggan hill. Rex could publish an Instagram post promoting a show *while* playing the bass at that same show. Rex could *almost* take a picture of themself without looking and have it appear as though someone else had captured them in a candid, carefree moment but still highlighted their best features—a skill that, as far as Rex knew, only Maggie had truly mastered.

They took a deep breath and focused on the screen, backing slowly away from the sculptures. The phantom figure appeared again, looming over the tiny sheep, blurred and fuzzy even as Rex's hands steadied and pressed Record. They had the impression of a grey-green snowsuit before the figure disappeared behind the manger.

"I'm just catching a Snorlax …" they whispered.

They'd backed up almost to the bend in the path when it reappeared, a tall human shape fully suited against the cold. It ran a gloved hand over the flowing hair of the drummer and Rex glanced up again in disbelief to confirm that it really was invisible to the naked eye.

When they looked back at their phone, it had halved the distance between them, its too-large body taking up the entire screen, and Rex caught a flash of vivid blue eyes under the cowl of its snowsuit before they turned and ran.

"Final question," said Jaymie, steering onto Fort Street. "Where do you see yourself in five years?"

"I don't think she'll ask that," said Aaron. He reached into his jacket to tuck his shirt and checked the mirror on the van's sun visor to confirm that his hair was no more or less dishevelled than usual. You didn't want to set expectations *too* high.

"You have to be ready for anything, Aar. Always on your toes! You can't let yourself get caught off guard—especially these days."

"Speaking of which, are you Jymmy?"

"No! Stop asking me that." Jaymie tapped the breaks in happy annoyance and turned the van into the winding streets of the Exchange District.

"Just checking. Because it crossed my mind that maybe all those thuds I heard on the porch roof were actually you and him in a fight, which he won, and now he's taken over your identity and decided to change the locks to stop you from getting back in the house."

"First of all, I only fell twice—I'm not *that* clumsy—and secondly, you'd have noticed by now if I had no idea who or where or why anyone or anything was, and all I talked about was porn." Jaymie nearly turned the wrong way onto a one-way, caught himself, and corrected the vehicle with a jerk. His brother appeared not to notice.

"What was the name of our first bicycle?" Aaron quizzed him.

Jaymie sighed and answered, "We called it Ronda because Mom was educating us on the Beach Boys, and the other one was Batman, but we totalled it right away by accident."

"*You* totalled it. What was the question? Five years?"

"Well, either way, we took them out one Sunday to show them off at Cruise Night, but they weren't ready for such an excursion, and we crashed them spectacularly into a vintage BMW on Portage Avenue. Satisfied? Yes, five years."

"In five years ... Well, I'd like to still be alive ... Beyond that ..." Aaron contemplated.

"I like your fighting spirit, Brzezinski. The job is yours," said Jaymie, pulling up to the curb. "OK, good luck!"

Rex rounded the bend, expecting the elf woman, and instead met with a group of massive, serenely smiling faces. Someone had spent many hours lopping at huge ice blocks until they had chipped away all the parts that weren't the seven Easter Island heads waiting to be revealed within.

Rex knew they'd taken a wrong turn but didn't dare backtrack. They darted between the giant faces. Ahead, the trail continued, winding deeper into the trees. Rex was sure Waterfront Drive was close by, but couldn't hear cars from either left or right, and knew that if they chose the wrong direction they'd end up on the deserted Red River. They had a vision of Aaron being drugged and dragged away on that empty expanse, and they shuddered and kept to the path.

They realized they hadn't seen a single person since they'd left the market, besides the wraith in their phone. They were alone. Cold needles of fear threaded through their chest, and they compulsively looked over their shoulder, knowing they would see nothing.

As they passed the last of the heads, a gash suddenly appeared in its face. Fragments of its eye and cheek cascaded to the ground in a tiny avalanche. Terrified, Rex raised their phone and saw a dark shape disappear behind the huge countenance.

They stumbled, unable to keep the camera in position.

"Little Bukowski ..." came the murmur, and a chunk of snow detached from the rounded nose and hurled itself at Rex, knocking their phone out of their hands in an explosion of white powder. Rex cried out, scrambled to retrieve it, and sprinted for the trees, no longer caring which direction they took.

The sunlight was obscured by the evergreen woods, but the trees were spaced widely enough that Rex could dodge between them. The undergrowth was packed down by snow, and their boots caught in hidden snares of wild grasses turned stringy and stiff as winter choked them. Rex wasn't sure how long they'd been running. They were certain they should've reached the street or the river by now.

They saw a patch of sunlight ahead and made for it, bursting out of the woods into a clearing full of huge sculptures made from a dense, impenetrable variety of ice that seemed to absorb the harsh sunlight rather than let it pass through.

The art pieces here were more abstract: geometric shapes with sharp angles and shiny reflective surfaces—perfect tetrahedrons and smooth cylindrical pillars, a pentagrammic prism, a doughnut-like torus balanced on its outer curve and, most impressively, three towering formations that looked like the metal climbing structures that were once a playground staple before too many children broke their necks falling from them. The beams looked like icicles welded together at the ends.

Rex stopped, gasping for breath. The woods were silent. They had no idea where they were. Then the softest whisper reached them.

"Bukowski ... Are you the one ...?" A tree branch snapped.

Rex circumnavigated the clearing, searching desperately for a path out and discovering there wasn't one; the area wasn't connected to the main display. A patch of snow fell from a tree far ahead, startling them, and they scrambled under the jagged shadows of the exhibit. From underneath, it seemed to Rex that the looming shapes made up a great angular labyrinth.

They skirted around a pyramid, ducked under the icicle beams of one of the immense climbing frames, traversed its gridwork of shadows to the other side, and crawled through the narrow space between the bottom of a perfectly spherical giant snowball and a thick pillar.

On the other side were rows of large, variously shaped ice blocks stacked on top of each other ten feet or higher, resembling minimalist interpretations of totem poles. At the bottom of one such tower was a cube reaching knee height, which had been hollowed out and left open at one end. Without thinking, Rex crept inside and curled up.

They waited, trying to quiet their exhalations. They could feel their nose running but didn't dare sniffle or wipe their face. The sun emerged from behind a cloud, causing the square-framed world outside their cave to coalesce into glittering TV static.

They'd almost decided to risk leaving the hiding spot when a sound reached them. Slow bootsteps squeaked against packed snow. Rex held their breath, staring transfixed out of the opening as the footfalls grew louder, their phone clenched inches from their face.

Just a stupid, freaky Snorlax ...

They nearly whimpered when a brown boot stepped into view. The leather ended at a dull grey-green pantleg; from Rex's vantage point they could see no higher than the long, snow-dusted shin.

The quiet voice came again—a man's voice, Rex guessed, speaking barely above a whisper, as though to himself.

"… I know you … I saw you …" Another boot stepped into view. "… And I remembered …" Rex clasped a mitten over their mouth and bit the fabric. "You play …" A hand hung loosely at his side, clad in a clean black glove with tattered fingertips. "The bass …"

It entered their mind in a slow trickle, like water from an ice-cold leak they were trying to seal before it could sink in and do damage, that they had met the city's murderer. A tear froze on their cheek. It occurred to them in a disconnected way—like an optical illusion their brain was paused on the brink of sorting out—that the hand hung too low for a normal person. And it was too big. Had it gotten bigger?

"Are you the one… the one chosen … to replace …" The hand was as large as a human head. Yellow-white nails began to protrude from the tip of each finger, shredding the fabric of the glove as they extended. Unable to watch any longer, Rex angled the phone away. The leg, hand, and claws remained, now fully corporal in the glimmering daylight. Rex squeezed their eyes shut.

"You should hope … not," whispered the man, and he continued through the sculpture maze, the crunching of his boots growing quieter and finally disappearing altogether.

49

Jaymie Mails his Manager

"I'm going to kill you someday," Jaymie whispered. He cowered in the corner of a snowy yard, occupying a tiny triangle of space hemmed in on two sides by a tall wooden fence and on the third by a set of snapping, bloodstained jaws.

Jaymie didn't share his brother's phobia of dogs, and on a few occasions he'd even approached a strolling dog, of his own volition, and petted it on the head as an expression of tolerance—especially if its owner was pretty or wore a hip band T-shirt. But that didn't mean he was fond of them.

"I know you've been waiting for me, asshole," he muttered, as the dog let out an ungodly ululation and thrust against the chain barely holding it at bay. "You think you're winning—well, you might have the advantage *now*, but I swear to god if you take so much as one bite of me, I'll sue to have you euthanized. Anything I do is self-defence—*I'm* in the right here! *I'm* the good guy! *Which of us do you think they're going to believe, you creepy motherfucker!*"

Since early November, Jaymie's assigned mail route had covered sections of West Broadway, where Jo lived, and The Gates, a neighbourhood that didn't exist on any map but was easily found by following an established algorithm of right and left turns. Its six square blocks, bordering the river, contained a café, a quaint library, and many large, ostentatious houses owned by mostly upper-middle-class professionals who expected their mail delivered on time whether their residences adhered to the laws of cartography or not. Jaymie liked his route;

it was scenic and enabled him to encounter people from a variety of walks of life.

Today, however, a series of sick calls and cases of rapid-onset ankle tendinitis had shuffled him to his least favourite part of the city, an area in the southeast corner of nowhere, where people you passed rarely returned a smile. His great dislike for the route was due in part to the beast he was in the early stages of being devoured by.

He'd forgotten to watch out for The Dog House, as he thought of it, and had gotten almost to the front door before the monster lazily emerged from under the steps. If he had to guess, he'd say it was a pit bull/rottweiler/velociraptor cross, regularly injected with anabolic steroids. (It was actually a mid-sized Doberman Pinscher.) Within seconds he'd been forced into the corner of the yard.

The brute lunged for him and came up a foot short, restrained by the leather band circling its throat. Jaymie flattened himself against the fence, certain he'd have been mauled to death by now if not for the collar and chain. A lance of anxiety-pain stabbed through his gut.

"Look, I don't know what kind of a deal you've struck up with the usual guy that he's survived giving you your fucking dog mail for this many years, but things are going to be a little different with me." The animal snarled. Eddies of saliva swirled through its teeth and ran from the ragged edges of its jaws, freezing into sabre-tooth icicles on the way to the ground. Distantly, from an alternate dimension slightly overlapping Jaymie's universe of fear, David Bowie was singing into his ear about letting all the children boogie.

The dog charged again, its chain pulling taut, and he eyed the hook where the other end was fastened. It was loosely attached near the front door; a jagged circle had been worn into the exterior of the house around it and the hook jerked closer to breaking free with every tug from the muscular animal.

Incidentally, the mailbox was mounted on the house only a few feet from the hook—not that Jaymie had any intention of delivering these wretched humans their mail.

His frustrated attacker let out a volley of vicious barking, spraying spittle across his jacket. He cringed. The hook wiggled precariously in the wall of the house. Jaymie took a deep breath, turned around, and jumped.

The hook snapped free. The dog surged forward. Jaymie clung to the top of the fence, pulling his boots out of reach of the gnashing jaws, shouting to God or sympathetic neighbours or anyone within earshot to come to his aid.

A woman's voice called from the house.

"What?" he yelled. He hoisted himself onto his elbows atop the fence and yanked his earbuds out. Now that he thought about it, "Starman" was not the right soundtrack to this ordeal. "I didn't hear you!"

"No, the dog!"

"Yeah, the fucking dog! What do I do?" he cried, heaving down on the pointed wooden slats to pull himself further from the claws scrabbling just beneath his boots.

"No, I was talking to the dog!" the woman yelled back. "Winnie! Winnipeg! Here!"

The monster trotted breathlessly back to her owner, tongue lolling with adoration, as Jaymie unleashed a tirade of swears and let himself drop back onto the snowy lawn.

"Leave the mailman—good girl, Winnie. Good!"

"The fuck is wrong with your dog?" he panted, wearily tugging mail from his bag.

"Goooood Pooh Bear. Who's a nice doggo?" the woman asked gravely. The dog grinned at Jaymie and discharged several litres of saliva onto the steps.

"Jesus. Here's your letter."

"Oh. 'S'the usual guy sick?"

"Tendinitis."

"What?"

"Sore Achilles."

"What?"

Jaymie replaced his earbuds, restarted the song he'd missed, and resumed walking, allowing Bowie's alien distractions to soothe his shaken nerves. The animal had interrupted both his listening experience and a text he'd been drafting to Daffodile about their upcoming "date," or whatever they were going to call it. He pressed Send, reached his next house, and was shoving a handful of mail through a slot in the porch door when a name on the top letter elicited a twinge of recognition and a pang in his already unsettled stomach.

He grasped for the envelope, but it slipped through his fingers to the other side. Cursing quietly, he turned the knob, found it unlocked, and stepped into the porch, careful not to tread on the mail he'd just deposited.

He stooped to retrieve the letter, then read the name and address twice to make sure he wasn't mistaken.

"Let all the children boogie," he muttered, and hammered savagely on the front door.

Rex waited at least ten minutes without moving. Then they heard the honking of a car horn on Waterfront, and realized they were very cold. They wiped their nose, dabbing gingerly at the freezing metal of their septum piercing, and finally climbed out of the snow cube.

They retraced their steps out of the garden of shapes, found their footprints in the deeper snow of the woods, and followed the tracks back to the main path. The sight of a larger set of prints overlapping with their own caused them to shiver harder as they tripped through the snow.

The return journey didn't take long, although Rex paused frequently to look through their camera. They came out of the woods by the vandalized manger scene, where the drummer was still jauntily poised for her next strike. Disgusted and uneasy, they jogged back to the market, which now bustled with activity. An intense relief began to melt over them as they joined the crowd and sat down to recover in the warmth of the mall.

They knew they should tell the police they'd sighted one of the city's active serial killers, but the thought of describing the unlikely stalker, filing a report that would probably never be followed up on, giving (or not giving) their pronouns, etc.—and hearing that subtle-nasty-weird tone at some point in the process—overwhelmed them. Maybe the cops would think them a videogame-obsessed misfit, trying to get attention; the thought awoke in them a familiar and trivial-seeming sort of ongoing misery that they didn't want to contemplate too deeply.

They considered calling their brothers. Both would surely drop everything if they knew Rex was in danger, but the danger had passed. The brightness of the day and the cheerful people around them had a surreal, calming effect, and they didn't want Jaymie to get in trouble at work or Aaron to panic needlessly. The situation was no longer dire. They could share the anecdote with them later.

Still, they weren't ready to be alone at home for the rest of the day.

Then they thought of Jo. Her apartment wasn't far, and Rex could take well-populated streets to get there. Was it alright to stop in on someone like Jo, unannounced, to say hello? The more they thought about it, the more it felt like the best, most exciting option.

What did someone like Jo get up to while unemployed on a Friday? Rex set out.

Jo was basking in the full glory of the cosmos.

When Rex rang the buzzer to her building, it wrenched her from a cyclical idea-loop that she had no idea how long she'd been caught up in. She kept her headphones on, ignoring the first few rings, and then wondered if at some point she could have ordered a pizza and forgotten about it. She buzzed Rex in and answered the door.

"Hi," said Rex.

"Very," said Jo. "I mean—hey, Rex!" She tried to remember the appropriate procedure for interacting with an impressionable individual while in a compromised state. She wondered if she should tell Rex she was tripping balls.

"What are you doing today?" asked Rex.

"Nothing," said Jo. An hour passed. "What are you doing?"

"Nothing," said Rex. "I got tired of listening to J and A cooing at each other all morning, so I went to see the ice sculptures, but I got freaked out … Long story. You're not busy?"

"Actually, um…" Jo sensed her face twisting into a pained expression muscle by muscle and wondered if it looked as strange as it felt. "I'm just having one of those days where … I have a lot of things …" Rex blinked inscrutably at her and Jo felt a chemically-amplified pang of remorse, certain she was already making her feel uncomfortable.

Making *them* feel uncomfortable. Oh no, oh shit! Jo had never made that mistake before. Drugs could really make you fall for life's illusions. You'd lose those perfect layers, you'd just get pulled in by appearances and before you know it you forget that it's what's beneath the surface that

"OK, it's fine," said Rex, scuffing at the carpet with one pigeon-toed boot.

"OK," said Jo.

"I just thought I'd stop by and see if you wanted to hang out, but."

"I …"

"Next time." Rex turned to leave, and as they glanced back down the empty hallway, a wary reluctance crossed their face, which Jo immediately misinterpreted as betrayal.

She saw that Rex had finally become disillusioned with her—that Rex was seeing her for what she truly was, an empty husk of a human, unable to open herself up to others. Rex must realize that Jo was a snob and a flake and had chosen to be alone doing nothing of value all weekend rather than spend time with the beautiful, potential-filled human that was Rex. Rex surely thought Jo scorned and looked down on them, and they'd regard her with hatred and resentment in return. But Jo didn't!

Her imagination assaulted her with a torrent of self-deprecating realizations. Also supplied by her imagination were a series of perfect little geometric windmills, blades interlocking in an Escher-inspired dance, spinning across every surface of the hallway. Jo suddenly worried that Rex would get swept up in them and blown tempestuously around the never-ending passageway like an untied balloon releasing its air.

"Bye!" said Rex. (In reality, Rex understood that adults—excluding Rex's brothers—had normal things they did with their time, and that Jo was probably doing her taxes and was trying express how busy she was without giving away the fact that she was doing something horrifically boring. Adults were always self-conscious about all the boring things they did.)

"Wait!" said Jo.

"It's fine, really," said Rex.

"I *do* want to hang out. I'm high as fuck is all. So like, if that doesn't bother you …?"

Rex's face lit up—figuratively, as in, their expression conveyed enthusiasm and relief, as well as literally, in that their head morphed into a floating orb of golden light—and they bounced past her into the apartment to get a look at her guitar collection.

50

Aaron Moves a Marble Urn

Even after forcing Jaymie to stay in the car and develop a five-year plan that didn't involve making it in the music industry, Aaron was early for his appointment at the bookstore on Arthur Street. He waited until exactly 9 a.m. and knocked on the glass.

"Come on in! I was just opening up." His employer held the door. "We don't have many customers this early in the day, so I can start showing you things. How are you?"

"Good, thanks. Um, I brought my resumé, if you'd like it …" He handed over a crisp folder.

"Thorough! OK, I'll put it on file. There's a hook in the back there …" She waited until he'd hung his coat, then continued, "You know the general layout, so I won't bother with that. Come around here and I'll show you the till. It's simple—you'll get it right away. The inventory system takes longer to get the hang of, but there's no big rush."

"So you're not going to interview me?" he asked.

"Interview you?"

"Like, what are my strengths and weaknesses?"

"What are your strengths and weaknesses?" she asked with amusement.

"I care *too much*—"

"OK, I get the idea."

"Or my five-year plan?"

"Have you *ever* had a five-year plan?"

"No, but Jaymie helped me make one in the car just now, and I practiced it while I was waiting."

"I don't think I need to know too in-depth what Jaymie's five-year plan for you is."

"So ... I got the job?"

"Seriously?" said Farida. "I've known you your entire life."

"Yeah, that's what I'm worried about," said Aaron.

His aunt laughed. "If you want to prove yourself, maybe you can help me move that thing." She pointed to a tall, ornate marble urn near the entrance. "It was here when I bought the store. No idea where it's from or what it's worth—I do like it, though. I want to add a new display there, and move it over by the books on early civilizations at the far end. Fit nicely in that corner, eh?"

"No, yeah, sure!" said Aaron, vowing to himself that he would solve the problem of the urn delivery by the end of the day.

"Excellent. It's heavy as hell, and my back's off-kilter again." She turned back to the till. "OK, I'll show you this, and then I have some errands to run. You can call me if you have any trouble, and don't worry about the inventory system—it won't be busy. If someone's looking for a book, you can always just check the section you think it would be in."

Aaron listened to her directions, carried out the process of selling a coffee-table Beatles biography and a compendium of queer theory to a hypothetical customer, and assured Farida he could handle the store on his own for a few hours.

"Can I look at your guitars?" asked Rex. "Can I try them?"

"The Jaguar is the best—you should try the Jaguar. It's over there." Jo settled on the couch, unsure whether she was coming down from her high or enjoying a period of relative lucidity between waves of stupefaction.

Rex picked up the guitar and struck a suspended chord. It sounded the way a seashell looks. "You're so good at that," Jo said in awe.

"I literally just hit all the open strings," Rex laughed. For a moment their features distorted, and a set of round, shiny alien eyes blinked up at Jo. She grinned in surprise.

"Rex, I like your face," she said serenely. "Your face looks like a little kitty face. —Not in, like, a *gendered* way—like, if Aaron was here, his face would be like a little kitty, too. Wait, is that inappropriate? I'm not really thinking the way I usually do ..."

"You're funny," said Rex. Their quiet strumming on the unplugged guitar was more like a texture than a sound. They paused mid-stroke. "Jo, can I buy some of your weed? I mean, I'm not trying to take advantage while you're messed up, but I can't go to the stores yet, and the stuff we get at school kinda sketches me out."

"I don't know what is the right answer to that."

"I just do it with Maggie sometimes, but we're careful, and we never drive, except Maggie sometimes, but she's a great driver. Can I buy just a little?"

"OK Rex, I respect you. Don't pay me, just take some, it's in the drawer." Rex put down the guitar and went to fish in the desk that held Jo's laptop and a chaotic pile of papers scrawled with incomprehensible notes about chords and song forms. Jo wondered if this was the kind of thing she was supposed to avoid when hanging out with a teenage friend. She wasn't sure—no one had ever tried to shelter *her* at seventeen.

"Hey, are you getting evicted or something? These letters are, like, kind of rude … Also, are you getting murdered? What's this postcard?"

"Oh, it's a joke. What's it say, something about 'jolly Quebec?' And my landlord's a dick. It's fine," said Jo, in no state to be concerned about the latest rent-related correspondence.

"Damn the man," said Rex gravely, and put a baggy with enough weed for approximately half of a standard-size joint in the pocket of their jeans. Jo smiled. The back wall of the cramped apartment tilted toward her. She shut her eyes and melted into her cushions. She remembered something. "You got freaked out earlier?" she mumbled against the pillow.

Rex pursed their lips and sat back down. They fingerpicked a few muted chords and sang, "OK, I know it sounds crazy, but I was walking around near Waterfront …"

Jo lapsed into synesthetic confusion, unable to tell the difference between Rex's voice and the pizzicato tones emanating from the guitar. "We're in a musical!" she gasped, as everything that had ever happened in her life suddenly presented itself within a grander context, imbued with purpose and narrative.

"Huh?" said Rex.

"I'm so sorry. For a second I thought we were in a musical, but you're totally just talking normally and everything is normal. Please tell me what happened. I'll shut up."

Rex shook their head, gave a crooked smile, and told her.

***

The urn was as tall as Aaron, and by his estimate at least as heavy. Ropy designs encircled its girth at even intervals all the way up, with an intricate pattern twisting in and out of itself all around the mouth's circumference. Aaron thought it was creepy, but Aaron thought that about most things.

He experimented with trying to lift it—unsustainable—gently tipping it to one side—unsafe—and drumming absently on its curved waist with his palms, producing very little sound—unsatisfying.

His first strategy was to procrastinate for as long as possible. He dusted the counter, made himself a map of the store, and put away a pile of non-fiction books in what he thought were the right places. He was, so far, killing it.

He heated a kettle in the back room and sent Jo a text that read, 'Hey I got a bookstore job. Now I know how to move books around like you!'

She responded a moment later, 'Cool except I got fired from that job cuz your band got me kidnapped by a cult lol. PS I'm hanging w rex.'

He read it with some surprise. 'Oh right, lol,' he typed back. 'Don't give Rex drugs pls ;)' Good news: Jo had responded, as she had each day since his mail delivery, and was therefore still alive; enough time had elapsed that the mail-order death threat could be confirmed facetious.

Time to take on that urn.

As Rex recounted what had happened that morning, Jo's face contorted into confusion and then alarm, and finally settled on fury. Rex wondered if they should have waited until she was sober.

"Asshole! How dare he!" She stood up. "Alexandre and Bob was one thing but if he wants to mess with *my band* I swear to god I'm going to make him wish he was never born—you're sure it was a guy? Of course it was a guy. Was he tall?"

"He was tall, yeah. He talked really quiet, but I think it was a dude. But … I don't know about a human dude. Like I said, I could only see him in my phone. And he grew that big hand …" Rex shivered.

"With nails. Fucking gross. And he had giant teeth? And shaggy fur?" Jo paced, running her hands through her wild black hair, easily the second most terrifying creature Rex had encountered that day.

"Um, no … No teeth. Or fur," said Rex.

"No teeth. I made that up. Sorry, my brain is doing things."

"That's OK. He had, like, a puke-green snowsuit." Rex forced themself to picture the phantom man. "And very blue eyes."

"Oh." Jo stopped pacing. "I met someone just like that … When was it … They tried to help me restart my car …" She paused. "*Or*, I just invented that story in my head a second ago, based on the details you gave me five seconds ago … Hmm …"

"I'm not sure how to help you."

"It was the day Aaron disappeared," Jo said confidently. "Damn it! If it *was* him, I could've taken the sucker out right then! … On the other hand. A lot of snowsuits in this city."

"Jo, he's really dangerous," said Rex, distressed again. "I don't think you should confront him. Like, no issuing challenges to him on the internet, please."

"Oh my god, I *was* thinking of doing that! Did I already do that?"

"No! I don't think so." Rex hugged their knees to their chest. "But seriously, he's a *for real* monster. Like the cult stuff. Like Jymmy but worse."

Jo sighed and joined them on the couch. "Yeah, I know. I guess we've known since the pumpkins, haven't we? Wait, the pumpkins really happened, right?"

"The pumpkins happened," Rex nodded. "Yeah, it'd be hard for a regular human to pull off."

"And if he can turn invisible, that'd explain how he stole the body …"

"Smashed up the pumpkins with his big claws," Rex added miserably.

"But that doesn't mean he can't appear as a human the rest of the time."

"We can't rule it out, knowing what monsters are like," Rex agreed.

"OK, so, this is probably stupid, but I started having suspicions about someone. Hear me out."

"OK, who?" said Rex.

"Just a second," said Jo. She went into the bedroom and didn't return, and Rex soon realized she'd forgotten what she was doing and fallen asleep. They rolled their eyes, checked the lock on the door, sat down, got up, checked the lock again, and then settled in, thumbing the strings of the Jaguar and tensing each time a passing set of boots cast a shadow across the little window of the basement apartment.

Aaron was finishing his lunch in the back room when he heard the chime of the front entrance. He moved behind the counter to greet the customer, who turned out to be Jaymie.

"Aaron, it's you! This is where you work! My brother-friend works here at this place, at his job, which I already knew, of course!" said Jaymie happily.

Aaron frowned. "Are you Jymmy?"

"Aaron, quit asking me that! Can't a guy come visit his brother at work without getting suspected of being an evil clone?"

"God, sorry. I'm just on edge because I don't want to fuck up again. Not that it's hard. Hey, can you help me move that—why are you laughing all creepy and silent like that?"

"Just kidding! I am Jymmy!" Jymmy grinned.

"Goddammit! How did you know I keep getting paranoid and asking Jaymie if he's you?" Aaron demanded.

"I didn't! I just guessed, because I got to know you so well in the car that one time. I thought, 'That's a thing he probably does!' And then you just went with it!"

Aaron was ready to bolt at any sign of violence. Jymmy vibrated with glee at the delightful coincidence of them crossing paths again.

"What do you want? Are you stalking me?"

"Ha! You're just as full of yourself as Jaymie! Did it cross your mind that I might actually have come in here in search of a—" He looked around, surveying the contents of the store, "—book?"

"Fine. What *book* are you looking for?" Aaron challenged, aware that knowing how to use the inventory system could enable him to get rid of Jymmy quite a bit faster. He decided he'd pretend to use it and tell Jymmy they didn't have whatever book it was.

"Well, perhaps not so much a *book* …"

"You cut your hair like ours." Aaron's fingers tapped a nervous march on the counter.

"Do you like it?" Jymmy beamed.

"Yes," Aaron admitted resentfully.

"So actually, the internet is down in my apartment," Jymmy confessed, "so I had all this time to think. And—irony—I thought of a question I wanted to ask the internet, *right now*. I thought, where better to find a smart person to answer my question than in a store with 'Books' on the label? I didn't expect it would be *you*! I didn't even realize you were smart!"

Jymmy's expression shifted; the clone was gazing at him with the same fond reverence with which Aaron had seen him behold Jaymie. He sighed and suppressed his impulse to run.

"I'm not that smart, but let's hear it. I can always look it up on my phone." He pulled the device from his pocket. "Impeccable logic, by the way," he muttered. "Go ask a guy in an indie bookstore …"

"Thank you, Aaron!" the clone said with surprising sincerity. "I'm going to get a phone soon, too, so I can call Big Niki, and also to watch porn on the bus!"

"Speaking of creepy shit you do, are you the murderer? I'm just asking because Jaymie made you like six months ago and I'm pretty sure the killings started around then." He quickly added, "And I'm not going to call the cops, because I'm terrified of you, and I'm also intimidated by cops. I just want to know. Jaymie thinks you're not, but I'm not sure."

"Noooo, I'm not it …" Jymmy fidgeted, poking at a title near the bottom of a high stack of books waiting on the counter to be reshelved. The stack gave a Jenga-tower wobble.

"OK, you sound *exactly* the way Jaymie does when he's avoiding telling me the entire truth because he thinks it will upset me, and then I make him tell me and it *does* upset me."

"Just the mini-donut lady, but it was an accident! I snuck in the truck for a little bucket of them, but the floor was all slippery with donut grease, and she saw me and blocked me from them but she slipped! The donuts went flying and I zipped around catching them in the bucket one by one! I missed the last one and it hit the heat dial on the grease machine, turning it to maximum hot, then bounced off and knocked a bottle of cleaning juice into the vat! It started on fire, so I pulled it out using the donut basket and I threw it out the takeout window, but as she slipped she'd grabbed the window for support and pulled it shut! So the flaming basket clonks off the window and the cleaning bottle pops out into my bucket of donuts, so I let go quick! It exploded in the air, sending balls of donut-fire whizzing around bouncing off walls, and both of us dodging them left and right! They finally fell into smouldering piles on the floor, and I grabbed a new donut bucket to eat. She was getting back up on her feet, and her eyes started getting bulgy, and her breathing all harsh, and I'd seen some movies and stuff so I knew she was about to change into her next, more scary evolution! … In retrospect it was probably a heart attack.

"I didn't tell anyone, because I was new and I didn't realize dying was a thing, and I was hungry and I didn't know about money so I thought people survived by outsmarting each other for all the scarce resources! I know better now. And it wasn't sexism," he assured Aaron. "I'd have accidentally murdered her if she was a man, too."

"Jesus Christ!"

"I won't do it again! My tummy hurts even just telling you that story!"

"I don't even know what to—you know what? Get the fuck out of my store, or I'll—"

"Aaaaaron! I don't kill people anymore! Just Spencer, and, OK, I almost murdered you, but that was just circumstances. I wouldn't do it again, because Jaymie likes you so much. And I watched all the Hallmark Christmas movies last month and learned about compassion! You have to let people learn from their mistakes! And then leave your big city job to open a bakery in your hometown and get married to your high school sweetheart, which *I* never even got to have."

"Ugh, I hate it—I don't want to deal with you—I can't—"

"Don't make me go to jail! You know it won't rehabilitate me. It'll just make me worse! It perpetuates the cycle of something something, I forget. People do bad scary things to each other in jail, which I learnt from all the jokes about it on TV, which is very, very confusing."

The door chimed again, and Aaron managed to stutter a distressed greeting to an older woman leaning on a cane. She stepped inside, shook the snow out of her hood, and stopped briefly on her way to the Biography section to admire them, exclaiming, "Ooh, twins!" Aaron grimaced. Jymmy winked sweetly.

"I just have one question I came in to ask. Please?" Jymmy implored, looking genuinely remorseful.

Aaron squeezed his eyes shut. It was true, he reminded himself, that many people are capable of improvement when given opportunities and education. And he hadn't been lying when he told Jymmy he was too afraid of him to call 911. "What's your question?" he asked.

"Are you ready?" Jymmy leaned tigerishly toward him over the counter.

"Ready for anything," Aaron winced.

"Who's Charles Bukowski?"

51

Jo Connors Vs. The World

"OK, hear me out," Jo said again, having regained some semblance of clarity after half an hour spent passed out in her room.

"Sure, tell me," Rex said gamely.

"Julio," said Jo.

"Who?" said Rex.

"… Leo?" said Jo.

"What?" said Rex.

"With the cute little beard?" said Jo.

"Lucas?" asked Rex.

"What did I say?"

"Julio," said Rex.

"Ha! Down by the schoolyard … Yeah, Lucas. This is so trippy."

"Jo, you're a mess! How are you even having this conversation?" Rex laughed, and Jo was glad they were distracted from their earlier trauma.

"I guess I've just been high enough times that I can function OK—part of the time, anyway." She shrugged sheepishly and added, "Rex, don't do drugs!"

"OK."

"How did you know I was talking about Lucas?"

"Because of Aaron. He was anxious the other day because apparently he told you not to worry about Lucas, and then he thought, what if you went back there all happy and relieved, and it turned out it *was* him after all, and you got murdered and it was all Aaron's fault?"

Jo put her head in her hands. "I'm sorry, I'm the worst. Did I give him a panic attack?"

"If it wasn't that, it'd have been something else."

Jo could tell Rex's nonchalance was forced. She felt another surge of anger and chose to direct it at the murderer this time, rather than herself. She rubbed her hands together. She had too many fingers. She started trying to count them, and then shook her head.

"I can't kick my suspicions about Lucas," she said. "Rex, can you take notes or something?" She was acutely aware that she was attempting to focus on the exact topics she'd drugged herself for the express purpose of temporarily forgetting.

Rex put down the jaguar and opened a memo in their phone.

"OK. *One*. I wanted to hang out with him after the tribute show, but he had an early morning the next day interviewing the mandolin player. He dropped me off at home. Shortly after, the mandolin player is found dead, *right there*, with all her bracelets stuffed in her case …"

"Bracelets—that reminds me, I'm pretty sure she was at our house concert, just FYI."

"Really? OK, let's write that down." Jo nodded. "Where was I? So, an hour later he texts me his interview was cancelled and he'd like to go for breakfast and, I assume, make out after. But they hadn't released her identity yet! How did he know she wouldn't be there! He said *she* cancelled. But is it a bit suspicious?"

"Not *that* suspicious. But it does put him at the right time and place." Rex tapped it into their phone. "But why kill her if they'd planned an interview? He's short a blog post."

"The bangles! Rex, remember what you said a while ago, about the mandolin girl being at the house show?"

"Like, thirty seconds ago?"

"The murderer could have seen her there—maybe found out she was a musician—and targeted her!"

"Yeah, that's why I brought it up."

"Lucas would have seen her there!" said Jo.

"So did Maggie. Maybe it was her!" Rex teased.

"Oh my god, would she?"

"No. And she was right in front of us, watching us play, when the pumpkin stuff would've gone down. The body getting swapped, I mean. As was Lucas," Rex reminded her.

"Right. But the killer could have an accomplice. Someone to help disappear the body."

"It's true. Hate ever bringing up that cult again, but it sure helps having a team."

"A band."

"Yeah, no, now that I think back, I think Lucas did leave for a little bit, actually. With bangles girl? It was a quiet audience—we could really see the room. Do you remember?"

"No. Must've been in the zone. Was it long enough to mess up all our pumpkins?"

"I wasn't paying attention."

"But even if not, Snowsuit could be working for someone, or vice versa—not necessarily Lucas, but, OK, the other thing is how he talks on his blog. Like it's this romantic, noble thing. It's, like, our responsibility to keep playing shows even though people are dying."

"Yeah. I noticed that," Rex agreed. "It's kind of a weird blog. You're reading it and you're like, this guy *really* wishes he was in a band. Right? Like, go learn an instrument, dude! It's not that hard. Again, bit of a Regina Cult mood, honestly."

"Huh. I didn't notice that. Do you think he could be bitter enough to go out and …?"

"Maybe? But lots of people wish they were musicians, and they don't become murderers. It's like they're helpless. Some capitalist conspiracy convinced them you just get born talented or not. And it's possible Lucas just … doesn't think about it."

"What?"

"About what he says."

"What do you mean?"

"He's just so into being in the scene and having musician friends and dating musician girls. It's his whole identity. Not that you should trust me about identity—I basically started figuring out mine like five months ago."

Jo blinked in surprise. "I'd trust you about it more than anybody," she said. "And you're right. He pointed out that it's his livelihood, but identity is the right word."

"So, he has to uphold this image, and keep creating content, and maybe he just doesn't worry about how that affects other people's actions or whatever."

"Oh," said Jo. "Right. Content."

"Not in a terrible way. Just, like the Youth Tambour scandal, where he got boycotted and had to take down those posts. Like, he seems like a nice person. But sometimes people can be nice, but they just ... don't think. I noticed that from having two brothers."

At Jo's questioning look, Rex added, "Oh, Youth Tambour—he just said they cashed in on PC trends and it was tacky that they switched to backing tracks and dropped two guys in the band ..." But another wave was coming on, and before Rex could finish they refracted into a fragile cherry blossom and the couch folded over on itself and Jo lost track of the world.

Aaron shifted the urn around on its base in an awkward semicircle that relocated it approximately one quarter inch westward. Farida had texted that she was delayed, and he'd confirmed that he was managing fine on his own. There was an hour left in his shift and he'd accomplished very little by way of urn conveyance. He swore under his breath.

He hadn't needed his phone to answer Jymmy's question. He recounted everything he knew of Bukowski's life and sold him three novels and a poetry book for further research. Jymmy had been amazed at his reservoir of Bukowski knowledge, and immediately promised to come back and test him out with more questions. Aaron asked him to please not, and then they both laughed with varying degrees of enthusiasm, and Jymmy went on his way.

So, back to the urn.

Late-afternoon sunshine poured through the tall windows at the front of the shop and highlighted a flurry of dust motes that swirled hesitantly in response to his efforts, like a crowd that only manages to get drunk enough to dance when you're midway through your last song.

He crouched by the base of the urn, wondering if a lower hold would allow him to get his arms around it more effectively.

"Need a hand?"

"Holy shit!" He lost his balance and fell backward, releasing the vessel in order to catch himself. "I didn't hear—did the bell—? Sorry, I—oh, it's you!"

"It rang, but you seemed really focused," Juniper laughed. "Sorry, didn't mean to sneak up."

She was vibrant—her face had no hint of the sickly pallor that had haunted it after her possession in the fall. She wore a wool coat and knitted dress over warm layered tights; her hair emerged in a braid from under a loose knitted cap, with a light snow-dusting over everything.

Aaron rose and returned an affectionate hug. "How are you finding the city? Did you find a place? Do you still hang out with the Bukowskiphiles?"

"It's good, and I did—in St. James—and I do occasionally, though I have some grownup friends now, too … This is one of my favourite downtown spots. I'm bi, and it has good queer stuff," she said. "I didn't know you worked here—it's usually a cool older lady."

"Oh! Cool. Yeah, my aunt owns it. Jaymie was pretending to be me at a family thing and apparently he did such an alarming job that she took pity and offered to take on a new part-timer, even if I'm not gay or anything. So, here I am!" He gestured around his domain, then patted the urn. "She wants me to move this beast. I know it's a test," he lowered his voice and leaned in. "I'm meant to accidentally tip it over and shatter it, and the ashes of the store's founder spill out and form into his angsty undead bust, which puts a curse on me so my soul gets sucked into a James Patterson novel, and also he tells me I'm fired."

"Really?" Juniper asked, astounded.

"Wha—no. Kidding. Sorry, forgot you have a bit of a culty, um … And I think the original owner was, like, also a lesbian, actually … Can I help you find anything?"

She bounced in excitement as she remembered the purpose of her visit. "Actually, today I'm looking for more Bukowski. I've been trying to read everything he's written."

"Oh … I just sold all of it." Aaron deflated. "I was helping an evil clone so he wouldn't get annoyed and kill me."

"Ah, kidding again." She chuckled wisely. "Well, I should've checked sooner—too bad! Anyway, can I help you move that?"

With Juniper steadying the top of the vessel, Aaron carefully tilted it forty-five degrees and lifted it by the base.

"Too … heavy?" he asked with effort.

"It's all right … I've got the … light end."

"Tell me if you need to …"

"I've been working … retail … so I'm … fine."

They maneuvered their way around the Canadian History aisle and the Queer Canadian History aisle, past the Local and Queer Local displays, down a passageway of Mystery shelves, over six stacks of Dean Koontz novels, through the labyrinthine Romance (Queer and Non-) sections, and into the Ancient World. They set it in the corner, entirely intact.

"Thank you so much. I think the real test was to see if I have enough friends that someone would come in and help me," said Aaron.

"Miranda used to say that any weight could be borne if you had enough good people around," Juniper said, and Aaron was surprised at the ease with which she mentioned her former cult leader.

"So, the urn was a metaphor after all," he said.

"Actually, we did all our own landscaping and renos, so we had to lift a lot of heavy things."

"Well, lucky for me." He was aware that the landscape of Juniper's old home had concealed quite a few decaying bodies, and was glad when she didn't elaborate.

"Happy to help! Maybe I'll just browse a bit and see if I like anything ..." She looked around the Old World, her gaze drifting over titles about Greek gods and Mesopotamia before resting once more on him. She smiled.

"You know," said Aaron. "We've got a lot of Bukowski at home. I could lend you some? If you'd like to come back?"

"I'll come back!"

"Or, hey, Jo's playing a show tomorrow night, if you want to come with us?"

"I'll come to the show!"

"Oh, good!"

"Great!" She took his number, said goodbye, and flitted out of the store.

Aaron tried to remember how old she was. At least twenty-two, he was fairly certain. A young twenty-two, but still.

Rex leaned over the girl on the couch, lifting hair out of her face to make sure she was breathing normally. Although Rex felt safer around Jo than nearly anyone else, they couldn't help noticing she looked more tired than usual. They picked up Jo's mail for a closer look, but tucked it behind their back when she spoke.

"OK, this is a little crazier than I'm used to," Jo murmured. "I'm probably being annoying. You can go if you don't like me like this ... Wait, don't go. Murderer ..."

"It's OK, I'm having fun," said Rex, much more content entertaining themself at Jo's than wandering the winter streets alone. They wondered if she had any snacks in the fridge, and went to look. Two sheets of paper pinned under a guitar magnet caught their eye.

"You made a suspect list with Anika and Michaud on it? But they're, like, super fun and nice! And Maggie?"

Jo opened her eyes with very apparent effort. "I was just trying to remember who was at those shows—I don't actually think they did it."

Rex looked at the second sheet, which appeared at first glance to give a rundown of one corner of the city's incestuous music scene. They silently read, "*Ballet Llama, Gunt, Lost the Show the Band, Shifty Principals, DZB, BMI Babies, Tornado Tornahdo*, Allene Elvira (solo vox/mando)."

"Wow, you're keeping track of all this?" they said, experiencing a subdued kind of excitement at the discovery. "Are these all the bands who've lost a member?"

"Member or affiliated musician," Jo confirmed drowsily. "I want to see if there's a pattern. Maybe it's a random monster, but maybe it's a … purposeful monster."

"Sick," Rex whispered, rereading the lists.

"The police'll never find him," Jo added. "They don't know the scene like we do. And also, fuck the police."

"Are they connected?" asked Rex. "The bands?"

"Some share members, but they mostly aren't even the same genre," Jo stretched out. "There's punk, Motown, indie, jazz-pop, singer-songwriter, shoegaze, scrunge, punk, Motown, indie … It's funny—I've seen most of these bands' albums somewhere, but I forget—I think I was pretty high at the time …" Jo's brow creased. "There was *Lost* and the *BMIs* …"

"Did you know Aaron once had a psychotic break auditioning for the *BMIs*?"

"Even I heard about that."

"He said the singer's German shepherd ran in, but I think he was just nervous."

"… Shit, I have a text! What do I do! Is it Lucas?"

"Give it here," Rex offered. "It's Aaron. He says he got the bookstore job and now he moves books around like you. What a dummy. What do you want to say?"

"OK, I'm thinking." Jo closed her eyes in concentration. "… Tell him his face is like a little freckly kitty."

"Wow, you guys text, like, every day, huh? ... OK, I told him we're hanging out."

"Thanks, Rex."

"No prob." Rex read Aaron's response, casually deleted the conversation to protect everyone involved, and passed the phone back.

Jo opened her eyes, unsure how long she'd been caught in another kaleidoscope of lost memories and thought-spirals. There'd been something about Quebec and a dead bird. She blinked and looked around for Rex. They were napping, curled into a ball at the other end of the couch. She was relieved they hadn't gone home by themself.

She checked the time and saw it was already late in the day. The couch undulated and tried to eat Rex, who rolled over and hummed softly. It masticated a few more times and then left the wiry bassist alone. Jo rated TwiLite a six out of ten: an interesting experience, but she could use more of the feel-good stuff to balance out the psychedelia.

She remembered that Aaron had texted her earlier, and she opened her messages to see how embarrassing her response had been, but was forced to conclude she'd imagined it. She sighed and set her phone down.

A vision entered her mind's eye of the first time she'd met him, gripping a steering wheel with pale fingers, panicking about a poorly-planned pumpkin heist which, now that she thought about it, probably could've gotten them all arrested. He'd been rubbing his forehead against the wheel, muttering about what a stupid idea it was, and all she'd done was shrug off his concerns and get annoyed that they hadn't put any music on. An ugly pang pulsed through her chest.

Jo sat up. She knew where she'd seen the names of those bands thrown together before. There *was* someone who listened to all of them—or at least most of them. She'd never bothered to find out who owned the car they'd used that night in October to steal thirty-six pumpkins.

52
Hey Jo

"What are you doing in my city!" Jaymie demanded.

"Mr. Bukowski, it's so nice to see you," said Miranda. "What are you doing in my house?"

"I'm delivering your goddamn mail!"

"Do you trample *all* the mail you deliver?" She pointed to the porch floor, where Jaymie's angry pacing had soaked the letters with muddy snowmelt.

Jaymie hadn't seen Miranda since fleeing Regina nearly two months prior, and although he'd accepted her offer of free band management and even exchanged several polite emails with her, it had been under the strict condition that she remain at least five hundred kilometres away.

"You're supposed to be in Saskatchewan!" he fumed. "What part of *'stay the hell away from my family'* wasn't clear? Are you stalking us?"

"No," she said patiently. "I needed a new start, and it's nice here. By the way, before I left, I helped lead the police to Sheena Wilder. I thought you'd be proud of me." Her expression indicated she wasn't particularly concerned whether or not he was proud of her.

"Sheena who?"

"Our leader—before you. She moved away to become an acting agent. I'd heard of some unexplained deaths on the Vancouver theatre scene …" Miranda bent to collect the letters and shake off the grime. "They were putting it down to people saying 'Macbeth' out loud too much—superstitious dears—but I realized she was using the chant again.

Apparently, the performances were amazing. Some might even have said it was worth the loss—"

"Pff, I hope they had plenty of understudies."

"*Some* might have said it was worth the loss," she continued, undeterred. "But I remembered your crusade to have us make *our own* art, and I did the right thing. I reported her and helped track her down. A bittersweet victory, but still, the right thing to do. The world is safe from Sheena and her incredible incantation." She nodded with wistful pride, before adding, "And her terrible management skills—I swear she wouldn't recognize a decent actor if one mimed hitting her over the head with an imaginary baseball bat."

"You didn't answer my question," said Jaymie, determined not to be redirected. "Why are you really here? And don't try to convince me it's *nice* here. I'm *from* here."

"When I said nice, I meant cheap. And despite my mixed feelings about the time your band tore my clan apart, I still very much believe in you and your music—"

"*Mixed feelings?* You were killing each other!"

"—And I don't exactly have an amazing reputation in Regina—"

"I told you to stay away from—"

"—And it's challenging—nay, *impossible*—to effectively manage a band when you're unfamiliar with their scene. There's only so much I can do, long distance. So, I rented a room to do some research—"

"You tried to sacrifice my baby sibling!" Jaymie seethed.

"—And I've already booked you a show with a four-hundred-dollar guarantee."

"… Come again?"

She shot him a prim smile. "At first they offered one-fifty. So, you're welcome." She slit the envelope with her pinky nail and adjusted her round glasses to read the sopping letter. "Is there anything else, Mr. Bukowski? I have a call with another client this morning."

"What kind of show?" Jaymie asked with suspicion.

"There's been a Battle of the Bands—"

"*I don't do Battle of the Bandses!*"

"Relax, Jaymie," she said with a longsuffering air that Jaymie didn't feel she'd earned. "Can you listen for thirty seconds? Good heavens, how did you lead us for two weeks?"

Jaymie scowled but quieted down, his mail route all but forgotten.

"There was a Battle of the Bands this past autumn—twelve groups competing—and they've narrowed it down to two finalists. You're simply opening for them. For money."

"When is it?"

"The twenty-fifth. I'll email you details." She turned to go back inside. Jaymie resisted shoving his foot in the door; displaying predatory behaviour wasn't the appropriate way to deal with a predator.

"Who are the other bands?" he asked.

"One is *Vampyres*, and the other … hmm …"

"OK, I don't care. We'll do it."

"Good choice, Mr. Bukowski. See what an advantage it is, having a competent manager? Still, best not to lose your day job just yet—aren't you behind schedule?" She squinched her nose and shut the door in his face.

Jo wandered down Wolseley Avenue amid the gathering shadows, meandering vaguely in the direction of a park she liked to visit.

The streetlights flicked on. During the summer, they were kept alight twenty-four hours a day; the neighbourhood was known for its towering elm trees, which by June bore enough greenery to obstruct all sunlight and plunge entire blocks into darkness for months at a time—a seasonal reversal of the unending night north of the arctic circle.

Now the darkening January sky was clearly visible through barren branches splintering heavenward like upside-down lightning strikes.

Jo stopped and looked around, trying to get her bearings. Rex ambled placidly at her side. She asked, "Where are we going?" and Rex rolled their eyes.

"Michaud's," they said. "Remember?"

"What? No."

"You were like, 'Jaymie's the murderer!' and I was like, 'Uh, he's probably not,' and you were like, 'Whose car did we use for the pumpkins?' and I was like, 'We borrowed Anika's, 'cause she wanted revenge on Garrett for cheating,' and you were like, 'Who?' and I was like, 'You know, Drummer Garrett with the pumpkins!' and you were like, 'Oh, duh!' and then we laughed and laughed …" Rex smiled in remembrance of a conversation Jo couldn't for the life of her recall. They turned down a side street and she obediently followed. "So we're going to ask Anika about it, and she's hanging at Michaud's."

"Right," said Jo, forcing herself to think back. "It came to me while you were napping. In the glove box, there was a *Gunt* album, and the *BMIs*, *Shifty Principals*, *Lost the Show*, and I think the mandolinist too. Also, the *Llama* and the *Bukowski* EP, but that just makes sense …"

"I mean, a lot of people are into multiple genres. And lots of people just enjoy being involved in local music," mused Rex. "But it *is* a little weird, because Anika's a cellist, and she mostly listens to classical and hip hop, and she goes to indie shows more for the social aspects."

"Do I suspect Anika?" Jo asked, embarrassed that she might have accused Rex's cousin.

"I doubt it," said Rex lightly. "She's a little mysterious, but she's not really the murdering type."

"Yeah, I don't really know her, but that's the impression I got," said Jo. She had a sudden recollection of Anika's knack for covert entrances and exits, but she pushed it from her mind. They passed an imposing basswood tree and cut through a back alley.

"Hey Jo, advice question: If I found out that some of the Bukowskiphiles have started writing fanfics about Jaymie, should I tell him? Shahla's little sister, Ayla, started it. Apparently there're a couple that get pretty NSFW. I don't even know who made them."

"Pfft," Jo spluttered. "Do you really think he'd mind?"

"No. But if he thinks my friends did it, he might make fun of me forever."

"Hmm. I guess what he doesn't know can't hurt you."

"That's what I figured." Rex tried to scoop a snowball, and the too-powdery snow streamed from between their mittens. "Hey, does our band name bug you? Do you feel left out, since you're not our brother?"

"I never really thought about it. Does it bother you?"

"No because I am."

"Right, duh."

"Hey Jo, what's the name of the girl who played drums at the *Ballet Llama* show?"

"Who? Oh, um. Hailey. No. Halsey. Helen. Why, have you seen her before?" For a brief moment Jo was certain that the girl must be the murderer, but then she remembered that they had moved on to entirely new subjects.

"Never mind," said Rex. "… Do you like the TwiLite?"

"Yeah," she admitted. "I like forgetting about real life for a while. Not that you should go and— Look, your brain on drugs, it's not *better*, it's just *different*, and it's the change that I like—I don't mean to condone—"

"Hey Jo, what's sex like?"

"What?" asked Jo.

"Just curious."

Jo hesitated. "It's like, you're two pieces of the same puzzle, and you're finally coming together."

"OK." Rex nodded contentedly.

"… But it's not quite a match. But you're not totally sure, so you try again, just in case the two pieces actually do go together, and then you keep trying a hundred or two more times, and hopefully one or both of you gets off during that process."

"I'm sorry I brought it up."

"I'm kidding. Why are you asking *me* this stuff?"

Rex shrugged and clapped a puff of snow out of their mittens. It formed into a ghostly aura around them, and Jo had to concentrate to make out their form behind the white veil without letting her mind disintegrate into TV static.

"If I wasn't tripping out, I could give you real answers. Why don't you wait till then?"

"Because then you'd remember that I asked," said Rex.

Jo softened. She remembered that Rex was shy, and both of their parents were far away somewhere being government spies (they weren't), and their brothers were two large cats. No wait, they were humans, they just weren't always brimming with healthy advice.

"I talk to Maggie, but she just pretends she's got it all figured out, because she's done so much random stuff. And I can't imagine things going down for me the same way that they do for her, you know?" said Rex. "And Auntie Dory and Farida are nice, but I'm worried if they learn anything about my life, they'll get freaked out and make me move back in with them, and I don't want to leave Jaymie and Aaron on their own."

"You can ask me anything. Whenever," said Jo, wishing that she'd have a wealth of wisdom to impart as soon as she'd sobered up, and feeling certain that she wouldn't.

"Hey Jo, what're you doing with that gun in your hand? Da-doo da doo doo."

"What? I don't have a—oh, you're singing Hendrix. OK."

***

"Did you know *DZB*'s playing tomorrow night, too? Probably steal your whole crowd—too bad!" Michaud handed mugs of steaming mystery liquid to Rex and a still befuddled Jo.

"We'll be at *your* show, though," said Anika, giving him an admonishing look.

"Thank you …" said Jo, attempting to integrate into the conversation.

"'Course we will," said Michaud. "*Tornahdo*'s a blast. I mixed their first original single—they should stick to covers, don't tell them I said that. But don't worry, Jo—*you'll* always have Nik's and my loyalties, covers or no." Then, lest she mistakenly think he was being kind to her, he added, "Better make it worth our while. I want to see some serious shredding, and I don't care if it doesn't fit the genre. Hey—would a *sell-out* say that?"

"That quote was out of context!" Jo protested, but Michaud laughed.

"That article was pretty bang on, honestly," he said.

"When's *DPZ* playing?" asked Jo.

"*DZB*, you fucking druggy!" snorted Michaud. "*Dead Zebra Beach*!"

"Ah Christ, *DPZ*'s that's di-psilo-something, isn't it. You know what I meant!" Jo grumbled.

"Doors are at eight," Anika offered. "But it's so close by, I bet a lot of people will hit both shows."

"I love *DZB*," said Rex quietly.

"I love your bass playing, little dude," said Michaud, popping the tab on his beer and turning his attention to Rex. "You want to play in the *Ballet Llama*?"

"What about Jake?" asked Jo. "Also, *what?*"

"He's busy. School or whatever. And yeah, we got offered to play Festival, in February. I was going to turn it down, but if we have a solid sub, and we find a drummer in time …"

"Me?" asked Rex. "Sub?"

"You were seriously grooving at that cover show last month. C'était magnifique, man. Tu parles français? Non? That's OK, neither does Jo."

"It better be safe, Mich, if Rex is going to do it," said Anika. "Putting *yourself* in danger is one thing …"

Michaud sighed. "Nik and I have been discussing the ethics of playing live," he explained. "I don't know what to do. I don't want to lose another bandmate." He set his beer on the coffee table and rubbed his tattooed forearms, which Jo knew was about the biggest display of vulnerability you'd ever get out of him. "It's not like it's the city's only murderer. People are making a bigger fuss because more of the victims are well-off hipster kids. It's obviously problematic. But still, if we *know* it only happens at music events, one solution is to cancel the music. This shit *is* preventable."

"On the other hand, your boyf's blog is pretty convincing," said Anika wryly. *"The show must go on."*

"Nik would never make the call to cancel a show—she's too afraid of being taken for a square," Michaud teased.

"Michaud's intent on pinning me as a wannabe radical just because I won't agree to the constraints of monogamy," Anika said easily.

"What can I say, baby? I've been splitting all my shit with seventeen other anarchists ever since I was a kid. I'm tired of sharing."

"I'm not your baby." She draped herself comfortably over the couch behind him and fluffed his hair. Then her face clouded. "But I don't know what the answer is. Not that it'll ever be my decision. Nobody's killing classical players. Jesus, poor Allene."

"Allene is who we have to thank for the *Ballet Llama* reunion," said Michaud. He absently massaged his bicep, distorting an image of a beautiful punk woman who also had many tattoos on her biceps. Jo wondered if among the tattoo-woman's tattoos was a teeny Michaud, with another teeny tattoo-woman, and so on, ad infinitum …

She focused, and noticed Michaud wasn't making eye contact with anyone. Normally you couldn't prevent him from talking directly into your face from as close a proximity as possible.

"She asked me to do production on her album. She's smart—nobody else would've hired a washed-up punk singer to produce a folk LP, but she was going for a *Weakerthans* vibe." He shrugged. "She wanted the backing band simple, so, on a whim, I called in Jake and Alexandre. Who's more willing to play sparingly than two guys who refuse to learn the note names? It could've bombed, but they were fucking perfect. That's when Jake suggested getting the *Llama* back together. I said sure, what the hell, but only for one show."

"Shit, I should contact him. I keep forgetting to get paid for that," said Jo.

"Now we've lost both Allene and Alexandre. We have to be more careful. But I don't want to stop playing, because …" He finally looked at Jo. "I have literally no other skills."

"Yeah," she said, returning his smile. "Me neither." She let her head fall back on the couch and looked around his neat, if scruffy, living room. It was the same house he'd been living in ten years ago when she'd first met him, only now he had three housemates who seemed fairly responsible, rather than a rotating troupe of ten housemates who were actually seventeen housemates, none of whom cleaned, paid a set amount of rent, or consumed food on a regular basis. She glanced over at Rex, cross-legged beside her, and wished they could have seen it in all its sloppy, zoo-like splendour. Her gaze fell on a collection of stringed instruments in one corner.

"Have you always had that mandolin?" she asked.

"It's a balalaika, and yes. I have."

"Sorry. I'm high."

"What else is new?" said Michaud merrily. "Rex, are you hungry? Are you vegan? Would you like some beans and rice?"

It wasn't until Rex was in Anika's car later that evening with a belly full of veggie stir fry that they remembered the original reason for their visit. They eyed the glove box.

"Are the bros home?" asked Anika, pulling onto Pandora Street. Rex had considered telling her about their scare that morning, but decided they didn't want to worry her or risk her passing it on to the aunts.

"I messaged Aaron, and he was on his way ... Do you think Jo's alright?"

"She's safe with Mich. Don't take their bickering seriously—they've known each other for ages. Rex ..." Anika hesitated. "Do you *want* to keep playing shows? I know Aaron says he doesn't, but I honestly don't believe him. And anyway, I don't interfere in his and Jaymie's ... world. And he's a adult, so. But if *you're* feeling pressured by Jaymie, or by your mom—"

"I want to play," Rex confirmed. "I'm careful at shows. I don't go anywhere alone." They gave their cousin a reassuring smile. They liked Anika, but she was the sort of person who was good at fixing things and always had a Plan, and though she could be protective, she wasn't always predictable (ex., the pumpkins).

They casually popped open the glove box and flipped through the CDs—*Gunt; Lost, the Show, the Band; the BMI Babies.* "Good album," they said, holding up *Shifty Principals'* eponymous 2014 release.

"God, I forgot those were in there. Mich loaned me them when we first started dating—he has every recent local CD, because of his job. He has to add them all to their database. I was organizing this chamber-pop indie crossover night, so I asked for recommendations. I booked *Lost*. Neat group—he was filling in with them before he committed to going solo."

"Cool." Rex filed the CD back with the others and swung their legs out of the car.

"OK, Rex, be safe."

Rex scuffled through the snowy yard. They thought of Jo, still on Michaud's battered couch, asleep or passed out or staring at a wall, and they had the feeling they'd made a mistake. She'd been incoherently describing the fabulous squalor of Back In The Day when Rex had reluctantly accepted a ride offer from Anika. Michaud had promised to keep an eye on her, which should have been fine, because they were old friends, and because Rex liked him, and loved the *Ballet Llama,* and wanted very much to ignore the fact that the *Ballet Llama* and its singer happened to be connected to every band permanently short a member.

Stupid. Rex pulled out the postcard they'd swiped from Jo's desk. It had a message glued in cut-out newspaper script on the back: "Joanna, you're next / comme dans le joli Québec," and then a phone number. Jo had the excuse of being temporarily obliterated, but Rex didn't. Jo should've been there on Pandora Street, with them, and not least of all because Rex wasn't sure they believed the card was a joke. They turned around and waved to stop Anika, not yet sure what they intended to say to explain the error, but the car had already slipped silently away.

53

The Bukowski Files

Jo was not the only one trying to find patterns among the killings. Another curious individual had taken on the case, in an effort to obtain bonus marks for her grade twelve computer science class.

While Shahla's approach had so far yielded no more results than Jo's, it was undeniably a more methodical one. She was developing a program that collected and analyzed data from a provincial organization that helped promote and fund local bands. Their website kept an up-to-date calendar of all the shows in the city, with the exception of small events like the house concert the *Bukowskis* had played in October. It was also, incidentally, where Michaud worked.

Her idea was that, since the murders were music-related, you'd be able to see everyone who was playing on any given night someone was killed. You could look for odd coincidences or evaluate the alibis of suspects who claimed they'd been playing a different venue across the city. It was the sort of thing you'd expect the police to be doing, if the police were, in fact, doing anything at all, but Shahla's program could potentially do it faster.

The concept had many holes. For instance, it assumed there was only one killer. It also rested on the shaky hypothesis that the killer was a musician or involved with bands. Lastly, it relied on a music-related motive more complex than Maggie's proposal of, "Some random person hates musicians and is showing up at random shows and randomly killing them"—because, obviously, the more random the crime, the more difficult it was to solve.

And then there was that infuriating, even-more-random mini-donut salesperson.

Either way, she'd get extra points just for programming the thing, which would bring her to a one-hundred-ten percent final grade. It was just an added bonus if she had something nifty to hand over to a detective at the end.

Ayla lay on the bed behind her, composing her fanfiction epic and listening, as usual, to the *BBBFB*.

While Shahla's genius had manifested itself early on as a penchant for taking apart and reassembling machines, Ayla's was of a subtler, slower-onset variety. And while Shahla's enthusiasm for her favourite local band expressed itself healthily in her social life and extra-curricular activities, in Ayla it had materialized as an all-consuming obsession that dominated her every waking hour.

Nobody in their family considered this to be reason for concern; Ayla was recently thirteen and had been to one concert in her life—an All Ages *BBBFB* show at the Park Theatre. Her zeal was an inevitable side-effect of processing such an event.

She was curled around her Bukowski Files—mostly a collection of photographs of Jaymie printed off the internet—and a bag of fries that Shahla had ordered for them. She'd just begun editing Chapter 53, in which Jaymie apologized to the female protagonist for his alcoholism, touch-and-go attitude, manipulative tendencies, unusual fetishes, etc., and they mourned his broken past and then fondled each other passionately for a while before heading into another spiral of possessiveness and abuse. It was, in a word, delicious.

Shahla rubbed her eyes, stretched, and answered a text from Maggie; they were formulating an elaborate plan to (sneak in and) catch *DZB*'s show the following night, and then walk the fifteen minutes to (sneak in and) join Rex in time for *Tornado Tornahdo's* second set.

She'd made a spreadsheet that showed what times the bands were purportedly playing, and then extrapolated the times they'd *actually* start playing. For instance, if *DZB*'s venue said the show would start at 9:00, it meant 10:45; if the more punctual venue of Jo's show said they'd start at 10:00, it meant 10:30. However, if they said 10:30, it only meant 10:40, etc. Shahla had developed separate logarithmic equations to express the two bars' projected showtimes.

With *Tornado Tornahdo* on her mind, Shahla reopened version 1.03 of her program. Occasionally the infant software still failed to scan social media and find the names of all the musicians in a given band, and each had to be input manually, which was Ayla's job. In between chapters of her saga, the girl was forced to compile data from Facebook and band websites—a dull task, but she had to pay off those fries somehow.

After a few minutes, Ayla reported the names of each *Tornahdo*, including both the dead guitarist and Jo. Shahla commanded the program to cross-reference them with the other bands, and found two members in common with *The BMI Babies*, who'd lost their substitute keyboardist at the *Bukowskis'* house show (and whose Motown jams she'd once danced the school night away to, with Maggie, in a basement bar on Osborne Street).

The *BMIs*, in turn, overlapped with the *Ballet Llama*, who overlapped with *Shifty Principals*, and so on and so forth. She tried out a few different graphic visualizer options and settled on a series of Venn diagrams. Then she sent a copy to the other chief Bukowskiphiles, Maggie and Stan, so they could take up the cause if she died at tomorrow's show. She wasn't a musician, but one couldn't be too safe.

She just hoped she could develop a more intuitive, user-friendly interface before then, if worse came to worst.

The sun had paced itself fairly well for most of the day, and it rewarded its own restraint by sprinting the last leg of sky, pole vaulting over the horizon, and passing out without setting an alarm. Darkness closed around Rex as they reached their front door. A movement from above caught their eye and made them momentarily forget their worries about Jo.

They squinted and made out a humanoid figure in the shadows of the porch roof. It swung around the side of the house toward Jaymie's window and slid out of sight. Rex froze. They had no idea whether it had seen them.

They bolted for the sidewalk, a series of plans already formulating in their mind: text Aaron to stay away, call Anika to come back for them, bang on a neighbour's door, hope it was just Jymmy back for another synth ...

Then Rex became conscious, in what felt like two or three jarring stages, of a low humming coming from the garage. The van was there, and running. Of course, Aaron would've arrived home by now.

They made for the vehicle, and then faltered. It was cold out, and Aaron had no reason to linger outside. They wondered if he'd seen the intruder and decided to wait for them in the van with the doors locked—

but that didn't make any sense; they knew Aaron, and if he was afraid, he'd have driven a ways away, phoned Rex, and returned to scoop them up. He wouldn't have parked in the garage. Rex gulped.

They reached the van on silent feet, longing to turn and run, and feeling an absurd sense of injustice at having to suffer twice in one day. The lightbulb in the garage had burned out recently and no one had gotten around to changing it yet.

Hugging their elbows, they peered in the driver's side window. A red glow emanated from the dashboard, where the speed- and tachometers formed lambent constellations. The neon green of the clock showed it was just after 6 p.m.

They thumbed the brightness up on their phone and held it up for light, which only cast an impenetrable reflection on the window. They flinched as the phone vibrated and a starry OMFG from Maggie blinked into the grimy glass. An emoji followed, in reaction to something Rex had sent earlier, its tears-of-joy expression twisted into a grimace by the window scum.

They withdrew the screen light and thought of calling their brothers from the street, but their eyes were already adjusting, and they could now see the shape of a head resting on the window, feathery brown hair nestled against the glass. With a lump in their throat, Rex grasped the handle and swung the door open.

"Aaaiiiihh motherfork ow!" Aaron tumbled out of the van.

"Ohmigod I thought you were dead!" cried Rex. "Why were you just sitting there?"

"You couldn't knock on the window, or something?" asked Aaron, brushing himself off. Realization dawned on Rex.

"I forgot to copy the key!" they said in dismay, and gave a small, hysterical laugh.

"No kidding," said Aaron.

"Were you locked out long?"

"Na, Jay was almost done work, so I waited around downtown to pick him up."

"And he's ..." Rex facepalmed. "... Breaking in through the bedroom window." There was a short yelp, a snowy thwump, and a round of swearing from the house.

"Trying," said Aaron. "But he actually Jymmy-proofed it pretty well."

"I've got it here," said Rex, digging in their pocket for the new key.

"Perfect. How's your day?"

"I was—this morning—I got—I saw the— ... Yeah, it was OK," said Rex. "You?"

"I ran into Jymmy. That guy's the fucking worst. Not the murderer, though, probably—Hey, Rex has the key!" he yelled. "The job's alright. I'll tell you about it."

Rex unlocked the door, only to be accosted by their three long-term tenants—all of whom vocalized that they were beyond ready for their evening dosage of canned mystery porridge—and Aaron's playful speckled therapist cat, who'd recently been examined by a vet and declared to be merely a large kitten. So much for quality psychiatric treatment.

Jo was seventeen years old and she'd had five drinks and too much of an edible, and now she was plastered to Michaud's couch, unable to string together a complete sentence. Inconvenient. It wasn't even the first time she'd made this mistake. *You'd think I'd have learned a lesson*, she thought, and giggled softly to herself.

Michaud's seventeen roommates, plus a few friends, were in the middle of an impromptu party she suspected she'd been participating in before she'd let herself go. The roommates were all drinking and smoking and hookahing and probably doing other things she hadn't tried or even thought of yet. *Sleater-Kinney* played loudly from a speaker in the kitchen.

On the bright side, her central location in the room meant there were enough raggedy punks of that mostly wild-yet-gentle variety milling around, who'd notice if she threw up, wigged out, or drew the attention of a creep.

Michaud was getting acrobatically wasted; he drank straight from a bottle of cheap rye, still self-aware enough to pose imperiously each time he took a slug. He had ten other teenagers enthralled by a bilingual tirade about the corrupt systems of oppression that—no, it was about the other band they'd just played with; he thought they were poseurs. At nineteen, he already had as many tattoos as his vegan frame could fit and about three times as much anger.

She'd lied to Lucas; she and Michaud *had* hooked up—not on this night or in this year, but after the band. Just a few times.

"It's fucking sad *Sum 41*-ripoff emo shit," he was saying, and the partiers agreed wholeheartedly that the opening band were worthless swill who deserved to die and have their pandering souls hacked from their bodies. Jo blinked up at him from where she lay immobilised. Oh yeah—they must have played a show earlier. She barely remembered it.

"I can't listen to shit like that anymore. It's been ten years," he said. The room quieted. The punks had drifted off. Jo tried to reach for them, to call them back, or follow them into the mists of their well-adjusted adult lives, but it was as though she were caught in a sleep paralysis.

"—Most of the pop bullshit that comes out these days—and I have to listen to them, and tell them, 'You just need to tweak your social media,' and 'This is how you make it as a band,' and not accidentally say, 'You're never going to make it as a band.' I know it's a musician's dream day-job on one hand, but it's fucking depressing. I'm just saying, sure, I made it pretty far, but it's not the glory it seems like you're imagining. I never asked to be a gatekeeper."

The living room was dark and empty. Jo rolled over on the couch. *I don't want to be high anymore*, she thought. *I want to wake up and make coffee and practice scales*. It wasn't a bad trip, exactly, but it had reached the phase where the fake epiphanies had lost their grandeur and begun to mock her, and her fatigued mind remained wired while craving rest. She vowed to stay away from the synthetic stuff from now on.

"That's harsh, man. Shit, is that how *I* sound? I mean, I just get pissed off sometimes. The stuff I play now, I can't take my anger out like with the *Llama*, you know? Maybe I am a sell-out. Ha ... Right, speaking of. I might take the gig, I found a sub. Glad you're not angry about it. And a little surprised. But like I said, it's just for one show, till it blows over." Jo heard him clinking dishes together, moving in and out of earshot in the next room. "... that new project? ... Sounds like exactly what I've been whining about, no offense ... Hey, can we not talk about Quebec? ... Sure, keep me posted ... See you."

Someone had covered her in a blanket and put an actual pillow—not a couch cushion—under her head. Michaud's free b'n'b had gotten classier over the years. She hugged her knees and snuggled in and woke up onstage.

Her eyes welled from the yellow glare in her face. The stage lights turned the rest of the room into a solid black wall, completely obscuring the audience that—presumably—stood in front of her.

She looked to her left, expecting a dreamscape diorama of the teenaged *Ballet Llama*, and was momentarily disconcerted when they weren't there. Her confused mind next sought the Brzezinski siblings, and she only recognized *Tornado Tornahdo,* finally, when they launched into the next cover.

Ah, it's the surf-rock show, she thought to herself. It was already tomorrow night. Tonight. Whatever.

She hoped she could remember the guitar parts to whichever song they were on, and was relieved to discover she'd already begun playing them. She exchanged friendly eye contact with the rhythm section, who gave no indication of annoyance at—or awareness of—her complete lack of mental presence. She flipped her hair out of her eyes. She recognized this song. It was "Telstar." It was in A major.

Rock and roll.

54

Hiberflipping Nation

By the time *Tornado Tornahdo* were finishing the first of their two sets, Jo had accepted that she wasn't dreaming and really had skipped an entire day of her life. It was the longest blackout she'd ever experienced.

Her gear was arranged exactly as she liked it, and the band seemed as untroubled as they had in their two rehearsals the previous week, which led her to believe she'd set up without assistance and given no more indication than usual that she was in an altered state.

She let the last chord ring, then set her guitar in its stand and looked around for her friends.

She could finally see the audience. The Brzezinskis were moving from their spots in front of the stage toward a booth Anika and Michaud had claimed off to one side. Accompanying Jaymie was a curvaceous woman wearing an exquisite scarf; it took Jo a moment to recognize her as the singer, Daffodile, and just as long to identify the familiar-looking girl beside Aaron as Juniper, the would-be pianist from Regina. Anika and Michaud's voices carried to the stage, arguing amicably. Lucas waited for her beside the table, tapping opinions into his phone.

What a lot of couples we are, she thought, and then wondered if a bird drawn from a single line of paint on the wall above the bar was going to burst into amorous recitative with Disney-musical lyrics. She looked away pointedly when it did so.

She noticed Rex perched at one end of the booth, waving her over, and she loped down the stage steps to join them. For a disorienting moment, the table seemed miles away, across a vast and exhausting expanse of black floor, but a few seconds later she was greeting her friends, accepting their compliments, and thanking them for coming.

She was at a remove from her surroundings. She heard herself saying normal-sounding words, and her friends replying with equally standard responses, yet none of it was real. It was as though there were a script she'd once memorized and forgotten, and now they were all enacting it with a déjà vu-like absurdity that made her want to laugh. She knew she shouldn't, though, because that would be weird. And she certainly didn't want everyone to think she was weird.

Jo suddenly felt the gut-wrenching grip of anxiety. What if they *did* think she was weird? What if the Brzezinskis secretly hated her? What if they thought *she* was the killer, because she was so big and awkward and friendless, and they were just too polite to kick her out of the band?

She looked at Rex, peacefully texting their high school friends, and just as quickly realized how ridiculous this was. Another of those crazy, stoned anxieties. What if all her sober, real-life anxieties were just as trivial as these ones? And she'd just gotten locked in the same thought patterns for too long and no longer realized the Truth? Was this the sort of revelation people talked about having while on hallucinogens?

She considered recommending it to Aaron, but he'd probably have a bad trip. Where was Aaron, anyway? Hopefully he hadn't gotten kidnapped again; she wouldn't be able to handle it in her current state.

She looked around and saw him at the bar with Juniper. Why did she think he was kidnapped? He waved, and suddenly his freckles multiplied, filling her entire field of vision, until she shook her head clear. Whoa, weird. She suddenly remembered him telling her that he'd briefly suspected Lucas, but he also might have suspected *her,* and then she wondered if the Brzezinskis secretly hated her and thought *she* might be the murderer—wait, hadn't she already worked through this? Funny how things kept coming around.

"Want a drink?" asked Lucas, and she realized she'd been speaking to him for several minutes. She wondered what they were talking about.

"A water would be great," she said.

"You got it." He went to stand in line, and Jo wondered if she could keep this up long enough to still have friends by the time this episode was over.

***

Rex watched Lucas leave for the bar, and then slipped out of the booth to take his place. Anika had texted them that morning to say she was at Michaud's for breakfast and that Jo had made it home safely. Their worries mostly allayed, Rex had spent the day with their bass, learning every *Ballet Llama* song ever recorded, just in case Michaud was serious about his invitation.

"Are you feeling better?" they asked.

"Well, it's not a huge deal or anything, but I've got kind of a bad feeling about all this. I can't sober up. It's been, like, thirty-something hours." Jo's tone was natural, but there was a feverish exhaustion in her eyes.

"You're *still* high?" they asked in alarm. "I'll google it."

"Feels like I got poisoned, ha … I wonder if Izzy gave me bad stuff. I wish I had an antidote, or something … Kinda tired of it …"

"Izzy? I've heard of her." Rex ducked behind Jo to avoid having their fake ID suspiciously eyed for the umpteenth time as a bartender collected empty bottles.

"I should've made sure she knew what she was selling me …" Jo mumbled. "But she just … She's kind of intimidating."

"Yeah, some of the kids at school know of her. She hangs out around Osborne, right?"

"I think it's getting worse. Man, if I'm stuck like this …" The dreamy demeanor of the previous day seemed to have been replaced by a mild craze. "Just need the remedy …"

"Maybe I should ask Jaymie," said Rex. "He's had friends who do stuff like this."

"Please don't tell him," Jo said quickly. "There's nothing he could do, and I don't want to cause a … and then Aaron would find out, and I don't want to make him—I mean, he might be uncomfortable with it …"

"Yeah, he would. OK, let me think," said Rex. They opened their phone and typed in "twilite." A series of cautionary articles and death statistics popped up. They scrolled to the more scientific sites, which provided lists of side-effects and long-term health risks, and then changed their mind and found a forum. The lights dimmed and the band began to congregate onstage.

Jo was murmuring to herself. "That little twerp. I wonder if she knows a single thing about her own product."

"I'll keep looking," said Rex, but Jo was already drifting back to the stage. They wished Maggie were there, but she and Shahla had gone to the

DZB show several blocks away. On the drug forum, a mother lamented that her son was experimenting with Twi and must certainly be hooked and doomed to die; a teenaged expert informed her that it sounded more like MDMA, but he might still die, who knows?

Jo was right—Rex wasn't sure to what extent drug dealers were obligated to read up on their wares, but if anyone would know anything about TwiLite, it was Izzy. And the bridge was only a ten-minute walk away, down a busy street. Rex could be there and back before the set was over. They pulled their coat on, checked that their family members were distracted with their dates, and headed out.

"How's clonehood treating you?" asked Lucas.

"What? Oh, good," said Aaron, glancing over at Juniper. He hadn't told her that he was officially a rehabilitated clone, or that Lucas and Jo, as his sponsors, were technically responsible for his behaviour. Fortunately, she was occupied talking to Daffodile. "Honestly, being Jaymie's clone hasn't altered my life all that much. Surprising, I know."

Juniper touched his arm. "I'm going for a quick smoke with Jaymie and Daffodile before the band starts," she said.

"You smoke? I mean, no, great, cool. I'll finish this drink and join you guys." Aaron had no desire to stand outside, missing part of a great instrumental rock set. Still, he was enjoying Juniper's company, and there was always the likelihood Jaymie would split a cigarette with him. He sipped his drink and shifted his backpack to his other shoulder.

"Hey man, can I ask you something?" said Lucas.

"I swear I haven't broken any laws lately. You don't have to worry."

"I'm not worried about the clone thing." He watched Jo tuning her guitar. The rhythm guitarist greeted the crowd and the drummer began a beat. "Is Jo … OK?"

"What do you mean?" said Aaron, raising his voice over the drums.

"Like, is she kind of … on drugs? Right now? All the time?" Lucas yelled into his ear.

"Oh, on drugs. Yeah," he shouted back. Two women cast wary glances at him as they jostled closer to the stage. He finished the last of his beer, missing the look of annoyance that passed over Lucas's face. "I mean, I think she smokes a lot of weed."

"I think it's getting to her head. It's like, a person needs a filter."

"Killed her? Killed *who?*"

"No, I mean, you need to be able to stay rational ... Does she seem paranoid, to you?"

"Um, I'm not someone who can pass judgement on that." Aaron deposited his empty bottle on a nearby ledge and forced himself to forget "killed her."

"What?" Lucas yelled, before continuing, "I mean, a couple times, we were talking, and I'm pretty sure she suspected *me* of being the murderer."

"Yeah, so did I for a minute."

"Jesus! *Why?* Just because I don't want to cancel music? Neither do you guys!" Lucas finished his own drink and set the bottle next to Aaron's with a forceful clunk that was lost beneath the driving beat.

"Yeah, but we're, like, *so* neurotic about it," shouted Aaron.

"What?" shouted Lucas.

"Neurotic!"

"Yeah, she is—" The music swelled by several decibels as the increasingly drunken band launched fully into "Misirlou."

"—just feel like, why be so suspicious about everyone—" His words were carried away by the notes of the double harmonic scale. "—wrong with just exercising reasonable caution? Not sure why she'd think *I'm the murderer*—" Jo's tremolo-picked lead line surpassed all other events in the room in both volume and importance. "—and acting strange—"

"What?" Aaron yelled, tearing his attention away from the music in time to hear "I'm the murderer," delete it from his overactive brain as per his CBT's instructions, and completely miss Rex slipping out behind him.

Lucas leaned in closer. "—kind of aloof all day. Do you think she's pissed with me?"

"She'd visit you? Like, in jail?"

"What? No, she's *pissed!*"

"Sorry! Na, she can handle her liquor—are you hearing this solo?"

"No, I think she's mad! I don't know what to do!"

"Oh, angry! I don't know ..." Aaron shifted uncomfortably and yelled back, "You could try saying things like, 'I care about you, and I don't want you to get murdered.' That's what we tell Rex when they're down about it. And we never let them go anywhere alone at shows—"

"What!"

"I said! We don't let them go out alone at shows! ... But I guess you can't really control that! With a girlfriend! So ...!"

"OK, thanks Aaron! Never mind!" said Lucas. Then he muttered something that coincided with a brief decrescendo and sounded suspiciously like "Fucking drummers," but Aaron opted to give him the benefit of the doubt. He realized that the more time he spent with Lucas, the higher his chances were of saying something that aggravated him, which was a bad move if Lucas actually was the murderer.

"I told Juniper I'd—I'm just—a quick smoke—see you later," he said. Outside, he zipped his jacket, adjusted his pack—heavy with Bukowski novels for Juniper—and admired the moon peeking over a building. It hung ripe and low in the sky, glowing with a ruddy, romantic hue.

Daffodile was chatting with a small entourage of friends or fans, and Jaymie turned away from the group to hand Aaron his cigarette.

"Juniper's not with you guys?" Aaron asked.

"You just missed her. Hey—turns out she's a Daffodile fan too!" said Jaymie. "Seemed pretty thrilled to converse with the Daff herself! As am I, obviously … But yeah, she made a kind of a quick departure."

"Why? Where to?"

"I don't know. She looked a little fidgety all the sudden, and then she said sorry and rushed off … I'm sure it's nothing to worry about. She's not inside?"

"No, I was just in there. I'll text her." He handed the cigarette back, his hands already going numb. Then he glanced around to make sure no one was listening. "OK, you're three dates in. One of an elite few with the inside scoop. You have to tell me, 'cause you know I won't leak it—what's Daffy's real name?"

"That's stupid, Aar. Obviously, it's Daffo—Well now. That's a good question."

"Unbelievable," said Aaron.

Rex crossed the Osborne Bridge under the wine-tinted glare of the full moon, which lurked on the horizon, flushed and bloated, giving the impression it had contracted an affliction of the inflamed and rashy variety.

They slowed at the end of the deserted bridge, feeling foolish. They had no idea how to locate Izzy, and they hadn't encountered a single person on the way, though the passing cars gave them a sense of safety. A pathway descended under the bridge into total darkness, and Rex eyed it warily, knowing the girl was rumoured to frequent the grottos below.

They'd already come this far. They texted Maggie the time and location of their death, just in case, and began to pick their way through the snow, down to the riverbank and under the shadow of the bridge.

It felt several degrees colder here, and the darkness was thick and otherworldly. Rex's phone light didn't penetrate far enough to illuminate even their own feet.

A snippet of conversation reached them, the words muffled, as though the stifling blackness had a muting effect. The sound of plucked guitar strings floated through from the other side—the first notes of an out-of-tune country ballad. But that was impossible; it was too cold for anyone to linger down there, handling icy steel strings. Torn between curiosity and fear, Rex stood rooted in the dark.

An unearthly wail pierced the stillness. Rex heard the cry, like a wendigo screaming toward them from somewhere across the river, and their nerves failed. They spun around and scrambled back into the bright moonlight.

The wind blew again, and they chastised themself; the keening was simply an effect of the breeze passing under the bridge, amplified by an overactive imagination. They shuddered, took a deep breath, and called, "Izzy?"

Their voice shook, and Rex was embarrassed at this clueless attempt to summon forth the bridge keeper. Yet sure enough, a small form separated itself from the shadows, wearing a hood that zipped all the way shut in the front and a coat that reached nearly to its ankles.

"Yeah?"

"Oh. Um … I wanted to—to ask you …" Rex stuttered, amazed that the girl could find her way around down there in the dark.

"Looking for something?"

"Actually, I need to know—my friend bought some stuff—"

"Yeah, I'm not sure you're ready for whatever your friend bought. Have you tried cigarettes? Let's start you with cigarettes. I'll give you a deal," said Izzy, the city's preeminent preteen drug dealer.

"No, I'm not shopping," said Rex, finding their voice. "My friend bought Twi from you, only it's gone wrong." Rex briefly explained how Jo hadn't sobered up, and that some kind of antidote was necessary.

"Antidote?" Izzy snickered. "Bro, there's no *antidote*. It's a drug, not a snake bite. It's not my fault if your bud hiberflipped and now she regrets it."

"Hiberflipped? I've never heard of it," said Rex. "Is that like when people do hippy flipping or candy flipping or whatever?"

"Hippy flipping? OK, boomer."

"I'm seventeen!"

"That explains it," the girl laughed. "You look younger. I thought you might be current."

"Sorry I haven't wrecked my brain yet!" snapped Rex. "What the hell is hiberflipping?"

"You sure you're ready?" Izzy teased.

"Explain like I'm five," Rex shot back.

"Hiberflipping—a.k.a. *winter flipping, quinzhee tripping, the Canada slumber, etc.*—" she said, as though to a child solemnly graduating from Froot Loops to the hard stuff, "is when you mix up a bunch of Twi with a bunch of DPZ—yum yum—and dream till springtime. Like a little old bear in hibernation. I don't recommend it to my clients, for health reasons."

"I'm pretty sure Jo wouldn't hiberflip …" said Rex, not at all sure whether or not Jo would hiberflip.

"Dude, you look familiar." Izzy's eyes narrowed through the zipper slit in her hood. "Do you play in *3BFB*?"

"Yeah," said Rex, surprised. "Bass. Do you … listen to us?"

She shrugged. "I used to. The new single sounds like a sell-out. Your early stuff was great, though."

"We didn't sell—we've made *one* EP—"

"I like the band name, even though it's kind of dated."

"Excuse me?"

"Problematic," she clarified.

"How are we problem—"

"Like, have you even *met* an actual broken family? Do they have those in your suburb?"

"We didn't mean that—it was just a play on—"

"Are you gonna buy something, square? I've got a business to run here. You want some meth, or no? Get out of my hair."

Jo was four songs into the second set when she realized Rex wasn't in the audience. Her eyes had adjusted enough to make out her friends in the front row—Lucas typing in his phone, Jaymie aerobically Instagramming her performance while maintaining a shouted conversation with his date, and Aaron, now on his own, politely engrossed in the music—and while it was possible that Rex had just stepped out momentarily, Jo somehow had the mental clarity—or perhaps the psychotropic telekinesis—to sense what had happened.

She remembered Rex's concern, and her own muddled rambling about an *antidote*—as if there were such a thing!—and she realized she might have inadvertently sent her friend on a dangerous, pointless mission, only a day after they'd been threatened by a murderer.

She'd just launched into a country-tinged solo that leaned heavily mixolydian, and she accidentally hit an ugly major seventh that there was no recovering from.

Ignoring the looks of incredulity from the band, she quit mid-solo, swung her guitar strap off her shoulder, and put the instrument on the floor. She thrust her way through the confused audience and out the door in a matter of seconds. Behind her, the rhythm guitarist clumsily picked up the solo on the wrong pentatonic scale, and the band played on.

55

The Garden

At around the same time Jo was making her dramatic exit, two teenagers slipped out the back door of a small, crowded venue several blocks away. *Dead Zebra Beach* had just started their penultimate song, but, according to Shahla's equations, they had to leave now if they wanted to reach the surf-rock show, meet up with Rex, and catch any of Jo's second set.

The door swung shut on the music with the effect of a volume dial being turned from eleven to five. Another pair of show-hoppers, a man and woman, walked ahead of them down the snowy back lane.

"What would you call this?" asked the man. "Meta-ethical soft-rock?"

"Post-environmentalism," suggested the woman.

"Postmodern emo-jazz."

"Post-post-punk deconstructivism."

"I liked their eyeliner," contributed Maggie, several paces back. "Love a guy in eyeliner."

"They might be the best band in the city," said the man. "Not counting *Noble Pirogue*, obviously, but they're huge. Best *new* band in the city."

"Fun fact," Shahla piped up. "A pirogue is a type of canoe, but seventy-three percent of their social media followers, when poled, thought it was an intentional misspelling of 'perogy.'"

"Dweeb," Maggie snorted.

"What about the *Bukowski Bros*?" the woman asked, ignoring the two teens. "I've seen you man-crushing on that guy." She adjusted her hat, a floppy woollen item that drooped around her face, hinting that it also served as a receptacle for a great deal of hair. She wore a wine-red coat, the collar of which reached just above her nose and left only her eyes visible. The bottom of the jacket fanned out, bell-like, to her knees. She had a tipsy way of walking—whether natural or alcohol induced—that gave Maggie the impression there might not be anything under the hat and coat but fluff or straw or goose feathers.

"They're good, but this music has *complexity*. Warmth. I still think Jaymie Bukowski is a nihilist," the man replied.

"You're a nihilist," said the woman.

"No, you." They sniggered into their face-coverings.

They turned down another alley, and Maggie and Shahla paused, deliberating whether it was smarter to reach the main street as quickly as possible, or bet on safety in numbers. They knew the killer had never struck a duo, but it was late and dark out, and a group of four provided greater security. They followed the pair.

"*DZB* are going to be massive," said the man. "They'll be one of the defining CanCon sounds of their generation."

"It's kind of amazing how they're virtuosic, but still fun. They've got to be the best on the scene," agreed the woman.

"OK, but the *BBBFB* are the best band, hands down," said Maggie loudly.

"Maggie ..." Shahla cautioned.

"Their music is good, but they're kind of cliché," said the man offhandedly. "Jaymie B has that tortured-artist thing, like, Look at me, life is hard and I'm an alcoholic and all I do is take drugs and try to get laid and then subtly insult the chicks I screw."

"It's *not* those things, it's a commentary," Maggie said icily. "It's *satire.*"

"Like, great, another self-pitying artist dude," said the woman, clearly not listening. "Hot, though. A bit scrawny, but wow."

"It's about how much our culture loves that *character* ..." Maggie tried.

"For satire to work, you have to be able to tell it's satire. The guy can sing, though, I'll give him that," admitted the man.

"Remember when we saw him at the *Ballet Llama* show and you asked him if he was a humanist, and he had, like, no idea what it meant?" the woman laughed.

"In his defense, it doesn't really mean anything," said the man.

"He's a good example of post-convinstagrimism," invented Maggie, who was good at identifying a person's point of insecurity early on.

"Perhaps," the man mused. "Or is he, rather, just a pale reflection of it?"

"Rather," agreed Maggie. "He refracts his societal milieu."

"You're cute, do you want to get a drink?" he asked, and she made a very audible retching noise.

Shahla tugged her arm, correctly identifying this exchange as the juncture at which the two parties should separate. "I don't like his balaclava," she whispered, pulling Maggie down a side street. "Like, show your face if you're offering a drink. And we are having *fun*. We're partying off your breakup."

"Ugh, his ironic snowsuit," said Maggie. "What a hipster. Disgusting."

Jo's friends knew she'd never bail on a performance so abruptly if something weren't very wrong. However, her departure had drawn their attention away from the music, and they immediately became aware of an even more pressing cause for alarm—Rex's absence.

When Rex didn't answer their phone, the family divided to scour the area. Anika and Michaud volunteered to search the venue top to bottom, while Jaymie and Aaron pursued Jo, wondering if she'd seen something from the stage and was already on the trail.

By the time they made it through the crowd, Jo had made significant headway, and they could only guess which direction she'd taken. At that point, Aaron decided Rex was definitely dead and broke his nine-days-without-a-panic-attack streak, and Jaymie couldn't leave him alone in the vicinity of the show—a potential death sentence—so he changed tactics and opened social media to contact Maggie and ask if Rex had gone to meet her. Then he dragged Aaron to the van, aware that their young DD was the one MIA and that certain risks might have to be taken.

And so, only Lucas saw Jo pelt across Portage Avenue and disappear down another street. Fortunately for him, he had even longer legs than she did.

"Hey! What are you doing!" he called.

"I have to find Rex!" Jo panted, slowing to a jog. He kept pace beside her.

"What? Weren't they back there?"

"They left. Under the bridge. They're under the bridge …" she mumbled breathlessly.

He seized her arm, which both of them immediately interpreted as threatening, and he let go just as quickly. "Jo, what's going on? I messaged you this morning, and you texted back—" He pulled out his phone and recited, still jogging, "'I'm practice for the show and not die but I don't know,' and then a little heart, and then you didn't respond all day."

"Did you hear me? I have to find Rex! I don't have time—"

"No. Stop. You're in a fucking T-shirt! What the hell is wrong with you?" He reached for her elbow again and she shrugged him off. "Did you smoke too much before the show and now you're, like—"

Jo let out a hollow laugh. "You have no idea. Hey—I made a mistake, but I'm not wigging out, if that's what you think—"

"Just relax for one fucking second, OK? Have you even texted Rex to see if they went for a snack? Before you go all berserk about it?"

Jo finally stopped and faced him, and her eyes had a demented gleam.

"How are you so chill all the time?" she demanded. "Aren't you scared *at all?*"

"So that's what it is? You're getting weird again because you're afraid of the killer?"

"I'm not afraid! I'm—maybe I am, but not for *myself!*" She glanced distractedly around the deserted street. The wind blew white veins of snow into her hair. "OK, a little for myself, but also for the people in the bands—and the—you know what? Don't make this about me!"

"It *is* about you! You're the one panicking right now!"

"I feel like I'm the only one who's sane right now!" she shouted.

"Funny, because it seems like you got high one too many times."

"OK, yes, but I didn't mean to, I just—"

"Hey, here's a novel idea, maybe being stoned all the time is affecting your brain? Making you, like, kind of reactive?" Lucas was steering dangerously close to accusing his new girlfriend of being crazy. Then again, she'd just ditched a show mid-set to run around in tights and a T-shirt in January, and he'd never been particularly tolerant of other people's drama.

"You said you didn't care that I smoke," said Jo coldly.

"You said you didn't let it get in the way of anything!" retorted Lucas. "And it kind of feels like it's getting in the way!"

"That murderer is getting in the way! And you keep changing the subject, which is kind of fucking suspicious! Are you gaslighting me?"

"What?" he asked in surprise. She rubbed her arms, appearing to finally feel the cold.

"You act like I'm hysterical every time I ask why you aren't worried! If you're not the killer, then why the hell aren't you scared like the rest of us!"

"Because I'm not a fucking musician!"

A silence hung in the air.

He continued, fumbling, "I mean, I'm … I know that you *are* a … But he only strikes when people are alone, and I figured if you stay around me, you'll be safe too. Like you said, the pattern—that they were all in bands—and I'm not, so I guess it finally has an upside."

"Rex is a musician," said Jo. "Aaron and Jaymie are musicians. My friends. Jake and Oli and Michaud and Anika and that little drummer Harriet."

"Yeah, but that's their choice, and people know the risks by now—musicians have had a higher mortality rate since long before the killer—that's just statistics—"

"And you get to sit back and enjoy the intrigue, knowing you're safe."

"That's not what I—"

"Do you feel *edgy*? Hanging out with people like us? Does this just increase the thrill?"

"Of course not!"

"You get to stream our music for free while we pay distro fees, and see our shows for cheap cover while we pay to book the venue, and you live vicariously through our destructive habits and mental breakdowns. Hell, *you* make ad revenue writing about if we were decent or embarrassing, and pass it all off as positive reviews. We put our whole *lives* into this—"

"OK, your *whole lives*? It's a fucking indie band, Jo."

"I'm sorry you never got to be in a band, Lucas, but if this as some kind of retribution—"

"*What?* Do you still think that *I'm* the—are you afraid of *me?*" He took in her maddened eyes and wild, snow-dusted hair, and realized what a stupid question this was. She raised her eyebrows. "Never mind," he said. "You know what—sorry for trying to keep a clear head while everyone is running around panicking. Sorry for trying to show an ounce of rationality—"

Jo scoffed. "Oh, perfect, let's look at the stats. Only point-zero-something percent of all people in the city got murdered so mathematically you'll only lose one finger off one friend—"

"—Instead of getting caught up in the drama or taking a hit of whatever your drummer is on and having a fucking hissy fit about everything—" He knew he'd gone too far.

"Go back to the show." There was finality in Jo's voice. "It's dangerous out here."

"Gladly," he said. "I hope, for your sake, you realize how ridiculous you're being and come back, because you're going to get frostbite."

"I hope, for your sake, that you're the murderer, because you've got five or six dark, lonely blocks ahead of you." She turned and started jogging again.

"Jo," he said, and she looked back. "I think we're done."

Maggie checked a text. "Quick detour," she said. "We're going to meet Rex first, if they're not dead. They're hunting a drug dealer under the bridge."

"Why?" asked Shahla.

"No clue. That's our Rex." They rerouted. A block away, the two students stopped and watched them. "They said they're looking for Izzy."

"That middle-schooler?"

"Yeah. She's a creep."

"Noted." They turned toward the river.

"God, quiet around here. Does nobody go out on the weekend anymore?" Maggie complained. "Is no one else breakup-partying?"

In the distance, the wind whistled its way under the bridge. A raggedy, floppy-headed form doubled back and began trailing the girls, lurching from the cover of one gloomy skeleton tree to the next. "Hey, did you solve the murders yet?"

"No. Based on the info, my program will probably land on Yarbrough, because he goes to every show. But that's his *job*. Also, it takes names from advance ticket sales, Facebook events, and our own input, but not from drop-ins paying at the door, so there's a lot of missing data."

The pursuer flickered out from the under the trees, its shadow growing and distorting.

"Bummer," said Maggie. The shadow spread over the heels of their boots. The girls paused their conversation to check Snapchat, which they did approximately every seven minutes. Neither saw the contorted shape descending.

It passed them and continued toward the bridge. As it went, its shadow faded away, and then its body did too. Lucas had been right about one thing: it wasn't interested in the fans.

Jo didn't reach Osborne Street. After five minutes of jogging, it became clear she'd taken a wrong turn. She was in the heavily-treed neighbourhood she and Rex had walked through the day before; she recognized the mammoth basswood they'd passed. She reoriented herself and hung left down Wolseley Avenue, on an alternate route to the bridge.

She'd walked this street many times and her steps were intuitive, yet soon her surroundings were once more unfamiliar. She turned in a circle, confused. The streets were more winding here, their trajectories dictated by the twists in the river to the south. The houses were somber and ostentatious. Jo realized she was in The Gates, the neighbourhood of Jaymie's usual postal route, which couldn't be found on any map and was generally encountered by outsiders only through a series of accidental spiraling turns whilst on an urban nature walk or high.

She turned south, knowing she'd hit the river and could follow the skating path to the bridge. A biting wind blew, and she realized for the first time that she was wearing only the sneakers, tights, and Pixies T-shirt dress she'd performed in. She lengthened her stride.

She gradually became aware that she was jogging to a beat, that her fraying imagination had built a hi-hat and snare pattern along to the bass of her footfalls. Fragments of an intricate lead guitar line intertwined with lush, richly harmonized synthesizer pads. A man's voice crooned above it all, too far away to make out the words, his tone raw with emotion and redolent of fraught teenage love.

Jo listened in wonder to the ethereal pop-punk symphony, amazed that her brain could have invented so complex a fantasia. A butterfly danced innocently past her face, unaware of the two amethyst eyes smeared across the backs of its wings, which gawked waggishly at her.

Oh right, I'm still totally ripped, she thought, and somehow this was very funny, and she laughed aloud. It crossed her mind that she was alone in the vicinity of two popular indie shows, which couldn't be good for her chances of survival. *I wonder if I'll meet the murderer,* she thought, and then she realized her prime suspect had just broken up with her, and this too was oddly hysterical. *As if Lucas could kill someone.*

She crouched to catch her breath, chuckling silently to herself. She had a vision of the scene, as though watching it from above—an Amazonian girl, crouched and wheezing with tangled black hair covering her face—and she suddenly couldn't imagine anything more frightening than herself. The murderer would think she was a mythical winter beast—a sexier adaptation of the sasquatch—and run for his life. She let out another volley of laughter, wiped tears from her eyes, and stood.

The trees had regrown their leaves. Rich jungle foliage in an endless spectrum of greens surrounded her. Unnaturally large flowers bloomed in vivid rainbows at her feet, ejaculating puffs of shimmering golden pollen. She giggled again. A flurry of bumblebees in shining armour met with the glistening spore-damsels in an elaborate mating ritual.

A meadow of marijuana plants twinkled mischievously from an empty lot, and a freckled golden-brown songbird swooped and nipped at the fertile buds, hoping for a subtle body-high. Jo held up a pallid hand and felt a childlike joy when it alighted. She marvelled at the radiance of its plumage against her ashen fingers.

The birdie opened its delicate beak and sang a guitar solo over a ii-V-I progression that modulated upward on each repetition. That was Jo's kind of guitar solo. Her fingertips had a bluish tinge, but she didn't worry, because a warm breeze was sweeping her along, and her T-shirt dress completely befitted the mystical garden.

The trees blossomed ever more aggressively, producing voluptuous fruits in unrecognizable varieties, while coquettish species of woodland fauna blinked provocatively at each other from behind strawberry-sequined bushes, all under an engorged, blushing moon.

And up ahead, in the middle of the road, lit by the red moon, stood a man in a grey-green snowsuit.

56

Ultimatum

The mysterious music actually wasn't a figment of Jo's delirium, though the rest of her tropical surroundings certainly were.

A few blocks west of her, *Dead Zebra Beach* were closing their set with an extended post-punk jam, at a volume that hurtled through the winter night, barged into houses where respectable people were trying to sleep, and seeped into Jo's fraying delusion to inspire the synesthetic visions she was experiencing.

Snippets of a jazzy keyboard solo also reached Rex, even further away, as they clumped up from under the bridge.

They texted Maggie to update her on their survival thus far, and found that, along with Maggie's message confirming that she and Shahla were coming to meet them, they'd missed two calls each from Jaymie and Anika; they hadn't even felt the vibrations in the stifling darkness of the bridge. They dialed a distressed Jaymie, assured him they were fine, and promised to stay on the line until they met up with Maggie and Shahla.

Then they set off on the fastest route toward their friends, listening to their brothers ranting over speakerphone about how Rex was never allowed out of the house after 8 p.m. again, and rolling their eyes.

Snow crunched behind them. They spun around, ambivalently hopeful.

"Izzy?"

There was no one.

"Stupidest decision you've made, honestly—murderer out there, poor Aaron thinking the uber-coyotes got you …" Rex resumed walking, but then had a horrible thought. They opened their camera and did a slow scan of their surroundings.

A ragdoll figure stood on the sidewalk half a block back. Rex let out a squeak, and it lolled behind a tree. They turned and ran.

They cursed the empty streets and the nearby shows and the fact that, even knowing all the necessary precautions, they'd managed to put themself in danger *again*, and for nothing—they hadn't made any headway on curing Jo.

They could still hear, distantly, the sounds of *DZB* closing their set. They veered in the direction of the music.

Their phone chirruped, "… is that band *Vampyres,* and guess what Adib's new band is called—did I tell you this already? Anyway, benefits of having a manager, I guess …"

Rex knew keeping tabs on the stalker would only cost them precious time, yet their eyes were drawn inexorably toward the monster-filled alternate world within their camera. They stared down helplessly, like a person discovering Facebook later in life without possessing the younger generations' hard-learned ability to not be conquered by their own feed.

"… miracle if we make it through that and we're all still human, right? Ha! —I'm kidding, obviously those are just their band names …"

There was nothing behind them but heaped snow-dunes and the empty street. An icy gust of wind numbed their exposed face. They were about to start running again when a silhouette high in the skeleton trees caught their eye. Their stomach lurched. The spook was perched on a branch twenty feet up, the skirt of her coat hanging like the head of a wilted tulip from her too-tiny waist, pencil legs kicking lazily at the violet sky.

"—hoping they don't hold a grudge against me from last spring. Probably not, right?" Rex tried to move, but something stopped them. A cloying feeling—whether from spiritual exhaustion or the delayed petrification of shock—overcame their self-preservation instinct, and they gripped their phone close to their face, observing the creature. It wasn't the man in the snowsuit, but Rex sensed the same careless, mocking pursuit, like it might *prefer* to catch up and butcher them, but it operated on artist-time and there was no huge rush.

"… and she goes, 'It would be better as a porn,' which I disagreed with for obvious reasons, but it does make you stop and think for a minute, doesn't it …"

They knew they should flee, but instead found themself wondering how many *more* monsters there were, after this one. How many more cults and clones were out there, misleading and preying upon people? How few fans who'd like their band's weird music? How few potential futures in which they found excitement and success? When you got down to it, how many groups in the world created pretty good music but then got distracted by arrogance or anxiety or insecurity, or by whatever it was that was eating at Jo, or just by pure *distraction,* or by any of the other things that Rex had to helplessly, uselessly watch getting in the way? And while they were at it, how few special people were out there who'd have anything in common with Rex and not be turned off by Rex's own unconventionalities—

"Rex, what the fuck! Are you there? I swear to god, if you're playing a trick …" Rex registered, with a dispassionate surprise, that they were still in the middle of a phone call. "Great, you made Aaron panic again. Hilarious, Rex, truly laudable. We're coming to get you. You're grounded forever, P.S." He said something to Aaron or Anika. "Where the hell are you?"

"There's no point anyway," they whispered.

A hot tear rolled down their cheek, elicited only partly by the tattered creature that had dropped from the branches and was taking deliberate, drunken dance steps toward them. Rex thought, detachedly, that if they were going to keep up this music thing, then they really, very badly, very soon, needed something *good* to happen, even if the good thing was proportionally tiny in comparison to all the bad things that had occurred over the past few months.

Something was emerging from the scarecrow woman's red collar and glowing white in the moonlight, and Rex realised it was a set of teeth, extending haphazardly in all directions like a time-lapse video of wild grasses growing. Grasses with thick, sharp blades.

Rex snapped out of it. They shoved their phone in their pocket and ran.

Somewhere ahead, the rock fusion band hit a series of syncopated shots and ended the performance on an unresolved dominant. There was to be no encore.

In a secret garden, surrounded by megaflora slavering with dew, orb-like fruits drooping indolently from over-burdened branches, and pairs of genteel white rabbits copulating elegantly, a young woman in a light T-shirt dress sat down to a faerie feast with a snowsuit-clad monster.

Vines crept in, snaking around the slats of a backyard fence, roiling across the alley, choking light posts, climbing garage-fronts, and breaking icicles from the rims of basketball hoops mounted there, all in the spirit of providing a leafy décor for the extemporaneous oasis. Attached to the stalks were thirty-six ripe, reincarnated pumpkins, nestled in the tentacular green fronds, as healthy as ever and shining with the orange-gold of an autumn sunset, with no regard for the fact that the Brzezinskis had severed and stolen them months ago.

Spread before Jo on a white paisley picnic blanket was a glorious pumpkin banquet of fresh pies and steaming breads and soups, interspersed with gaily flickering candles.

A dog barked down the street, and even that harsh sound was sonorous and complex; Jo saw in her mind's eye layer upon layer of the harmonics that formed the timbre of the woof, stacked on top of each other in tidy fractions, an octave, under a fifth, under a fourth, under a third, on and on into infinitesimality.

"So, what do you think?" murmured the creature across from her.

"Pardon?" said Jo.

"What do you think?" He sat cross-legged, hands resting on his knees. He spoke in a hoarse, understated mewl, and Jo concluded that Rex's assessment had been correct—this guy was definitely a creep.

"Of the pumpkins?" she asked. "Pretty good. Bread could use salt."

"What? Is that slang?"

"Slang?" Jo sampled a stew with her fingertip.

"Like, you want to be paid?"

"Paid for sitting here? Wait, is this a date? Are you *hitting on me?*"

"Hitting on you? God, you haven't changed at all. Pumpkins … Are you talking about that show months back? What are you talking about?" His tone had the grating testiness of a voice intentionally altered, but there was something familiar under the put-on gruffness.

"Nothing. What are *you* talking about?" she asked warily.

"Seriously?" he hissed. Greyish nails peeked from the frayed tips of his gloves. "Were you not paying attention for the last five minutes?"

"The murders?" Jo tried to make out his eyes under the alley's dim streetlamp. They were a smudge under his balaclava.

"My offer."

"Your offer. Right." Jo inwardly chastised herself for not listening. In her defence, if you want to make a business proposal, you shouldn't surround your target with lavish distractions only minutes after their boyfriend has dumped them. She took a bite of pumpkin pie.

"Stop eating the snow! Are you listening to me?" snapped the man.

"Snow," Jo cooed. A giant pumpkin-flower bloomed overhead, and she gazed into its syrupy yellow sunburst. She realized where she was. She'd made it through The Gates and come out in Garrett's back alley. She used to smoke out here, back when they jammed at his house.

"This. This is what I couldn't stand about the *Ballet Llama*."

"Excuse me?"

"Did you even get my card?"

"The postcard? I figured it was a joke. I thought one of the guys sent it, like we used to."

"I *did* send it."

"OK … OK, it is you, then." The familiarity in his voice clicked into place. "Hey, how come you never said Hey or offered me a ride when my car broke down?"

"I thought it was funny you didn't recognize me—I've had the same bass case for ten years. I was just there to pick it up. And something else I'd left."

Jo had a sudden, manic sense of victory. "Damn, I knew this whole thing wasn't just, like, a random hungry monster! That'd be so … campy! Or … is it still?" As she said it, she realized it was just as well that she'd missed his entire exposition; she was far too high to negotiate a death threat. But even as the thoughts occurred, disjointed and fuzzy, something was rallying within her, insisting on coherence, accessing the anger that had plagued her for months, harnessing its power of focus to guide her failing attention to the blue eyes that flashed under the balaclava. She said, "And I *do* want to be paid. You owe me one-fifty."

"Fuck you, Jo."

"Jesus, Jake! What's your deal, anyway? Since when do care about music again? Did you kill Al?"

"I've always cared about music—I thought *you*, of all people, would see that. I thought you might have noticed the damn hypocrisy! I mean, it was your speech that convinced Michaud to turn down our *one* chance." At her nonplussed expression, he continued. "Do you think your *Bukowskis* would refuse label representation? They'd snap it up at the first opportunity!"

"Yeah, because they're an *indie pop* band. And it wasn't just Michaud's decision—we were a democracy, as I remember—Oh my god, *that's* what this is about? You know it's different with punk—you can't go commercial so easily! Political bands who go big have to find a whole new audience because their fans feel all betrayed. Do you really think a fucking French bilingual band could hit the mainstream off a couple weeks of drama? That was frontpage Reddit shit, not top forty radio shit! We'd have lost everyone! We went over this! Do we have to talk about this now? The walls are dripping in my brain! Why are your nails all fucked! Why are you doing that with your voice! And did you fucking kill Al!"

Her former bassist sighed. "Al joined Michaud's project right after we recorded Allene. After all those years out of the scene. I'd thought we had an understanding! The *Llama* ended, and we accepted it. But here you all are, washed up, trying to *make it*, a decade later. It's pathetic. Michaud and his little empire of Twitter followers. Self-righteous Alexandre insisting we stay indie, and suddenly he's too busy for my band because he's backing up Mich's fucking Dallas Green sad-boy pop act?"

Jo blinked, forcing herself to maintain focus on him, on anything but the waving vines clutching at the edges of her vision. *"Your* band?"

"Well, you were all making a comeback, so I thought I would too."

"We all—? Oh, because I joined the *Bukowskis*. I'm selling out or whatever."

"I saw you posting last winter that you were looking to play out again, and I knew it was only a matter of time. You, at least, I'd thought I could count on not to let go of the *Llama*. I mean, you accomplished fuck-all for nine years."

"Thanks."

"And this after your big rant in Montreal about avoiding the corporate fuckers—I should've known you wouldn't even remember that, considering you were so wasted you fell off a bridge. God, we really had something, if you all just hadn't been such losers! That passion—do you remember? I miss that. Now I just think and think and think and think …"

Jake leaned back on his gloves, and Jo tried to delete the hallucinated picnic from her visual field. It refused to budge, and the effort left her exhausted. The bassist must know she was too out of it to fight him— maybe he'd been counting on it. She felt a spasm of shame, and it turned into a shudder of alarm when she looked down and realized, for the second time, that she was only in a T-shirt. She blinked away her disorientation, then closed her eyes as he monologued, "Watching my fellow artists—*my friends*—turn into these cheap little content creators … You think you can use the system for anything more than making a buck for the Big Five? I want to be there when it spits you all out … So. I'm putting together the perfect Spotify-algorithm band. Two-minute songs, hook up front, one verse, no bridge. A philosophical experiment—a statement. Of how far music has come. Songs that laugh in the faces of those who love them."

"That just sounds like a good business plan, not that I'd ever listen to it in my life," Jo mumbled. Still, there was something that echoed all the way down into her heart. *That passion, do you remember …*

"You *have* changed."

She gritted her jittery teeth; she wouldn't let herself fall into a despair spiral thinking about content creation. "And the other victims?" she asked.

"They couldn't fit it in their schedules."

"You killed them because they *wouldn't be in your band?*"

"Well, I had to keep it a surprise."

"What about Casio Bob? That guy doesn't even know how Spotify works, much less how to make a listenable two-minute song."

"He guessed what I was doing! Can you believe, him of all people? But he knew the scene, kept in touch with Al. Confronted me at the reunion. Too loyal to the *Llama*, anyway."

"Fuck. What about Oli?"

"Mel from *Tornahdo* was my first choice for rhythm, but you know how that turned out. But Oli's on board, after he saw what happened to Al. And before you ask, the other players all had to be skilled and close to Michaud, so if anybody caught on, they'd think he did it. For now."

"You're planning to kill him, too."

"Sure, after he's had some time to appreciate my work. I told him a little about the project, just not all the … details. Who knows—maybe he'll turn out to have Oli's good sense. Question is: do you?" He'd stopped altering his voice.

"Ah. I was supposed to call the number on the card and then you make me an offer I can't refuse." A snowflake-filled breeze fluttered her hair across her cheeks, disturbingly failing to produce any sensation in them.

"As I explained earlier, Druggy-Jo Armstrong, I'll need a lead guitarist."

"No solos, I'm guessing. Hey—Jake, if you miss the *Llama* so much, why'd you turn down Festival? Does it really interfere with your Ph.D. more than your murder-band does?"

"I didn't. Mich asked me to sit out a show after I gave away a few non-Advils at the reunion. He's replacing me, can you believe it? You can't replace me! Seriously—after putting *me* on medic duty! After *I* organized it all! Everyone had fun, but I guess some of the kids who tripped were underage and the word got around. He's paranoid about getting cancelled."

"Huh. Didn't stop you guys sharing anything with *me*, back then."

"See, you get it. I knew we'd still see eye to eye."

"No. Nope."

He laughed, and it sounded almost normal, almost the laugh of a kid she'd written riffs with in a gear-strewn garage. He said, "Well, sorry you're lower-case-t traumatized from almost-fame and too much fun. Speaking of drugs, do you want to know how I invented Twi? I mean, it was an accident, but a useful one. That *is* what you're on right now, right?"

"That was *you!* Fuck, I forgot you did some weird Anarchy Master's degree in Calgary."

"Edmonton. And it was scientific ethics. Where do you guys get this stuff?"

"God, I can't believe you've been slaughtering people. 'The bass player did it' is so 'the butler did it.' And why these indie kids who just want to make art?" Jo's attention had coalesced briefly into a razor of pure focus with a bit of static at the edges. She felt for whether her legs still had enough blood in them to stand up on. She heard the dog barking again.

"It isn't art, and it doesn't have to be slaughter, now that I have the formula right. See, last winter I was feeling experimental and, even with my philosophy focus, my science major provided me twenty-four-hour access to the labs. I knew my thesis would benefit from a practical element—it should have been a simple molecular alteration …"

Jo zoned out. This was not music-related, and it had by now fully registered that she was in the process of being murdered. She'd already begun to freeze, which left only fight or flight on the table, and she was too tired to run. The pumpkins pulsed encouragement at her, and the ground was fairly solid despite the snow, and someone had conveniently left her Jaguar propped against Garrett's fence. Maybe Oli was supposed to show up for a rematch guitar-off?

"The possibilities—I've barely scratched the surface! Microdosing, for instance. Just a pinch in my coffee every morning … And of course, a lite, commercial variety for consumption by the general public, so don't go worrying your one hit will do you in. Not like *you'd* worry … Funny it all comes back to you, since you're the reason we ended. The tour. The band. The *movement*. Here we are, full circle." The bassist's eyes widened in his woolly mask. His nails extended and retracted. "And by the way, the *Bukowskis* are too weird to get big. So I hope you appreciate this is your last chance." He stood and loomed over her. "Think about it, Jo."

Jo munched a final piece of fictitious pumpkin loaf and then wiped her cold hands on her dress and stood. "I've thought about it," she said.

"Where the hell are you? ... Rex! Rex!" Jaymie's phone was silent, and he was only spared from mirroring Aaron's second panic attack gasp for gasp by the fact that he'd been keeping pace with Daffodile drink for drink, and the woman had a tolerance. A filmy tequila haze had settled on his mind, numbed his stomachache, and left him calm—calm for Jaymie Brzezinski, anyway. "OK. OK. OK. Maybe their phone's dead."

"When has that ever happened in their entire life!" cried Aaron. The two had been sitting in the front seat of the van, keeping warm while Jaymie stayed on the line with Rex and Aaron recovered his nerves and tried to reach Jo.

"OK, they were walking back from the bridge. There's not that many routes. They'd have stayed on a main street," said Jaymie.

"Except they'd turn into the neighbourhood to meet Maggie at *DZB*."

"We know where that is. OK. OK, Aar, let's go find them. Rex and Jo. Both of them." The surf-rock band was still playing inside, lead guitarless. Jaymie tapped his fingers in time on the dash. "I shouldn't drive," he said. "I feel OK, but I've had like six drinks in the last couple hours."

"Responsibility," said Aaron vaguely.

"Or rather, I might not feel OK. I'm a little—never mind. I'm feeling it, though."

"OK, I think I'm not panicking anymore." They got out and switched places. Jaymie tried the stereo to see if the CD in rotation would help Aaron's nerves. It was the *Ballet Llama*, and it would not. Aaron pulled onto the main street.

"Turn here," said Jaymie, and Aaron did so, and then both of their attentions were briefly wrenched away from navigating, because for an instant they witnessed one of the biggest and most bad dogs either of them had ever seen in their life, completely leash- and collarless, loping into the darkness beside an old warehouse building.

"Oh my god, oh my god," said Aaron, involuntarily hitting the breaks. "Giant coyote."

"For Rex," Jaymie reminded him.

"For Rex," said Aaron.

"For Rex," said Jaymie. Aaron performed a shaky lane-change and managed to avoid running a stop sign. "Everything is fine," intoned Jaymie. "Most chill car chase."

"For Rex," said Aaron. The bar hosting the other show came into sight, and he slowed to a crawl to scan for Rex or Maggie. A siren shrieked, and he yelped and slapped the wheel in frustration. "Jesus! Startled me."

"Shit. That's for you, dude," said Jaymie.

"What? I'm going like five kilometers!"

"Yeah, that's probably what did it."

"No. Not now."

"Pull over. Pull over. We can't do a for-real car chase right now." Jaymie said. "Fuck fuck fuck."

"I can't get in trouble. I'm on clone probation!"

"Shit! No, we'll just explain."

"What, our kid sibling might be getting eaten by a monster?" Aaron's emotional status was reaching a six on the Richter Scale, but he pulled as smoothly as he could onto a side street, leaned back against his seat, unrolled the window, cleared his throat, and said, "Hey, Officer. Is there … Is there a problem?"

Rex's breath plumed in front of their face. They didn't dare look back as they pounded over the pavement. Without the music to lead them, they relied on their sense of direction. They thought they could hear footfalls sounding out with a sickening patter behind them.

They swerved around a corner and saw a quinzhee in the next yard, chest-high and made of hard, packed snow. A child-sized crawlspace entrance beckoned. Hesitating only a second, Rex shoved their backpack through the tunnel and slithered after it into the backyard fortress.

The entrance didn't let in the light, and as they crawled blindly to the back of the cave they half expected and wholly wished to tumble into Wonderland, or be transported, by that rare beneficent magic responding only to deep necessity, into wintery Narnia. Of course, neither miracle occurred, and they grasped their pack against their chest and held their entirely black-screened phone camera in front of them like a lost arctic explorer clutching a faulty compass.

They would make their last stand.

57

The End

Jo's guitar was safely in her hands once more. She was comforted by the familiar weight. It wasn't just an intimately mastered apparatus, extending her abilities, so much as an actual part of her body—a detachable wing that twitched at the edges of her perception like a phantom limb when not pressed up against her ribs. She was whole again. She looked down.

Wow, wrong-o! It wasn't even her guitar! It was a huge fucking literal battle axe she'd never seen before in her entire life! So much for somatic awareness. She coiled her fingers tighter around the wooden handle, getting a feel for the instrument. She could work with this. She looked up.

There was a creature in front of her, at least seven feet tall, each of its ten claws almost as long as the neck of her Jaguar. It gave a laugh that sounded like every string in a grand piano breaking at once. The Enemy.

Jo planted her feet as the creature lashed out, its claws flickering scarlet under the fever-stricken moon. She lifted her weapon, and the claws met metal with the scream of nails on a chalkboard. She lost her balance, stumbled, and thumped the axe head into a lush flower garden (a snowdrift) to right herself.

The man lunged again, and she spun around, wrenching her weapon free of the drift and blocking him. Then she held it at full length before her, keeping as much space between them as she could. The creature made a grab for the axe head, pushing it aside and slashing at her. She leaned into the shove, ducked the nails, and wrenched upward with her blade, scraping a tear into an already tattered leather glove. She feinted right, closed the space between them, and punched the axe into the belly of his snowsuit. He crashed down face-first into a pile of sweet sleeping hummingbirds, which buzzed up into the sky in irritation.

Jo stayed close, warily aiming the edge of her blade at her old friend's neck, ready to grapple with the mercy-vs-revenge dilemma surely about to assault her from within her own heart. It didn't come. She lifted the axe high and brought it down with a nasty crunch into the space where snowsuit met balaclava. Victory!

Before she could savour the win, her eye caught movement from behind her. A human-shaped thing in a knee-length coat was lurching forward, face obscured by a high collar except for a set of jaggedy teeth protruding upwards at all angles. A frayed scarf wisped out behind it.

Jo was getting the hang of this. Real battle was very different from trying to take down a cult member with a fist to the face; it was easier to really fight for your life when all the facets linking life to reality had been stripped away one by one. She'd lost hope of a mortal enemy she could fathom and cope with—for instance, the unlikely but at least believable scenario of a boyfriend who was also a serial killer. She'd lost her grasp of the setting, because it was supposed to be winter, wasn't it? And even before that, she'd lost the fiery spirit of her old band and the community that enabled her to understand where she was and what she believed in and where she might be headed, and in fact she wasn't sure when those parts had started to fall away, whether it was when she took Twi yesterday, or if it was weeks or months or years before that.

With all that losing, she was probably better off not trying to calculate the odds of a win tonight.

She swung at the scarecrow girl, who caught the axe head in her great teeth and shook it like a terrier playing tug-o-war, emitting a shrill warble that could've been either a giggle or a scream. Jo was jerked toward the creature, and it took all her strength to keep hold of the wooden handle. The cloaked waif was too strong for her size—too strong for a human—and Jo lost her footing and tumbled toward the quivering teeth, crying out in alarm. The jaws released the axe and opened wide.

Still off balance, Jo used her momentum to kick the monster in the shin and dodge past. Teeth snapped shut inches from her neck. She caught herself and mustered her strength. Then she lifted her weapon, swiveled, and connected it with the creature's narrow waist. A spray of goose feathers erupted, the red coat collapsing brokenly to the earth in a rainfall of fluffy down.

Jo gasped in exertion, but staggered over to the figure to make sure it was dismantled. The teeth had retracted, and she winced, reached in, and tugged the collar down to a reveal a face she only recognized because of her recent social media detective research: it was the singer from *Lost, the Show, the Band*, who'd been killed outside a shoegaze show months ago.

A snow-muted sound came from behind her, and the breath she was trying to catch became a cough of dismay. The clawed bassist stirred and wheezed. He lifted his head from the flowerbed, planted his hands under his chest, and pushed himself to one knee. Chunks of dirty ice were caught between his nails, turning into daisies that died in his hands and fell amongst the feathers.

Jo slammed her axe into the snow in frustration. "You jerks *regenerate?*"

"Give it up, Jo," he said.

"Why are you like this? Why isn't she dead? Why are you invisible sometimes and why do your nails do that and your eyes are like—and your voice is all—"

"I'm not explaining everything to you three times! It's the drug. I told you already: I have the formula."

"Formula? I thought you meant verse–chorus–verse–chorus–bridge–chorus–chorus!" Her voice finally broke on the last chorus.

"I meant everything. Musical formula, chemical formula, biosocial, ethical, retributive-compensational formula!"

That was the thing, with punks—you couldn't tell if they were a peppy, feisty kid or a full-on psycho until it was years too late. Jake set his stance and cracked his neck. "We had to die ... on the Twi ... And you will too."

With aching muscles, she lifted her implement to defend herself, the blade shedding grey fuzz and something else—a slim cardboard item that had been tucked in the *Lost* singer's coat, and that now fell at her feet. Ignoring the restored enemy, she leaned and picked up the familiar postcard, which unfolded to reveal a patterned baggy holding a tiny amount of weed. It was a common means of packaging, but she recognized this particular satchel, because she'd seen Rex fill it from her own supply a day earlier and then put it in their pocket.

A cluster of people exited the *DZB* show, walking toward their cars or homes or to the terrible and impossibly cheap pizza-by-the-slice place a few doors down. Some lingered to smoke, eyeing with interest the police car parked around the corner.

The officer placed a gloved hand over the unrolled window of the van and said, "I believe you're drunk."

"Sorry, no, I'm stressed out," Aaron replied calmly. "My sibling. Our guitarist ran away. And I saw this dog."

Jaymie must have intuited that Aaron was in over his head, because he leaned in and said, "Actually, *I'm* drunk. He's just having a panic attack. It's at its quiet stage, so you might not be able to tell, but I can. Not ideal, I know, but we have to get to the emergency room, because my appendix is bursting, and I'm in a lot of pain, which I was foolishly trying to drink away, and that's why I'm drunk and he's panicking. Ow."

"You're going forty under the speed limit and in the middle of two lanes. I'll have to do a breathalyser, and then we'll see about the ER."

The brothers exchanged pained looks and exited the van, Jaymie holding his stomach in feigned agony, or rather in real agony, because as it would turn out, Jaymie wasn't entirely lying.

And Aaron, as it turned out, *was* drunk. In all the chaos, he'd completely forgotten, and as he handed over his license and was placed under arrest for his first-ever DUI, Jaymie clasped him by the shoulders, said, "We will come get you from jail. It's going to be OK," and ran into the dark to find his sibling.

Jo knew she couldn't fend off both enemies for long. Even her drug-enhanced fantasy-fighter alter ego had limits. Her fingers were so cold she couldn't feel the wooden handle, her shoulders ached from the weight, and her neurons sparked in and out as she looked from the mini stash in her hand to the twitching creature in the snow.

The man had risen. She was out of time. She shoved the baggy into the top of her dress. As he lifted a clawed arm, she stepped forward and swung, slicing a short rip through the front of his suit and knocking him back to one knee. She grunted in desperate annoyance that the heavy blade hadn't done more damage—the thing looked sharp enough to dismember someone. The man brushed a twig out of the tear in his suit.

Snow crunched behind her and she spun again, in time to take a spiraling club at the other creature. The axe thunked into the side of the scarecrow woman's head, sending her tottering off balance. Jo's heart sank, and she closed her eyes for one brief, deep breath, opened them, and looked down at her tool. It was quite obviously a tree branch.

No time to mourn the axe—she hefted the stick and turned back toward the man, leaving the ragdoll creature teetering on its little feet.

Then a new sound came.

The barking dog could still be heard, insistent and high-pitched, but the noise was swallowed by a guttural cry that swept through the lane, wilting Jo's monstrous flowers, infecting and deflating the pumpkins with inner rot, and sending the last of the concupiscent fauna skittering away for greener pastures.

And an animal appeared. Following on the echoing heels of the howl, a massive dog detached itself from the darkness of the alley. It was sparsely covered in shabby brown fur, its black soulless eyes burning under dangling mats of hair. Jo stared: a wolf, but all wrong; an expanded hyena without the sense of humour. She dropped the branch. The snowsuited man shrank away down the lane. The scarved monster righted herself, just in time to be grasped in the impossible maw of the beast. Dripping teeth sank into red fabric.

Jo stood in puffs of feathers as the animal chomped. Then she backed away until she hit the fence. Then she decided to run, while at the same time, her body decided to give out. She sank onto a bed of baby's breath. The smaller, more feasible dog down the alley still barked madly, losing its shit at the moon, which was failing to fill it in on the action.

And the silent, scandalized moon watched the red scarf stream through the air and come to rest, blanketing Jo's knees like a bloody river, as the monstress was torn limb from limb.

"Hey, I'm OK to go to jail. It honestly sounds like the safest place for me at the moment. But my brother just left for the Misericordia Hospital on foot, and I'm worried he's going to get lost in The Gates and killed by his own appendix, so can I make an appointment with jail for later?" Aaron jangled his handcuffs disconsolately as the officer led him back to his police car.

"Not how it works, kid. But you don't go to prison for a first offense. By the way, do you know how many cases of appendicitis I hear about every Saturday night?"

"I bet. My dad worked for the police at one point," said Aaron. This unexpected and seemingly ludicrous setback had distracted him from the urgency of finding Rex, and given his panic a faded, washed-out quality. "So I understand there are … challenges. I support the drunk driving laws. And um … I appreciate that you have a helicopter." Two truths and a lie.

The officer narrowed his eyes and shone a flashlight over Aaron's face. Aaron cringed. "Do I know you?"

"I hope not?" he replied. Then the cop laughed.

"You're that guy that lost his brother a while back! I still listen to your interview when I need a pick-me-up."

"Right ..." said Aaron.

"Obviously it wouldn't be so funny if you hadn't reported him found."

"So funny."

"Hang on, I have it here." He pulled out his phone and tapped a few times, and a voice recording began to play.

'Or it's like, you know when you've been invited to more than one party at once, and one is clearly better, but the other one is a birthday you're obligated to go to ..." Aaron's mind caught up and fitted the officer's comments into context. "This is a missing person report?" he asked dubiously.

"Seriously, so sweet," the man chuckled. "Wait, I like this one ..."

'It's like you know when you can't decide what to watch, and there's something you want to see but you're embarrassed because it's dumb or soapy or whatever so you need someone you can kind of lead into it, like inception them into thinking it's their own idea and you're just humouring them. What do the rest of you people do? Watch it all by yourself in secret, just sitting there feeling ashamed? As I'm saying it now, I'm realizing that must be the case."

"That fucker," said Aaron.

"You said your dad's with the force? ... Well, I actually know what it's like to have an unwell family member. We wouldn't want you to lose your brother again. I'm keeping your license and you'll have to come in to pay the fine. Obviously you can't drive. OK?"

"What? Oh! OK. Gonna go retrieve him. Thanks, officer." Aaron rubbed his freed wrists, picked up his heavily loaded backpack, muttered "So problematic," and sprinted after Jaymie.

If Jo were in her right mind, she might have forced her tired body to creep away while the dog savaged the defeated monster. Or she might have waited until she saw it lift its head to sniff in the direction Jake had taken and then lope away into the dark, and then she might have risen quickly and knocked on the nearest door, or tried to find her way back to the bar.

If she'd still had a grasp of reality, she might have noticed she was freezing to death. Perhaps the threat of the various creatures she'd been dealing with might now pale in comparison to that of the minus-thirty-four temperature, which, while not interested in intimidating, slashing, or eating her, was indifferent to her under-dressed and over-inebriated condition.

She sat against the fence and tossed the red scarf aside in distaste. The little dog barked on, and she realized it was probably the same one that had frightened Aaron headlong into her lap all those months ago. She wondered where he was now—Jake was gone, and she wanted to share the abandoned fay feast in celebration. She tried to manifest her band, and only succeeded in materializing a pumpkin-flavoured ladyfinger, which she ate. It tasted like nothing.

"Rex," she said to nobody. "I would *love* for you to join the *Ballet Llama* … Is what I *should* have said." She tried to get up and found that her feet no longer existed.

Maybe the pumpkin buffet had been cursed, binding her to this enchanted faerie mound, where she'd be forced to spend eternity eating magical pseudo-food and playing reverb-y minstrel-rock for elven royalty. On the bright side, it was difficult to imagine anyone more akin to mystical pixies than the Brzezinskis, and she'd never minded being around *them*.

Sitting on her white paisley picnic blanket with her tree branch axe close at hand, she suddenly had the impression that her friends must be just behind the fence, about to appear, laughing, with a fresh load of pumpkins in their arms. OK, she'd go meet them. She *did* have feet, and she *could* get them under herself. She made a move to rise.

But she was holding something, and she finally allowed herself to look at it, wheezing in surprise at the sight of her hand. It was stark and shaking, as was the arm attached to it. She squeezed the little baggy in unfeeling fingers.

The weather closed in. It wasn't entirely indifferent, after all; though unaware of the two indie shows nearby (it didn't follow that kind of thing), it was so angry about the Jets losing against Minnesota that it was ready wring the life out of someone.

Jo knew she should get her mind in order, but then she'd have to think about that weed stash and what it meant and whether it was her fault, and by now she was far away from the ephemeral picnic; the leafy forest floor was so comfortable, and there was a cushion of vines covered in soft pine needles and smelling sweetly of cinnamon and brown sugar.

She lay down in the moss. Perhaps it was alright to take a rest from the disappointments and failed bands and corrupted bandmates and lost jobs and dead friends and loves that never got a fair chance. *To rock or not to rock*

… Did it matter? She curled up in a cradle of newborn flowers, sprouting before her eyes to remind her of the infant joys that were possibly still to grow, provided she nurtured the seeds she'd planted and didn't do something idiotic to ruin it all.

The wind blew a light dusting of snow over her still form, and the moon moved on to find more interesting displays of suffering, winking out of sight like the stand-by light of an amplifier being switched off. The barking dog fell quiet in exhaustion, and the winter exhaled and curled over the scene like a white cat tucking its nose into the end of its tail and nodding off after a long evening playing with its food.

58

Appendicitis

"Which is another reason I had to break it off," Maggie was saying. "Like, don't fat-shame me and try to pass it off as being concerned about my health!"

"Gross," said Shahla.

"You're so lucky you don't have to deal with these douchebags."

"I mean, you could just be single for a while."

"Boring."

A man came into view in front of them, and Shahla grabbed Maggie's arm. "Yarbrough."

"Oh, shit."

"It probably wasn't him," Shahla whispered.

"Rex said Jo said he was right there when Allene got killed."

Lucas reached them and nodded as he passed, then stopped. "Hey, I think I know you two."

"Oh, hi," said Maggie. "We were just talking about how much we aren't musicians."

Shahla caught on immediately. "Yeah, I can't even carry a tune. So sad."

Lucas sighed. "I'm the same," he said, and the girls realized, too late, that their survival tactic had just engaged him in one of his favourite guilty-pleasure conversations. "I played a little as a kid, but I had to decide between that and hockey, and back then it was the sports kids who got all the respect—I'm ashamed to say I fell for the popularity game …"

Shahla tried to extricate them. "Sorry, but my friend here just broke off a three-month relationship yesterday and we were having kind of a vulnerable, um—"

"No shit! I just had a breakup, like, ten minutes ago!"

Maggie said "I'm sixteen," and Shahla said, "I'm asexual," and Lucas backpedaled.

"No, no, I wasn't—I was just commiserating! I would never—but hey, you guys know Jo, right?"

"Yeah, we're going to meet Rex and catch the end of her show. And Rex is out here on their own so we should definitely hurry." Shahla inwardly kicked herself as soon as she said it.

"Oh … Yeah, Jo was looking for them, but it didn't seem like she knew what she was doing …" Lucas sighed again. "Shit. Maybe I should come with you."

"It's really fine, I think we're—"

"No, it'd be irresponsible of me—you're kids."

"I'm eighteen now," Shahla clarified, but it was too late, he'd committed.

"Oh for god's sake," muttered Maggie, as he filled them in on his breakup. Shahla rolled her eyes. The group was nearing the intersection Rex had texted to Maggie some time ago, when Shahla got a notification; her program had finished compiling data and experimentally landed on its first culprit: as predicted, it was Lucas. She silently showed Maggie.

"Wow, our lucky night," Maggie whispered.

The two girls warily made their way onwards, as Lucas expressed his doubts and misgivings about whether breaking up with Jo had been the right decision.

"Wait, but isn't she playing right now?" asked Maggie.

"She ran out with no explanation in the middle of a solo, totally baked. I had to leave her wandering around looking for Rex. She wasn't listening to reason."

The girls exchanged another look. "This is the spot," said Maggie, glancing at her map. "We must have missed them. And they haven't messaged again." There was no one to be seen, and on the off chance Shahla's program *was* right, it was possible the worst had befallen Jo during her and Lucas's "breakup."

"I'll get their GPS," said Shahla.

"You can do that?" asked Maggie.

"Yeah, I've got copies of all your phones'—you know, don't worry about it."

"Why am I even asking."

"One sec."

"Oh wow!" On a sudden stroke of inspiration, Maggie widened her eyes at Shahla. "New text from Rex! They're back at the bar, and Daffodile is about to go onstage to sing an impromptu Joni Mitchell cover and go down in local short-term herstory! But aw, we can't go because it's my curfew and my mom says she's picking us up *right here* in five minutes!"

"Oh gosh, I wish so hard that we could see it! Or at least read about it tomorrow from someone reliable!" said Shahla.

"The Insta stories are gonna be just FOMO City."

"I see what you're doing," said Lucas, with slight uncertainty. "But I respect that you had your own plans tonight, and I'm getting really cold, and I'm going to choose to believe you."

"'Kay, bye!" The girls waved him away with vigour, and he reluctantly turned back.

He made his way toward the surf rock show, thinking about the past month with Jo, and about what could have caused their connection to unravel so quickly. It wasn't as though he didn't believe in the murderer. He knew the victims; he'd seen most of them perform at some point, before they'd been lost forever.

It was more a defense mechanism—a desperate need to cling to the illusion of control over his beautiful, music-filled world—that gave him the misconception that a bit of vigilance was all that was required to avoid a similar fate. And so far, nobody had tried to murder *him*.

He wasn't being vigilant at all as he passed by a large quinzhee and gave it a kick.

Quinzhee-making was one of the city's most popular culturally-appropriative winter activities. A well-made quinzhee, allowed to sit at just the right temperature and hollowed out before its creator fell to exhaustion, was a formidable structure. The snowsuited bassist, in flight from the giant canine that had mauled his undead companion, had seen in it the same defense potential Rex had, and crawled inside to wait out the danger. It was there that the coyote-thing had found him, flattened itself like a bulgy-eyed cat sliding under a door, and slithered through the small entrance to finish its work.

Lucas's kick loosened a chunk of ice, which he booted across the street before walking right past the showdown, arriving safely at the bar, and still catching the last song of the show—lucky bastard.

His departing bootsteps left the street quiet. Opposite the quinzhee was a row of houses, and beyond that was a still alley, and then a fence, behind which a drummer stood with a glass of whiskey in one hand, his phone in the other, and a mistrustful look on his face.

"I don't know, I literally just got outside," he was saying. "This little mutt's been barking like a goddamn maniac, so I went to check—yeah, I'm pretty sure she's just been eating snow and talking to herself ... OK, fine. And listen—just because I don't want your wasted guitar player to die of exposure, doesn't mean I don't still think you're all complete assholes."

Jaymie made it four blocks in the direction of the bridge, where Rex had last been in contact, and then threw up into a prickly hedge. He had no idea what appendicitis actually felt like, but it couldn't be more painful than whatever (hopefully) psychosomatic ailment was expressing itself in his guts at that moment.

He made a deal with himself—thirty seconds curled up on the ground moaning, and then back to finding his sibling. His phone rang.

"Rex?" he asked desperately. But it was Garrett, informing him that his (Jaymie's) guitar player had passed out in a T-shirt in his (Garrett's) back alley, and could he (Jaymie) come remove her please? "For christsake," said Jaymie, and croaked out a promise to be there soon.

He pushed himself to his knees, vision polka-dotted with pain-spots. Then a hand closed around his bicep and pulled him the rest of the way up. He leaned into his helper in relief. "You're not arrested! Did you talk your way—aw, not *you!*"

"Jaymie! How come every time I see you it's like your whole life is falling apart! It's like your face is doing this thing that's—it's like this—"

"Stop doing that. I don't look like that."

"Did you misplace Aaron again?" If it was commendable that Jymmy remembered Aaron's name by now, Jaymie did not acknowledge the effort.

"No, he went to jail." Jaymie gave an agonized sigh. "It's Rex this time."

"No way, I was literally just talking to Aaron about jail yesterday!"

"What are you doing here?" Jaymie swayed on his feet, and Jymmy took his arm and slung it across his own shoulders.

"I was researching Jo on Instagram, not in a sexism way, and I saw she was playing tonight, so I came and stood at the back because I was shy and all of you had a friend. But you all left so I came out to see where you went. I tried following Jo but I got stuck in The Gates."

"Understandable," Jaymie wheezed.

"You lost the little guy?"

He winced as another fist of pain pinched his stomach. "I did," he said.

"Do you want help?"

"I … Yes. I need to find them. And then I think I need to go to Emergency."

"OK, Jaymie. I'll walk you there. I know where it is because somebody took me there for my donut burns. Kindness of strangers."

Jaymie nodded his gratitude, unable to look directly at Jymmy because he was distracted by something large and achy in his throat that was threatening to turn into another vomiting bout, but which elapsed into nothing. "Rex first," he said, swallowing thickly.

"Did you try calling them with your phone?" asked Jymmy, effectively erasing any generous thoughts Jaymie might have been having about him.

"Yes, I tried fucking call—you know what? I'll just …" Jaymie pulled out his phone to try Rex for the twentieth time as the two of them made their way down the street, Jymmy steering them surreptitiously toward the hospital.

There was no sign of Jaymie—Aaron had thought he would catch up in minutes, but either his brother had made faster time than estimated, or Aaron had turned off toward the bridge too soon. In fact, there was no sign of anyone, and the houses had grown tall and judgemental. He was already lost in The Gates, because of course he was.

He dialed Jaymie and got voicemail—the phone was busy or dead. He looked around for an indicator of direction and couldn't even find the moon. Yet as he stood in the stillness, a sound reached him, and he promptly sat on the curb and put his head in his hands.

Something about the noise, wet crunching blended with canine snuffling, told him he was on the right track, because his sibling was missing and his friend had fled into the night underdressed and defenceless, and his brother was alone and possibly in danger too, and so obviously there was going to be a dog involved at some point. He waited a minute for the sound to fade, then rose and sighted the exit Gate, which had smugly appeared behind him, wiggling a Gothic crest in self-satisfied "yoo-hoo." He'd jogged right past it. He recognized where he was, sighed, and pressed on, drawn by some sense of cosmic full-circle significance to Garrett's alley.

He found Jo curled up in the snow against the fence, deathly pale and in a deep hibernation. He dropped to his knees, dog-threat temporarily forgotten, and shook her shoulders.

"Jo, wake up! Hey! Please be alive!"

Her eyelids twitched but didn't open. He felt her forehead and swore quietly. Then he became aware of a sound. There was a slow, snowy *shhhhhh*, as though the winter night was shushing him, urging him to let the woman sleep for god's sake, she'd been up for forty-odd hours. Aaron touched her cold face and implored her more urgently, but the weather had been playing the long game, kiss-of-death-wise, and wasn't about to release the fallen warrior without another fight or, at the very least, an inappropriate demonstration of fairytale romance.

Aaron looked around, trying to work out what had happened. A tree branch lay nearby, its end smeared in a substance like sap or blood.

"Jaymie, psst!"

He started at the whisper-shout, then made out a stocky silhouette standing in the doorway across a plain of garden boxes. The remnants of autumn's harvest made soft waves under the snow, the undulations giving the yard's surface the appearance of a pot of water flash-frozen whilst boiling. Aaron raised a hand gratefully, not caring that this man definitely hated him. Garrett stared back wide-eyed and jabbed his finger out in useless warning.

Before Aaron could open his mouth, the shushing swelled, and from the darkness a creature appeared. It was pulling the soiled remains of what appeared to be a headless, flattened person, its arms raised mid-snow angel and one leg doubled back at the waist; it took a moment for Aaron to register it as a tatty snowsuit. When the animal was within a few feet of Aaron, it deposited the polyester epidermis on top of another, less recognizable form that was lying a few feet from the freezing guitarist. Aaron had been too preoccupied trying to wake Jo to notice the red fabric that ribboned through a pile of something like cotton batting or feathers, jagged protrusions sprouting from the jumbled mass like fronds on some aquatic abomination washed up from the depths. And the thing that was dragging the suit like a well-loved chew toy—Aaron had to blink, certain his mind had invented it, for surely it had come from his own worst nightmares—was the largest, most hideous dog he had ever seen. The animal, which looked like a breeding error involving a wolf and Gollum, nosed through its spoils. A pool of bloody saliva trickled out of some part of its face to steam in the snow.

Aaron stared at the impossible beast, unable even to panic, for surely this was a hoax. It was almost funny, so awful was it, and he emitted something between a laugh and a gag.

The mutant coyote swung its head up from its kill and beheld him with empty eyes. Aaron understood that the only option was to flee, to make for Garrett's doorway. Yet when he moved to run, he became jarringly aware of his own body, which was still crouched in the cold, holding the head of someone who couldn't. The door thudded shut.

"Jo," he croaked. "Please wake up." A low growl sounded. The beast, disappointed at the miserly caloric payout from the defeated monsters, was interested. It shook its matted head and stepped toward them on hairless paws that extended farther than paws should, their knuckly, elongated pads tapering to neat black nails.

And Aaron did the only thing he could, which was to rise to his feet and stand over his unconscious friend. He faced the animal. His jacket was unzipped—he must have been about to transfer it onto Jo—and he grasped its sides, pulled it wide, and yelled "Aaaaaaaaaa!"

He slid his backpack from his shoulders and swung it in frantic figure eights in front of him. The overburdened pack split at the zipper, and a cascade of Charles Bukowski novels arced out and spilled into a crescent-shaped boundary across the ground. *The Most Beautiful Woman in Town* landed inches from the animal's ungodly paws, and the dog sampled the book's cover with a huge, evil tongue.

Aaron's chest heaved. The dog lifted its muzzle and stared at him for a long moment devoid of time or sense or feeling. Then it grinned, nosed the book away, shook its head as if to say, "TL;DR," and, seizing one of the frondy bits of its trampled prey, ambled back down the lane.

Aaron dropped back to his knees. He covered Jo with his jacket. He shook her shoulders and rubbed her freezing hands. Finally, she coughed and opened her eyes.

And, as though The Gates had decided to belatedly cough up an extra reward for his bravery, another scuffling sound came, and then a voice.

"Aaron?"

He groaned in relief as Rex stumbled into sight and dropped down beside him. "Holy shit," he said. "Happy to see you."

Rex hugged him, then turned to Jo. "What happened? Is she OK?"

"She's conscious. Hypothermia, maybe. Can you call Anika?"

"Our Bukowski's getting ruined," Rex commented, pulling out their phone and nodding at the scattered library.

"I'm tired of him anyway."

"*Hot Water Music* is not gonna make it to Juniper." The book lay in a muddy slough of tracks. "Nik—yeah, hey, I'm fine, we need a ride."

Aaron's own call went to voicemail. "Fucking fuck! Where the fuck is Jaymie!"

"Oh, he's at the Miz! He said to come to Garrett's and save Jo from freezing because Garrett was being a dick and wouldn't bring her in. See, I was hiding in this quinzhee, because this lady monster chased me, and I threw my weed so it looked like I kept going, and she went past and I just waited for ages in the dark, I was so scared. No service in there, even. Then I tried to go back to the show but I got lost in The Gates, and then Jaymie called." They carefully placed Aaron's empty backpack under Jo's head and petted her hair. "Oops, missed so many messages from Maggie. She says they found our van back by *DZB*."

Jo looked up blearily, took Aaron's hand in her own icy ones, and said very seriously to Rex, "Don't worry, I avenged you."

It took five minutes to revive Jo to relative lucidity and another five to rub some feeling into her arms and convince her they weren't pumpkin faeries. By then Anika's headlights had bathed the alley in light. She and Michaud helped them into the car, and they drove to collect Jaymie, who explained that he'd tolerated the short, painful walk to the hospital but not the twenty-minute wait in triage without a book, and insisted he was fine and had just been experiencing a quick When-The-Body-Says-No episode due to anxiety. Jymmy was thrilled at the reunion and requested a ride downtown.

It took them a few more minutes to fit seven people into a car built for five, but they succeeded, because by now almost all of them had been on tour at least once. Anika dropped them at their van, where Maggie and Shahla waited, and then she and Michaud said goodnight. Garrett had not reappeared since witnessing the awful animal confront Aaron, and one could only assume he had, understandably, never had opportunity to build up the courage of a family band who'd braved weather, supernatural menace, and dogs, simply in order to remain a four-piece.

59

The Other Pumpkin Thieves

Jo woke up in a comfortable bed in a room she didn't recognize. She wore her long underwear and a borrowed hoody that was slightly too small; her tights and dress were piled on a chair by the bed, looking damp. Her hands and feet felt stiff, and there were white patches on her fingers, indicative of a frostbite she hoped would blister away in a day or two. She had a headache. Most importantly, she was sober.

She sat up slowly and tried to get her bearings. The walls were a pleasant maroon, adorned with paintings, in various styles and sizes, of eccentric-looking birds. On the dresser sat a collection of knick-knacks, including an extremely quirky clock, a Pegasus figurine, and a child's plasticine impression of a saxophone. Jo wondered if all these things were clues as to where she'd ended up, and her now perma-fried brain was simply failing to combine the evidence and solve the mystery.

She looked for more hints. On the bedside table were a framed finger-painting of something vaguely guitar-shaped, with the words "A BAS HAS 4 STRNGS" scrawled at the bottom and, beside it, a staged photograph of two very small, furious toddlers dressed up as nineteen-twenties jazzers, wearing pinstripe suits and sporting fedoras and huge cigars—an unfortunate artwork that could only have been born from the conspiring of a doting, irony-loving mother and an exploitative photographer.

Jo relaxed. Somehow, she'd made it through her TwiLite ordeal and landed safely in Leonora McLeod's bedroom on Pandora street.

She got up and made her way downstairs, where she found a grown version of one of the cigar-smoking infants seated at the kitchen table, gnawing an unlit cigarette, gripping a half-eaten toaster strudel, and perusing Twitter with a febrile intensity.

"You're alive!" he said, rising. "Coffee?"

"Please." She took a chair. "Thanks for bringing me here. I've been an idiot."

"No problem, Jo. You were very cooperative." He handed her a mug. "You know how you'll have that really wasted friend sometimes, and you're like, *It's time to go home!* and they're like, *But I heard a dog!* and you have to drag them out with all your strength? ... You were nothing like that." He held up the box of strudels and, at her nod, popped one in the toaster.

"Everyone's OK? Aaron and Rex ...?"

"Unscathed. Rex is sleeping, as per usual. Aaron and I just got back from the police station—he's prepping for a drum lesson he rescheduled like five different times. He lost his license and his clone income, and you and Lucas will probably get calls from the government requesting you take him for semi-regular check-ins and supervise him more effectually."

"Shit. I'm so sorry I put you guys in danger. When I realized Rex was gone ..."

"In all fairness, we should've taught Rex that drugs don't have antidotes, so that's on us. You never know what gaps you've left in a kid's education." He shrugged and gave a rueful smile. "And anyway, we're always in danger. We just stay together and we do our best." The toaster popped. "Here—it's pumpkin pie flavour!"

"Thanks. Glad you're all OK. Did I tell you it was my old bassist in the snowsuit?"

"Jake! Yeah, you said you fought him before the coyote came? We can't wait to hear the sober version! Poor Rex got chased by the other freak too. Aaron and I reported it all this morning, but the police'll probably stop by to talk to you later today. Honestly, I'm not sure they believed us ... Hey, did you find out how he swapped the body with the pumpkins?"

"I forgot to ask," said Jo, trying to retain the details of the previous night. "But the claws, the powers ... I think it's an effect of the drugs he's been experimenting with."

"Intense. My latest theory is that the murdered door guy was actually a pumpkin *all along*, enchanted to be human for the duration of our show, and at the stroke of midnight he turned back into his true form ..."

"Ha." She still felt a knot of shame at the night she'd put them through; it had been ages since she'd last been the guy who has to be brought home and put to bed. She stirred her coffee self-consciously. "Well, guess I should be at home for the cops. Good strudel—I'll just eat quick and be out of your hair."

"Out of our hair? Oh. No …" He laughed lightly and widened his eyes at her. "No, Jo." Her evident confusion only caused his unhinged smile to grow, and she was reminded that he'd recently spent two weeks leading a cult. "You live *here* now."

"Sorry?"

"We thought it would be best."

She considered the possibility that he was actually Jymmy, but the thought quickly passed. This was classic Jaymie Brzezinski. "I see," she said carefully, blinking away a brief, confusing flashback of a hallucinated, pumpkin-bedecked faerie mound.

"Rex told us you're on the verge of eviction and you're flat broke—no need to be self-conscious! I realize I'm not entirely blameless for that situation—"

"I got fired from my job because I was stuck in your cult, and I got fired from my next job because I no-showed, because Aaron was missing, because you cloned yourself."

"Like I said, not entirely blameless. Anyway, Rex says all your things are boxed and ready to go—"

"I was working on unpacking—"

"—so we thought we'd go get them this afternoon! Sunday is a perfect moving day."

"—and I may have made a bad choice or two, but think I get to retain some agency in where I *live*—"

"And it's not *just* because you're broke and depressed and on drugs and you got dumped and you're, apparently, prone to near-suicidal late-night shenanigans, it's also largely—"

"I'm not—I don't—"

"—for Rex's sake! They want to keep an eye on you. They like having their favourite people close by—that's why they've been living with *us*, instead of enjoying stability and proper mothering at our aunties' place. I think it's an abandonment complex, but what do I know? Anyway, they want you here and, if you haven't picked up on it, we like to keep them happy so they continue eating meals and going to school. There were some concerns for a while—dysphoria stuff. It evened out with the name change and pronouns and everything, but we're still pretty careful with them. And also, I didn't say anything and you don't know that, if anyone asks—"

"Rex wants me to stay …?"

"There's more than one kind of monster out there, Jo. And the poor kid barely knows their father!"

Jo was quiet. Jaymie poured himself more coffee and composed a tweet announcing the date of their next performance.

Finally, she said, "Well, it'd make practices more convenient."

"Excellent," he beamed. "So glad you still agree. Especially since I took a video of you when we got home last night and we first suggested it, and you kept hugging us and saying how happy you are to be finally part of the band, and I posted it to our socials! Stan is thrilled."

"What."

"Plus, we're recording a new album. Our first release with you on it—the full band! Free rent until we're done. We can split bills once you're back on your feet."

"I … Thanks. I'm … glad I have you guys looking out for me."

"It's our pleasure—and not just because you're underground famous. Though there is one thing you could do in return." He paused to gauge Jo's reaction and then leaned in hopefully. "Tell me what broke up the *Ballet Llama*? What, am I exploiting my position of power?"

Jo laughed. "Oh, it was me, I drowned in the fucking St. Lawrence!"

"Get the fuck out!"

"I was making a dumb speech about the death of the music industry, but I was drunk and fell in! Apparently my heart stopped. They did the whole thing, though. CPR. Brought me back pretty quick. I got sick for a while but I'm OK. Wow, though! Trauma!"

"Fuck yeah!"

"Right?"

"I had mouth-to-mouth once too! Aaron kicked me in the pool. I didn't die though."

"Cheers."

"No shit. The St. Lawrence. Legendary."

"I know. I was in the hospital and they couldn't play without me—people had expectations by then. We cancelled the rest of tour, but we never said why, so the intrigue built up and we just let it ride until this indie label caught wind and tried to sign us … And then we broke up. We couldn't agree on anything anymore. I was secretly relieved, at the time. I was really exhausted, on a few levels. But sometimes I still wonder how far we could've gone."

"Of course, naturally. That's wild—I won't pass it around."

"Please don't—it's embarrassing, and plus we still make like five bucks each whenever the mystery resurfaces online and people go check out the album." Jo finished her coffee. "Hey, speaking of the ER …?"

"Right, so, they gave me an appointment this week to go in and get a peptic ulcer treated, and I may need a driver, but the dear siblings think I just mistook a panic attack for a heart attack—that's standard around here—so how about you keep my secrets and I'll keep yours?"

"Happy to drive."

"Great. Let's get you moved in! Word of advice: any belongings you treasure, hide them now. My brothers *will* use all your shit. They have this 'what's yours is mine' mentality, I don't know what it is—maybe it's a younger sibling thing. Anyway, welcome to the band!"

"Rock and roll," said Jo.

A frantic beat rose from the basement. Someone was having a 200-bpm tantrum. Rex folded their pillow over their head. It wasn't even noon.

After ten minutes of groggy frustration, they accepted that the noise wasn't showing signs of abating, and lay back, letting the beat wash over them. It was louder than Aaron's playing, and messier; he'd have to be practicing drunk and midway through a meltdown. And it was far too early in the day for all that.

Rex headed downstairs, thumbing their phone for missed messages. Jaymie and Jo, they learned, had gone to pick up a load of boxes and escape the noise of the drum lesson.

They sleepily scanned the cereal collection for the sugariest one, then poured a bowl and checked that the milk wasn't too severely expired. The rhythmic onslaught ceased abruptly, and Aaron's voice drifted up from the basement, "Getting there, but seriously, you're going to have to practice it slow at some point or it's never going to be clean."

"Ugh, fine," his student responded.

"Using a metronome for tempo practice is a good—"

"Yeah, I'm just not going to do that."

"OK … Think that's good for this week …"

There were footsteps on the stairs, and a moment later the drummer flung the door open and stepped into the kitchen. Rex froze, a spoonful of cereal marshmallows unswallowed in the back of their mouth. A rivulet of milk ran down their chin. They became acutely aware of their oversize Rocky Horror PJ shirt, boxers, and faded cherry hair sticking out in all directions.

The girl cocked her head and tapped her thighs with her sticks. Recognition crossed her features. Behind her, Aaron listed meaningless homework instructions that neither she nor Rex heard. Herman jumped shakily onto the table and thrust his face into the cereal bowl.

"It's you," said Hannah. Rex stared. Then they gulped down their marshmallows, wiped the milk off their face, and went to introduce themself.

It took only one van trip to transport all of Jo's belongings. She and Jaymie attached her mattress to the roof, piled boxes on the seats, and loaded her guitars and gear into the trunk.

Back at the house, Aaron had finished his lesson, and the three of them carried everything in. The entire process took barely more than an hour.

Her new abode was a spare room that Leonora had used as a practice and teaching space when she lived there full-time. Jo positioned her mattress on the floor, estimating that she had approximately one square foot more room than in the bedroom at her apartment. She was moving up in the world.

By the time she'd arranged her boxes, she was feeling optimistic; a new space was a fresh start, and she resolved to smoke less, practice more, and resume her job hunt.

She didn't feel ready to process what had happened with Lucas, though she had a dull, angry-ashamed feeling at the thought of him, and she knew that at some point they'd probably have to talk things over. She pushed it to the back of her mind, carried her gear down to the jam space, and returned to the porch to untangle a box of her patch cords that had spilled there.

As she collected the last one, her hand brushed a paper coffee cup out from under the couch. She picked it up, remembering the morning her car had broken down outside the coffee shop where they'd held their secret show. She'd run into Jake, with his shapeless snowsuit and bass and a messenger bag stretched oddly spherical, and she realized—or maybe he'd told her, while she was too high to remember—that he'd left the bass there as an excuse to return in the morning and collect another, smaller thing he'd stashed. Her chest panged. Poor, headless Alexandre. She wondered again how her old bandmate had become such a monster.

She brought the cup inside and was about to dispose of it, when another memory hit her. *Just a pinch in my coffee every morning …* Come to think of it, she *had* had some weirdly vivid dreams in the Brzezinskis' porch that day. Had he microdosed her on purpose? There was no way of asking him now.

What a dick, she thought, and she tossed the cup into the recycling. Then she carried the box of neatly coiled cords to her room, and began in earnest, for the first time, to unpack.

"I can't decide if this is, like, cosmic nihilism, or he's just trying to get attention."

It was October of 2019, and Jaymie was midway through the chorus of "Professional Drunk."

"Well, the real Bukowski would never have considered himself a nihilist. There are certainly themes of pessimism and absurdism in his writing." Two college students occupied a far corner of the room, *Daft Punk*ian helmets covering their faces, taking in some good old indie rock.

A few feet away, a petite woman could be heard drawling to her equally petit boyfriend, "They sound like *Vulpix*, but with words, you know?"

A girl in the front row sang along; the drummer missed a beat; two ex-lovers bickered near the back.

"Well, this guy's read the Charles Bukowski Wikipedia page, I'll give him that." The man in the helmet sipped his drink, half listening to the flippant lyrics of the song. He decided Jo's new band was OK. He decided to brush up on his Bukowski.

Lucas Yarbrough slipped back in from the hall, speaking over the music to a young woman wearing an ocean-blue onesie and many gold bangles. "I meant every word—send me the final mix when it's done and we'll do an interview before the release." As the woman moved to find a seat, Jake caught her shoulder and jerked his helmeted head. She raised her eyebrows and followed him back out into the hallway.

"Who's in the mask? Oh, it's you. Look, I changed my mind about the band," she said.

"You'll change it back," he replied easily.

"Kenton told me some things you *forgot* to mention."

"Say, where *is* Kenton?" The blank black sheen of the helmet hid a cruel smile.

"He's working the door—" She peered toward the front entrance, where a person in leopard print slouched near the cash box, playing on their phone. "Or he was. But anyway, you don't even want mandolin—if you just need a backup singer, you could get anyone—"

"But we like your pretty voice."

"Creep." She laughed, but fidgeted with her bracelets.

"I think we can work in the mando. Mumford vibes."

"Ew. I'm out. End of convo." She pushed past him, back into the living room, where Jaymie was in the middle of his onstage costume change, i.e., wearing only his underwear.

"Keep thinking, Allene," he called after her.

"What is wrong with these people?" asked his companion. She was a philosophy major, singer, and performance artist, and he'd killed her outside a shoegaze show several weeks earlier. She wore a silver suit and carried a red coat over her arm, and the muffle of her headpiece gave her voice a tasteful Brit-rock crunch.

"They don't get it yet," said Jake, and his own suit glittered in divine campy villainy. "But they will."

He took in the scene before him in the living room. The *Bukowskis* hit a hard stop at the end of "Don't Do It" and launched into "A Place in the Heart." Several besotted teenagers gazed up at Jaymie from almost between his feet. Lucas adjusted his glasses and tapped his phone. A critic who claimed to give only positive reviews; it might be worth killing him just out of irritation. Jake turned away.

"Ready?" he asked.

His friend nodded and pulled her coat over her silver suit, and they made their way upstairs, passing the petite couple engaged in a distinctly non-PG performance against the banister. They entered a bedroom, where the body of a man was barely visible in the moonlight, laid out on a mattress.

"So they didn't even call the police?" asked the undead singer.

"No. This is only the first or second show these kids have put on."

"New promotion group, right?"

"Yeah. Bit of a desperate vibe ... Hey, it's almost Halloween. I have a good prank."

"The pumpkins?" she guessed. "They're still under the stairs." She began to fade, her form leeching away into the moonlight until it could only be seen from a certain angle, or perhaps captured by the flash of a phone camera.

"There's no help for that," sang the frontman beneath them. The drummer harmonized a third above, *"N-n-n-n-no, no help for that!"* As they retrieved the pumpkins, the heartbeatless girl felt sad to be missing the end of the set. She hoped she'd see this band again. The floor rumbled with a fill executed by the bass player. It took the two creatures very little time to claw, chew, and shape the pumpkins into human form, and by then the newly deceased keyboardist was sitting up, looking ahead with vacant eyes. He was stark white, the top of his shirt wavily bloodstained like red icing around the rim of a cake.

The monstress quietly escorted him out the front door while the band finished, and Jake made his way out the back, stopping only to ask Jaymie, for fun, if he considered himself a nihilist. In the porch, Jake's stoned former guitarist was shamelessly ogling the idiot blogger as he babbled some fanatical drivel to try and impress her.

"One show I was at, your bass player's strap came off, and he was too fucked up to get it back on—he ended up sitting on his amp like he was meditating!"

"Yup. Sounds like Jake. He fell off near the end, right?"

"Yes! His leg fell asleep, or something. He played the last however-many songs lying on his back on the floor!"

"Those were the days," monotoned the guitarist.

"Nice suit—*Daft Punk,* right?" Lucas called after him.

The vapid flirtation faded as he stepped into the autumn air and smiled to himself. A dog barked. The monstress reappeared at his side, leading her empty-faced ward.

"So, how many more?" she asked. "Must be almost a full lineup."

"Lead guitar."

"Sick." The chatter from the house party diminished and the night closed in around them.

"Wait till you meet your bandmates," she told the chthonic keyboardist, who moved stiffly beside her. Then she gave a contented sigh that emitted no breath. "I love a good art project," she said. And, "I love a good band."

The dog down the street bayed mournfully, wishing it too could be at the indie show.

"Yeah, me too," said the bassist, clicking his teeth to an imagined beat. "It's gonna be killer."

60
Epilogue

Shahla had survived to see her masterpiece through to the end, even if it was too late for a revelation. She and Maggie had been dropped off by the *Bukowskis* late the previous night, and had slept long into the day. Now she was back at work, staring at a "loading" symbol shimmering across the updated version of her program.

"I wish I could go to shows," said Ayla from the usual spot on the bed behind her, continuing an entirely one-sided conversation. "Eighteen is so many years away."

"I see the problem," said Shahla, engrossed in her project.

"I'm going to try out 'they/them' now, like Rex," said Ayla.

"That's great, kid," said Shahla. "Come on ... the bassist from the *Ballet Llama* ..."

Their mother knocked on the bedroom door. "Dinner," she said. "Go tell your sister."

"Sibling," Shahla corrected, without moving her eyes from the screen. "They're in here. They use 'they-slash-them' now."

"Oh," said their mother, from the hall. "... Dinner time." She would spend the next six months adapting.

"Who is it?" asked Ayla.

"It's your mother," said their mother.

"No, the murderer." Their mom accepted she wasn't part of the discussion and went back downstairs. "Who does it say?"

"One sec," said Shahla, infuriatingly. "It's ..."

"Did your bot get it right?"

"For fuck sake, it still says Lucas! He's the only one responsible enough to buy advance tickets or get on a guest list."

"Ugh, I don't even remember what their bassist looks like. I hate real life. Fanfiction is so much more fun. I need the *BBBFB* to get big so people will read my book."

"Who were you hoping the murderer was?"

"Maybe the lead singer. He's so hot and French." Ayla rolled onto their back, knocking their Bukowski Files to the floor.

"You growing out of Jaymie?" Shahla left the program to its eternal analyzing and swung around in her computer chair, beholding her sibling with a deep and impervious fondness.

"No, I'm just not exclusive right now," they replied. "And I like a bit of scruff."

"Alright, bud. Keep your options open. No murderers though."

The two went to join their parents, for whom family dinners were a non-negotiable daily tradition. Behind them, the failed AI chomped away on social media accounts and bandcamp releases and the Manitoba Music Live Events Calendar, consuming fresh data and the latest singles from everyone in town until it achieved sentience, perfected an algorithm that produced an indie pop song so perfect you'd never need to listen to anything else again in your life, and decided to start a band.

This project could not have been completed without help! Many thanks to Lesley Glendinning for proofreading, Alexis Flower for cover art and design, Domo Lemoine for editing Michaud's French, Theresa Thor (in advance) for producing the future audiobook, Virginia McClain and Sam Beiko for sharing publishing knowledge, and the folks at Transistor 66 for help with the release. And thanks to all the rest of the friends and fam who read this book back when it was a weekly-updating internet web serial and encouraged me to keep writing weird stuff.

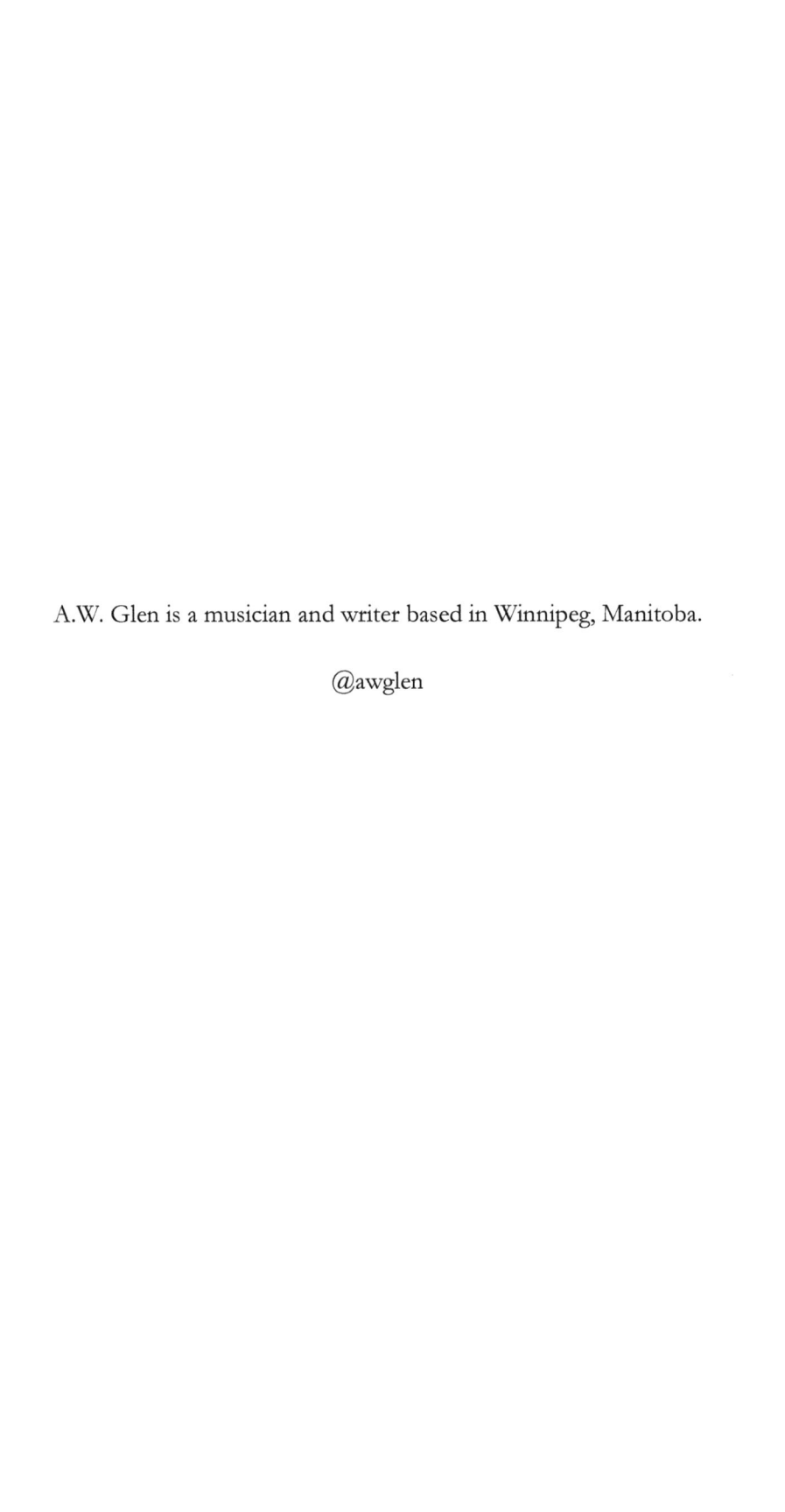

A.W. Glen is a musician and writer based in Winnipeg, Manitoba.

@awglen

Milton Keynes UK
Ingram Content Group UK Ltd.
UKHW031001261124
451585UK00005B/570